TRAVELLERS' INN

When Bethany and her mother are left destitute following the death of her father, they are forced to leave their home. With little more than the clothes they are standing in, their last hope is to prevail upon Bethany's Great Aunt Sarah, who runs a coaching inn. But the inn has seen better days, and Sarah's cold welcome is matched by her lack of sympathy to their plight. However, she allows them to stay, and Bethany's attitude and hard work impress Sarah. When Bethany encourages her to build up the business again trade increases. But troubles loom with rumours of plans for a railway, and in the form of labourer Zachary Brown, who takes a shine to Beth, but who is not all he seems . . .

Th
la
pe

0135993778

Elizabeth Jeffrey lives near Colchester. She began her writing career with short stories, more than a hundred of which were published or broadcast. In 1976 she won a short story competition which led on to writing full-length novels for adults and children. Elizabeth is married with three children and seven grandchildren.

ELIZABETH JEFFREY

◆

TRAVELLERS' INN

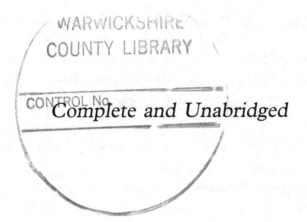
Complete and Unabridged

CHARNWOOD
Leicester

First published in Great Britain in 2006 by
Judy Piatkus (Publishers) Ltd.
London

First Charnwood Edition
published 2009
by arrangement with
Little, Brown Book Group
London

British Library CIP Data

Jeffrey, Elizabeth.
    Travellers' inn
    1. Widows- -Fiction. 2. Posthouse- -Fiction.
    3. Large type books.
    I. Title
    823.9'14–dc22

    ISBN 978–1–84782–691–6

Published by
F. A. Thorpe (Publishing)
Anstey, Leicestershire

Set by Words & Graphics Ltd.
Anstey, Leicestershire
Printed and bound in Great Britain by
T. J. International Ltd., Padstow, Cornwall

This book is printed on acid-free paper

1

'No, Mama, you know very well you can't take your silver candelabra. Mr Jones, the solicitor, made it quite plain that we could only take our personal possessions, and strictly speaking, that means the clothes on our backs,' Bethany said firmly.

'But they are *mine*. They belonged to my grandmother,' Emily said, her eyes filling with the tears that for the past dreadful weeks had never been far from the surface.

'Mama, nothing is yours,' Bethany explained for the twentieth time. 'You know perfectly well that the law said all your possessions became Papa's when you married him. Now the law says everything he owns must be sold to pay his creditors. Including, I'm afraid, your candelabra.'

'Perhaps we could buy them back,' Emily said doubtfully.

'We could if we had any money. Which, of course, we haven't, except for the few pounds we were allowed to keep.' Bethany sat down on the sofa and pulled her mother down beside her. 'Now, Mama, we've been over this a hundred times. Papa embezzled all that money so that he could continue to give us the lifestyle we're used to.' She caught her mother's hands and gave them a little shake. 'What you must always remember is that he did it because he loved us; because he wanted the best for us. He always

1

intended to pay it back, I'm sure of it.' It was the right thing to say to her mother but Bethany suspected there was more to it than that. She was sure that her father had hoped a good win on the horses would take care of his debts, instead of which, continued losses only increased them.

'Well, committing suicide was hardly the best thing for us,' Emily said bitterly. 'I shall never get over the shame of the funeral! No plumed horses, no purple-draped funeral carriage; nothing but a hole-in-the-corner burial early in the morning in an unconsecrated part of the churchyard. How shall I ever face Lady Armstrong and her set again? I'm sure we're the talk of society.' She freed her hands and dabbed her eyes with a black-edged handkerchief.

'Since we shan't be here in London to face anybody, let alone Lady Armstrong and her set, that's the least of our worries,' Bethany said, getting to her feet. She looked round the elegant drawing room, with its duck-egg-blue walls and spindly furniture. 'Mr Jones said we could stay one last night in this house and that we should leave everything as it is; tomorrow he will send in the men to clear it, then everything will be sold to pay off at least some of Papa's debts.'

'He's very trusting,' Emily said, her voice heavy with sarcasm. 'How does he know we won't steal the spoons?'

'Because an inventory has already been taken. Everything is listed, down to the last inkwell. Don't you remember? Two men came last week to do it.'

Emily nodded, then suddenly, she crumpled. 'Oh, Seymour,' she sobbed, 'how could you do this to me? How could you go and leave me in this horrible, horrible mess? We've always been so happy . . . '

Bethany bit her lip against her own threatening tears, but she knew one of them had to be strong, so she swallowed hard and said briskly, 'Now, is everything packed? We must be up early in the morning because the cab is coming at seven to take us to The Bell to catch the coach.' She managed a watery smile. 'Come mother, it's not that bad. We were allowed enough money to buy decent mourning clothes and we are to be allowed to keep the rest of our wardrobe, so that's something.'

Emily made a noise that was something between a snort and a sob but said nothing, so Bethany continued, 'I'm really looking forward to meeting Aunt Sarah and Uncle John; you've told me so much about them, Mama. And I've never been to the country before so I'm really quite excited. I'm so glad you wrote and asked if we could go and stay with them.'

'Well, we've no other relatives,' Emily said gloomily.

'It's a little strange that you've had no reply,' Bethany said with a frown.

'Oh, I expect it will be all right. They live in an inn, so there's sure to be plenty of room for us. And it's out in the country where nobody will know our shame.' Emily gave a shudder. 'The wife and daughter of a man who committed suicide can hardly expect to be welcomed into

3

polite society, can they. We'll have to think up a plausible story . . . '

Bethany waved her hand dismissively. 'Oh, I'm sure we shall think of something. Now, I'll go to the kitchen and make us both a hot drink and then we must retire. We have to make an early start in the morning and Lovatt isn't here now to call us and bring us breakfast in bed.'

'No, everything's changed,' Emily said woefully. 'All the servants have gone. Oh, Seymour, what have you brought us to!' She dabbed her eyes again, a short, rather plump woman in her mid-forties — a well-preserved mid-forties until the trauma of her husband's untimely death early in March 1840, and the desperate position he had left her and Bethany in, had drained the colour out of her cheeks and sharpened her features. Under the widow's cap she was only now becoming adjusted to wearing her fair hair parted in the middle and neatly coiled over her ears. It was the last task Lovatt had performed for her before tearfully taking her leave that morning.

Bethany left her mother to wallow in her misery and went down to the kitchen. She was not at all like Emily, being tall and willowy, with copper-coloured hair that refused to be tamed into any of the fashionable hairstyles of the day but hung in riotous curls round her shoulders. Her features, too were gentler than her mother's, grey eyes under neatly arched brows, a slightly tip-tilted nose and a wide mouth that appeared permanently on the verge of breaking into laughter. Unlike her mother, too, she had never

4

mastered the art of being ladylike and at eighteen rather resembled an unbroken colt, and was uncomfortable, not to say impatient, with tinkling teacups and polite conversation. Sometimes Emily despaired of her but in recent days she had been glad of her daughter's matter-of-fact approach to life and her strength of character.

Emily looked up as Bethany returned. 'The kitchen range has gone out and although I can speak to it in French and German I don't know how to light it,' Bethany said flatly. 'You could have some cold milk, that's what I'm having. Or water. There's nothing else, except half a loaf of bread and we shall need that for breakfast.'

Emily shuddered. 'No, thank you, dear.'

They went to their separate rooms, Emily to weep herself to sleep at the cruel blow fate and her husband had dealt her, Bethany to go over in her mind the circumstances that had led to them being turned out of the elegant London home where she had been born and had lived for the whole of her life.

She had led a pampered life, she realised that. Music lessons, art classes, dancing lessons, French and German as well as the three Rs under a private governess. There had even been talk of a finishing school in France although that hadn't come to anything. Lately, her mother had begun taking her along when she paid her afternoon calls, which Bethany had considered a complete waste of time.

Then, out of the blue, had come the dreadful news that her father had been found dead in his office at the bank. Hanged. She had had nightmares picturing the scene. It appeared he had run up debts and used clients' money to pay them — always, of course, meaning to set the record straight when funds improved. As he explained in a letter, he had never meant to steal the money, only to borrow it until such time as his fortunes improved. He was an incurable optimist, an optimism sadly misplaced as far as his affair with Lady Luck was concerned, because he was an inveterate gambler; cards, horses, anything that moved was worthy of a wager. Bethany's mouth twisted wryly. Ultimately he had gambled his family's well-being.

And lost.

After the first, terrible, shock had come the realisation that she and her mother were virtually penniless and without a home, since everything, including the roof over their heads, would have to be sold to pay off Seymour's debts. Mr Jones, their solicitor, had been very kind, allowing them to stay there until they could make 'other arrangements'. In effect, until they could find someone to take them in.

It had been Bethany who had thought of Aunt Sarah and Uncle John. Emily had told her so many stories of the wonderful times she had spent in the Essex countryside with her aunt and uncle as a child that Bethany had persuaded her to write and ask if they could pay them a visit. It would, at least, give them a breathing space whilst they decided what to do next. The fact that there had been no reply was understandable; the posts were notoriously unreliable and slow.

The next morning, in spite of bright, early April sunshine, the two women got up to a cold house, since there were now no servants to light the fires. They helped each other with their numerous petticoats and laced each other's stays, Bethany in fits of giggles and Emily even managing a wan smile from time to time. Then, after Bethany had done the best she could with her mother's hair, which fell far short of Lovatt's expertise, much to Emily's irritation, they went downstairs to the kitchen and a miserable breakfast of bread and butter and cheese, washed down with water.

They were both relieved when the cab arrived to take them to The Bell, so that they could leave behind the house full of memories of happier times that was no longer their home.

The Bell yard was full of hustle and bustle, with ostlers attending to the horses, servants running hither and yon at the beck and call of travellers and grubby, underclad and underfed urchins getting under everyone's feet trying to earn a copper, carrying bags or messages or holding the horses' heads. Bethany managed to find a young lad to transfer their luggage from the place where the cab driver had dumped it when he saw the meagre tip, to the coach. It consisted of two small trunks, containing everything they owned in the world.

The young lad obviously felt sorry for the two ladies dressed all in mourning black, their faces covered by veils, and made them as comfortable as he could inside the coach.

'Thank you for your help,' Bethany said, handing him a penny.

He touched his forelock. 'Thank you, Miss. Won't be long now an' you'll be orf.'

The coach swayed alarmingly as luggage was loaded and the passengers travelling outside climbed up to their seats. A woman with a squawking hen in a basket and a man in a stovepipe hat squeezed inside the coach opposite Bethany and her mother, obviously annoyed at the amount of space taken up by their voluminous black skirts. Then with a blast on the horn the coach began to move.

The first stage took them to the outskirts of the city, then, after a change of horses, it was on to Brentwood and another stop before going on to Chelmsford, where there was time for a hot toddy and a bun before resuming their journey again, this time with two elderly, card-playing men as their companions.

'Tell me about the place we're going to, Mama,' Bethany said, to relieve her mother's constant complaints about the state of the roads and the discomfort of the coach.

Emily gave a cry as the coach lurched over a particularly deep rut before answering, 'It's out in the country — on the road to Harwich — between two villages, Mistley and Bradfield. It used to be a coaching inn years ago, like the one we've just left, but gradually the inn at Manningtree, on the other side of Mistley, became more popular. All the same, people travelling along the road could always be sure of a welcome. Aunt Sarah's ale was quite famous in the district, I remember. And so were her mutton pies.'

'What did you do when you stayed there?' Bethany asked, anxious to keep her mother talking so that she shouldn't begin complaining again. 'Was there dancing? And visiting?'

Emily gave a little mirthless laugh. 'Oh, bless you, no. Aunt and Uncle worked all the time. They were always busy with the comings and goings at the inn. But I was never bored. I played in the fields and down by the river with the farm workers' children. It didn't matter to me that they were poor and had no shoes; we were simply children playing together and Uncle and Aunt encouraged it.' She paused. 'Understandably, my mother was quite shocked when she found out, but of course it's different in the country. At least it seemed so to me.'

'How long is it since you saw Aunt and Uncle?'

'I last went there just before Seymour and I were married. About twenty years ago.'

'Are you sure they'll still be there?' Bethany asked anxiously.

'Oh, yes. They would never move from such a lovely spot.'

Emily sounded so confident that Bethany didn't remind her that there had been no reply to her letter, a fact that was becoming more and more worrying the nearer they got to their destination.

Eventually, they reached the King's Head at Colchester, tired and hungry.

'This coach goes on to Ipswich,' Bethany told her mother as she helped her down, stiff and aching from the jolting. 'The Harwich coach leaves in an hour. That gives us time for a meal.'

They left the trunks in the care of a stable lad and tried to find their way through the jostling crowd to reach the dining room of the inn.

'Who d'you think you're a-shovin' of?' a tipsy, rat-faced man shouted, spilling porter down Emily's dress.

'Aye, where d'you think you're orf to?' his companion added as they tried to edge past to look for the dining room.

'I — we're looking for somewhere where we can get a meal,' Emily said, nervously looking round for Bethany.

'Well you're goin' the wrong way. This is the way to the public,' a third man pushed his way forward.

'Then perhaps you'll be good enough to tell us which direction we should be going in,' Bethany said, stepping in front of her mother and very conscious that they were now almost surrounded by quite a crowd of rough-looking men.

'P'raps you'll be good enough,' another man mimicked. He thrust his face near to Bethany's so that she could smell his beery breath. 'An' why should we do that? Are you gonna make it worth our while?' He caught her arm and another man got hold of Emily.

'Let go!' Bethany said between clenched teeth. She was too angry to be frightened. 'Or I shall call . . . '

'Who will you call? Ain't nobody here'll take

any notice,' they jeered. 'They're all too busy lookin' after theirselves. Now, come on, two well-britched widders like you must hev a bit to spare. Give us . . . '

Suddenly, there was the crack of a whip on the cobbles and a voice shouted, 'Be off with you! Leave these two defenceless ladies alone or I'll call the constable! You can see they are in mourning.' A whip pointed at a tall, gangling youth. 'Beckwith, I'd have thought better of you. You should be ashamed of yourself.'

Almost before he had finished speaking the assailants — and there were more of them than Bethany had realised — had melted away into the crowd and she found herself standing with her mother and looking up at a distinguished-looking man in a top hat and long frock coat.

He doffed his hat, revealing a shock of dark brown hair. Then he smiled, a smile that lit up his face and crinkled the corners of his eyes and Bethany realised he was younger than she had first thought, probably in his late twenties. 'Did I hear you say you were looking for food?' he asked.

'Yes, we left ho . . . London quite early this morning and we've hardly eaten since,' Bethany answered. 'And we have to wait an hour for the Harwich coach so there's plenty of time.'

'Then allow me to find you a room where you can eat without further fear of being molested.'

Before they could protest he led them into the inn and through several passages to a small room at the end where there were two settles, one each side of a bright fire and with a table between

11

them. 'There, you should be quite comfortable here,' he said, looking round. 'And quite private. I'll make sure you are attended to without delay.'

'You are very kind, sir,' Bethany said. 'It was quite alarming, suddenly finding ourselves surrounded by those men.'

'Yes, I'm sure it must have been. I assure you they won't trouble you again, ladies.' He doffed his hat once more. 'Now, I wish you good day and a safe journey to Harwich.'

'Oh, we're not going as far as Harwich,' Emily said quickly. 'Our destination is just the other side of Mistley.'

He frowned, then raised his eyebrows. 'Really? I wasn't aware . . . ' Then he smiled again. 'But you're waiting for your meal. Excuse me, ladies, I'll have something sent to you directly.'

He was as good as his word and five minutes later two steaming plates of stew and dumplings and two mugs of mulled ale were brought by a fresh-faced girl, whose gingham dress was cut a little too low in the bodice for Emily's approval.

'This is not at all what we're used to, Bethany,' she complained, picking up the cheap knife and fork and pointing to the rather battered pewter plates. She looked round at the comfortable but by no means luxurious panelled room and sighed. 'I can hardly believe it's less than two months since we were sitting on Mrs Jackson's balcony, watching our dear Queen's wedding procession drive by and hearing the church bells pealing all over the city. Oh, it was such a wonderful occasion. And the dinner the Jacksons held afterwards! Twenty courses before I lost

12

count!' She pushed a dumpling round distastefully.

'You'd better eat it, Mama,' Bethany said, her mouth full. 'It's really a very tasty lamb stew and we don't know when we shall get another meal.'

Emily looked up, her fork halfway to her mouth. 'What do you mean, you don't know when we shall get another meal? My Aunt Sarah always keeps a good board and we haven't got much further to go, have we?'

'About twelve miles, I believe. We should reach Travellers' Inn soon after six, I should think.'

'Oh, thank goodness for that. I'm very tired and I believe every bone in my body has been shaken up in that coach. I hope the next one will be a little more comfortable.'

They finished their meal, which even Emily had to admit was delicious and Bethany went to find the landlord to settle up.

'It had already been paid for,' she told her mother when she returned. 'That kind man must have paid for it. I looked for him but he's gone, so I can't thank him, and we shall probably never see him again.'

'I daresay he could afford it,' Emily said comfortably. 'He was quite well dressed, although of course my Seymour would never have worn a coat of that cut.'

'Mama, you really are a terrible snob,' Bethany chastised, giving her arm a little shake.

'Well, dear, there are standards,' Emily said unrepentantly. 'Ah, look, is that our coach? It says Colchester to Harwich but it looks rather crowded.'

'I'm sure there'll be room for us,' Bethany said.

It was not, as Emily had hoped it would be, a comfortable ride. The coach was old and crowded with people anxious to catch the boat from Harwich to the continent and the road, unlike the turnpike roads, was rutted and rough. They did manage to find seats inside but only because two men gave up theirs and rode outside beside the driver. The prospect of heaving Emily up on to the top of the coach had made Bethany smile quietly to herself but she was glad it hadn't come to that. All the time, as they watched their luggage being stowed and before they boarded the coach, she looked out for the dark stranger who had bought their meal for them but he was nowhere to be seen.

It was nearly six o'clock when they stopped to change horses at Manningtree.

'Oh, dear, we've still got another three miles or so to go, if I remember rightly,' her mother said. 'We shall know the inn when we see it because the sign is brightly coloured. In any case, it's the only house along that stretch of the road. The coachman said he knew the place so he'll know where to stop.' She heaved a sigh. 'Oh, I ache in every bone from this journey, Bethany. I shall be so glad of a comfortable bed tonight. That's one thing I remember about Aunt Sarah's feather beds, they are filled with goose feathers and so soft you can sink right into them.'

The coachman blew his horn and they lurched off again into a misty April dusk.

2

They left the town and the coach creaked and trundled its way along a lonely road, bordered mostly by blackthorn hedges studded at intervals with tall elms or gnarled oaks. Over to the left the mist hanging in the river valley spread its tentacles up over the fields and wisped round the coach windows like ghostly fingers.

Suddenly, there was a shout from the coachman and the coach stopped.

He climbed down from his perch and opened the door. 'Here y'are, ladies,' he said. 'The Travellers' Inn. On'y that don't look much of a inn and from what I hear there ain't many travellers.' He didn't wait for them to alight but busied himself with their trunks. By the time they had helped each other down and were standing on the grass verge beside their belongings he was back up on his seat and with a quick flick of the reins the coach was on its way again and fast disappearing into the gathering gloom. The whole procedure had taken less than five minutes.

Frowning at the coachman's words, Bethany turned and looked at the house behind her. It stood at the roadside, a square, greyish building with a tiled roof and a heavy domed porch over the front door. To each side of the door, six on one side, five on the other, were windows of varying sizes, which all seemed to be set at different levels so it was difficult to gauge with any certainty which were on the upper and which were on the lower floor. Above the door, which was badly in need of a coat of paint, swung a sign, so weatherworn that it was impossible to read what was written on it. There was no sign of life to be seen anywhere.

She turned to her mother. 'Are you quite sure this is the right place?' she asked doubtfully.

Emily nodded. 'Oh, yes. This is definitely the place. I remember it well.' She lifted her black veil so that she could see more clearly and peered, frowning in the gathering darkness. 'But it wasn't at all like this when I used to visit. There were always people about. It was always busy . . . ' her voice trailed off.

'But that was over twenty years ago, Mama,' Bethany reminded her, trying to keep the irritation she felt out of her voice. She sat down on her trunk. 'Oh, I knew I was right. We should never have come until we heard from Aunt and Uncle. Obviously, they're both dead and the place is derelict.'

Emily sat down beside her. 'I'm afraid you may be right, Bethany,' she said in a small voice. 'Oh, dear, as if we haven't trouble enough! Now what shall we do?'

'Well, I suppose we'll just have to walk back to the village and find a bed for the night. How far did you say it was? Three miles? Although I must say it seemed like more in that rattly old coach.'

'Oh, I couldn't possibly walk that far, Bethany. Not after that dreadful journey. And what about our things?'

'Ah, yes.' Bethany gave a sigh. 'Very well, you'd better stay here with them while I walk to the village and get someone to come and fetch you.'

'No, you can't do that. You can't leave me here alone, Bethany. Not in this lonely, godforsaken spot.' Emily hugged herself, shivering. 'Think of the robbers; the highwaymen . . . '

'I thought you said it was a marvellous place, where you had such a wonderful time when you were a child,' Bethany said, tiredness and disappointment making her waspish. 'All right, then. What are you going to do, stay here by yourself or walk back to the village with me? You'll have to do one thing or the other.'

'I'll walk back with you,' Emily said.

'Then let's go and have a look round the back and see if we can find somewhere safe to leave these trunks while we're gone. We can pick them up in the morning, when we've decided what to do next. We're too tired to make any decisions tonight.'

'I wish now I hadn't let you persuade me to come here,' Emily said petulantly, getting to her feet.

'And I wish you hadn't painted the place in such glowing colours,' Bethany snapped back. 'However, we're here now, Mama, so we must make the best of it, for tonight, anyway. Come on, let's have a look round and see if we can find a way into the place. I suppose we might even be able to stay here for the night.'

'Oh, no, Bethany, I could never stay in an

17

empty house with no beds.' Emily gave a shudder.

'Well, we shan't find a bed anywhere if we don't make a move.' Bethany led the way down the cobbled yard by the side of the house and round to the back, dragging the trunks behind her. Now she could see that the house was in fact L shaped, the short arm of the L a single storey at right angles to the main building. Beyond this wing and separated from it by the slightly sloping cobbled yard was the shadowy bulk of a stable block and outhouses.

Suddenly, Emily caught Bethany's arm. 'Look, I can see a light,' she said, pointing to a window. 'That's where the kitchen is . . . was. See? In that window at the end, near the stable block?'

Bethany let out a long breath. 'That means *somebody's* here,' she said, 'even if it isn't Aunt Sarah. I'll go and knock at the door.'

'No, wait. Supposing it's a thief. Or a burglar,' Emily tightened her grip.

'Well, we haven't got a lot for anyone to steal apart from a few clothes, so I don't think that's much cause for worry,' Bethany said cheerfully, shaking her off.

'We could be murdered.'

'That's true.' She looked round and noticed a rusty old pitchfork propped against the wall. 'I'll take this with me,' she said, getting hold of it, whereupon the prongs fell away from the handle. She picked them up. 'Never mind, it's still a useful weapon.' She went forward, holding the remains of the pitchfork before her like a talisman.

'You'd better knock,' Emily said nervously from behind her. 'It's only polite.'

'What, to warn whoever might be inside that I'm going to spear him with a pitchfork?' Bethany said over her shoulder. 'Oh, very well.' She rapped on the door with her knuckles, then stood back. From what she could see in the gathering darkness the door had several pieces of wood nailed on at odd angles to stop it falling to pieces and another piece of wood was pushed into the hole to form the latch.

After several minutes this makeshift latch moved and the door opened a crack.

'Who is it?' A woman's voice asked. 'What do you want?'

'Oh, Aunt Sarah! Thank goodness you're here,' Emily said, stepping forward eagerly. 'It's me. Emily. Your niece. And my daughter Bethany.'

'What do you want?' Aunt Sarah repeated, not opening the door any further.

'We'd like to come in, please, Great Aunt. We need a bed for the night,' Bethany said.

'I've got no spare beds,' Aunt Sarah said shortly. 'Anyway, what have you come to me for? I haven't seen hide nor hair of you for the past twenty years.'

'We've come to you because we've nowhere else to go,' Emily pleaded. 'I thought you'd be pleased to see us. Please, Aunt Sarah, let us in.'

With obvious reluctance Aunt Sarah opened the door far enough to let them through. Bethany followed her mother, leaving their luggage just inside the door.

Sarah eyed it up and down with obvious distaste, then resumed her seat at the end of the long, scrubbed table in the middle of the room. It was a large kitchen, with a huge dresser filling the wall opposite the window, a large kitchen range at the end of the room where Aunt Sarah had her chair and a single bed covered with a patchwork quilt at the other. Various chairs and small items of furniture filled any remaining space and everywhere was cluttered with books and papers, coats, boots, and heaps of clothing, whilst the table — which needed a good scrub — held the remains of her meal, plus a lump of cheese, half a loaf of bread and a jug of milk. All this Bethany took in by the flickering light from a rusty looking candelabra with one arm missing that was standing in the middle of the table.

She threw down her hat, peeled off her gloves and ran her fingers through her unruly, copper-coloured hair. 'It's so nice to meet you, Great Aunt Sarah,' she said, smiling at her and ignoring the icy atmosphere. 'Mama has told me so much about you that I already feel I know you.'

Sarah stared at her coldly but said nothing. She was a tall woman without an ounce of spare flesh on her bones. High cheekbones and the curve of her jaw spoke of beauty in the past, a beauty that even now would be apparent if she were to smile and if her thick, iron-grey hair, dragged into a tight bun on the top of her head, were to be allowed to have its way and wave gently like the stray tendril that had escaped capture and fallen across her forehead.

'Do you think Mama might sit down?' Bethany's courage was beginning to fade in the face of this formidable woman but she tried to keep her voice light. 'We've come an awfully long way since eight o'clock this morning and I know she is very tired.'

'She can sit if she likes,' Sarah said, with a shrug. 'But I've got nothing to give her. Or you.' She nodded at Bethany.

Bethany moved a pile of clothes off a chair so that her mother could sit down but remained standing by her chair, her hand on her mother's shoulder.

'Where's Uncle John, Aunt Sarah?' Emily asked, with a puzzled frown. This was not at all how she remembered her aunt's house. Nor her aunt, if it came to that.

'Died. Five years ago.'

'Oh, I am sorry. Poor Uncle John. So that means you're here all alone?'

'Looks like it. But you needn't think . . . '

Emily wasn't listening. 'Oh, dear, I wish you had let me know, Aunt. You know how fond I was of Uncle John.'

'Hmph. You wouldn't have come if I had. Once you got married to that man and went off to live the high life in London you didn't have time for the likes of us.' She looked Emily up and down and then gave Bethany the same treatment. 'I see you're both in mourning. Is he dead?'

Emily nodded, biting her lip. 'Yes, a month ago.'

'An' I s'pose he didn't leave you well provided for.'

'No, I'm afraid he didn't.'

'I'm not surprised. He didn't look the sort that would; him with his curly whiskers and fancy weskits. All show and no substance, I could see that at a glance.'

'You never liked him, did you, Aunt,' Emily said sadly. 'But you didn't know him. Seymour was a wonderful man and I loved him. It was just unfortunate . . . '

'Seymour! What sort of a name is that!' Sarah spat the words out. 'I'll tell you what sort of a name it is. It's the sort of name that belongs to a man who lives beyond his means and leaves his wife and child destitute. And I'll wager that's exactly what's happened.' She looked from Emily to Bethany and then back again. 'Yes, I thought as much. I can see it in your face. Well, you needn't think you can come to me begging for charity. You made your bed when you married him, so you'll just have to lie on it now he's dead.' She turned away and poked the fire. 'I never asked you to come and I don't want you here, so you can go back to where you came from as quick as you like.'

'This is not like you, Aunt,' Emily said, bewildered and near to tears. 'You never used to be so hard and unyielding. You were always loving and full of fun when I stayed with you as a child.'

'That was a long time ago. Folks change.'

'Well, surely you won't grudge us a bed, just for tonight? It's a long walk back to Mistley and we're very tired.' Emily lifted her veil and dabbed her eyes.

'I don't take lodgers any more,' Sarah said stubbornly, folding her arms and putting her elbows on the table. 'And you needn't think you can get round me by crying. I never did like cry-babies.'

'I'm not crying and we're not *lodgers*, Aunt Sarah,' Emily said, pulling herself together with an effort. 'We're *family*. I'm your niece, remember. I used to spend a lot of time here with you and Uncle John when I was younger.'

'Well, you're older now and so am I and I still don't take lodgers.' Sarah's mouth was set in a grim, straight line.

Bethany had been standing beside her mother's chair watching the exchange between the two women with horrified amazement but suddenly, with a little cry, she crumpled to the ground in a dead faint.

Immediately, Emily knelt down beside her and supported her as the impact with the floor began to bring her round. 'Oh,' she said weakly, passing her hand across her brow, 'Did I faint? How stupid of me. I'm really sorry, Mama.'

'It's all right, dear. I expect it was just tiredness. It's been a very long day.' Emily raised her voice. 'Can I have some water for her, please, Aunt?' she asked, without looking round.

'Yes. Here you are.' Sarah came over with a cup of water, most of which she threw in Bethany's face. 'That should bring her round,' she said unsympathetically.

Bethany brushed the water off her face with her arm and took several sips of what was left in the cup. 'Thank you, Great Aunt Sarah,' she said. 'I feel much better now.' With Emily's help she got to her feet, although still staggering a little.

'Since Great Aunt Sarah is so unwilling for us to stay here, Mama, I think we should start to walk back to Mistley,' she said quietly, gripping her mother's arm for support. 'But perhaps we could leave our luggage?' she nodded towards the trunks standing in the doorway, then looked enquiringly at Sarah.

Sarah looked her up and down as she leaned on her mother. 'Hmph. I suppose I shall have to let you stay here tonight,' she said grudgingly. 'The state you're in you don't look as if you'd make it halfway back to Mistley.' She wagged a finger. 'But only for tonight, mind.'

Bethany smiled weakly. 'Oh, thank you, Great Aunt Sarah. We would be most grateful, wouldn't we, Mama.'

'Yes, indeed we would, Aunt,' Emily said with a sigh of relief.

Sarah went to the mantelpiece and took a stub of candle and rammed it into a pewter candlestick. Then she lit it from the candelabra on the table.

'You'd better take this.' She thrust it at Emily. 'You can sleep in your old room; you know the way. And you'll need to keep your clothes on because I expect the bed's damp. It hasn't been slept in for a long time.' She nodded towards the door in the corner when she saw Emily hesitate. 'Well, go on. I don't keep late hours and that girl looks as if she needs her bed.'

Emily thanked her aunt and led the way along a dim and dusty passage that still bore a faint aroma of old ale and pipe smoke, mixed with damp and decay. The stairs were at the end of the passage on the left. Two steps up and they twisted back to run parallel with the passage itself, then three steps from the top they twisted yet again. There was a door off this bend and Emily pushed it open.

'This is it. This is where I used to sleep as a girl,' she said, holding the candle high. 'I loved this room because I could see right across the field to the river. I'll show you in the morning.' She patted the counterpane, patchwork, like the one downstairs. 'Do you know, it doesn't seem to have changed at all. Everything is just as I remember it.'

Bethany lifted a corner of the counterpane. 'Except there aren't any sheets or blankets and the bed feels damp,' she said briskly. 'I'll have a look and see if there are any in the chest of drawers.'

'Shouldn't you be lying down, dear?' Emily asked anxiously. 'I don't want you to faint again.'

'Oh, I'm perfectly all right, Mama,' Bethany said, turning to her with a laugh, 'You didn't really think I fainted, did you? I only pretended to.'

'Of course I did. I was quite worried about you.' Emily said, slightly annoyed that she had been taken in. 'You were very convincing,' she admitted.

'Well, it was the only way I could think of to make sure we got a bed here for the night. I could see there was no other way she would let us stay, miserable old battleaxe. Anyway, it had the desired effect; we have a bed, although nothing to eat.' She pulled out another drawer. 'Ah, I think I've found a rug or something we can cover ourselves with. Shine the candle over here, Mama.' She pulled out a thick rug and shook the dust and moths out of it. 'It's a bit damp and moth-eaten but at least it hasn't got a mouse's nest in it,' she said cheerfully.

Emily shuddered. 'Oh, Bethany, don't!' she begged.

'Well, we might as well go to bed,' Bethany said. 'That candle won't last much longer and we've had a long day. If we cuddle together and cover ourselves with this rug we shouldn't be too cold.'

'I really think we should remove our dresses,' Emily said doubtfully. 'They'll be like rags by morning if we sleep in them and we need to keep them nice. There's no telling who we might come into contact with in the days to come.'

Bethany yawned. 'I'll let the days to come take care of themselves. I intend to keep on everything I'm wearing, including my shawl. I can't sleep if I'm cold.' She climbed into bed and pulled the rug over her. After some hesitation, Emily removed her hat and shawl and, with some difficulty, her dress and several petticoats and unlaced her stays, before climbing in beside

26

her. Bethany's last thought, before she fell into a deep and dreamless sleep, was to wonder where she had left her own hat.

She woke in the morning to find her mother shivering beside her.

'I'm so cold, Bethany,' she said, through chattering teeth. 'This bed's damp. I think I must have caught a chill.'

'I told you to keep all your clothes on, like I did,' Bethany said unsympathetically. Nevertheless, she felt her mother's bare arm. It was burning. She sat up in bed. The sight that greeted her was not encouraging. The curtains at the windows were full of holes, the ceiling was peeling and festooned with cobwebs and there was a pall of grey dust and dead flies on every surface, although underneath it the furniture looked quite good. She lifted the rug which had been covering them and saw that they had been lying on a bare mattress. What else they might have been sharing the mattress with she preferred not to speculate. She put her hand on it. It was decidedly damp and her mother was still shivering.

'Come along, Mama. You must get up and put your clothes on,' she said more gently. 'Then wrap yourself in both your shawl and mine and get back into bed. I'll go and see if I can persuade Great Aunt Sarah to warm some bread and milk for you.'

'Thank you, dear.' Emily gave her a weak smile. 'Oh, what wouldn't I give for my nice warm, comfortable bed with its silk sheets and my dear maid Lovatt to look after me. I really do feel most dreadfully ill, Bethany. I hope Aunt Sarah won't turn us out. I don't believe I could walk any distance.'

Bethany patted her hand. 'I'm sure she wouldn't be so cruel as to do that, Mama,' she said with a smile. 'Not when she sees how ill you are.'

As she went down the narrow staircase to the kitchen she could only hope and pray that she was right.

3

As she made her way downstairs Bethany tried to think what she could do to make her mother more comfortable. Perhaps there was a room where a fire could be lit so she would at least be warmer. She knew there was no question of Aunt Sarah sharing her warm kitchen.

In the gloom at the foot of the stairs she noticed that there was a door at the end of the passage. Feeling more than a little guilty she pushed it open and found herself in a large room that looked as if it covered the entire front of the house. Clearly, this had once been the public room, although the bolts on the big front door were so rusted that it looked as if it hadn't been opened for years.

The room itself was filthy. Everywhere was thick with dust and grime. Chairs were carelessly piled on beer-stained tables and several wooden settles stood at odd angles as if they had been pulled out from the wall and couldn't find their way back. The walls and paintwork were drab, dark and peeling and the boards were bare except for dirt, bits of plaster, mouse-droppings and a rusty old spittoon. On one wall a picture of Nelson's flagship had slipped to an angle that made it look as if it was about to sink. There were no curtains at the windows but a coating of grime and cobwebs did very well instead.

She closed the door on the depressing sight

29

and tried the only other one she could see, which was halfway down the passage. This looked more hopeful. It was very much smaller and looked out on to the cobbled yard at the side of the house. There were two steps down into it and she realised from the levels that it must be directly under the room she and her mother had slept in. She paused, pinching her lip. It looked as if it had once been a private parlour, although at the moment it was dirty and uncared for. But the original plush curtains still hung at the window and there was a matching table cover and several rugs on the floor. The room was quite well furnished; there was even a comfortable-looking chair by the fire covered in the same rust-coloured plush. She was sure she could make her mother quite warm and snug in this room if only Aunt Sarah would agree to a fire being lit. She nodded to herself. Yes, she could make Mama very comfortable here. Thoughtfully, she carried on to the kitchen at the end of the passage.

Sarah was sitting at the table eating porridge, a man's cap, with the peak at the back, on her head. Standing by the door was an old man, almost as wide as he was tall, in a smock and gaiters and with a dirty, floppy-brimmed hat on his head. He snatched the hat off when he saw Bethany and gave her a friendly smile, revealing toothless gums.

'Good morning,' Bethany said brightly, including them both in her greeting. She looked out of the window. 'It's a pleasant day, isn't it.'

'It'll rain before long,' Sarah answered,

spooning porridge without looking up.

'Marnin', Miss,' the old man said, inclining his head, pinkly bald and rimmed with a fuzz of white hair, in Bethany's direction. He turned to Sarah, 'Well, I'll chop ye a few logs afore I go, Sary. Anythin' else you want?'

'Oh, can you wait a minute?' Bethany said, stepping forward eagerly. 'If Aunt Sarah doesn't mind I should like to light a fire in the little room just down the passage so it would be nice if I could have some logs, too.'

'Oh, you'd like to light a fire, would you!' Sarah said, looking up in angry surprise, with her spoon halfway to her mouth. 'And who gave you permission to go poking around in my house?'

'Well, I . . . '

'What next, I should like to know! You told me you only wanted a bed for the night and then you'd be leaving me in peace.' She stared at Bethany. 'It was against my better judgement that I agreed to let you stay, I might tell you. I wouldn't have done if you hadn't collapsed, although I must say there doesn't look to be much wrong with you this morning.'

'I was tired last night,' Bethany said with perfect truth. 'But I'm better now. And it's true, we hadn't intended to impose on your hospitality for more than one night when we saw how unwelcome we were. But you see, Mama is not at all well this morning. She's quite exhausted after all she's been through plus that long and uncomfortable coach journey from London yesterday. Added to that I think the bed was a little damp and she's caught a chill.' She spread

31

her hands. 'I really don't think she's fit to travel — especially as we don't know where we shall be going — so I thought if I could light a fire in that little room and keep her warm for a day or two . . . ' her voice trailed off as she saw the look on Aunt Sarah's face.

'Ha! Just as I thought!' was all she said. She turned to the old man. 'What did I tell you, Reuben? Now they're here they'll keep finding excuses to stay and they'll be like rats in a barn, I shall never get rid of them.'

Reuben scratched his bald head. 'Well, they'd be comp'ny for ye, Sary,' he said diplomatically.

'I don't *want* company. I prefer my own.'

'Well, I don't see as you can turn 'em out. Not if th'owd lady's outa sorts. That wouldn't be a Christian thing to do, now, would it.' He turned to Bethany. 'I'll fetch ye a bit o' kindlin' for the fire, Miss. I dessay the chimley might be a bit damp so you'll hev to watch the smoke till that clear. Come to that, I'll light it for ye, if ye like.'

'I'd be very glad of that,' Bethany said eagerly. 'You see, I've never actually lit a fire, so perhaps you could show me what to do. Then I'll know for another time.'

''Course I will, dearie,' he said, clearly glad to have been asked.

Sarah was looking from one to the other, open-mouthed. Suddenly, she slammed her porridge spoon down on the table. 'Am I to have no say at all as to what goes on in my own house?' she demanded.

Reuben put his head on one side. 'Well, Sary, seein' as how you don't use that part o' the house I don't reckon thass gonna make that much difference to ye whether they go or stay,' he said sagely. 'T'ain't as if they'll be in your way.'

'They'll want feeding,' Sarah said, as if that clinched the argument.

'That's true,' Bethany said. 'In fact, I was going to ask if I might buy a little bread and warm milk from you for Mama.' She laid a small but definite emphasis on the word 'buy'.

'Oh, you've got money, then,' Sarah said, unbending slightly.

'A little. Not very much, but enough to pay our way while we're here. That is, if you'll allow us to stay for a few days,' Bethany added hurriedly.

'Well, perhaps a day or two,' Sarah conceded grudgingly. 'Till she's better.' She gave a disparaging snort. 'She's gone soft, married to that popinjay, that's her trouble. Catching a chill through sleeping in a damp bed! I never heard such rubbish.'

Bethany came to her mother's defence. 'Mama has been under a great deal of strain, lately,' she said. 'She's very upset at losing Papa; I know she misses him terribly. It's also been hard for her having to leave the house because they'd lived there for twenty years. It was a lovely house,' she added wistfully.

'And what about you? Weren't you upset, too?' Sarah demanded, watching her closely and showing something of an interest in her great-niece for the first time.

'Of course I was. I still am. I loved my father

33

very much, whatever his faults. But it must have been worse for Mama.' She gave a slight shrug. 'And one of us has to be strong.'

Sarah nodded but said nothing.

Bethany went on, 'I admit I've never done much in the way of housework because we've always had servants, but I'm willing to try and clean that little room up, if you have a broom I could borrow. You see, it's very dirty and full of cobwebs.' She hesitated. 'That is, of course, if you wouldn't mind.'

'I'll git the kindlin',' Reuben said, scuttling away with a grin before Sarah could answer.

'I expect you'll find cleaning stuff in the stable,' she said finally, waving her arm in the direction of the window. 'You can clean the place up if it gives you any pleasure but I can tell you it will soon be as bad again after you've left. I never go through there. I live here, in this kitchen.'

Bethany smiled, and in that smile Sarah saw, fleetingly, disconcertingly, a vision of her own younger self. 'Well, perhaps you will, Aunt, once I've made it habitable again,' she said. She pulled a coin out of her pocket and laid it on the table. 'Might I have some bread? And a little warm milk for Mama?'

'There's half a loaf and a pat of butter. You can take that.' Sarah nodded to the remains of the loaf on the end of the table. 'And there's milk in the jug. Reuben will fetch me some more. You can warm it on the stove there. And eat something yourself. You'll need it if you're going to clean that room.'

34

'Thank you, Aunt. I'm very grateful.' She hesitated. 'And could I put a brick in the oven to warm the bed for Mama?'

Sarah glared at her. 'Are you trying to make her more soft than she is already?' she said. Then she shrugged and jerked her head towards the stove. 'All right. Anything to make her better so you can leave me in peace.'

'Oh, thank you, Aunt. You're very kind.' Bethany gave her a grateful smile.

While she was warming the milk Reuben came back with wood to make the fire so after she had taken her mother the bread and milk and eaten some herself, she made sure Emily was as warm and comfortable as it was possible to be in such a dank and cheerless room and hurried back to the little parlour, anxious to discover what every little kitchen maid knew from the age of ten, namely, how to light a fire. She realised with some misgiving that she had an awful lot to learn if she and her mother were to survive without the help of servants when they had managed to find somewhere to live. She pushed the thought from her mind; they wouldn't be going anywhere until her mother had recovered.

She opened the door to the little parlour and choked as smoke billowed out.

'Thass all right. The chimley was damp so I burnt a few wood shavin's to dry it out.' Reuben's voice came through the smoke. 'That'll soon clear. You can come in. Best open the winder, I should think, to let the smoke out.'

This proved difficult and by the time they had between them, managed to prise open the casement most of the smoke had dispersed into the passage.

'Thass better. The fire'll draw now.' Reuben hawked and spat into the cinders. 'Now, this is what you do. You put some shavin's in first, then some small kindlin', then, when thass caught, you put bigger bits o' wood on. Then a bit or two o' coal if you've got it. When thass goin' nicely you put yer logs on.'

'It sounds simple enough,' Bethany said doubtfully.

'I'll show yer. The secret is, don't put the bigger bits on till the little bits are well alight.' Deftly, Reuben built the fire in the grate and lit it. Before long it was crackling merrily and the flames were curling round the logs. 'There. You'll be as warm as toast in here in five minutes,' he said, sitting back on his heels and watching the flames dance.

'Thank you, Reuben.' Bethany held her hands out to the blaze. 'Oh, it's lovely. But I mustn't stand here warming myself all day. I must clean this room up so that I can bring Mama down to sit here. Aunt Sarah said there was a broom in the stable.'

'Aye. There's brooms an' brushes an' plenty o' rag for polishin'. Everything you're likely to need, my gal.'

She gazed round the room, neglected for so long, and gave a rueful smile. 'I've never done anything like this, but I expect I shall manage. It's difficult to know where to start, isn't it.'

'You start at the top and work down,' he advised. 'Get the cobwebs out, sweep the ceilin' an' the walls, then the floor. That way you won't put dirt back on what you've already done. Then you can clean up the furniture. I got a bit o' beeswax an' turpentine somewhere. That'll give it all a bit of a shine. That an' a bit o' elbow grease.'

She frowned. 'Have you got any of that?'

'Aye. Plenty.' He touched his elbow. 'An' so hev you, dearie.' He made a polishing motion.

'Oh, I see.' She chuckled. 'Oh, dear, I have got a lot to learn, haven't I.'

She set to work with a will, pulling down cobwebs so thick and black they could have made a suit for an undertaker's mute; sweeping everything in sight; beating the dust out of curtains and cushions; shaking rugs and the table cover out of the window; coughing and spluttering when the dust got thick and singing to herself when it cleared. At one point, out of the corner of her eye she thought she saw a shadowy figure in the doorway, but when she looked properly there was nobody there so she decided it was a trick of the light. Or perhaps there was a ghost, she thought happily, although she had never heard her mother speak of one.

She worked harder that day than she had ever worked in her life but by the time she had finished the room looked warm and welcoming and the firelight glinted on the freshly polished furniture. Pleased with her efforts she went wearily upstairs to her mother.

'Do you think you can manage to walk downstairs, Mama?' she asked the wan-looking figure huddled in the bed. 'It might be good for you to sit in a chair for a while.'

'Is it warm down there?' Emily asked weakly.

'Yes. Warm and cosy.'

'Then I'll try.' Still swathed in the two shawls Emily struggled out of bed and allowed herself to be helped down the stairs to the little parlour.

'It's rather small,' she said, looking round disapprovingly.

'That's why it's so nice and warm,' Bethany said, hiding her disappointment at her mother's lack of appreciation. 'Come and sit by the fire, Mama.' She helped her mother to the chair by the fire and put a footstool at her feet. Then she stood back, brushing a strand of hair away from her forehead.

Emily looked up at her as if she had only just noticed her, a horrified expression on her face. 'Bethany! What have you been doing! Look at your dress! It's filthy! Your best mourning dress, which cost me a great deal of money, as you very well know. Now, look at it, all streaked with dirt and dust. And is that a tear in the lace I can see? And where are your petticoats? How can you go about with your skirts clinging round your . . . your nether regions like that? You should be ashamed of yourself.'

'And so should you, Emily,' a peremptory voice came from the doorway.

Emily looked up and Bethany turned round to see the tall figure of Aunt Sarah standing there. She went on, 'Don't you realise how hard this girl has worked to make this room habitable for you? I know what a state it was in, even though I seldom come to this part of the house and I can

38

tell you two servants working together wouldn't have done as much as she has today. She must be worn out. Yet all you can do is complain that she might have spoiled her mourning clothes. I would have thought better of you, Niece.' She nodded towards Bethany. 'I expect you're hungry after all this effort, child. Well, I've made some vegetable soup. It's good, nourishing stuff. You can have a bowl if you like.' A ghost of a smile fleeted across her face and was gone. 'I shan't charge you for it.' She turned to Emily, her expression hardening. 'Do you want some, too?'

Emily leaned her head on her hand. 'No, thank you, Aunt. I feel much too ill to eat. But perhaps a little beef tea?'

'You're not in your London house now, my girl. It's vegetable soup or nothing. I grew the vegetables myself. Take it or leave it.'

'I'll leave it, thank you.'

'You'd do well to eat a little, Mama,' Bethany said gently. 'You'll never regain your strength if you don't.'

Emily nodded wearily. 'Very well, a spoonful or two, perhaps.'

Bethany went to the kitchen with Aunt Sarah, who ladled a generous helping of soup into a bowl for her and a few spoonfuls for her mother.

'Emily never used to be such a namby-pamby creature when she used to visit me as a child,' she said irritably. 'That man she married did her no good. Made her soft and gave her ideas above her station.' She looked at Bethany. 'I always knew when she picked up with him no good would come of it. She should have stayed in the country and married into good farming stock. Like I did.'

Bethany bit her tongue. Aunt Sarah's marriage didn't seem to have done her much good, either, judging from the way she lived, but she could hardly comment on it.

'Mama was sorry to know Uncle John had died,' she said instead.

'Aye. He was a good man and could turn his hand to anything.' She handed Bethany a tray with the two bowls, some chunks of bread and two pieces of cheese. 'Now, go and get that inside you. I can see you're not afraid of hard work, child. Nor am I, but there are some things a woman can't manage by herself.' She nodded towards the door. 'Well, go on, then, go and eat it before it gets cold.'

Bethany went back to the little parlour. Her mother looked up as she opened the door.

'Oh, I'm glad you're back, Bethany. It's getting a little chilly in here. The fire needs more coal, or logs, or something.'

Bethany gave a sigh. 'You'll have to learn to do these things for yourself, Mama,' she said, carefully placing two logs on the fire. 'We shall never again have servants to wait on us hand and foot, remember.'

Emily shuddered. 'Let's not talk about that.' Delicately, she took a sip of soup. 'I've never liked thick soup,' she said, pursing her lips. 'It's so . . . so . . . *agricultural*, don't you think, Bethany?'

Bethany smiled at her. 'Actually, Mama,' she

said sweetly, 'I think it's quite the most delicious soup I have ever tasted. In fact, I think I shall ask Aunt Sarah if I can have a little more. Unless, of course, you're not going to eat yours? In which case . . .'

'No, having tasted it, I find it's not too unpleasant,' Emily said quickly. 'And one must eat something if one is to keep one's strength up.'

Bethany rolled her eyes to the ceiling. 'I'm glad you're feeling better, Mama,' she said, with only the faintest trace of sarcasm.

4

That evening, as she sat with her mother in the small parlour, in front of a fire she was having to tend herself because there were no servants she could command to do the job for her, Bethany felt that every bone in her body was screaming with tiredness. Yet she was happy; happy with a sense of achievement such as she had never known in her life before. Looking round the little room, which was bathed in the soft glow of the oil lamp Reuben had found in the stable and shown her how to trim, the firelight was reflected in the polished wood of the tables and chairs. Remembering how dirty and neglected it had been when she first saw it, she was filled with quiet satisfaction. She, who had never before in her life lifted anything heavier than a book, had moved furniture, beaten carpets and polished furniture and windows till her arms and back ached. And she had enjoyed every minute of it.

'I think I shall give the bedroom the same treatment tomorrow,' she said, thinking aloud.

Emily yawned. 'Oh, dear. I mustn't yawn like that, it will stretch my skin into ugly wrinkles,' she said, smoothing her face. 'What was that you said, dear?'

'Nothing, Mama,' Bethany said with a sigh. 'Are you ready for bed, now?'

'Not yet.' Emily wriggled deeper into her chair. 'It's very comfortable down here. I've no desire to go back to that horrid cold bedroom and that dreadful damp bed.'

'It isn't damp any more. I put another brick in when you came downstairs so I'm sure it's quite aired now,' Bethany told her. 'And I helped Reuben take the trunks upstairs while you were dozing by the fire, so you can put on a proper nightgown tonight.'

Emily sat bolt upright. 'Who is this Reuben? And when did you allow him into our bedroom?'

'Oh, calm yourself, Mama,' Bethany said wearily. 'Reuben is Aunt Sarah's friend. I think he's a farmhand and he must be nearly seventy, I should think. But he's as strong as a horse. He could have carried the trunks upstairs by himself if I hadn't insisted on helping him.'

Emily raised her eyebrows as the significance of the trunks dawned on her. 'So we're to be allowed to stay?' she asked eagerly. Then her face resolved into its habitual disapproving expression. 'Not that I want to remain in this godforsaken spot, you understand. This is not at all as I remembered my aunt's house. I'm sure, given time, we can find something a little more congenial.'

Bethany suppressed a smile. 'Then you won't be disappointed to know that the trunks were only taken upstairs because they were in the way, standing by the back door. And they can just as easily be taken back down again,' she said wickedly.

'Oh.' Emily's face fell. 'I see.'

A little later, when Bethany helped her mother up the stairs to the bedroom, she was as surprised as Emily to see a pile of bedding — sheets, blankets, pillowcases — stacked on the bed. And even more surprised to find that the brick she had put in earlier in the day had been replaced by a hotter one.

She hummed quietly to herself as she made up the bed with sheets which, although patched, were spotlessly white. A small shaft of hope that Aunt Sarah was unbending and just might allow them to stay on at Travellers' Inn shot through her.

She was not to know about the conversation between Sarah and Reuben that had brought about this apparent weakening.

It was the trunks that did it.

'They're in the way,' Sarah told him when he came up from the mill with flour for her to make bread. 'See, you could hardly squeeze through the back door. Take them out to the stables for me, will you?'

'Thass damp out there,' he said, sitting down at the table and slurping the soup she had saved for him. 'I'll take 'em upstairs.'

'No, you can't do that,' she snapped, horrified. 'Once they get their luggage up there I shall never get them out.'

He mopped his whiskers with a large red handkerchief. 'Well, what of it? That little gel's a hard worker, Sary.'

'I don't want them here! Can't you get that into your thick skull, Reuben Scales?'

'What for you don't want 'em here, Sary Pilgrim?' He grinned. ''Fraid they'll find out suthin' you don't want 'em to know about ye?'

'Nothing to find out,' she said with a shrug. 'They can see all there is to see.'

'Well, then why don't you let the poor critters stay? From what I can make out they ain't got nowhere else to go and from what you've said, that mother couldn't cook water she's so helpless. That'll put a rare burden on the little gel.'

'Hmph. You've taken quite a shine to her, haven't you, you old reprobate,' Sarah said, nearly smiling.

'Well, she remind me o' you when you was May queen that year,' he said with a sigh. 'I'd hev married you meself if my mate John Pilgrim hadn't got there afore me an' swep' you orf your feet.'

'Yes, well, that's all in the past.' A dull flush spread over Sarah's face, but whether it was from annoyance or pleasure at the remembrance of things past even she couldn't tell.

He got to his feet and raised his white bushy eyebrows. 'So will I take them boxes up the stairs, Sary?'

Sarah gave a deep sigh. 'I suppose so. If you're so eager to take them up you won't have any trouble in fetching them back down again in a day or two when they leave.'

As Reuben dragged them through the passage to the stairs, Sarah heard Bethany's voice and knew she was helping him. But she studiously avoided joining them.

Nevertheless, she was ready to question him the minute he returned. 'What did she say?' she asked, almost pouncing on him.

'Who?'

'You know very well who. Bethany, of course.'

'She said, I'll help you with them trunks, Reuben. They're heavy an' you're a owd man,' he said, his eyes twinkling.

'Rubbish.' But Sarah was too proud to question him further.

He reached the back door but turned before he lifted the latch. 'That'd be a Christian thing to do to give them ladies some sheets an' a blanket or two,' he remarked. 'That bed ain't fit for a dog to sleep on. The room ain't much better, neither. Don't you never do no cleanin' up there?'

'You mind your own business, Reuben Scales.'

He shook his pink head before ramming his hat back on. 'Ah, you're a hard woman, Sary Pilgrim.'

'I'll see you in the morning, Reuben Scales.'

'Aye. You will. If I'm spared.'

'You'll be spared. You're too wicked for the Lord to take you overnight.'

It was their usual way of saying goodnight.

After he had gone Sarah went to the oak chest in the corner and dragged out linen that hadn't seen the light of day since her husband died. She took it upstairs, but she stopped short of making up the bed. She didn't want them to feel too welcome.

But Bethany knew nothing of this as she made up the bed and replaced the hot brick. Then she helped her mother off with her myriad array of petticoats and corsets and laid her black bombazine carefully over a chair.

'Ah, it's such a relief to wear a proper nightgown again,' Emily said as Bethany helped her into bed. 'There's nothing quite like fine lawn.' She sank back on to the pillows, then made a grimace of distaste. 'Oh, dear, these sheets are dreadfully rough,' she said as she pulled them up round her ears. 'And I do believe I can feel a ridge where they've been patched! Oh, what wouldn't I give for my lovely . . . '

'Remember how we slept last night and think yourself lucky we've got sheets at all,' Bethany said crisply, cutting her off.

'There's no need to snap at me, Bethany. I was only remarking . . . '

'Well, don't, Mother. I'm too tired to listen.' Bethany slipped into bed beside her mother and was asleep almost before her head touched the pillow.

She woke early to the sound of the rooster proclaiming that it was morning and the birds twittering in the trees outside the window. She got out of bed and padded over to open the casement and looked out. It was a beautiful April morning; and she could see the dew glistening on the new corn shoots in the field beyond Aunt Sarah's garden fence. Beyond that, the river sparkled in the early morning sunlight as two boats made their way slowly upriver, with just enough wind in their sails to keep them moving. It was a peaceful sight. And so quiet. There were no street vendors crying their wares; pie sellers vying with fish sellers; ballad singers with lavender sellers; chimney sweeps with their sweeping boys calling 'Sweeeeep!' And no clop of horses and rattle of iron-rimmed cart wheels on the cobbles.

She drew in gulps of fresh country air, sharp and clean as the day. She realised now that she had never before tasted fresh clean air and she couldn't get enough of it. She had always been used to the atmosphere in London, where the air was permanently thick, polluted with horse dung and sewage, smoke and fog, rotting vegetation and the ever-present stink from the River Thames — smells she had never even noticed when she lived among them.

'Oh, Bethany, do come away and close that window,' Emily's petulant voice came from the bed. 'You'll catch your death of cold and you're letting all the cold air into the room. And look at you, still in your nightgown and leaning out like that! Supposing someone should see you!'

'There's nobody out there, Mama. This is not London, remember. There are no passers-by. But you go back to sleep. I'm going to get dressed and go for a walk, then I'll bring you some breakfast. Are you feeling better today?' she asked as an afterthought.

'I can hardly tell, after being woken like that,' Emily said.

'Well, no doubt you'll know by the time I get back.'

Bethany rummaged in her trunk and found a dress of pale blue muslin with a darker blue underskirt and bodice. Dispensing again with the many petticoats that would have made it stand out and hinder her activities, she threw a shawl round her shoulders and left the room quickly so her mother shouldn't notice.

Aunt Sarah was in the garden, digging, her brown skirts hitched up above her ankles, revealing a pair of men's boots on her feet. She looked up when she saw Bethany, and tucked a stray strand of hair back under her back-to-front man's cap.

'Ah, that's better, I'm glad to see you're wearing a bit of colour,' she said, nodding approvingly. 'A young girl like you shouldn't be wearing unrelieved black, it makes you old before your time.'

'I'm not sure Mama will agree with you, Aunt,' Bethany said, smiling. 'But she was not happy yesterday when I wore my black dress to clean the little parlour, so since I intend to give the bedroom the same treatment today I know I can't avoid offending her one way or the other.'

Sarah threw her head back and laughed. 'Well said, child.' She became serious. 'And just because you're not swathed in black doesn't mean you grieve any less for your father. It's not outward show but inward feelings that count.'

'That's what I think. But unfortunately, Mama sets great store by appearances. She always has,' Bethany remarked thoughtfully. 'It was a great blow to her when we had to leave our lovely house in London, so it's kind of you to let us stay for a few days so that we can decide what to do next.'

'Have you any ideas?' Sarah leaned on her spade.

'I think I shall have to find some kind of employment. Mama will object, of course, she'll tell me young ladies don't soil their hands working for a living, but I don't know how she thinks we'll live if I don't work; what little money we have won't last long.'

'What do you think you'll do?'

She shrugged. 'I daresay I could teach a little French and German and perhaps give music lessons.'

'Not much call for that sort of thing round these parts,' Sarah said bluntly.

'Then perhaps a Dame school?'

'Perhaps.' Sarah resumed her digging. 'Ah, well, I suppose you'll have to stay here till you decide,' she muttered, her words almost lost in the sound of the spade in the earth.

Bethany carried on to the end of the garden.

'If you go through the gate and along the side of the field you'll come to the river,' Sarah called after her. 'But don't trample the farmer's wheat, whatever you do. Keep close to the hedge.'

It was a hawthorn hedge and tiny tight buds were just beginning to form, clouding the bushes with a green haze. Beyond the hedge cows grazed in a field dotted with buttercups and daisies. Everywhere Bethany looked there were signs of new life, green and lush. Under the hedge clumps of primroses were beginning to open their delicate yellow flowers. Having been brought up in the city Bethany had never seen anything quite like it and she was enchanted.

She carried on walking along the edge of the field, accompanied by the sound of grazing cows tearing at the grass on the other side of the hedge, and down the slope to the river. The tide had turned now and the water had left the bank of sea-lavender and sedge and was sliding back over its bed of black mud. Little popping noises were coming from the tiny creatures that lived in the mud and seagulls had already begun to pattern its smooth, black, shining surface with their footmarks. She stood for several minutes, watching the gulls, watching the sails of the boats disappearing in the distance and savouring the quiet, country air, then turned and made her way back to the house.

'You've been a very long time,' Emily complained when Bethany arrived with her breakfast of porridge and freshly baked bread. 'I've been waiting for you to come back because I need the chamber pot and I'm afraid to get out of bed because I feel so weak.'

Her mother was still very weak, Bethany admitted to herself as, a little later, she sat on the bed and watched as Emily ate her breakfast, leaning back exhausted after every few mouthfuls.

'I feel so lifeless,' she complained. Her eyes filled with tears. 'And I worry so much because I don't know what's to become of us, Bethany.' She turned her head on the pillow. 'Oh, Seymour, why did you leave us like that? I do miss you so.'

Bethany stroked her brow. 'We'll manage, Mama. And Aunt Sarah says we can stay until you're quite better and we've decided what to do.' She knew this was an exaggeration but she felt that her mother needed some comfort, some stability in this harsh world into which she had been so cruelly thrust.

'That's kind of her,' Emily said without enthusiasm. Suddenly, her eyes opened wide. 'Bethany! Why are you wearing that blue dress? Where is your mourning dress? Have you no respect for your poor, dear, dead papa? I'm ashamed of you!' She spoke with more animation than she had shown ever since their arrival.

'Since nobody will see me I thought it better to wear something that wasn't important. You were unhappy because I wore my best dress yesterday to clean the little parlour, Mama. Well, I intend to do the same thing with this room today, so I shall get equally dusty and dirty.'

Emily gave a slight shrug. 'I thought perhaps I might spend the day in bed, today. It's very . . . well, it's quite comfortable and I don't feel strong.'

Bethany regarded her mother thoughtfully for several minutes. 'Very well, Mama, if you don't feel well enough to come down to the little parlour, I shall light the fire and spend the day there by myself. It's a pleasant little room.'

Emily moved on her pillows. 'Well, perhaps, if you were to help me to dress I might manage to come downstairs again . . . '

'I'll light the fire first.' Bethany left the room smiling to herself. She was fast learning how to handle her mother.

Later, with Emily ensconced in the little parlour, Bethany spent another happy day cleaning and polishing. It was something she knew she needed to do, not only to make the rooms habitable for her and her mother but it was as if in getting the dirt out of the rooms she was also cleansing herself of all the dreadful things that had happened to her recently and getting ready for a new start.

'But I still don't know what kind of a new start,' she said to Aunt Sarah when she went to the kitchen for a bucket of water to scrub the floor and told her of this feeling.

'Time enough to decide,' Sarah said. She was standing at the table kneading dough, her sleeves rolled up to the elbows showing brown speckled, sinewy arms. 'I looked in on Emily a little while ago. She says she's ill but I told her what she needs is a walk in the fresh air.' She banged the dough down on the slab. 'Mind you, it'll take her a while to get over the shock of having to leave London like that. I reckon it's only now beginning to really sink in and that's why she feels so under the weather.' Sarah suspected that there was more to the flight from London than she had been told, but she was not one to pry. She looked up at Bethany. 'You're coping with it by doing all this cleaning, but at the moment she's not coping at all.'

Bethany laughed. 'I can't see my mother cleaning a room, Aunt Sarah. She wouldn't know where to start.' She became serious. 'Neither did I, come to that. Reuben told me how to go about it.'

'Speak of the devil, you'll hear the flap of his wings.' Sarah nodded towards the window, where Reuben was just crossing the yard.

'Well, what do you want?' she asked rudely

when he pushed open the door.

'A drop o' rabbut stew, thas what I want,' he answered, equally rudely and Bethany realised that this way of speaking to each other covered a very real affection between them.

'You bring me a rabbit and I'll make a stew,' she said, shaping the dough into loaves.

'Here y'are, then.' He threw a dead rabbit on to the table. 'Still warm. I jest caught it.'

'Well, you might have skinned it, man.'

'If I'd done that you mighta said I was bringin' ye a dead cat.'

'Oh, get away with you, you old devil.' She waved a floury hand at him. 'Go and do some work. You can come back at seven for some stew.'

'I shall want a good helpin',' he said as he went out of the door. 'Time that git to seven o'clock my belly'll be stickin' to my backbone.'

'He's nice. I like him,' Bethany said, as she poured water from the kettle into her bucket.

'He's all right,' Sarah conceded, nodding. She watched as Bethany crossed the room to go upstairs again. When she reached the door she called, 'If you don't feel you've cleaned your troubles away by the time you've finished that room there's another six through there that want doing.' Then, so quietly that Bethany wasn't even sure she had spoken, 'But there's no hurry.'

5

Over the following weeks Bethany was happier than she had ever been in her life. Most days she walked down to the river and was quite surprised to see how far the tide rose and fell. Sometimes the water lapped right up to the bank whilst at others it could be little more than a thin stream between two banks of thick, black mud. She found it quite fascinating.

She was able to watch the corn in the field grow and begin to ripen and she picked peas and cherries with Aunt Sarah. In between times she cleaned out more rooms and made them habitable.

'Why don't you sleep upstairs, Aunt Sarah?' Bethany asked one morning as the two of them were companionably shelling the peas they had picked. They were sitting in the garden in the sunshine whilst Emily reclined in the shade of the apple tree a little distance away, fearful that too much sun might spoil her complexion. 'Now that Mama and I are here you wouldn't be lonely upstairs. And as far as I can see it's only in the room at the far end that the roof leaks.'

'Bless you, child, I'm never lonely,' Sarah said with a laugh. Then her face changed and became grim. 'It wasn't loneliness that drove me to live in that one room, child, it was necessity.'

Bethany looked up, frowning. 'Necessity?'

She nodded. 'It was cheaper. It meant I didn't

have to light fires in any of the other rooms. And I didn't have to keep them clean. After all, what did I need with such a rambling place? I'd got all I needed in the kitchen. So I more or less shut the rest of the house off.'

'But Mama said how prosperous the inn was when she used to visit you,' Bethany said, puzzled.

Sarah nodded, gathering up the pea shells. 'Aye, it was, when John was alive. He could turn his hand to anything, that man. He was blacksmith, ostler, wheelwright; I don't believe there was any job he couldn't tackle. He did all the outside work and I made the ale and the mutton pies and looked after the travellers.'

'Oh, yes, Mama told me about your delicious mutton pies,' Bethany said. 'Don't you make them any more?'

Sarah shook her head. 'No call for them. No call for my ale, either. Folks don't come to Travellers' Inn any more.'

'Why not, Aunt Sarah?'

'You can see for yourself. There's nothing here for them. I just about manage to keep body and soul together, with a bit of help from Reuben — he brings me flour and the odd rabbit and bit of chicken feed and I give him a meal and a few eggs, but I've no money to speak of. I grow my own vegetables and what I can't grow I do without.' She looked up. 'That was why I didn't want you here. I couldn't see how I could provide for you.' She looked down at her shabby dress under the sacking apron she was wearing. 'I didn't want you to know I was only a step

56

away from the workhouse,' she added quietly.

Bethany laid her hand over her aunt's. 'Just as we didn't want you to know that the reason we had to leave London in such a hurry was that my father committed suicide.'

Sarah's head shot up and her mouth dropped open. 'Suicide!'

'Ssh!' Bethany put her finger to her lips, nodding in Emily's direction. 'Mama would kill me if she knew I'd told you. But it's true, all the same.'

'What happened?'

'He embezzled money from the bank where he worked so that he could provide us with the life we . . . Mama wanted. When that wasn't enough he began to gamble. Or maybe the gambling came first, I don't know.' She gave a shrug. 'What I do know is that he got badly into debt and the house and everything in it had to go to pay off some of it. He couldn't stand the shame of it so he took his own life.' She paused. 'Leaving us to sort out the mess as best we could,' she added with a trace of bitterness. She spread her hands. 'That's why we came to you, Aunt Sarah. We had nowhere else to go.'

'I see. Thank you for telling me, child.' Sarah took a deep breath. 'It just shows, however much you think you know a person, you can never be sure.' She was quiet for several minutes, then she went on, 'I thought we were quite comfortably off, John and me. We both worked hard and the inn was doing well. Or so I thought. But when John died — and it was sudden, he simply dropped dead in the yard one day, I suppose his heart gave out — I discovered there was hardly any money in the house. Just enough to pay for a decent funeral but not much more.'

'Oh, Aunt Sarah!' Bethany's face was full of consternation.

A brief smile flitted across Sarah's face. 'You soon learn who your friends are when you're in trouble. Gradually, the customers stopped coming. Well, the drink ran out and I couldn't afford to buy the malt for more and I hadn't the heart to make pies. I suppose you might say my heart was broken. You see, I thought John was saving to provide for us in our old age; that's what he'd always told me. 'We shan't never need to worry about the workhouse, Sarah,' he used to say. 'I've made sure of that.' But it wasn't true. Either he'd spent it all or we hadn't earned as much as I thought, hard though we'd worked. Either way, he hadn't provided for me.' She paused. 'I don't know how I would have managed without Reuben,' she said, shaking her head. 'Well, I do, I'd have been in the workhouse by now, perish the thought.'

Bethany was silent for a long time; the only sound between them the plop of the peas as they fell out of their shells into the bowl. At last she said, her voice tentative, 'Perhaps, if I can find some kind of work, it would benefit us all if you let us stay on here? You see, if I was earning a little we would be able to pay our way so you would at least have some money coming in. Paying guests, you could call us,' she smiled hopefully at Sarah.

Sarah nodded. 'We'll see. The thought had

crossed my mind.' She looked up at the sky and began to gather up the basins that held the peas and the shells. 'This sun won't last the day out. There'll be a storm before nightfall, you mark my words,' she said, changing the subject.

'How can you tell that?' Bethany asked, surprised.

'See those little puffy clouds?'

Bethany looked up and nodded.

'Well, there wasn't a cloud in the sky when we came out. And the air is getting heavy. If we don't have a storm before the day is out I shall be very surprised.'

'Should I tell Mama to come indoors?'

Sarah glanced over at her without much interest. 'No, she'll be all right there for an hour or two.' She paused, regarding her niece. 'I know it was a long time ago but Emily's changed a lot since she used to come and stay with us as a girl. She used to love to play with the farm children and help with the harvest. Out in the fields from morn till night, she never worried about getting her dress torn or the sun spoiling her complexion in those days. Most of the time she ran about bare footed.' She shook her head sadly. 'That father of yours must have given her ideas above her station; now all she thinks about is spoiling her smart clothes and worrying about what people will think about her. Not that she's likely to meet anybody here. I don't entertain.' These last words were said in a mincing, mocking manner.

'Oh, Aunt Sarah!' Laughing, Bethany followed her into the house. She was beginning to like the tall, gaunt figure striding ahead of her.

Bethany had intended to spend the day cleaning out the little room behind what had once been the public room. Sarah had told her it used to be John's office and little snug where he entertained his special friends but over the years it had become full of clutter and rubbish. She looked inside. The heat hit her like a blanket from the sun streaming in at the window and she could see motes of dust dancing in the sunbeams. It was too hot and oppressive to cover herself in dust and dirt from this filthy little room so she closed the door and left it. There was no hurry, it wasn't a room that needed to be used. Instead she went upstairs and prepared the room that Sarah had shared with her husband until his death, determined that her aunt shouldn't spend the rest of her life living in the muddle of the kitchen. She fetched bed linen and made up the bed and even put water in the ewer on the wash stand and a bar of soap in the soap dish.

'There,' she told her aunt when she came downstairs again. 'You'll be able to sleep in your old room tonight.'

Sarah smiled. 'You're a good girl, Bethany. Thank you. I must say I shan't be sorry to get back to my old bed again. But I shall keep the little bed in the kitchen. I might need it when the winter comes.'

'Oh, Aunt Sarah!' Bethany said, a hint of reproach in her voice.

Sarah shrugged. 'Well, you never know,' she said enigmatically.

She was right about the storm. As the day went on the sky darkened to a dark blue and then purple as the clouds banked and the atmosphere became more and more oppressive and sticky. By evening the thunder that had rumbled in the distance for most of the afternoon grew louder till it was crashing overhead and jagged forks of lightning streaked into the little parlour where Bethany and her mother and aunt were eating their evening meal of bread and cheese and Aunt Sarah's home-made apple jelly.

'We should cover the mirrors,' Emily said, visibly starting with every flash. 'And the knives.'

'Whatever for?' Sarah asked with a frown.

'Because they're bright. They'll attract the lightning.'

'Rubbish. Ah, here comes the rain. That's better. I don't like lightning without rain, but I never heard such nonsense as covering up the mirrors,' Sarah said, relaxing in her chair as the first huge drops of rain fell on the window, followed almost immediately by a deluge.

Bethany said nothing. She regarded it as something of a triumph that she had managed in the last few days to lure Aunt Sarah out of her kitchen to sit and eat with them in the comfort of the little parlour. But it was a triumph that would be short-lived if she, Bethany, didn't soon find some occupation that would earn her some money, because what little she and her mother had brought with them was nearly gone. Already Bethany had walked the three miles into the little town of Manningtree and sold a brooch belonging to her mother that she had hidden in her reticule before they left London, for far less than it was worth. She still had a necklace and a bracelet that could be sold, but her mother was adamant that she wouldn't part with her rings. Sometimes, Bethany was exasperated by Emily's refusal to face up to their reduced circumstances. She still insisted on dressing each morning — with Bethany's help — in her stiff stays and black bombazine widow's weeds, despite the increasing heat and she never stopped complaining because Bethany had discarded her mourning, together with most of her petticoats, in order to give herself more freedom of movement.

The storm reached its height, the lightning, thunder and rain together forming a heavenly cacophony of noise.

'Perhaps I should take another pan upstairs to catch the rain,' Bethany said suddenly, raising her voice above the sound. 'The one already up there must be full to overflowing.'

'I'll fetch a bucket,' Sarah said, getting to her feet. She cocked her ear. 'Hark. Is that someone banging on the front door?'

'No, of course it isn't,' Emily said, shuddering. 'Nobody would be out in this. In any case, you'd never hear it over the noise of the thunder.'

'No. Listen. There it is again.' Sarah lifted her finger.

'Yes, I heard it that time,' Bethany said. 'Goodness, whoever is out there must be soaked to the skin. I'll go and see while you see to the leak in the roof, Aunt Sarah.'

'No, Bethany. Don't open the door. We could all be murdered in our beds,' her mother's anxious voice followed her as she took a candle and went along the passage to the front door.

It was so long since it had been opened that the bolts were stiff and it was a minute before she managed to draw them back and drag open the door, equally stiff on rusty hinges.

A man in a sodden cape, with water running off the brim of his hat, stood there, with an equally bedraggled-looking horse.

'Can you give me shelter from this storm for a while? My horse has cast a shoe and I've still several miles to go.'

Sarah came down the stairs as he spoke. 'We'll give you shelter from the storm, it's our Christian duty in weather like this, but we don't take travellers any more,' she said brusquely, 'the inn has been closed for several years.'

'Oh, I was not aware that it was an inn,' he said in some surprise. 'I was merely seeking shelter from the only house I've passed in the last half hour.'

'Take your horse round to the back,' Bethany said, pointing. 'You'll find stabling there.'

'There's not much in the way of feed, I'm afraid, except a few carrots,' Sarah said, 'But you'll find sacking to rub him down. Then you can come in the back door. The kitchen's warm so you'll be able to dry your clothes. You look wet right through,' she added.

Half an hour later the man, divested of his hat and cape, which were hanging on the clothes airer above the stove, but still wearing trousers wet up to the knees and a shirt that was so wet that it stuck to his shoulders, was sitting at the table in front of a bowl of steaming soup, with bread and cheese to follow.

'I can only offer you milk, or water from the well. We have nothing stronger here,' Aunt Sarah said. She was still slightly hostile towards the visitor.

'Water will be fine. I thank you,' he replied. He took a draught of the water she poured. 'This is the sweetest water I've tasted in years,' he said, surprised. 'Is it from your own well?'

'Aye. It's fed from the spring.' Sarah flushed with pleasure in spite of herself.

Bethany had been watching him from the other side of the table. Suddenly, she said, 'Excuse me, but aren't you the man who was so kind to us at Colchester back in April? At the King's Head? You found us a room and bought us a meal.'

He looked up at her, frowning. Then he smiled as recognition dawned. She remembered his smile, how it lit up his rather stern face and crinkled the corners of his eyes. 'Yes, of course. I remember. You were being harassed by some youths, as I recall.'

'That's right.' She nodded eagerly. 'I looked for you when we'd finished our meal but you'd gone, so I was never able to repay you and thank you for your kindness.'

He frowned. 'But as I remember it there were two of you. Your mother . . . ?'

'Yes, she's in the little parlour. I'll go and fetch her and tell her she's quite safe.' She laughed.

'When she heard the banging on the door she thought it was someone intent on murdering us.'

'What? On a night like this?' It was his turn to laugh. 'I assure you I was only intent on getting shelter from the infernal rain. There's not another house on this road for miles.'

'No, but the farm is only half a mile or so from here, over the fields,' Sarah said, 'I'll get Reuben to take your horse there when he comes tomorrow and get it shod for you, Mr . . . ?'

'Oakley. Matthew Oakley. That's very kind of you Mrs . . . '

'Sarah Pilgrim. And this is my great-niece, Bethany.' She looked towards the door, where Emily had appeared like a black wraithe. 'And my niece, Emily. Recently widowed, as you can see,' she added without enthusiasm.

He stood up as Emily came forward and languidly offered him her be-ringed hand as if she were bestowing a great favour.

'You're still very wet,' she remarked, frowning.

'Mama! He was out in all that torrential rain. What more can you expect!' Bethany turned to Matthew, whose dark hair was still clinging to his forehead in tight, wet curls. 'I was telling Mama that you were our guardian angel at Colchester, Mr Oakley. It's so nice to think we are now able to repay you a little for your kindness.' She waved her hand. 'Oh, please sit down and finish your soup before it gets cold.'

'Thank you.' He resumed his seat and his meal. 'Since we are so formal, perhaps I should tell you that it is Dr, not Mr Oakley,' he said, looking up with a disarming smile. 'But I would prefer to be known as Matthew, if it's all the same to you.'

'Ah, so you're the doctor man I've heard tell about,' Sarah said darkly.

'Nothing bad, I hope,' he remarked, helping himself to more bread.

'No, nothing bad,' she said. She went to the door that led to the rest of the house. 'I think I'd better see if I can find you a pair of dry trousers and a shirt,' she said, more to herself than anybody. 'You'll be about the same height as John, I'd say.'

She came back after about five minutes. 'You'll find dry clothes in the bedroom, the door on the right at the top of the stairs. They may not be overly smart but they'll keep the rheumaticks at bay while we dry your things. There's a nightshirt there, too, since you'll be staying the night. But you won't be needing that for an hour or two.'

'Do you think it's really wise, Aunt Sarah? Allowing a strange man to stay under our roof? Three women alone?' Emily asked anxiously when he had gone upstairs to change.

'Oh, really, Emily!' her aunt said scathingly.

'I'm sure Matthew is a perfect gentleman, Mama,' Bethany said.

'But if you're so worried you can always take the poker to bed with you,' Sarah nodded towards the hearth.

'Thank you, Aunt Sarah, but I don't think it will be necessary.' Emily was clearly offended.

'When he said he was Dr Oakley you said you'd heard of him, Aunt Sarah,' Bethany said.

66

'What do you know of him?'

'I've heard tell that he's a good doctor. And Reuben says he's not quick to collect his fees from them as can't afford to pay. He seems to be well thought of in the district.'

'Where does he live?'

'On the far side of Mistley, I believe.'

'Does he live alone?'

Sarah looked at her thoughtfully. 'You're mighty inquisitive, my girl. But since you ask, yes, I believe he does, except for his housekeeper. I'm told his wife died in childbirth just before he came to the district. That's all I know so it's no good you asking me anything else.'

A faint flush spread over Bethany's face. 'That's quite a lot of information for someone who hardly ever leaves the house,' she said with a smile.

'Reuben keeps me informed,' she said shortly.

'Well, all I can say is, it's a good thing I'd got your room cleaned and ready for you, Aunt Sarah, because at least we can offer him somewhere decent to sleep,' Bethany said.

'Hm. Just as I was looking forward to sleeping in my own bed again.' She gave an exaggerated sigh. 'But I reckon it won't hurt me to sleep in the kitchen for one more night.'

Bethany went over and put her arms round her, much to Emily's surprise. 'Dear Aunt Sarah,' she said, giving her a kiss.

Sarah pushed her away. 'Get away with you. There's still work to be done.' But she couldn't hide a smile of pleasure.

Five minutes later Matthew Oakley reappeared. He had towelled his hair dry and was dressed, quite unselfconsciously, in the thick moleskin trousers and flannel shirt Sarah had found for him.

'Trousers are a bit short,' Sarah said, frowning. 'You're quite a bit taller than my John was.'

'They're dry. That's the important thing,' Matthew said with a smile. 'And I'm very grateful to have them to wear while my own are drying. It really was quite a storm, but it seems to have passed now.'

'All the same, you'll not be leaving tonight. Not with a lame horse,' Sarah said firmly.

'Thank you. I shall be more than glad to stay,' he said and smiled at Bethany.

6

When Bethany walked into the kitchen the next morning Matthew, dressed once more in his own clothes, was sitting at the table companionably eating porridge with Aunt Sarah. He got to his feet when he saw her.

'No, please, sit down,' Bethany said, smiling at him. 'I have to take mama her breakfast.'

'Not till you've eaten your own. There's more on the stove. Help yourself,' Sarah said, nodding towards the blackened saucepan. 'If Emily can't get up to eat breakfast with the rest of us then she can wait for hers until we've finished ours. It's time she stopped wanting to be treated as an invalid. She's been moping about feeling sorry for herself for nigh on three months now.'

Bethany said nothing, but she did as she had been told and helped herself to the thick creamy porridge and sat down to eat it.

A minute later the door opened and Reuben came in. 'Mornin', all,' he said. Then, seeing Matthew, he snatched off his old hat. 'Ah, mornin', Doctor, Sir.'

'I expect you'll want feeding, too,' Sarah greeted him in her usual caustic manner. She nodded towards the stove. 'I've made plenty.'

'No, thankee kindly,' he said, obviously uncomfortable in the doctor's presence. 'I jest called to see if there was anything you wanted, Sary. If there ain't then I'll be on me way.' He turned back to the door, anxious to be gone.

Sarah frowned. It was not like Reuben to refuse breakfast. Then understanding dawned. The old man wouldn't deem it right to sit at the table with the doctor, whom he regarded as very much his superior.

'There is something you can do, Reuben,' she called before he could escape. 'The doctor's horse is in the stable. He cast a shoe in the storm last night. Will you take him to the smithy and get him re-shod so he can be on his way, please.'

Reuben touched what would have been his forelock if he hadn't been bald and rammed his hat back on his head. 'I'll do that right away,' he said, giving Sarah a look, half shocked, half admiring, to think that the doctor had actually spent the night there.

'Thank you, Reuben.' Matthew felt in his pocket and drew out a coin. 'I think this should cover it. Keep the change for your trouble.'

Reuben's eyes widened when he saw the value of the coin. 'Thankee, sir,' he said. 'I'll be back 'ithin the hour.'

'Good man.' Matthew nodded. 'I need to be on my rounds as soon as I can.' He turned to Sarah as the door closed behind Reuben. 'Not that I wouldn't enjoy staying longer with you, Mrs Pilgrim. You've been most hospitable. Yet I believe you said you no longer run this place as an inn?'

'That's right,' Sarah replied firmly. 'I couldn't manage it on my own after my husband died.'

'That's a great pity,' he said. 'I would have been very happy to recommend you to friends and acquaintances. The food you've given me has been excellent and the bed was clean and comfortable. It's not often a traveller finds that, you know.' He gave a rueful grin. 'Usually, one finds oneself itching and scratching after a night at an inn.' He smiled at Bethany as she came back into the room after taking up her mother's breakfast. 'I was just complimenting your aunt on the hospitality I've received,' he told her.

'Matthew thinks it's a pity I no longer run the place as an inn,' Sarah said, gathering up the dirty crockery. 'I told him, I couldn't manage it on my own.'

'No, of course, I can see it would be a great deal of hard work for one,' Matthew agreed, dismissing the subject. 'Now, I must collect my belongings so that I'm ready to leave when your man comes back.'

'Reuben's not 'my man', whatever you might mean by that,' Sarah said sharply. 'He's an old friend.'

'I beg your pardon, ma'am. I assure you I meant no offence,' Matthew said, surprised at her tone.

He went back upstairs and Bethany sat down and leaned her arms on the table. 'We could do it, Aunt Sarah,' she said thoughtfully.

'Who? Could do what?' Sarah asked, listening with only half an ear.

'We could run this place as an inn again.'

Sarah swung round. 'You don't know what you're talking about, child. You've no idea what it takes to run a place like this. It's hard work. And it needs money. I can't make ale because I

71

can't afford to buy the malt. I can't make mutton pies because I can't afford to buy the mutton. And you can't feed travellers on soup and bread and cheese all the time.'

'No, but that's what you could give them to start with,' Bethany insisted. 'It's good wholesome soup. Matthew ... Dr Oakley had no complaints.'

For a moment Sarah looked interested. Then she shook her head. 'I couldn't do it. Not on my own.'

'Could you do it with my help?' Bethany asked.

'Only if you could look after horses.'

'I don't know anything about looking after horses.'

'Well, there you are, then. It needs a man.'

'Reuben's often around.'

'He's old.'

'He wouldn't like to hear you say that, Aunt Sarah. Anyway, he's not much older than you, is he?'

'No. But he's often up at the farm.'

'He could come and teach me what to do.'

'Looking after horses is no job for a woman.'

'It is if there's nobody else to do it.' Bethany leaned forward. 'We could do it, you and me, Aunt Sarah. We could make a go of it, I know we could. We might even get Mama to help.'

Sarah threw her head back and laughed. 'Now I know you're talking nonsense, my girl.'

Matthew came back into the kitchen as the

clop of hooves heralded Reuben's return with his horse.

'Thank you again for your hospitality, Mrs Pilgrim,' he said. He took out a guinea and laid it on the table.

'There's no charge,' Sarah said, pursing her lips. 'You only had the same as us.'

'I would feel badly if you wouldn't let me pay for the inconvenience I've caused you,' he replied. 'And I would like to think I could recommend your hospitality to others.'

'Yes. Please do,' Bethany said firmly, ignoring the look her aunt shot her. 'We can at least offer a simple meal and a clean bed.'

He bowed his head slightly. 'What more could a traveller ask?' he said with a smile.

After he had gone Sarah rounded on her.

'What did you say that for? You've no idea how much trouble it is, looking after travellers. And we've no money to buy extra food. What happens when my vegetable patch is empty so I can't make soup? We shall be a laughing stock, turning travellers away because we've nothing to feed them on.'

Bethany held up the shiny coin. 'There's money here to buy malt. You can start making your ale again, Aunt. And there's Mama's necklace and bracelet. We could sell them. I don't suppose they will fetch a lot but it will help.'

Reuben came in after seeing Matthew on his way.

'Hev you two fell out?' he asked, looking from one to the other. 'You look like thunder, Sary.'

'No, we haven't fallen out but this stupid girl wants to open up the inn again. I've told her we can't do it . . . '

He sat down and slapped his knee. 'Don't be daft, Sary. 'Course you can do it. Thass a wunnerful idea.'

'Oh, you would take her side,' Sarah said huffily. 'But who will do the outside work? Who'll look after the horses? Tell me that. Will you?'

'Reckon so. Hang a towel outta the attic winder. I can see that winder from my cottage so I'll know when I'm needed an' I'll come.'

'You might be up at the farm.'

'I ain't up there all the time an' anyway I can still see that winder. An' if thass dark you can put a candle up there.'

'Hmph.'

Emily wafted down, if a rather short, plump woman could ever be said to waft.

'What's going on?' she asked breathlessly, sitting down after the effort of negotiating the stairs.

'These two are trying to persuade me to open up the inn again,' Sarah said shortly.

'Oh, no, you can't do that!' Emily was shocked. 'We could all be murdered in our beds!'

'You said that last night, Mama, and we were perfectly safe with Dr Oakley under our roof,' Bethany said with some impatience.

'Yes, but he's a doctor. That's different,' Emily said primly. 'Anyway, that kind of thing is not what we're used to. You never know what kind of ruffian might want to stay. When we lived in London . . . '

'But we don't live in London any more, Mama,' Bethany said gently. 'Things are very different for us now.'

'And it's time you appreciated that and stopped playing the lady.' Sarah cut across her words. She turned to her great-niece and with stubborn perversity said, 'On second thoughts, I think it would be a very good idea, Bethany. I think I might like to start brewing my ale again.' She smiled to herself. 'Folks used to say it was the best in the district. That's because the water from my well is so sweet.' She rubbed her hands together. 'I'll have to get all the tubs out. You'll help me scrub them, won't you, child?'

Bethany's eyes sparkled. 'Indeed, I will, Aunt.'

'And we'll leave you to wash up the breakfast things, Emily. There's hot water in the kettle and the bowl is on the shelf.' Sarah saw Emily looking with horror at her smooth hands. 'And you'd better remove your rings. If the stones fall out you'll never find them again,' she said wickedly.

★ ★ ★

Dr Matthew Oakley rode off towards Manningtree deep in thought. In the two years since he had arrived in this corner of Essex he had passed the shabby-looking house many times on his wide-ranging rounds. It was obvious it had once seen better days and in truth, when he had hammered on the door, desperately looking for shelter from the torrential rain, he had half-expected to find the place abandoned.

It had been something of a surprise, then, to find the place occupied by three such different characters; the elderly woman, clearly the owner, reluctant at first to give him lodging, yet perfectly capable and obviously used to hard work; the girl, her great-niece, eager and enthusiastic to embrace whatever life had to offer, and the girl's mother ... quite different from the other two, she had an air of genteel superiority quite incompatible with her surroundings. It was clear the loss of her husband had affected her badly. He could understand that. It was only his work that had kept him going after Celia and the baby died. He had always felt guilty over that. He was a doctor, for God's sake, yet he hadn't been able to save his wife from dying while giving birth to their stillborn child. It was a long time before he could attend a confinement without trepidation after Celia's untimely death.

He deliberately turned his mind away from those painful memories and back to his night's lodging. The place had been shabby — threadbare might be a better description — but everywhere was scrupulously clean and the food simple but tasty. It was quite plain the inn had fallen on hard times after the old woman's husband died. Understandably, she hadn't the heart or the energy to carry it on without him. But the position was good and with the energy and enthusiasm of Bethany — what a nice name, it suited the girl, too — and the knowledge and expertise of the old woman he was confident Travellers' Inn could once again thrive if the will was there. He hoped he hadn't been over-persuasive in suggesting it. After all, it was none of his business.

Nevertheless, he decided to keep an eye on the place and if they did take his advice and open it up again he would call in from time to time to see how they were faring. Especially Bethany. He drew in a quick breath. That was the first time since Celia's death that he had given even a passing thought to a pretty girl. Not that Bethany was exactly pretty, she was too tall and strong-featured and her copper-coloured hair too unruly to be what he would call pretty. 'Pretty' smacked of 'demure' and there was nothing demure about Bethany; she was more like an unbroken colt, full of unbridled energy. He went on his way, smiling at the analogy.

★   ★   ★

Sarah and Bethany spent the morning in the old brew house throwing out all the rubbish that had accumulated over the years. Then they scrubbed all the benches and racks, scoured out the wooden casks and barrels, washed stone jars and cleaned out the big copper in the corner where the water would be heated.

'John built all these benches and racks on different levels because it's more efficient to make use of gravity where you can,' Sarah explained. 'But of course, in the first place, all the water has to be carried from the well in buckets.'

'I can do that, Aunt,' Bethany said, her eyes

shining with enthusiasm.

Sarah regarded her thoughtfully. 'Aye. I guess you can.' She nodded towards the wooden yoke standing in the corner. 'You'll have to get used to that. Halves the journeys if you hook a bucket on the chain at each end. But it takes a bit of time to get the hang of carrying two buckets; you have to make sure they're equally balanced.'

'I'll learn.'

'Aye. There's plenty for you to learn, child.'

By the time they were ready to leave the brew house, scrubbed clean in readiness for the first brew, Bethany's back felt as if it was breaking in two and her hands were red and raw, the fingertips wrinkled from being so long in hot water. Her head was reeling from trying to remember all she had been told. She knew the smallest barrel in the rack was a 'pin'; the next size up a firkin; then a kilderkin; then a barrel. After that came a hogshead, a puncheon and finally a butt, which held a hundred and eight gallons. The biggest one Aunt Sarah used was a barrel, which held thirty-six gallons, but Bethany had scrubbed out several half butts, which would be used to hold the liquor as the beer went through its various stages.

'You have to be careful not to overheat the water before it's poured on to the malt or it will spoil the mash,' Aunt Sarah said at one point. 'Then it has to be left overnight before it's strained and the wort — that's the strained-off liquid — is boiled with hops.' She straightened up and rubbed her back, frowning.

'What's the matter, Aunt Sarah?' Bethany

rubbed her own back and pushed her hair back out of the way.

'I was just remembering. I reckon there are still a few hop plants growing in the hedge at the bottom of the garden. It only takes a few wrapped in a muslin bag. Helps the flavour.'

'We'll look, later. What comes next?'

'It has to be cooled and the yeast added. Then it's left to ferment before it's put in the casks, there.' She nodded towards the iron-bound oak barrels ranged along the wall from the smallest to the largest. 'The kilderkin is generally big enough for one brew, that's eighteen gallons.' Her shoulders sagged suddenly. 'Not that we shall need that much. Who do we think is going to come here after all this time? Nobody will know we're brewing again. And if they know, will they care?'

Bethany laughed again. 'They'll know if you tell Reuben. We'll have the farm workers queueing up at the door.'

Sarah sniffed. 'We shall see.'

'Well, if your beer is as good as you say . . . '

'Aye, I know what you're thinking. A good wine needs no bush.'

Bethany frowned. 'I've never understood that. Why should wine need a bush?'

'In the olden days they would put an ivy bush over the door of a tavern to show that wine and ale were sold there. If the ale was good people soon heard about it.'

'Perhaps we'd better put an ivy bush over the door, then,' Bethany said with a laugh.

'No, like you say, Reuben'll let people know

we're brewing again.' She took a deep breath and let it out slowly. 'I must say it feels good to be back in the brew house again, Bethany. I always enjoyed making my beer, although I rarely touched a drop, myself. I'd rather have a cup of tea.'

Bethany took her arm. 'A cup of tea. What a good idea. I think we've earned it, don't you?'

They walked across the yard together, much the same height and build and with the same easy stride. The thought flitted through Sarah's mind that this lovely girl was just the kind of daughter she and John had always hoped for but had never been blessed with.

7

When Bethany and Sarah reached the kitchen they found Emily sitting huddled by the kitchen range.

'You didn't light the fire in the little parlour, Bethany, so I was forced to sit here,' she complained as soon as she saw them.

Sarah strode over to the range. 'There won't be a fire here, either, if it's not made up,' she remarked, feeding it from the wood pile and venting her irritation with the poker.

'You know I don't know anything about keeping fires in,' Emily said plaintively 'I've never had to . . . '

'Well, you'll have to learn, Mama,' Bethany quickly cut across her words as she saw the expression of scorn on Aunt Sarah's face. 'If we're going to make the inn pay we shall all have to work at it.'

'I really don't know what you think I can do,' Emily said distastefully, regarding the rings on her white hands. 'I don't think serving beer to yokels is quite in my line.'

'I'm sure we shall find something for you to do that won't offend your delicate nature,' Sarah snapped, pulling the kettle forward and straightening up. 'If it's only emptying the slops.'

'Oh, I couldn't possibly do that!' Emily said, too horrified to notice the sly wink her aunt had exchanged with Bethany. 'That's a kitchen maid's task.' She shuddered. 'If you want my opinion, I think this is altogether an ill-considered idea. Just because you gave shelter to Dr Oakley for one night doesn't mean you should open up the house to all and sundry. You never know what kind of ruffian might want lodgings. We could be robbed while we sleep or . . .'

'Murdered in our beds,' Bethany and Sarah chanted in chorus with her.

She looked at them both with a mixture of surprise and anger.

'Well, Mama, you have said it all before,' Bethany said with a sigh.

She bridled. 'That's as may be. It doesn't make it any less true and I really don't think I want any part of it.' She turned away, having said her piece and went to sit at the far end of the table to register her displeasure.

'Well, would you rather starve, Mama? Or be reduced to living in one room in a lodging house while I try to eke out a living teaching children from the village for a penny a week?' Bethany asked, her voice rising with impatience. 'We can't live on air, you know. What little money we had won't last much longer and then what do you intend we should do? Live on Aunt Sarah's charity?'

'No, of course not,' Emily said irritably. She was silent for some time. Then she gave a long-suffering sigh. 'All right, I'll do what I can to help. But I fear it won't be much. I'm simply not used to it. My darling Seymour . . .'

'Well, your darling Seymour isn't here now, so

having made your point perhaps you'd like to begin getting used to it by making us a cup of tea, Emily,' Sarah interrupted rudely, flopping down on to her chair. 'Bethany and I are tired and hungry and in no mood for your theatricals.'

Emily's eyes filled with tears. 'Don't be so unkind, Aunt. Don't you understand? I miss Seymour terribly. Sometimes I just don't know how I can carry on without him.'

'I miss him, too, Mama,' Bethany said gently. 'That's why I try to keep busy. Maybe it would help you if you found things to do to keep you occupied.'

'Like making the tea,' Sarah persisted. 'My tongue's hanging out for a drink.'

Emily turned to Bethany with something of a frightened look. 'You'll have to show me, Bethany,' she whispered. 'Do you put the tea in the water or the water on the tea?'

Sarah rolled her eyes to the ceiling but said nothing and was eventually presented with a cup of tea that was, if not quite as strong as she liked it, at least drinkable. With commendable tact, she didn't point out that Emily had forgotten to use the tea strainer.

*　*　*

The next day, Bethany helped Aunt Sarah to start the brewing process by fetching water from the well. She found the yoke — crafted to fit Aunt Sarah's shoulders and therefore quite comfortable for her own — made carrying two buckets at a time less difficult, once she got used to it, because the weight was evenly distributed. She lost count of the number of journeys she made in order to fill the big copper, under which Aunt Sarah had already lit a fire. When the water was hot enough it would be poured on to the malt that Reuben had fetched from the maltings in the village.

'Can't do anything more now,' Sarah said when they had finished.

'Then I shall start work on the public room,' Bethany said, still full of energy and enthusiasm.

'No need to be in a hurry for that,' Sarah told her, refreshing herself with a draught of the cool, clear water from the well. 'The beer won't be ready for a week or more.' She shook her head. 'And then I don't suppose there'll be anybody here to drink it,' she finished gloomily.

'Then we'll drink it ourselves,' Bethany said cheerfully. She refused to have her spirits dampened by anything her aunt or her mother said because she was finding, much to her surprise, that she was happier than she had ever been in her life. She was busy; she had a purpose; in truth there were never enough hours in the day for all she wanted to do. It was a far cry from her life in London, when she had often been bored and looking for things to do to fill her days. Things that met with her mother's approval, that was. But now, she climbed into bed every night beside her mother, exhausted but happy, and fell asleep planning what she would do the next day. High on her agenda was to clear another bedroom so that she could have a room to herself, because although it was something Emily would never admit to, she snored. Sometimes quite loudly and in a most unladylike manner. Bethany would have found it quite funny if it were not for the fact that it sometimes woke her up.

There were, in fact, six bedrooms at the inn, three facing the front of the house over the public room and two smaller rooms facing to the back, with a view over the fields to the river. Then there was the room she shared with her mother. She had already earmarked the little room at the very end of the corridor for herself. But this was the room with the leaking roof and she knew there was no money to repair it so she resigned herself to putting up with her mother's snoring for a while longer.

'Perhaps I could prepare the vegetables for the soup today,' Emily said tentatively the next morning. After the previous day's outburst she had realised that she would have to make an effort if she was not to be excluded from Sarah and Bethany's plans. And Emily didn't like to be excluded. 'Of course, you'll have to show me how,' she added, suppressing an expression of horror when Sarah dumped a pile of potatoes, onions and carrots in front of her.

'You can boil these up with the chicken in that big saucepan on the stove. I killed an old hen that had gone off the lay so it'll make us a stew that'll last for several days,' Sarah watched for several minutes as Emily struggled to look as if she knew what she was doing then sat down beside her. 'Look, I'll show you.'

Smiling broadly, Bethany took herself off to

make the large public room habitable. In spite of the fact that this had four windows, two each side of the big front door, it was a gloomy room because the windows, rather small and leaning drunkenly in all directions, were covered in a curtain of dirt and grime and the peeling paintwork was dark brown. But she worked with a will, using the system Reuben had shown her, starting with brushing the cobwebs off the ceiling and cleaning the walls and windows before scrubbing the floor. Then she washed and polished all the chairs and tables and settles, including the long table near the door to the passage, where the beer had been served. After some experimenting, she placed four settles back to back with tables in between to form little private alcoves, put benches along one wall and chairs round the other two tables. When she had finished she called Aunt Sarah in to view her day's work.

'Still looks a bit bare, I'm afraid,' she said, gazing round the room.

'It'll do for now.' Sarah went over and straightened the picture of Nelson's flagship. 'But there are more chairs and benches in the snug.' She nodded towards it. 'They can be brought out if they're needed. Not that they will be, of course.'

'Yes, they will,' Bethany said firmly. 'I'll fetch them out tomorrow.'

Sarah shook her head. 'Oh, I shouldn't bother. That room is in a dreadful state,' There was something almost like agitation in her voice. 'It's where we put all the stuff we didn't know what to do with.'

'But I thought it was Uncle John's snug,' Bethany said, in surprise.

'Yes. Yes, it was. But after he died . . . No, leave it. I'll do it, when I get time.'

Bethany shot her a glance. She looked quite flustered and Bethany got the distinct impression that she didn't want her to touch the room, although she couldn't imagine why.

Sarah had got as far as the door by this time. 'Leave all this, now. Come and eat some of the stew your mother's made. It smells all right.'

'It smells delicious,' Bethany said, following her along the passage to the kitchen.

It tasted delicious, too and Emily, pink-faced and beaming, basked in their appreciation.

Reuben dropped in, as he very often did around meal times, and showed his approval by eating three helpings.

'I'll ketch a rabbut for ye in a day or two, Ma'am,' he said, slurping the last of the gravy. 'That'll make a nice tasty stew, too. I'm very fond o' rabbut stew.'

'You're very fond of anything we cook,' Sarah said, sharp-tongued as ever with him.

He ignored her and gave Emily a wicked grin. 'I'll teach ye how to skin it. You jest hev to slit . . . '

Emily shuddered. 'Oh, I don't think . . . ' she began.

'He's only teasing, Mama,' Bethany said, doubled up with laughter.

'I ain't teasin' about the rabbut,' he said innocently. 'But I will skin it for ye.'

'Thank you. I'll be glad of that,' Emily said, giving him a somewhat sickly smile.

★ ★ ★

The next day, in spite of Aunt Sarah's reluctance to let her into the snug, Bethany fetched out the things she needed to make the public room look less sparsely furnished and more welcoming. She had no intention of disobeying her aunt by tackling the snug itself, she simply wanted to make the public room look nice. Reuben had already provided her with a sack of sawdust to be put down on the floor when the time came for customers. She had polished up the brass spittoon she had found but when she saw a second one in the snug, on a shelf above the old bureau in the corner, it occurred to her that it would do no harm to provide more than one — after all, it was quite a large room.

She pulled an old chair over and stood on it to reach the spittoon but the chair was rickety and one of the legs gave way. She never quite knew what happened next. Thinking about it afterwards, she decided she must have caught the pocket of the voluminous apron she wore for cleaning on the corner of the bureau as she stretched up to reach the spittoon, although she was never quite sure. But whatever the cause, the front of the bureau dropped open and the heaps of papers that had been crammed into it spilled out on to the floor.

Horrified that Aunt Sarah might think she was prying Bethany began to scoop them up and push them back where they had come from. But she couldn't help noticing that there were a number of official-looking letters that had never been opened. There was also an envelope addressed to Mr and Mrs Pilgrim, in her mother's handwriting. That, too, had never been opened. Puzzled, she picked up more of the papers and suddenly realised that she was holding a sheaf of accounts on paper headed *Essex and Suffolk Bank*. She frowned. Bank statements? She had never seen a bank statement but she couldn't think what else it could be. And whatever it was, on each one, the column of figures added up to over three hundred pounds. But whether this belonged to Aunt Sarah or was owed by her, Bethany had no way of knowing. From the state of the house it was most likely the latter.

She sat back on her heels. So that was why Aunt Sarah hadn't wanted her to touch this room. She didn't want to risk her discovering that she owed money. She pushed a strand of hair back behind her ear, wondering what she should do. Her first thought was to put everything back as she found it and say nothing. But if Aunt Sarah owed the bank three hundred pounds she could be turned out of this house just as she, Bethany, and her mother had been turned out of the London house. Then all three of them would be homeless. The thought made her feel physically sick.

No, some way must be found to pay this money back, even if it was only a little at a time.

'Ah, there you are!'

Startled, she looked up and saw Matthew Oakley standing in the doorway.

She scrambled to her feet. 'My goodness, Dr Oakley, how you startled me!' she said, guiltily smoothing down her dress.

He came into the room. 'Oh, I do beg your pardon. I was quite sure you'd heard me come in.' He jerked his head. 'You've certainly made a transformation out there. You've obviously been working very hard.' He smiled at her. 'But I thought we'd agreed that you would call me Matthew.'

She nodded. 'What? Oh, yes, of course, Matthew.' She ran her hand through her hair distractedly, not looking at him.

'What's the matter, Bethany? Is something wrong? Have I come at a bad time?' he asked, concerned.

'Yes. No. I mean, I'm not sure,' she said, shaking her head.

'What is it, Bethany? Can I help?'

She studied him for a moment. 'Where is Aunt Sarah?' she asked, seemingly inconsequentially.

'In the garden. I saw her as I was passing and decided on the spur of the moment to call in to see how you were all faring. Your mother is with her; they're picking raspberries to make jam, they told me. They also told me how hard you had been working here, so I asked if I might come and see what you'd been doing. I'm sorry if I startled you.' He took a step towards her. 'There is something wrong, Bethany, isn't there.' It was a statement, not a question.

She nodded, then shook her head. 'I don't

know what to do, Matthew. I don't even know whether I ought to tell you.'

He regarded her thoughtfully. 'Far be from me to press you to tell me anything, Bethany, but I can assure you I never break a confidence. It's a requirement of my profession. And if I can help . . . '

She sat down on the windowsill and stared down at her hands, twisting them nervously in her lap. 'I must talk to somebody, because I really don't know what I ought to do.' She was quiet for a minute, then she looked up at him. 'You see, Matthew, it's like this. Quite by accident I've found some bank statements — at least I think that's what they are but I'm not sure because I've never actually seen one before — naturally, Papa always looked after that kind of thing and then, after he died, the solicitor took charge of things . . . ' She paused, then took a deep breath and continued, 'If I'm right, it looks to me as if Aunt Sarah owes quite a lot of money. She told me some weeks ago that Uncle John had left her without any money when he died, but she didn't say she was actually in debt.' She bit her lip against threatening tears. 'Mama and I have been through all this. We lost our house in London because of my father's debts. I don't think I could bear to go through all that again.' She turned away. 'And I think it would kill Mama.' She sniffed and brushed her hand across her eyes. 'The trouble is, I can't speak to Aunt Sarah about it because I found these documents quite by accident. They were in this bureau; it fell open when I fell off that chair and she'd told me not to touch anything in here.' She rubbed her hand across her forehead, leaving a dirty streak. 'Now, of course, I can see why. Oh, Matthew. I don't know what to do.'

He was silent for several minutes. Then he held out his hand. 'Would you be prepared to let me take a look? Maybe they're not what you think they are. Or they could be very old, or out of date.'

'I never thought of that.' She waved her hand. 'You can look if you like. They're all here. Most of them fell on the floor but some are still in the bureau.' She watched as he began to read through the papers. 'Oh, dear. Whatever shall we do?' she murmured, half to herself. 'And what will Aunt Sarah say? She'll think I've been prying into her affairs. But if she owes a lot of money . . . '

Matthew wasn't listening. Suddenly, he looked up, smiling. 'You're quite right about them being bank statements, Bethany. That's exactly what they are. But your aunt isn't in debt. She doesn't owe anybody anything. In fact, it looks to me as if her bank balance is very healthy.'

'Really!' Bethany beamed at him. 'Oh, thank goodness for that.'

'You should smile more often, Bethany. You've got a lovely smile,' he said quietly, smiling back at her. He tapped the papers in his hand. 'Yes, as I was saying, her bank balance is healthy to the tune of over three hundred pounds. That's quite a lot of money. But I'll admit these statements are rather old. And all those envelopes that have never been opened have the bank imprint, so it looks as if they might contain the more up-to-date statements.'

'She didn't open the letter Mama sent, either,' Bethany said, puzzled.

He stroked his chin. 'I wonder . . . ' He began again. 'Has it occurred to you, Bethany, that she might not have opened all these letters because she can't read?' he said thoughtfully.

'Aunt Sarah unable to read? No, I would never have thought of that,' Bethany said in surprise. 'All the people I've ever known could read . . . well, not the servants, of course, but everybody else . . . ' her voice trailed off.

'It might not be the reason,' he said hurriedly.

'No, but now you come to speak of it, it would make sense. All those unopened envelopes pushed out of the way. Every time a letter came she put it in the bureau so that she didn't have to face the fact that she didn't know how to deal with it.' Bethany warmed to her theme. 'So she never found out that she had money in the bank.'

'And now you'll be able to tell her that she has,' he said, smiling.

'But how?' she asked, in something akin to alarm. 'How can I tell her that without admitting I've been looking through her private papers? And how can I reveal that I know she can't read — if, indeed, that is the case — without embarrassing her?'

'Well, in the first place you must explain how the bureau fell open and the papers fell out . . . '

She studied him for several minutes. 'Will you talk to her, Matthew? After all, if you hadn't been here I would have gone on thinking she was in debt.'

He stood up and held out his hand to her. 'Come on, let's be partners in crime and do it together.' He cocked his ear. 'It sounds as if the raspberry pickers have returned to the kitchen so there's no time like the present.'

She took the hand he offered and got to her feet. 'I'm so glad you're here, Matthew,' she whispered. 'I don't think I could manage this on my own. I hope Aunt Sarah won't . . . '

'Of course she won't.' He squeezed her hand and propelled her firmly toward the door. 'And if she does, just remember, I'm right here beside you.'

He was amazed at how much pleasure those last words gave him.

8

Sarah listened in silence as Bethany confessed what she had found in the bureau, her expression changing from alarm to annoyance and finally to studied nonchalance.

'Yes, of course I knew they were bank statements. I just hadn't got round to looking at them,' she said airily when Bethany finished speaking.

Bethany and Matthew exchanged glances. 'So in that case you wouldn't have realised that there was quite a lot of money in the bank?' Matthew asked gently.

'Money in the bank?' Sarah's jaw dropped and with it her guard, revealing for a split second a frightened and vulnerable old woman.

'Over three hundred pounds,' Bethany said.

'Probably more than that,' Matthew added. 'There are quite a number of what I assume to be bank statements that have never been opened, so there could be quite a bit of interest as well.'

Her face creased with anxiety, Sarah opened her mouth and closed it again, without speaking.

Matthew saw her difficulty. 'These things can be very complicated, you know. If it would help, I could take you to Colchester and come to the bank with you and get it all sorted out,' he offered, still speaking gently.

She hesitated for several minutes, then she nodded. 'I think I might be very glad of that,

Matthew. I don't know anything about banks and suchlike and it's a long time since I was in Colchester. You see, John always managed all the money so I never bothered my head about it.' She plucked at her apron, still obviously not happy. 'Would I . . . would there be papers to sign?'

'Possibly. Well, yes, I'm pretty sure there will be.'

'Ah.' She chewed her lip.

He went on, keeping his voice casual, 'But, of course, not many people are able to do that, so as long as a mark is made and witnessed it's usually sufficient.'

'It wouldn't be sufficient for me. I should want to sign properly. I should want everything above board.'

'Oh, there's no question . . . '

Bethany cut across his words. 'Perhaps I could help you with that, Aunt Sarah,' she said carefully, 'Just to make sure you don't feel nervous when it comes to doing it in front of strangers.'

Sarah nodded, obviously relieved. 'Yes, you see, I don't have much call to write these days so I'm a little out of practice.' She turned to Matthew. 'Do you think you could sort all those papers for me? I get . . . muddled when I see a lot of writing and figures and things.'

'Of course I will, Sarah.' He smiled at her. 'And shall I make an appointment with the bank for next week?'

'So soon?' She looked apprehensive.

'Well, the sooner it's done the sooner you'll

have money to spend,' he reminded her.

'Money to spend.' A faraway expression crossed her face. 'John always said there was money but dying so sudden and unexpectedly he never got round to telling me where it was, so I thought he must have been joking,' she said sadly. She shook her head. 'It's always puzzled me because it really wasn't like my John to leave me so badly provided for.'

'No, I always remember him as a very kind and caring man,' Emily said, adding sadly, 'But sometimes it isn't until after they are dead that you find out what people are really like.'

Bethany said nothing but leaned over and squeezed her mother's hand. Emily smiled at her gratefully.

Matthew left, taking the contents of the bureau with him and promising to arrange a meeting with the bank manager. After he had gone, Sarah was very quiet for a long time, idly picking over the raspberries in the basket on the table.

At last, she swallowed and said, 'It's not just that I'm out of practice with writing, Bethany. I can't write at all. And I can't read, either. John did try to teach me, but there was never much time and there always seemed to be something in my head that wouldn't sort out the letters. They were all of a jumble, however I looked at them. Figures, too. So in the end I gave up and didn't bother.' She pulled back her shoulders. 'But I manage all right. Most of the time I don't need to.'

'It must have been very frightening for you

when the letters started coming from the bank,' Emily said, sympathetically. 'I know how it frightened me when I began to get all those official letters after Seymour died. Of course, I can read a bit, but I couldn't manage all those long words on official things. So I was grateful when the solicitor took care of everything and I didn't have to worry any more.'

Sarah shrugged, but it was a shrug very akin to a shudder. 'When the letters started arriving I put them in the bureau so I wouldn't have to look at them. After a year or two they stopped sending them. I expect they thought I was dead.'

'So that would be why you didn't answer my letter,' Emily said thoughtfully. 'I often wondered why you didn't reply.'

'Was it from you? I knew it was a different kind of envelope but I didn't know it was from you.' She spread her hands. 'Well, there you are. Now you know the whole story of why I was so reluctant to let you stay here. As well as not wanting you to know I was only one step from the workhouse, and God knows, that was bad enough, I was scared you'd find out I was so stupid I couldn't even write my name.'

Bethany got up and went to her. 'Oh, Aunt Sarah, as if all that matters,' she said, giving her a hug. 'And you're a long way from being stupid. Look at all the things you've taught me to do!'

Sarah looked up at her in surprise. 'Things I've taught you to do?'

'Yes. More things than I can count. You've taught me the names of the birds in the garden and the wild flowers in the field; you've taught

98

me to make bread and how to brew ale and soon you're going to teach me to make mutton pies. Oh, there are so many things. And I'm so grateful to you for letting us stay with you because I love it here. George, the old cockerel, wakes me every morning and I get up and look out of the window at the cows in the field and the boats on the river and I feel glad to be alive.' She gave her another hug. 'I'll teach you to write, Aunt Sarah. And read. It will be something I can do to repay you for all the things you've given me.'

'Yes, we're very grateful for your hospitality, Aunt Sarah,' Emily agreed, although her tone was a little less enthusiastic than her daughter's because she was still missing the luxury of her London house, with servants to attend to her every need. Strangely, although she hardly admitted it, even to herself, the only thing she missed about Seymour was his generosity, a generosity for which she had ultimately been forced to pay a high price.

★ ★ ★

A week later, when Matthew arrived in a hired gig to take Sarah the twelve miles to the bank in Colchester, she could not only sign her name and read a little but could recognise numbers — which she had never found any difficulty in calculating in her head — when they were written down.

She went off nervously clutching her small carpet bag, which she carried to boost her confidence rather than for what it contained, wearing the black bombazine bought second-hand for her husband's mourning and a black bonnet which Bethany had trimmed with flowers and ribbons to make it look a bit less funereal. Her boots, though down-at-heel, were polished to a high shine.

'She doesn't look right, dressed up like that,' Bethany said, waving her off.

'That's only because she never wears anything but an old brown skirt and that striped shirt of Uncle John's,' Emily replied. 'She's quite a striking-looking woman when she smartens herself up.'

Bethany laughed. 'I suppose she thinks there's no point in dressing herself up since she never sees anyone except Reuben. And he isn't exactly the height of sartorial elegance, is he.'

As she spoke he came round the corner of the house with a face like thunder. 'Where's she orf to, then, all dressed up like a dog's dinner?' he demanded, jerking his thumb in the direction of the departing gig.

'Who do you mean? Aunt Sarah?' Emily asked coolly.

'You know very well who I mean.' Reuben gave a sniff and wiped his nose with the back of his hand. Emily annoyed him. To his mind she was neither use nor ornament with her London airs and graces; turning up her nose and flapping her little fat, ring-bedecked hands at the idea of skinning a rabbit or plucking a chicken. It would do her good to get her hands into some of the things he'd seen Sarah tackle at times; that would teach her a thing or two.

'Matthew's taken Aunt Sarah into the bank in Colchester,' Bethany said, sensing the antagonism between the two of them.

'Why for?'

'I can't see that's any of your business,' Emily said sharply.

'Come inside, Reuben. We can't talk out here,' Bethany said. 'There's still some porridge left in the pot and I'll tell you while you eat it.'

'And do try to eat quietly,' Emily said, distastefully. 'There are times when you sound for all the world like a pig eating cinders.'

'Mama! Don't be so unkind!' Bethany said, shocked.

'I don't know how you'd know that, I'm sure,' Reuben remarked. 'I ain't never seen you anywhere near a pig sty. It'd do you a power o' good to muck out a pig sty,' he added under his breath.

'Oh, that's enough, you two. Here's your porridge, Reuben.' She turned to her mother. 'You can go and tidy up the little parlour, Mama, then you won't be offended if he slurps.'

Reuben ate steadily while Bethany told him all that had happened. When he'd finished he put his spoon carefully down on the table. 'Well, I'm glad to hear John had looked after Sary, arter all,' he said. 'I was ollus surprised he'd left 'er 'ithout any money at all.' He got to his feet. 'But now she's found she's got money I reckon she won't want me traipsin' round here all the time to keep a eye on 'er 'cause she'll be able to manage for 'erself.' He rammed his old hat on. 'Thankee for the porridge. Now I'll bid you good day, 'cause I got work to do.' Before Bethany could speak he was out of the door.

Emily came back into the kitchen as he left. 'What's got into him?' she said, her eyebrows raised as she stared after the figure hurrying across the field to the farm.

Bethany shook her head, frowning. 'I can't imagine.' She watched the retreating figure for several minutes. Then, suddenly her face cleared. 'Ah, yes, of course. I think I know what's troubling him.' She hurried out of the door, then picked up her skirts and began to run after him. He was halfway across the field before she caught up with him.

'You're wrong, you know, Reuben,' she called breathlessly, when he was near enough to hear. 'You're wrong in thinking Aunt Sarah can manage without you.'

He stopped and turned round.

'However much money she's got she'll still need you,' Bethany said, without giving him a chance to speak. 'It's not just that you've made sure she hasn't starved over these past years, although I know how grateful she is for that, but it's much, much more. You're her friend, Reuben. And a very good friend; one she values.'

He opened his mouth but before he could speak she went on, 'You don't really think she'll change now she's discovered Uncle John didn't leave her destitute, do you? You don't really think she'll drop you like a hot coal and say, 'I don't need you any more, Reuben Scales. You looked after me when I didn't know which way to turn but I'm well provided for now so, off you go, I don't need you any more.' You don't really think Aunt Sarah is like that, do you, Reuben?'

He hung his head and scuffed a tuft of grass with his boot. 'No, I don't reckon she is,' he admitted.

'I'm glad to hear it.' She paused for a minute, then said quietly, 'Do you think you might be just a tiny bit jealous? Oh, not because she's got a little money now, I know that wouldn't bother you; no, because you're afraid she might not need to depend on you quite so much?' She gave him a playful punch to take the sting out of her words and he had the grace to look sheepish. 'Well, she might not have to *depend* on you quite so much but that doesn't mean to say that she won't still need you. After all, she's got to have somebody to argue with and insult!'

He nodded, still scuffing the tuft like a schoolboy caught scrumping apples by the farmer. ''Spect you're right,' he conceded.

'So you'll be along tonight, won't you? We've got the rest of the chicken stew to finish up. I'll get Mama to put a few more vegetables in it, so there'll be plenty.'

He lifted his head and gave her a toothless grin. 'Even if I do sound like a owd pig eatin' cinders?'

She waved her hand impatiently. 'Oh, don't take any notice of Mama. It was very rude of her to say that. You must come. Aunt Sarah will be disappointed if you don't. And so shall I.'

'Orl right.' He gave a theatrical sigh. 'I 'spect I'd better come an' help finish the stew 'cause

103

you'll all be livin' off the fat o' the land from now on, I dessay.'

'Not if I know Aunt Sarah. We shall still be living on bread and scrape if she has her way,' Bethany said with a laugh.

He went off and she watched him with affection as he carried on across the field. He was a proud man who had known nothing but hard work all his life, out in all weathers, wresting some kind of a living from the often unforgiving land. She had heard the phrase 'the salt of the earth'. Watching Reuben, she knew what it meant.

★ ★ ★

Sitting round the table that evening and eating the succulent chicken stew, which Matthew had not taken much persuading to share with them, Sarah, dressed again in her old brown skirt and striped shirt, outlined her immediate plans.

'They told me at the bank that the money John left isn't enough for me to live on for the rest of my life,' she said. 'Well, I'm not daft; I knew that. But it'll make things a lot easier for us all.'

'You'll be able to have the roof mended, Aunt Sarah,' Bethany said eagerly, planning her escape to a room of her own.

Sarah nodded. 'I called in at the builders with Matthew on the way home and asked them to send somebody to do it,' she said, clearly pleased with herself. She turned to Reuben, who was mopping up the last of the stew gravy with a lump of bread. 'And I've got a nice little job for you, Reuben Scales.'

'Oh, hev ye, indeed. An' what might that be?' he asked suspiciously, without looking up.

'The old dog cart in the barn could do with a coat of paint to freshen it up. We bought some paint in Colchester. A nice, bright blue. And on market day I'd be glad if you'd come with me to buy a pony to put in the shafts.'

He looked up. 'I dunno as we'll be able to get a nice, bright blue pony,' he said seriously, shaking his head.

She ignored that remark and leaned back in her chair. 'A pony and cart'll make things a lot easier for us all.'

He sighed heavily. 'Easy come, easy go. No wonder you've never got a penny to bless yerself with, Sary Pilgrim,' he muttered, half to himself, with a sly wink at Bethany.

'*What* did you say, Reuben Scales?' Sarah glared at him.

'He's only teasing you, Aunt Sarah,' Bethany said, trying hard not to laugh.

'I'm only trying to make life easier for you as well as for the rest of us, Reuben Scales,' Sarah said huffily.

'And I persuaded her to buy a nice joint of beef at the butcher's,' Matthew said. 'I thought she deserved a little celebration.'

'Ah, thass a long time since I had a nice bit o' roast beef,' Reuben said wistfully.

'And if you carry on the way you're doing it'll be a long time yet,' Sarah said sharply. 'What makes you think you'll be asked to join us?'

'Bright blue paint. Thass what. If I don't get a taste o' roast beef, you won't git your cart painted, Sary Pilgrim.' Reuben gazed round at the assembled company with a self-satisfied grin on his face. 'An' I shan't come with you to buy a bright blue pony to go with it, neither.'

'Oh, keep quiet, you old devil,' Sarah said, 'and get this bowl of stewed apple inside you.'

Bethany caught Matthew's eye and they exchanged smiles. It was good to know that Sarah's money wasn't going to spoil the relationship between the two old friends.

9

A week later, the builder arrived and replaced the slates on the roof.

When he had finished, assuring her that the whole roof was now completely watertight, Bethany went upstairs and spent the rest of the day claiming the room she had earmarked for herself. It was right at the end of the passage and under its air of dirt and neglect the furniture in it was substantial. She worked very hard, heating and carrying buckets of water, moving things around, cleaning and polishing everything in sight. When it was all done and with pretty china set out on the washstand and dressing table she sank wearily on to the bed, rubbing her aching back and surveyed her handiwork, pleased with what she had achieved. After a brief rest she finished the task she had set herself by transferring her meagre belongings from what would now be her mother's room and put them away in her own. Then, satisfied with her day's work, she opened the window and leaned on the sill, gazing out over the patchwork of fields stretching towards Bradfield. Beyond the pasture where cows grazed among the buttercups there was a field of ripening corn, separated from it by a thick bramble hedge that Aunt Sarah promised would yield blackberries for both wine and jelly in the autumn. Beyond that was a field full of sheep. And if she leaned out far enough she could see the river winding its way towards the sea.

She smiled contentedly to herself and went downstairs. She loved it here. There was always so much to look forward to, so much to do; yet at the same time life had its own rhythmic pattern and nobody ever seemed to hurry. Her years in London seemed like another life.

'You look pleased with yourself, child,' Sarah said when she entered the kitchen.

'I am. My room looks nice. And I'm sure Mama will be pleased to have her room to herself.'

Emily turned from stirring a saucepan on the stove and pushed a strand of hair back under her widow's cap. 'I've never complained,' she protested, adding, 'but it's true. It will be nice to have a room to call my own.'

'Of course, if we get a sudden influx of visitors I may have to move back with you for a night or two,' Bethany warned. 'But I expect we'll be able to put up with that.'

'Visitors? Yes, I expect we shall,' Emily replied. Clearly the thought of visitors worried her more than sharing a room with her daughter.

They all sat down to eat.

'Mm. This pie is tasty,' Bethany said as she took a mouthful.

'It's a mutton pie. I made it,' Emily said proudly.

Bethany raised her eyebrows in Aunt Sarah's direction.

Sarah shrugged. 'She's not a bad cook. She's always got cold hands, which is good for making pastry. It'll be as well for somebody else to know how to make my mutton pies. The time will come when I can't.'

'I can't imagine that time ever coming, Aunt Sarah,' Bethany said with a laugh. 'I think you're immortal.'

'It comes to us all, my girl, in the end,' Sarah reminded her. She looked up as Reuben came in the door, spattered with bright blue paint from where he'd been painting the dog-cart. 'Except for him, of course. Wicked old devil, he'll never die.'

'I shall. I shall die o' thirst if I don't soon get another drop o' beer. I never knew sech a dry owd house. Leavin' me out there, parched and workin' me fingers to the bone paintin' that owd cart, with never so much as a 'wouldee like a drop more, Reuben?' jest so's you can hitch up the mare and go swannin' around the countryside, showin' everybody what a bargain you got at the market.' He banged his empty tankard down on the table.

Sarah put her knife and fork down with a clatter. 'Bargain! I paid over the odds for that mare and you know it, you old rascal. Did you look in her mouth?'

'Now then, you two, you're not still arguing over poor old Peggy, are you?' Bethany said filling Reuben's tankard from the jug. 'You know perfectly well you wouldn't have bought her if you hadn't thought you'd got her at a good price, Aunt Sarah. And you, Reuben, wouldn't have let her. Now, sit down and have one of Mama's mutton pies and stop teasing

109

the poor old woman.'

'Not so much of the old woman, my girl,' Sarah said.

Bethany burst out laughing. 'Why not? Only a minute ago you were implying you were at death's door.'

'I really don't think you should speak to Aunt Sarah like that, Bethany,' Emily said, looking at her anxiously and not quite understanding the banter. 'It's rather rude to speak to your elders like that.'

'Yes, it is.' Bethany bowed her head contritely, but there was still a smile on her lips. 'I'm sorry, I shouldn't have called you an old woman, Aunt Sarah.'

Sarah sighed. 'Ah, but it's no more than the truth. I am an old woman.' But the twinkle in her eye proved that she didn't really accept the fact.

Reuben ate his pie and slurped his beer. When he had finished he hiccupped gently. 'Well, I reckon I'd better get back to paintin' that owd cart or I shan't get finished afore nightfall.' He got to his feet swaying gently. 'My word, thass a rare strong brew you've made, Sary Pilgrim. If I hev any more I shall be puttin' the paint on the cart upside down.' He looked down into his empty mug. 'Well, I might jest manage another drop . . . '

'That you will not!' Sarah said, waving him away fiercely. 'You've had more than your fair share already.'

He went off, grinning aimiably, and after a while there were voices in the yard. With a knowing look at Sarah, Bethany picked up the jug of beer and two mugs and took them out to where a couple of farmhands were sitting on a bench outside the stables, enjoying the evening sunshine and throwing the odd word to Reuben as he finished painting.

It was a habit that had begun quite casually. One evening, after a particularly hot day, two of the farm workers had called in at the yard on their way home, ostensibly 'for a word with owd Reuben'. Reuben had suggested to Sarah that a mug of beer might be 'jest the thing after a hard day's work' and this had gone down well. After that, as news of Sarah's brew spread and whether Reuben was in the yard or not, there would be at least two or three who called in 'for a word with Reuben' on their way home. Soon it was three or four, then six or seven and before long another bench had to be found, and then a table for the game of dominoes that somebody — nobody knew quite who — had produced. Soon, the yard became a regular meeting place during the long summer evenings and Pilgrim's beer once again began to make a profit.

Still Sarah clung to her insistence that she was not intending to open up the inn to the public again and that the price the drinkers paid was only to cover the cost of brewing.

But one evening, in the middle of a game of dominoes, it began to rain. It was a heavy summer storm that both Harry the shepherd and Sid the cowman had watched rolling in, saying anybody with half an eye would have seen it coming if they hadn't been staring so hard at the dots. But there was no time to argue. The dominoes were swept up and they all piled into the public room to continue their drinks and their game.

Whether Sarah liked it or not — and secretly, although she wouldn't admit it, she liked it very much — Travellers' Inn was back in business.

Emily was less enthusiastic. She was happy enough to spend time in the kitchen, a voluminous white apron covering her black mourning dress, making Sarah's famous mutton pies and to experiment with cooking various other delicacies, but she refused to even set foot in the public room, let alone serve the beer there.

'It's no place for a lady,' she said primly. 'And I don't like the idea of Bethany being in there with all those men, either. What you yourself do, Aunt Sarah, is, of course, none of my business.'

'You listen to me, Emmy Proctor,' Sarah said, using Emily's childhood name. 'The men who come to Travellers' Inn behave themselves because they know very well if they don't they'll be out on their ear and never allowed back. They know I don't allow foul talk and bad language and they respect me for it. They respect Bethany, too, although if it makes you feel any better I can tell you I don't let her stay in there when I'm not there. Not because I don't trust the men, but she's still only a young girl and it wouldn't be right. There. Does that satisfy you?'

Emily shrugged uncomfortably. 'I still don't think it's right for women to run an establishment of this kind,' she said, but she didn't sound convinced.

'Plenty of women do,' Sarah retorted.

'Not well-bred women,' Emily said. 'My Seymour . . .'

Sarah wagged a finger at her. 'Let's hear no more of what your Seymour would or wouldn't have allowed, Emily. Your Seymour left you in no position to choose, remember. But if you don't like living here, the door is never locked. You're free to go whenever you like.'

'I've nowhere to go to.' Emily shook her head sadly.

'There's always the Spike,' Sarah said cruelly, using the local name for the workhouse.

Emily stared at her, her face a mask of horror. 'Oh, I couldn't . . .'

Sarah nodded complacently at her reaction. 'Then you'll have to make the best of living here. Just as Bethany's doing.'

'Bethany likes it here,' she said feebly.

'Yes, and so did you, once upon a time, before your head was filled with big houses and big ideas.' Sarah waved her hand dismissively. 'Bah, I haven't got time for all your airs and graces. I've got work to do. And so have you, Emily.' She nodded towards a pile of washing up.

★ ★ ★

Sometimes, when he was passing and had a few minutes to spare Matthew Oakley would drop in for a mug of ale and a brief chat. This didn't happen very often because he was the only doctor in a wide area so he was always busy. There was another reason, too, although he

113

rarely admitted it, even to himself. He realised it would be very easy to fall in love with Bethany; he was full of admiration for the way she was coping with a new and unfamiliar way of life, a way of life which obviously suited her now that she was becoming used to it because each time he saw her she seemed to have blossomed and grown even more lovely. Or was it just in his eyes?

One evening, returning from a visit to the Squire, who was suffering from a painful attack of gout, which he refused to admit might be aggravated by rich living, Matthew gave in to temptation as he was passing Travellers' Inn and called in to slake his thirst with a mug of Sarah's best brew. He had refused port wine from the Squire, saying he made it a rule never to drink when he was out on his rounds, but he had finished for the day now so the rule no longer applied.

He left his horse to graze on the grass verge and went in through the open door of the public room. This was something new. Previously, the front door had always been barred and bolted, but now the companionable buzz of men's voices could be heard as he approached. He glanced up at the sign above the door. It could do with a lick of paint; the coach and horses were so weatherworn as to be barely distinguishable.

The buzz of conversation ceased as soon as he entered.

'Oh, don't mind me, boys, I've only come for a drop of Sarah's best,' he said, taking off his hat and mopping his face with a large white handkerchief. 'This heat gives a man a thirst.'

'Aye. That it do, Sir,' one or two mumbled into their mugs.

Sarah jerked her head towards the kitchen. 'Perhaps you wouldn't mind stepping this way, Doctor,' she said. 'Emily's not feeling too well. I'd be glad if you'd take a look at her.'

'Certainly, Sarah.' He followed her through into the passage, ducking his head as he went through the door. 'What seems to be the trouble?'

Sarah turned and winked as she led him into the little parlour. 'I'm sure you won't mind, Matthew, but I'll bring your drink in here. I think the men in there feel a little uncomfortable in your presence, you being the doctor.'

'You're very perceptive, Sarah,' he said. He grinned at her. 'I wouldn't want my presence to inhibit their drinking. Ah, good evening Emily,' he said as he saw Emily sitting by the window with her embroidery. 'And how are you today?'

'A little tired. I've been busy baking all day.' She gave him a deliberately wan smile. 'You might like to try one of my fairy cakes with your ale.'

'They're quite delicious,' Bethany said, coming in with his drink and nodding a greeting. 'I'll fetch you a couple, Matthew.'

She came back with a plate of cakes, sat down and took one herself after offering them to him. 'I must remind Aunt Sarah to get a couple of the boys to bring in another barrel before they go, so it will have time to settle before we tap it.' She automatically refastened the slide that held back her unruly coppery hair as she spoke.

'You've quite taken to the role of inn keeper, I can see that,' Matthew said, smiling at her.

'No. That's Aunt Sarah's role. I simply help where I can,' Bethany answered seriously. Then her face broke into a smile. 'But I enjoy it, just as I enjoy everything these days.'

He nodded approvingly, thinking what a lovely smile she had and how it lit up her face. He pushed the thought away, saying, 'I'm glad to hear it. It's better than any doctor's medicine.' He drained his mug and stood up. 'I must be off.'

'Have you still got work to do?' Emily asked.

'No, I've finished for today, thank goodness. It's been a long day.' He yawned as he thought about the empty house he was about to return to and the meal that would have been left for far too long over a saucepan by Mrs Weston, his housekeeper. At the door, he turned to Bethany.

'Of course, it's none of my business, but have you given any thought to repainting the sign over the door? I noticed as I came in that the paint is so weather-worn that it's impossible to see what it says.' He shrugged. 'I shouldn't think it would cost too much to have it repainted and it would brighten the front of the place up no end.'

Bethany's face lit up. 'Oh, what a good idea. I'll get someone to take it down and I'll repaint it as a present to Aunt Sarah.'

'You?' He raised his eyebrows in surprise.

'Why not? It would put the art lessons my father paid such a lot of money for to some use.'

116

There was the barest trace of bitterness in her tone.

He shook his head. 'The number of things you can turn your hand to never ceases to amaze me, Bethany,' he said admiringly.

Bethany flushed with pleasure, but she tossed aside his remark with, 'Maybe you should wait and see what kind of a job I make of it before you say that, Matthew.'

After Matthew had gone and the barrel had been fetched and put in place, Bethany went over to Reuben, who, with an eye to future winters, had commandeered the chimney corner for his own, and quietly asked if he would ask someone to remove the sign discreetly and take it round to the stables so that she could paint it.

'I reckon Zack's the man for that,' he said, nodding towards a young man with a shock of black hair who was busy with a game of dominoes. 'He's a strong as a horse and he never mind what he does.' He leaned towards Bethany. 'I dunno where he come from but he's a nice enough fella. He's turned up ready to help with the harvest for the past couple o' years. He's a good worker, too. I think he'd like to settle in these parts, but the Gaffer's got enough hands most o' the time so he won't take him on permanent, like. I'll hev a word with him an' get him to fetch a ladder round.'

Bethany put her finger to her lips. 'Don't let Aunt Sarah know,' she said. 'I want to paint it as a surprise for her.'

'There's plenty o' that blue paint left over

117

from the cart,' he chuckled. 'You can use what you want o' that.'

'Thanks all the same, Reuben, but I've got something a little more artistic in mind than slapping on a coat of blue paint.'

Things worked out very well. When Aunt Sarah took Peggy and the bright blue dog cart on its first outing she was happy for Bethany to go with her. While Aunt Sarah was busy shopping for her needs Bethany bought paint from the ironmongers and hid it under a blanket in the back of the cart. Riding back, with Peggy trotting happily between the shafts, Aunt Sarah gave her the reins and dozed in the sunshine, knowing that Peggy would give no trouble. Sitting up in the driving seat Bethany could look out over the fields of nearly ripened corn and she was filled with a quiet contentment.

'Mama should have come with us,' she mused, half to herself. 'She would have enjoyed this.'

'Hmph,' Sarah said, waking up. 'If I know your mother, she still has visions of a carriage and pair, my girl. I don't think she's quite ready to be seen travelling in a dog cart.'

Bethany grinned. 'You're probably right. But I still say she doesn't know what she's missing.'

10

Zachary Brown was a tall, muscular man, clean-shaven, with regular features, a ready smile and deep-set, steel-grey eyes that missed nothing. He had a healthy tan from being out in all weathers, summer and winter alike. He had been brought up in the Essex port of Harwich by his grandmother, his mother having died when he was a child. He had never known who his father was and privately, from what he had heard, he doubted if his mother had, either. After his grandmother died, when he was about twelve, he was left alone in the world, with two choices; the workhouse or fend for himself. He chose the latter. Living in Harwich, there was always work to be had, loading cargo on to ships, carrying bags for wealthy passengers, holding horses' heads for a penny. He even did a bit of crossing sweeping so that the Quality didn't get their boots soiled as they went between the hotel and the packet boat.

That was what he did in the winter, being allowed to sleep in a tiny room under the eaves at the back of The Jolly Sailor in return for humping casks and barrels, sweeping floors and emptying spittoons.

But in the summer he liked a change from working at the busy port and he made his way inland to help on the farms. He enjoyed this. He loved the wide open spaces, the sun on his back as he hoed turnips, the smell of the grass and corn, and the camaraderie of the reapers at harvest time. For the past three years he had worked for Isaac Walford at Marsh Farm, sleeping in the barn and eating in the farmhouse with the regular workers. He always kept himself clean and well shaved, worked hard, never minding what he was asked to do, never made trouble and was always cheerful. Because of all this he was never out of work.

Having reached the age of twenty-four he sometimes had an idea he ought to consider settling down, with his own fireside, a compliant wife to do his bidding and look after his every need and a clutch of children to look after him in his old age. But so far, he had never met anyone worth sacrificing his freedom for.

He was intrigued when old Reuben asked him to take down the inn sign because the coppery-haired girl was going to repaint it. That was a man's job in his view and he was interested to see what sort of a fist she was going to make of it. Therefore, he made a point of slipping into the stable when he knew she was at work there, just to take a look and possibly to have a quiet laugh at her expense.

He was amazed, however, as he watched the transformation from what was little more than a greyish board with a few pale colours streaked here and there, to a picture of a brightly coloured coach with steaming horses, a coach-man in his thick greatcoat and tall hat and the outside passengers similarly attired. The guard seated at the back of the coach even had the horn to his lips, blowing a warning that the coach was approaching.

'My, thass clever,' he breathed as he watched Bethany putting the finishing touches. 'Where'd you learn to do that?'

'I went to art classes before I came here to live,' she answered absently. Then, as if suddenly realising he was there, she turned to look at him, frowning. 'But what are you doing here? Why are you always watching me? Shouldn't you be at work?'

'I've finished for today. An' I think thass clever, what you're doin', so I like to watch.' He grinned at her. 'What time will the Big Room be open?'

'Big Room? What do you mean?' she looked at him blankly.

'The Big Room, where you sell the beer. I'm fair parched.'

She wiped her brush on a rag. 'Well, if you want a drink you can work for it,' she said briskly. 'We need water from the well. Mr Isaac has asked us to supply beer for the harvesters and also for the harvest home so we've got a lot of brewing to do and that means we'll need a lot of water from the well. The yoke is over there, see?' she nodded to the corner where the yoke was propped.

'Who usually fetches the water for the brewin'?' he asked, fitting it across his shoulders so that it sat comfortably.

'I do.'

'Thass powerful heavy work for a young woman,' he remarked.

121

'That's why I've suggested you should do it,' she answered coolly.

'How many bucketfuls?'

She pursed her lips. 'About twenty, I should think, to begin with. Have a word with Aunt Sarah, she'll tell you.'

'Twenty! Thass ten journeys!'

'Congratulations. You can count.' She spoke without looking up, concentrating on putting the features on the coachman's face.

'Don't you be saucy or I'll . . . '

She looked up, her eyebrows raised. 'You'll what?'

He grinned. 'I'll go an' fetch the water.'

Bethany sat back on her stool after he had gone, a half smile on her face. She had never spoken to anyone quite like him before. It was obvious he admired what she was doing. Or was it perhaps herself he admired? She wasn't sure. Thoughtfully, she watched out of the open door as he carried the buckets into the brew house, then went back to the well for more at a smart pace that didn't seem to alter whether the buckets were empty or full. It seemed he was tireless.

After that, he always seemed to be on hand when water was needed from the well or when barrels needed changing in what had come to be called the Big Room. And he fixed the newly painted sign back over the door, almost as anxious as Bethany to see Aunt Sarah's reaction to it.

They stood in a line on the opposite side of the road, looking up at it, Sarah, Bethany,

122

Reuben — who never liked to be left out — and Zack. Even Emily came out to see what all the fuss was about.

Sarah shook her head. 'It's a bit too eye-catching,' she remarked, turning the corners of her mouth down. 'We shall have all the coaches stopping here.'

'Since there are never more than two coaches a day, and they won't always stop here, I don't see that as a problem, Aunt Sarah,' Bethany answered.

'They might want to put up for the night,' Emily said nervously.

'Oh, Mama! What if they do? That's what an inn is for, for goodness sake.' Bethany turned to her impatiently.

'Well, we might . . . '

'If you say we'll all be murdered in our beds once more, Mama, you'll be the first victim, I promise you that.' Bethany spoke through gritted teeth.

'I think it looks real nice,' Zack said, as proudly as if he'd painted it himself.

'Well, if we find we've got a stable full of horses to be fed and watered and bedded down, will you come and help Reuben to look after them?' Aunt Sarah said, her voice sharp. She wasn't sure whether she liked Zachary Brown; he was a bit too forward, a bit too familiar, for her liking. But she had to admit he was a worker.

'Yeh. I'll come an' help. Any time. I like horses. I'm good with 'em.'

Sarah winced. She wished he wouldn't boast. She also wished he wouldn't wink at Bethany when he thought nobody else was looking.

*   *   *

The corn had grown tall and golden. Everyone's eyes were turned to the sky, hoping and praying the good weather would last until the harvest was in and there was an air of anticipation and muted excitement in the men from the farm when they came in for their evening drink. Harvest was a time when a man could earn the extra money to pay for winter clothes for the family and when wives and children could also take their part and earn a little.

When the day came for reaping to begin, Sarah and Bethany donned their oldest clothes and bonnets with deep frills at the back to protect the backs of their necks from the sun. Then, wearing boots to prevent the stubble from tearing their ankles they went to the first field to be cut. The reapers were already out, their great scythes swinging rhythmically as they cut swathes of the long-stemmed corn, expertly cutting so that it fell neatly for the binders to come along and tie it into sheaves ready for traving, which was what Sarah said was the term for stacking the sheaves into stooks. Bethany and Sarah would be traving, behind Reuben and another man, who were binding and tying the sheaves. Zack, a younger man, was wielding the heavy scythe, which was carefully tailored to his height and reach, stopping in his rhythmic swing only to hone the blade on his rub-stone to keep it razor sharp.

It was hard and hot work. The corn was

prickly and dusty and the insects bit mercilessly, but Bethany refused to admit she was tired while the others kept working, especially Aunt Sarah, who was over three times her age. Nevertheless, she was grateful when the time came to stop for a drink and something to eat.

Emily had declined to come and work in the fields; the horrified expression on her face when it was suggested revealed that she thought it was beneath her dignity. Hearing the laughter and banter from the workers and seeing the children singing and playing together, because the whole village had turned out to help, Bethany thought sadly what a lot her mother was missing. But Emily relented sufficiently to bring along the pasties she had cooked and they sat by the hedge — Emily on a small stool she had brought with her, Bethany and Sarah on the grass — and ate their pasties and drank beer from the cask Zack had carried down on his shoulder. A little further along, in the shade, several mothers sat together suckling their babies before replacing them in the nests they had made for them in the long grass, and other groups of women sat laughing and talking together. The men tended to congregate in a different place, either talking and drinking or lying back in the sun gathering their strength for the rest of the day. Work wouldn't finish until it was too dark to see and it would begin again next morning at dawn.

'Can I get you another drink, Ma'am?' Zack was at Sarah's shoulder, holding out his hand for her mug.

'No. If I have any more I shall want to sleep

instead of work,' Sarah replied. She hadn't heard him approach and she didn't like it.

'What about you, Miss Beth?' He cocked an eye at Bethany.

She blushed. Nobody had ever called her Beth before and it rather pleased her. She shook her head. 'No, thank you, Zack.'

Sarah intercepted the look that passed between them and liked it even less.

By the time the reapers stopped for the night Bethany felt as if her back was breaking and her arms were aching so much she could hardly lift the spoon to eat the broth her mother had prepared for them. Even Aunt Sarah admitted she was tired and would be glad to go to bed. But it had been a good day. And as the reapers worked their way round the field and the amount of standing corn grew less and less Bethany had been amazed at the number of rabbits that had run out from their hiding places among the tall stalks, only to be knocked on the head by the young boys waiting for them with sticks. Even as young as seven they were adept at catching them and sometimes it was difficult to see who ran the faster, the rabbits or the boys.

The following days took on the same pattern. The only difference was that gradually Bethany found she was less tired at the end of the day and by the time the last load of the harvest was loaded on to the wagon and the horkey bough, which would be tied to the topmost beam of the barn to ensure a good harvest the following year, had been hoisted on to it, she was able to dance behind the wagon and sing with everybody else.

Everyone was in high spirits and looking forward to the Harvest Home provided by Mr Isaac at the farm. A long table was laid out in the yard and the farm workers and their families sat down to the best meal they would have in the year. Some thirty people sat round the table, with Reuben, who had been selected as this year's Lord of the Harvest, at the head. Mr Isaac and his elderly housekeeper, Mrs Kraft, waited on table, serving lavish helpings of roast beef, and vast quantities of suet pudding and vegetables, to be followed by huge apple pies and cream. The people, who rarely saw meat apart from the odd rabbit, ate till they could eat no more and washed it all down with Sarah's ale.

Then the dancing began, with Billy Shovel, the fiddler hired for the purpose, playing as tirelessly as the dancers danced. Little children fell asleep under the table, while the bigger ones joined in the dancing until they were too weary to dance any more and crept into a corner to sleep like their younger brothers and sisters.

'Come on, you'll dance with me, Miss Beth, won't you?' Zack came over and held out his hand.

'Shall we take a turn, too, Sary Pilgrim?' Reuben asked as Bethany got to her feet.

'No, that we shan't,' Sarah said sharply. 'You're too old to go prancing round the floor and so am I.'

'Ah, don't be daft. If the young 'uns can do it, so can we.' He pulled her up and put his arm round her waist and twirled her on to the floor. They were an incongruous pair, the tall, upright woman, not quite so thin as she had been six months ago, and the short, fat, bandy-legged man in gaiters and smock, but before long she was laughing as much as he was at their efforts to keep up.

Emily sat watching, her eyes mostly on her daughter, dancing with Zack. They made a handsome pair and it occurred to her, not for the first time, that it would be nice if Bethany could meet a suitable man and marry him. Not Zachary Brown, of course, the daughter of Seymour Stanford deserved better than an itinerant farm worker.

'You're not dancing, Ma'am?' Mr Isaac came and sat beside her. He was a thick-set man of medium height, with a craggy face and greying hair and whiskers. His blue eyes, as he looked at her questioningly, were shrewd but kindly.

She smiled, a little nervously. 'No. I think it wouldn't be appropriate. You see, I'm still in mourning.' She plucked at her dress. 'It was only at my aunt and my daughter's insistence that I left off my weeds, but they said I should.'

'Yes, I'd heard your husband had died, Ma'am. I'm sorry to hear that, but that dark blue colour suits you very well, if I may say so,' he said gallantly. He smiled. 'And I don't see why you shouldn't join in, if you feel like it. The steps are not difficult.'

She still hesitated. 'Well, I don't know . . . '

He leaned towards her. 'To tell you the truth, Ma'am, I feel I should take the floor but I don't know who to ask. I would have asked my housekeeper, but as you saw, she's getting on in years and today has been hard work for her so she has gone home to bed. The problem is, if I ask one of the workers' wives to dance I'll have to dance with them each in turn or I'll be accused of favouritism.' He sighed ruefully. 'Years ago I might have quite enjoyed it, but nowadays I don't think I'm quite up to that much activity.' He opened his hands towards her. 'But if you would consent . . . '

'Well, if you put it like that.' Emily got to her feet, secretly glad to have a legitimate excuse to dance with this rather nice farmer.

The beer flowed freely and the noise level rose until the fiddler could hardly be heard above the shouting and singing of raucous songs.

'Take no notice, Ma'am,' Isaac Walford said as he danced with Emily for the tenth time. 'It's good for them to let their hair down once in a while.'

'I can't hear what they're singing,' Emily admitted, wondering if she looked a sight since some of the pins had come out of her hair.

'That's as well, Ma'am. Their songs are not for the ears of ladies.'

Bethany had danced every dance, the young men of the village taking it in turns to spin her around. She couldn't remember when she had enjoyed herself so much.

'My turn now?' As a boisterous young lad twirled her round at the end of a particularly strenuous barn dance she almost fell into the arms of Matthew Oakley.

She laughed up at him. 'Matthew! I didn't realise you were here.'

'I only arrived a few minutes ago. Mr Walford suggested I should drop by but I thought it best to wait until the beer had run freely. I didn't want to inhibit the proceedings.' As he spoke they joined in with a rather ramshackle attempt at Sir Roger de Coverley, ramshackle because half the dancers were drunk and the rest didn't know the steps. The dance ended with everyone sitting on the floor, too weak with laughter to dance another step.

All too soon it was time to leave. Reuben, as Lord of the Harvest, was hoisted precariously on to the shoulders of two of the strongest men and proposed a toast to Mr Isaac, thanking him for the best Harvest Home in living memory — he had to make three attempts to say this because the amount of beer he had drunk muddled the words as they came out. But everyone got the gist of what he was trying to say and they all cheered in agreement before staggering off to their beds and the day off Mr Isaac had awarded them for all their hard work getting in the harvest.

When the last straggler had gone Isaac invited Sarah, with Emily and Bethany, into his large, stone-flagged kitchen for a last drink. Matthew was invited too.

'A cup of tea is what I'd like more than anything,' Sarah said, easing herself carefully down on the settle in the inglenook. 'It's been an exhausting evening.'

'I'll do it,' Bethany said quickly, going over to the immaculate kitchen stove and pulling the kettle forward, before getting cups and saucers down from the dresser and laying them out on the scrubbed table.

'Thank you,' Isaac said. 'I'm not very good at hospitality when Mrs Kraft isn't here, but I hate coming in to an empty house when all the revellers have gone. Everything seems so flat, somehow. And I'm always too keyed up to sleep because I've been so anxious that everything would go right.'

'I'll wager none of the workers would ever imagine that,' Matthew said with a smile.

'Probably not,' Isaac said, gratefully accepting a cup of tea. 'Any more than they realise that paying their wages is not my only expense and that if I don't get a good price for my crops I don't have money to buy more, as well as paying them. To tell you the truth things are not as rosy as I might like them to be.'

'Would you be willing to sell some land, if the railway comes?' Matthew asked.

Isaac drank his tea as he pondered. 'I'm not sure,' he said. 'Once the land's gone the potential for crops goes with it. It's a bit like eating your own tail.'

'Do you think the railway will come?' Emily asked.

'No, not to these parts,' Sarah said firmly.

'I must beg to contradict you, Ma'am,' Matthew said. 'I think before many more years we shall have a railway network all over the country. There is already a proposal to bring the railway through from London as far as Colchester, and if that happens it will only be a matter of time before a line goes through to Harwich . . . '

'Some long time, I should think,' Isaac said a little uneasily.

'But who will use it?' Emily asked. 'I've heard the carriages are open like cattle trucks. One could catch one's death of cold simply travelling on them at such high speeds. Far more comfortable to travel by coach, I'm sure.'

'You didn't say that when we travelled here by coach, Mama,' Bethany said with a laugh.

'Well, we can only hope the railway won't come,' Sarah remarked. 'Because if it does, it will be the end of the coaching inn and all your hard work, Bethany, in persuading me to open up Travellers' Inn again will be for nothing.' She got to her feet. 'Now, I'm going home to bed.'

Matthew and Isaac both got to heir feet as the three women prepared to leave.

'I wouldn't worry, Bethany,' Matthew said quietly. 'I'm sure the inn is safe. It will be several years before the railway reaches these parts. But I'm sure it will. Eventually.' He smiled at her. 'But who knows where you'll be by then?'

11

A few nights after the Harvest Home, about nine o'clock on a windy night towards the end of September, there was the sound of horses' hooves and the rumble of coach wheels on the cobbles outside the kitchen.

'I know what this means,' Sarah said. 'They'll be wanting a bed for the night.'

'Our first coach! Oh, how exciting!' Bethany said, restraining herself with difficulty from clapping her hands.

'I don't know about exciting, it's hard work, as you'll soon find out,' Sarah said dryly.

A moment later there was a banging on the door.

'Three ladies and two genl'men require beds for the night, Ma'am,' the coach driver said, tipping his tall hat to Bethany, who had got to the door first. 'They had a rough crossing from Holland and they need to sleep afore they go any further. And I could do with a meal and a bed for the night, meself, Ma'am.'

Standing just behind Bethany, Sarah nodded. The meal and a bed was what a coachman expected in return for the business he had brought to the inn. 'I'll get somebody to see to the horses,' she said. She laid a hand on Bethany's arm. 'Is Reuben still here, in the Big Room?' she asked briskly, immediately calling on her past experience of running Travellers' Inn.

'No, I think he's gone back to his cottage. But Zack's still in there. Shall I fetch him?'

'Yes. Ask him to come right away. He said he knows what to do with horses, now he can prove it. Then go upstairs and make sure the beds are aired. I'll ask Emily to put soup to warm and to heat some pies in the oven. It's a good thing she baked today. Oh, then you can lay the table in the little parlour. That will be the best place for guests. Can't ask them to eat in the kitchen with the coachman.'

She turned back to the coachman, who was helping the occupants out of the coach; three rather ill-looking women and two men who didn't look much better. Only one of the women spoke English and that not very well, but they managed to make Sarah understand that they were grateful to be on dry land after their terrible crossing and would be glad of a little food and a bed for the night.

Later, when she took the soup and hot rolls into the little parlour, Bethany discovered that the foreign languages she had been so scathing about learning were useful after all, because she was able, in a mixture of fairly fluent French and German, to ask the visitors where they were bound for. Relieved to find someone who could understand what they were saying, they told her that they were making for Ipswich, where they had friends. By the time she took in the hot pies and some mulled ale the soup and rolls had vanished and they were all looking considerably better and talking animatedly to each other.

'Please ring the bell if there is anything else

you need,' she said, pointing to the little bell she had placed on the table. 'Then, when you are ready to go to bed, I'll show you to your rooms.'

She left them to their meal. She was flushed with excitement. These were their first visitors. Travellers' Inn was back in business. She almost skipped back to the kitchen, where the coachman was eating a substantial meal, washed down with Sarah's best ale. Emily had taken herself off to bed, a bed she would have to share with her daughter tonight because Bethany had given hers up to one of the foreign ladies.

The next morning, after a good night's rest and a hearty breakfast, obviously fully restored to health, the party left. They were full of praise for the treatment they had received and promised to return and also to recommend the inn to other travellers.

Bethany was ecstatic and even Sarah allowed herself a nod of satisfaction at the way things had been managed. Emily stayed out of the way; she had been happy to receive praise for the lightness of her pastry via an intermediary but she was unwilling to allow herself to actually be seen by the visitors. She had not yet come to terms with being the server rather than the served.

Reuben came in to the yard in time to see the coach leave.

'There's porridge left in the pan. You might as well come and help us finish it up,' Sarah said by way of greeting, turning back into the house.

He followed her, glowering, and sat down at the table without speaking. The three women sat down with him, animatedly discussing the night's events as they ate their breakfast. Even Emily was pleased with things, now that the visitors had left.

'They seemed a very good class of people, from what little I saw of them,' she remarked. 'Well dressed and well mannered. Of course, I couldn't tell whether they were particularly well spoken since they didn't speak our language.'

'And since you didn't get near enough to them to find out,' Bethany said wickedly.

'I didn't find it necessary. There were quite enough people running back and forth at their beck and call without me joining in,' she replied. 'Quite frankly, I don't see myself as some kind of menial.'

Sarah caught Bethany's eye and raised her eyebrows without speaking. Bethany stifled a giggle. Her mother really was incorrigible.

Sarah looked across at Reuben. He was slurping his porridge, still with a face like thunder, and hadn't said a word. 'What's the matter with you, Reuben Scales?' she said sharply. 'Cat got your tongue?'

'Nope.' He carried on eating.

'Then what's put your nose out of joint?'

'Nawthin'.'

'Rubbish. I can see you're ratty over something so you might as well tell me what it is, first as last.'

He glared at her and deliberately put his spoon down. 'All right, then. I'll tell ye.' He took a deep breath. 'I thought as how you was gonna give me a shout when there was a coach to see after,' he said. 'If I don't misremember, I did offer to look arter the horses and you said when you got a coach in you'd hang a towel outa the winder or put a light in it, so's I'd know to come. Well, you got a coach in last night, but did you call me? No, you never did. I 'spect you found somebody better to do it.' He sniffed and took a drink of tea.

'Oh, don't be such a silly old fool,' Sarah said, helping herself to toast and marmalade. 'You said you were going home early because you were tired, so you wouldn't have seen a light if we'd put one up. And if you had seen it, you wouldn't have thanked us for getting you out of bed.' As far as she was concerned that was the end of the matter. But Bethany could see that Reuben wasn't placated.

'Of course, it wasn't that we found somebody better, Reuben,' she told him. 'It just happened that Zack was still here, in the Big Room. He'd been shifting the barrels for us after everyone else had gone, so we asked him to do it. And then he offered to come back early this morning to harness the horses up.'

Reuben sniffed again but said nothing. Then his curiosity got the better of him and he asked, 'Did 'e make a good job of it?'

'The coachman didn't complain,' was all Sarah said.

'Hmph.' Reuben scraped up the last of his porridge and got to his feet. 'If you find Zack such a help I wonder you don't ask him to stay here and work for ye, Sary Pilgrim,' he said vindictively.

'Maybe that's not such a bad idea,' Sarah said,

goading him. 'I must say he's been very useful to us, lately, with the heavy work.'

'Well, you'll hev to get a move on. He'll be orf in the next day or two, now the harvest's done.'

'Where's he going?' Bethany asked.

He shrugged. 'How should I know? I ain't his keeper.'

'Oh,' Bethany feigned surprise. 'I thought you'd know. You usually know most of what's going on. We rely on you for our news.'

He chewed his gums, torn between telling what he knew and keeping his own counsel. Telling what little he knew won. 'He ain't got no partickler plans as I know of. I 'spect he'll end up back at Harwich if nothin' better turns up. He's a bit of a rollin' stone.'

'You wouldn't really like it if we asked Zack to come and work here, would you, Reuben,' Bethany said gently. 'You'd think we were trying to put him in your place. Or worse, that we were trying to get rid of you, which is something we would never do.'

Reuben shrugged. 'I wouldn't ezackly mind,' he said grudgingly. 'Tell ye the truth, I'd rather you took on Zack than some stranger. I can work with Zack. He's a handy bloke an' he don't mind tacklin' the jobs I find too heavy nowadays.' He gave his gums another chew, then added, 'I'll hev a word with him, if ye like.'

'That would . . . ' Bethany began.

Sarah banged her fist on the table. 'Just you hang on a minute before you start employing people on my behalf,' she said, glaring at them. 'There are matters to be thought out. For a start, if we took him on where would he live?'

'I reckon he could make hisself a comfy little billet over the stables,' Reuben said. 'There's plenty of room there.'

'You seem to have it all worked out,' Sarah said suspiciously. 'Have you already spoken to him, Reuben Scales?'

He looked a little sheepish. 'Mighta put in the odd word.'

'And what was his reaction?' Bethany asked, trying not to smile at the old man's deviousness.

'Reckon he'd be willin' to give it a go,' he replied. 'For his keep an' a bit o' baccy money.'

'You old devil!' Sarah said. 'You've got it all cut and dried, between you.'

'Well, he's a rare good worker,' Reuben pointed out.

'I'll think about it,' Sarah said huffily, annoyed that the initiative had been taken out of her hands.

Reuben went to the door. 'Well, don't take too long. He'll be gone by the end of the week,' was his parting shot.

Emily had been looking from one to the other as they spoke, saying nothing. Now she said, 'I like Zachary. I think he's nice. He works hard, speaks nicely and he keeps himself looking respectable.'

'So you think we should take him on, if he wants to come?' Sarah said, raising her eyebrows.

'I don't see why not. It will mean Bethany won't have to carry those heavy buckets of water up from the well on that dreadful yoke thing.' Emily made a prim little mouth. 'Yokes are for yokels, not for well-brought up young ladies.'

'Oh, Mama!' Bethany said, exasperated.

'I'll think about it,' Sarah repeated.

★ ★ ★

She didn't think for long, because by the end of the week Zachary Brown had been offered the job and was happily settled at Travellers' Inn. He had made himself a snug little home in the room over what had once been the tack room, with a few odd bits and pieces of furniture that were not needed in the house and the truckle bed that John, Sarah's husband, had occasionally used if he had to stay up all night with a sick horse. He even found a reasonably sized piece of a broken mirror to hang over the chest of drawers. He had discovered this last in the chicken house. It was filthy, because the hens had roosted in it and there was even an addled egg at the back of one of the drawers. But he scrubbed it out and gave it a coat of the bright blue paint left over from the dog-cart, then, with half a brick propping it up in place of the missing foot it was quite adequate for his few possessions.

He was as happy as a lark in his new home and his new job. He went about the place whistling, happily carting water and shifting barrels, chopping wood and carrying coals, glad to have a room that he could call his own, plenty to eat and free beer, as long as he didn't drink too much, which he was careful not to do.

He was also careful not to upset Reuben, deferring to him, learning from him and on the

140

odd occasion when Reuben had taken a drop too much, taking him home and putting him to bed. Reuben began to look on Zack as the son he had never had and Zack treated Reuben as something of a father.

'I was a bit dubious at first,' Sarah confided to Bethany one day when they were busy in the brew house. 'I wasn't sure how Reuben would take it if Zack came here, because he's a funny old codger.'

Bethany frowned. 'But it was Reuben's idea that you should ask Zack,' she argued.

'Ah, you don't know him like I do. He's artful. He goaded me into it,' Sarah said. 'Pushed me to see how far I'd go. Then he'd be able to sit back and say, 'I told you so' when it didn't work out. Crafty old devil.'

'Well, it has worked out,' Bethany said with a laugh, 'So you can both claim credit for it.'

Sarah nodded. Then she looked thoughtful. 'How do you get on with Zack, Bethany?' she asked.

'Me?' Bethany tossed her auburn curls. 'Oh, we get on all right. I'm glad I don't have to carry the water any more.'

'Is that all?'

'What do you mean?'

Sarah shook her head. 'Nothing.'

Bethany continued with scrubbing a wooden vat, keeping her head down so that Aunt Sarah shouldn't see the flush that had spread across her face. She was not going to admit to anybody that she found Zack's presence unsettling, disturbing, in a funny, rather nice way. She found herself looking out for him and when she caught sight of him her heart would give a little lurch. She liked the way he shortened her name to Beth, nobody had ever done that before and it seemed somehow intimate, something shared between them and nobody else.

Of course, Zack knew nothing of all this. She guessed that, in truth, he only shortened her name because he was too lazy to call her Bethany, the same reason he called Emily 'Emm', much to her pretended annoyance; pretended because he was inclined to flirt with her and she clearly enjoyed this. But he didn't try to flirt with Sarah. He didn't use her Christian name, either, but always called her Mrs P. in a mixture of deference and familiarity.

Zack could charm a bird off a tree when he put his mind to it. Bethany knew this. But she still liked him.

Matthew dropped by about a month after Zack's arrival. He usually managed to pay a visit to Travellers' Inn about every four weeks or so; a busy practice that took in outlying districts didn't allow time for more frequent visits.

Over the months they had known him he had become what Sarah called 'kitchen company'; quite comfortable sitting with them in the big, warm kitchen and sharing whatever meal was on offer. It had begun because the men in what Zack had renamed the Bar were obviously ill at ease drinking in the company of the local doctor. There was a definite village hierarchy; the farm workers didn't drink with the farmer who employed them, nor with the local shopkeepers.

Neither were they comfortable in the presence of the doctor.

Matthew respected this. In any case, he was far happier being entertained in the kitchen, in an atmosphere of homely friendship which was a far cry from his own empty house and a meal cooked by his housekeeper and left to keep hot over a saucepan of water, which had more often than not boiled dry by the time he got to it.

'Our young friend seems to be making himself useful,' he remarked, nodding towards the bar, where there was a hum of male conversation interspersed with outbursts of somewhat raucous laughter. 'I heard you'd taken him on as handyman when the harvest finished.'

'It was Reuben's idea,' Sarah said with a shrug, doling more shepherd's pie on to his plate. 'I think he feels he's getting past sawing logs and chopping wood. And now we're brewing again we need a strong man for the heavy work. It seems to be working out all right,' she added, unwilling to admit how useful he was. 'He can turn his hand to most things.'

'It's good to have a man about the house,' Emily said firmly. 'I wasn't happy about some of the things Bethany was having to do, like rolling barrels and carrying water.'

'Oh, Mama, I never had to roll barrels, there was always someone here who offered to do that,' Bethany protested.

'Well, you had to carry all that water up from the well,' Emily insisted. She gave a little shrug. 'Anyway, it's nice to hear him whistling as he works. He's always cheerful.' Her voice dropped.

'And have you noticed? Since he's been here his speech has lost that awful drawl. What I mean is, he's beginning to speak more like we do and less like Reuben.'

'Nothing wrong with the way Reuben speaks,' Sarah said quickly. 'My John spoke the same way. It's the way most Essex people talk.'

'Yes, I know,' Emily said with a trace of smugness. 'But it's nice to hear Zack speaking . . . well, properly.'

Matthew smiled to himself. Clearly, Emily was quite enchanted by Zack. He wondered how Bethany felt about him. He was a young man; handsome in the rugged kind of way that appealed to women, from what he had observed. He glanced at Bethany, busily collecting up the plates and placing a large apple pie on the table. Her face was partially hidden by her mane of chestnut hair, hair he had a sudden urge to run his fingers through.

She looked up, almost as if she had read his thoughts and he felt a flush spread under his tan.

'You'll have a piece of Mama's apple pie, won't you, Matthew?' she asked, her voice quite matter-of-fact. 'She makes the most delicious pastry.' She smiled as she spoke.

He pulled himself together with an effort. 'Thank you. Yes, I will. And some of that succulent-looking cream to go with it.' He smiled back at her.

Later, as he rode home along the country roads, although he was trying to put his mind to a difficult case in one of the outlying villages, his thoughts kept turning to Bethany. She was young, at least eight years his junior, he told himself; she probably regarded him as nothing more than a kindly, over-worked, middle-aged widower. Which was exactly what he was. But there could be nothing wrong in taking an interest in her well-being; she was so young, so unspoiled, so ready to take on new challenges, yet so vulnerable. He would hate her to get hurt. What she needed was a good husband to love and care for her. Not that he himself had any thoughts of remarriage, of course. But it wouldn't be difficult to love and care for a girl like Bethany.

12

All through the autumn and winter Travellers' Inn was steadily busy. Coaches called on their way to and from Harwich in the knowledge that they could rely on a warm welcome, a good meal and a comfortable, clean bed. Thanks to Zack there was also good stabling and care for the horses.

When he had first come to Travellers' Inn Sarah had sometimes been a little short with Zack, almost as if she resented his presence, but as the months wore on and the weather worsened she came to appreciate his worth, because even in the foulest weather he could be heard whistling about the yard as he did all the heavy tasks and cheerfully saw to the horses whatever time of night the coaches arrived. It was also his job to harness up Peggy and take the trap into the village for the supplies that they could afford now that the inn was becoming more prosperous.

Sarah had particular cause to be grateful to him when Reuben contracted his yearly bout of bronchitis. Every year, despite, or perhaps even because of the fact that he had been used to being out in all weathers from an early age, the old man went down with bronchitis.

'It's that filthy old pipe you smoke,' she warned him, when once again the tell-tale cough developed.

146

'Thass got nothin' to do with it. I jest got a bit of a tizzick in me throat,' he insisted, when he got his breath back.

'You should get off home and take yourself off to bed. There's snow in the air. Look at the clouds over to the east,' she said. 'I'll give you a can of Emily's soup to take with you.'

'I've got another box o' kindlin' to chop for ye afore I go,' he said stubbornly.

'Don't be daft. We've got enough firewood to last us till the middle of next summer, already.' She began ladling soup into an enamel can.

'I'll go when I'm good an' ready.' He began to cough again. When he had finished he wiped his brow. 'I'll jest finish . . . '

Sarah rattled the can at him. 'You *have* finished. Now, home you go. Bank up your fire and don't come out again until you're better.'

'You're a nag, woman. You're worse'n a wife.'

'How would you know that? You've never had a wife.'

'I don't need one. Not with you naggin' at me all the time.'

'Oh, get off home. I shall come and see you tomorrow.'

'You won't need to. I shall be back here.'

But he wasn't. The next day there was a foot of snow on the ground and it was still falling.

Bethany looked out of the window at the white landscape, marked only by the footprints of the birds walking among the crumbs she had put out for them, tiny prints that were rapidly being covered by the snow that was still silently falling out of the leaden skies. A row of icicles, some of them nearly a foot long, hung from the eaves of the barn and the brew house.

'I wonder why it is that the snow seems so much whiter here in the country,' she mused, leaning on the window sill. 'In London it was grey and slushy almost before it hit the ground. I suppose it was the soot from the chimneys.'

Emily was busy making pastry. She loved cooking now that she had found she was good at it. She looked out at the wintry scene and gave a little shiver, although standing in front of the big range with the kettle singing on the hob she could not have been at all cold. 'I'm glad Zack brought us in a good supply of logs and coal last night,' she said. 'At least we shall be nice and warm, whatever the weather.'

Sarah came and stood beside Bethany, looking out at the snow. 'I wonder how that old fool is this morning,' she said, half to herself.

'Who? Zack?' Bethany looked at her in surprise. She didn't normally refer to Zack as an old fool.

'No. Not Zack. Reuben, of course,' Sarah said impatiently. Then, more thoughtfully, 'I hope he won't try to struggle along here today. He always does, you know, when the weather's bad. Likes to make sure there's nothing I need.' She turned back into the room and took her old black coat off the back of the door. 'His chest was quite bad last night, you know, although he wouldn't admit it. I think I'll go along and make sure he's all right this morning. I can take him some porridge. I don't suppose he'll have made himself any breakfast.'

'Oh, I don't think you should go out in this weather, Aunt Sarah,' Emily protested.

'Rubbish. How do you think I've managed all these years? I've always had to go out, whatever the weather.' She opened the door, letting in a blast of cold air, and nearly cannoned into Zack, who had come across the yard from the brew house with an old sack over his head and shoulders and his head down.

They both came back inside and Zack closed the door against the icy wind.

'Oh, do come in and get warm, Zachary. You must be frozen,' Emily said. If Emily had her way Zack would be living in the house with them, but Sarah was firmly against that idea.

'No, I'm not at all cold, Emm. I've been in the brew house, boiling up the wort. There's a good fire there, under the copper.'

'Did you put the hops in?' Sarah asked quickly.

'Yes, Mrs P, I did. It's all under control. It'll be a good brew. You'll see.' He grinned at her. 'You can take your coat off. I've taken care of everything. Peggy's been fed and watered and I've put an old blanket over her. And I've got a good fire going in the tack room . . .'

'Aunt Sarah's not worried about that, Zack,' Bethany said quickly. 'It's Reuben she's worried about. He wasn't very well last night, and she was just on her way to visit him.'

'Oh, no need for that, Mrs P, I'm all wrapped up against the weather. I'll go and see if the old chap's all right,' Zack said easily. 'He did look a bit peaky last night, now I come to think of it.'

He looked round the room. 'Is there anything I can get for you ladies before I go?'

'No, we've got everything we need, thanks to you, Zachary,' Emily said, smiling at him.

'You can take Reuben this pot of porridge,' Sarah said, putting the lid on a blackened saucepan with a basin inside. 'Be careful how you go with it because I've put it over a pan of hot water to keep it hot.'

'Would you like some porridge, Zack, before you go?' Bethany asked.

He held up the pan. 'I'll have some of this with Reuben. It feels as if there's enough here to feed four or five people,' he said with a grin.

Zack was gone for nearly two hours. When he came back he told them that Reuben was indeed quite ill.

Divested of his snow-caked sack and sitting at the kitchen table drinking hot cocoa, he told them, 'I made him a good fire and made him eat some porridge. But I reckoned he needed a doctor; I could hear his chest rattling as soon as I opened the door. So I went along to Matthew's house and left a message for him to call and see him. I hope I did the right thing, Mrs P.' He looked enquiringly at Sarah.

Sarah nodded, looking anxious. 'Is he warm enough?' she asked. 'Has he got enough blankets?'

'Oh, yes. He's as snug as a bug in a rug,' Zack said. 'Don't worry, Mrs P. I'll go back and see him later on. Make sure he's got everything he wants.'

She gave him a wintry smile. 'Thank you,

Zack. The silly old fool needs somebody to keep an eye on him.'

'I'll do that, never fear.' He finished his cocoa and wiped his mouth with the back of his hand. 'In fact, I might stay there with him tonight. I can kip down in front of the fire, make sure it doesn't go out.' He got to his feet. 'Now, I'll go and check the brew and then I'll fetch you some more logs.' He shrugged the sack back over his shoulders and went out into the snow, which was now falling in large, soft flakes.

'Large flakes. That's good. It means it'll stop snowing before long,' Sarah said when she saw it.

'We're lucky to have Zack,' Emily remarked. 'I wouldn't want to go out in this weather.'

Sarah nodded. 'Yes, he's proving his worth,' she admitted.

The snow lasted a week, turning from pristine white to a grey slush, which froze each night as more snow fell, making it treacherous underfoot. During this time Zack stayed with Reuben, only returning to make sure nothing was needed at Travellers' Inn and to be plied with hot food to take back to Reuben's cottage. There was little custom at the inn; most of the men were busy at home, or out gathering wood to burn to keep themselves and their families warm. In any case, with the ground frozen solid and covered with snow there was little prospect of work; and if they didn't work they didn't get paid, so there was no money for beer and precious little for anything else. The few coaches that passed the door didn't stop.

One afternoon Matthew arrived, on foot. He

was wrapped in a large coachman's caped overcoat and wore a hat with a wide brim to keep the snow off his face. He carried his leather bag.

'Have you called on Reuben yet?' Sarah greeted him before he could take the heavy coat off.

He grinned at her. 'Yes, Sarah, I have. Several times. And I can tell you he's mending nicely. Zack is looking after him well.'

'You'll stay and eat with us, won't you, Matthew?' Bethany asked eagerly, glad to see a different face.

'Yes, please do. You don't look as if you've had a good meal for days,' Emily said, frowning at him. 'When did you last eat?'

He shrugged. 'I don't remember. I've been busy, as you can imagine. And I didn't think it fair to make Major carry me, with the roads nigh on impassable.' He sat down at the table and put his head in his hands. 'A cup of tea would be very acceptable, thank you, Emily.'

'Come into the little parlour. There's a good fire and a comfortable chair in there,' Bethany said. 'I'll bring you some tea and toast.'

'Thank you. That would be lovely.' He followed her into the little parlour and sank gratefully into the armchair by the fire, stretching out his legs. 'This may be a mistake,' he said with a sigh. 'If you make me too comfortable I shan't want to leave.'

Bethany smiled at him. 'You know you're always welcome, Matthew.' She went to the door. When she reached it she turned back. 'We've got rabbit pie for supper tonight. Zack caught a couple before the snow came and they've been hanging in the barn. Why don't you join us?'

He yawned. 'No, I'd better not stay. I've one or two more calls to make.' He smiled back at her gratefully. 'Tempting though it is, I'll forgo Emily's delicious pastry and settle for tea and toast.'

A little later, when Bethany took the tray with tea, toast and honey into the little parlour, Matthew was sound asleep. She crept away, shutting the door behind her. An exhausted doctor was no use to his patients; the sleep would do him good.

He slept solidly for three hours and when he woke, with the succulent aroma of rabbit pie in his nostrils, it was not difficult for the three women to persuade him to stay and eat with them.

'You spoil me, ladies,' he said, sheepishly holding out his plate for a second helping.

'It's a good thing somebody does,' Sarah remarked. 'That housekeeper of yours doesn't seem to bother very much.'

'Well, she has her own family to care for. She does what's necessary,' he said, defending her.

'If you came to see us more often we'd be able to spoil you even more,' Emily said archly, as she gave him another generous helping.

'Mama!' Bethany said, shocked. 'Remember, Matthew is a doctor. He has his patients to attend to. The fact that we enjoy his company is no excuse for keeping him from his work.'

Matthew looked up at Bethany's words. She

was smiling at him, but her smile was completely without guile; there was no hidden meaning or message in her words. He realised he had been a fool to think there might be.

He finished his meal and got up to go. Sarah accompanied him to the door.

'You'll be calling on Reuben again tonight?' she asked.

He nodded. 'I'll drop by, although there's no real need. He's mending nicely, thanks to Zack.'

Sarah cleared her throat nervously. 'He's to have whatever he needs, Matthew,' she said. 'Whatever medicine . . . ' she nodded at him, meaningfully. 'You understand?' She cleared her throat again. 'Send the bill to me. You needn't tell him.'

He patted her arm. 'I understand, Sarah.'

'Good. He's looked after me for a good number of years. The least I can do is to see he has what he needs. So whatever it costs . . . '

'There'll be no charge, Sarah,' he said, buttoning up his coat. 'Your hospitality more than repays me for any professional help I've given Reuben.' He pulled his hat down over his ears and went out into the bleak night.

Sarah watched him disappear into the darkness, sniffing the air.

'I do believe it's getting warmer,' she announced when she went back into the kitchen. 'You mark my words, all this snow will be gone by morning.'

She was right. When Bethany looked out of the window the next morning a steady rain was falling, washing the last of the snow away from the cobbles in the yard and uncovering the tufts of grass growing between the stones. The icicles on the barn had already dripped away to nothing and in the road the icy slush had turned to mud. Puddles of brown, muddy water filled the ruts left by old coach and cart tracks. In the hedgerows the trees and bushes were beginning to lift their branches again as the snow that had lain so heavily on them for days began to melt.

After two days the rain stopped and the sun came out, its rays catching the raindrops on the tips of the leaves and sparkling in them like jewels.

'I think I'll walk along and see how Reuben is, now the snow has gone,' Sarah announced in the middle of the morning. 'I'll take him a drop of beer. I expect he's missed his beer, drunken old reprobate.'

'Oh, Aunt Sarah!' Bethany said with a laugh. 'You know that's not true. Reuben isn't a drunkard.'

'No, perhaps not. But he likes his beer, you can't deny that.'

But before they could argue any further the door was pushed open and Reuben walked in. He was wearing his habitual smock and gaiters and a battered old hat but round his shoulders was a brown horse blanket.

'What are you doing here, Reuben Scales? You're not well. You should be at home by the fire,' Sarah greeted him sharply.

'I'm better,' he announced. 'I couldn't sit lookin' at them four walls any longer. I wanted a bit o' fresh air. An' a mutton pie, if there's one goin'.' He winked at Emily. 'An' a drop o' beer. I've missed me beer.'

'Oh, we can tell you're feeling better, the way you're throwing your orders around,' Sarah said. 'Anybody would think you owned the place. Well, I suppose you'd better sit down while I fetch you a mug of beer.'

'An' a pie. Don't forget the pie, Sary Pilgrim,' he ordered, sitting down at the table.

Bethany smiled at them both. She knew that a very real affection lay under the banter.

Zack came in with the coal hod in one hand and a bag of logs in the other.

'What are you doing here, Reuben? I was coming to see you as soon as I'd got the coals in,' he said, looking at him in surprise.

'Well, I've saved you the trouble.' Reuben grinned a toothless, smug smile. 'I'm better an' I'm here.' He jabbed a finger in Zack's direction but directed his words to the three women. 'He looked after me a treat while I was under the weather,' he said. 'He'll make somebody a wunnerful wife.' He began to chuckle at his own joke. But the chuckle turned to a cough.

'Ha! Maybe you're not quite so recovered as you thought you were, Reuben Scales,' Sarah said sternly.

He waved his hand dismissively. 'Give over, woman. Stop your naggin'. I'm all right,' he said.

'I've got to take the trap and go into the village before long,' Zack told him. 'If you can bear to stay here for a few more minutes I'll drop you off at your place when I go.'

Reuben chewed his gums. 'I was gonna walk

home,' he said, frowning. 'I don't want you treatin' me like a invalid. Thass on'y half a mile.'

'Don't be daft, man,' Sarah said. 'Don't be so independent. Let the boy take you. He's practically going past your door.' She was busily putting a loaf of bread and two mutton pies in a bag, which she banged down on the table. 'You can take these with you and if you agree to go with Zack I'll add a basin of that stew bubbling on the stove.'

'If you're tryin' to bribe me you're goin' the right way about it,' Reuben said with a grin.

'Can I come, too?' Bethany asked. 'I need some more wool for my tapestry stool cover and it's no use asking Zack to go to the haberdashers for it.'

'No, that's a woman's shop, you won't catch me in there,' Zack said quickly, straightening up from stacking the logs by the stove. 'You'll have to come along and do your own shopping.'

Bethany went upstairs and put on her pelisse and bonnet and picked up her muff. By the time she went downstairs again Zack was at the door, with Reuben sitting behind him in the back of the trap. He reached down to give her a hand up beside him, smiling at her as he did so.

The trap rattled off along the road. Sarah and Emily watched it go.

'Do you think Zack and Bethany . . . ?' Emily began tentatively.

'Good heavens, no,' Sarah interrupted her. 'He's only a hired hand. She wouldn't look twice at him.'

'He's very handsome,' Emily ventured.

'That's as maybe. Handsome is as handsome does. I'm quite sure Bethany will look a great deal higher than Zachary Brown for a husband. After all, even though you've both come down in the world she's still a lady.' Sarah banged the washing up bowl down on the table irritably. 'I'm surprised you should even think of such a thing, Emily. I'm sure Bethany hasn't.'

Emily looked at her aunt, surprised at her vehemence. But she realised that in spite of his hard work and usefulness Sarah still had slight reservations about Zack. Maybe it was simply because she was afraid Reuben might feel left out.

13

The snowdrops that bloomed under the kitchen window were the first sign that winter was on its way out. They were followed by yellow, white and blue crocuses, and after that the daffodils began to appear.

Each day, as the weather improved, Bethany took a walk down by the side of the field to the river, eagerly watching for the primroses and wild violets that Aunt Sarah assured her she would find in early April on the bank under the hedgerow.

'You need to go to Farthing Wood for primroses,' Zack said, the day he saw her return with a little posy, the first she had found. 'You'll find hundreds of them there.'

'Where's Farthing Wood?' she asked.

He pointed to a stand of trees on the other side of the road at the top of the rise. 'Over there. Just behind those trees. I'll show you, if you like.'

'When? We need to go while the primroses are still flowering.'

He thought for a minute. 'I s'pose we could go tomorrow afternoon when I've finished digging this patch ready for Mrs P to plant her potatoes.'

'Thank you. I'd like that.'

She went indoors and put her posy in water.

'You could do with a few more. When I was a girl I used to collect a lot more than that,' Emily said, looking at them disparagingly.

'It's the first I've found. But I'm going to get some more tomorrow afternoon,' Bethany said. 'Zack says there are a lot in Farthing Wood. He's going to show me.'

'Oh, that's where we used to go when I was a girl,' Emily said, her face lighting up. 'We used to take picnics, Aunt Sarah, Uncle John and me.'

'We could do that tomorrow, if you like,' Bethany said, although even as she spoke she felt a small stab of disappointment. She would rather have gone with Zack on her own.

Emily laughed in delight. 'Oh, what a good idea. We'll take a picnic just as we used to. I daresay Aunt Sarah will come, too.'

But Sarah declined. She wanted to plant her early potatoes now that Zack had dug the ground for her.

In the event, Emily didn't go, either. She was confined to bed all day with a bad headache.

'Does your mother often get bad headaches?' Zack asked, as they made their way up the hill the following afternoon. He looked quite smart, having washed under the pump and tamed his rather unruly hair. He had even had a shave.

'No, not often. In fact, she was looking forward to coming with us today. We were going to bring a picnic, just like she used to when she was a girl.'

'Well, where is it then?' he asked with a grin.

'Where is what?'

'The picnic.'

She flushed. 'I thought it wouldn't be right to bring it as Mama wasn't coming.'

'No, you're probably right. Anyway, I'd rather it was just you and me, even without the picnic.' He went ahead, whistling and she followed, picking her way carefully.

Farthing Wood was an ancient wood, ringed by a wide ditch with a stream at the bottom.

'Ah. I forgot about the brook. But never mind, we'll just have to jump over it,' he said as they stood looking down at it.

'I don't think I can manage that,' she said doubtfully, looking across to the woods on the other side. 'It's too far across.'

'Well, if we scramble down the bank to the edge of the stream it won't be so wide for you to jump. Do you reckon you could manage that?'

She nodded. 'I think I might.' But she didn't sound very sure.

He smiled at her. 'Come on, give me your hand. I'll help you down.'

He steadied her as she picked up her skirts and half scrambled, half slid down the bank, laughing, her hat falling back so that it was only held on by the ribbons. Then he jumped over the water in the brook to show her how easy it was.

'Come on,' he encouraged, holding out his hands. 'Now it's your turn. It's not all that wide.'

'What if I fall in?' She asked nervously.

'Don't worry, I'll fish you out. But you won't fall in because I'm going to catch you.'

She took a deep breath, gathered her skirts and took a flying leap, relieved and a little surprised when her feet touched dry ground and he caught her hands. But she had landed on the very edge of the stream and it began to crumble under her heels so that she teetered on the brink. Zack quickly grabbed her round the waist before she over-balanced into the water.

'That was a near thing,' he said, smiling down at her without releasing his hold. 'And after cleaning the stream so well, too.'

Relieved, she relaxed against him. 'Oh, thank you for catching me, Zack,' she said, a little breathlessly. 'I can't imagine what Mama and Aunt Sarah would have said if I'd gone home with my skirts all wet.' She hardly knew what she was saying because he was still holding her closely.

'I guess they would say I hadn't been looking after you very well. And I wouldn't like them to say that, Beth, because they might not let you come with me again,' he said softly.

She glanced up at him. He was still looking down at her and his expression was serious. She licked her lips. 'Oh, I don't think they would ever say that, Zack.'

'I hope I would never give them cause to.' As he spoke he lowered his head and his lips brushed hers, as gently as a butterfly wing. Then he straightened up and slowly took his hands from her waist and caught her by the hand, his mood changing. 'Come on, I'll help you up the bank.' He grinned at her. 'I almost forgot. We're here to gather primroses.'

She managed to smile back at him as he helped her to scramble up the bank. When they reached the top he waited, watching her as she refastened her hair where it had escaped its pins and replaced her hat.

'You've got beautiful hair. You shouldn't cover it up,' he remarked thoughtfully. Then he turned from her. 'This way. Follow me.'

He led her through the wood, following a barely discernable track, to a shady clearing through which another stream ran, this one no wider than a man's stride. Yellow primroses covered shallow mossy banks on either side of the stream.

'Look, the water's so clear you can see the pebbles in the bottom of the stream,' she said, looking down into it.

'Yes, it's fresh, spring water. Good enough to drink. Are you thirsty?' He knelt down and cupped his hands and drank from them.

She copied him, and took a drink of the clear, sweet water. 'Mm. It's nearly as good as the water from Aunt Sarah's well. And almost as cold.'

'Same source, I shouldn't wonder,' he said. He sat back on his heels. 'Well, here we are, I've brought you to where the primroses are.' He grinned at her. 'You'd better pick some or your folks'll wonder what we've been doing all afternoon.'

'Aren't you going to help me?' she asked, flushing for no reason that she could think of.

He rolled over and sat up, resting his elbows on his knees. 'No. I'm just going to sit and watch you. It's my reward for bringing you here. In that pretty blue dress and with your hair tumbling all round your shoulders . . . '

'It isn't tumbling round my shoulders, is it? I thought I'd pinned it back up.' She put her hand up to make sure it was secure.

He leaned forward and in one movement pushed her hat back and removed all the pins from her hair so that it fell to her shoulders in heavy waves. 'It is now. No, leave it, it looks nice like that.' He caught her hand as she made to twist it up again. 'You make such a pretty picture I could watch you among the primroses all day.' He leaned back and picked a blade of grass and began to chew it, never taking his eyes off her.

She tossed her head, both pleased and embarrassed. 'That was a pretty speech, kind sir,' she said, trying to make light of his words as she bent towards the primroses.

He didn't answer and when she glanced at him his expression was serious.

She picked primroses and wild violets and put them carefully in the little basket she had brought with her, conscious that his eyes were on her all the time.

'Haven't you finished yet?' he said at last as she tried to make room for a few more violets in the basket. 'There'll still be some here another day.'

She straightened up and pushed her hair back. 'Yes, the primroses will but I won't, will I,' she said, looking round at the now somewhat depleted yellow carpet at her feet.

'I don't see why not. We can come again if you like,' he said carelessly. 'I'm due an afternoon off a week, although I don't always take it, and this is as good a way to spend it as any.'

She shot him a glance but he had rolled over on to his back and was looking up at the dappled sky through the leaves of the trees so she couldn't see his expression. She went and sat down beside him.

'You're right. I've picked enough. We should be getting back,' she said, looking at the little fob watch she wore at her waist and realising that it was almost two hours since they left home.

Suddenly, he caught her hand, at the same time putting his finger to his lips. 'Listen. Can you hear the thrush singing?'

She listened. 'How do you know it's a thrush?' she whispered. All birds sounded alike to her.

'You can tell by the song,' he whispered back. 'And there she is, look.' He pointed. 'On the end of that sycamore branch.'

'Ah, yes, I can see her. She's lovely.' She turned to him delightedly and found his eyes not on the thrush but on her.

'Oh, yes, she's lovely, all right,' he said with a smile, tracing the line of her jaw with his finger.

Then, abruptly, he stood up and pulled her to her feet. 'Time we went home,' he said briskly. 'Your folks'll wonder what we've been up to. It doesn't take two hours to pick a few primroses.'

'But we had to find them before we could pick them,' she said, laughing. 'And now we've got to find our way back.'

'That's no problem. I know these woods like the back of my hand.' He began to lead the way. 'We'll come again when the bluebells are out. The whole wood is like a blue carpet. But that won't be for a few weeks yet.'

'I shall look forward to that.' She followed him for some distance, then stopped in dismay as they reached the stream. 'We've come out at a different place,' she said, dismayed. 'The stream is much wider here. I couldn't possibly jump.'

'You don't have to.' Suddenly, he took off his boots, swept her up in his arms and stepped into the brook.

'No, you mustn't . . . you'll drop me. Put me down,' she said in alarm.

He stopped in mid-stream. 'Do you really want me to put you down? Right here?' he said with a grin. 'The water's nearly up to my knees so you'll get your dress pretty wet and ruin your shoes into the bargain if I do. But, come to think of it . . . ' He made a quick movement as if he was going to let her fall.

She gave a little scream and put her arms round his neck. 'No, no, don't drop me, Zack. Take me across,' she begged, feeling totally helpless.

'Please,' he prompted, clearly enjoying himself.

'Please, Zack.'

'What will you give me if I do?' He was still making no attempt to move; holding her in his arms as if she weighed nothing at all.

She laughed a little uncomfortably. 'I don't know. What do you want?'

He put his face close to hers. 'A kiss. A proper kiss this time, I think.' He bent his head and kissed her, his lips gently moving to part hers. 'Sweet sixteen and never been kissed,' he murmured eventually.

'I'm eighteen,' she replied weakly, hardly aware of what she was saying.

'But still never been kissed.' He bent his head again. 'Until now.'

She had no idea how long they remained in the middle of the stream, nor how they got to the bank. She only knew that his lips were still on hers as he gently put her back on her feet. 'There. Back on dry land,' he said. He smiled. 'Or should I say, back to earth?' He looked her up and down then leaned over and straightened her hat for her. 'Must make sure you're looking respectable or your dear mama will wonder what you've been up to,' he said with a wink.

She managed a smile in return but she was beyond words as she watched him wade back for his boots. She knew that life would never be the same for her again.

★ ★ ★

It was Bethany's job to keep Travellers' Inn clean and tidy. All except the bar, which Zack swept and put clean sawdust down as necessary. As she went about her work, cleaning and polishing, making sure that the rooms were ready for travellers wanting a night's lodging, with fresh, lavender-smelling bed linen, furniture polished and the china all washed and sparkling, she was surprised — and a little annoyed — that Zack's attitude to her didn't seem to have changed at all since that day in the woods. He never so much as by a look or a smile betrayed that he even remembered the kiss they had shared, let alone attempted to repeat it. And she gave him every opportunity. It was always she who called him in

167

for his meal, whether he was in the brew house, the wood shed, or right at the bottom of the garden. But he invariably said, 'I'll just finish this and then I'll be along,' sometimes without even looking up at her.

She began to wonder if she had imagined what had happened. Or perhaps dreamed it. But the feelings that even the memory of it aroused in her, feelings such as she had never experienced in her life before that day, convinced her that it had been no dream.

But life was too busy to dwell for too long on this. With warmer spring days and dryer roads there was more incentive to travel and more coaches pulled in for the good meal and clean bed for which Travellers' Inn was rapidly becoming known. Bethany was kept busy making sure that the clean beds they were famous for lived up to their reputation — the bed linen was always changed between visitors, there was no climbing into grey, stained, many times slept-between sheets at Travellers' Inn. Aunt Sarah wondered at the wisdom of this; she felt that Bethany was wearing herself out changing the sheets *every* time and suggested that perhaps every two, or perhaps three consecutive visitors, especially if they were men, could share the same bedding. Bethany's answer to this was to engage a laundry woman to wash the sheets — the wife of one of the farmhands who could do with a few extra pennies. Sarah said no more; in truth she was gratified at the high reputation the inn enjoyed.

The little parlour had been turned into a cosy

dining room, and visitors knew they could look forward to a good meal, served by the pretty wench with the lovely hair. From time to time Bethany received a lewd suggestion from a guest slightly in his cups, but this was swiftly dealt with by Zack, who usually kept an eye on what was happening from his position in the bar.

Emily had taken over most of the cooking, a task which she obviously enjoyed, especially when there were overnight guests, who could always be relied on to compliment her on her pastry or her tasty fruit crumble. Since finding a purpose in her life she had become far less prone to measuring everything against how things had been in her Seymour's time. In fact, although she didn't admit it, she was beginning to see her late husband for exactly what he had been, a clever man who had not been quite clever enough to succeed in juggling his — and other people's — finances in order to sustain a lifestyle far beyond his means. She was also finding that the simple life had other benefits; being much more active, with less time to sit and read novels whilst dipping into expensive chocolates, meant that she had been able to pull her corset in by several notches and still feel quite comfortable.

Zack was invaluable. He had willingly taken on all the heavy work: the digging, fetching water from the well, humping barrels, sawing logs and looking after Peggy, the mare. Twice a week he would harness her to the dog cart, brasswork gleaming, and trot her into the town to fetch any supplies needed. Sometimes, Emily and Bethany would go with him if they needed embroidery silks or items from the haberdashers. Occasionally Sarah would go too, but she much preferred to stay at home and work in her garden.

She spent quite a lot of time in her garden, planting and hoeing among the vegetables, tending the flowers, or simply sitting on the bench outside the woodshed in the sun talking to Reuben, who was happy to smoke his old pipe in the sunshine and leave Zack to do most of the jobs he had previously done for Sarah.

Sarah left most of the brewing to Zack, too, although she kept a watchful eye on him to make sure the beer was always up to her rigid standards. He didn't appear to resent this and went about his work whistling, always cheerful, flirting gently with Emily because he knew she liked it and deferring to Sarah when there was the slightest problem for the same reason. He continued to treat Bethany in the same friendly, almost brotherly way he had always done.

Bethany was puzzled and a little annoyed. But more than anything, she was disappointed.

14

The primroses had hardly wilted in their bowl before the memory of the afternoon in the wood was pushed firmly to the back of Bethany's mind.

It was late one afternoon on an April day that was giving a foretaste of high summer; hot and sunny with cloudless blue skies. The Colchester to Harwich coach drew up in a cloud of dust and its occupants, some of whom had been travelling since early morning with several changes of coach, climbed out, hot, stiff and exhausted. There were two elderly ladies who seemed to spend most of their time bickering and immediately began to complain at being forced to stay at such a ramshackle place; a rather bad-tempered middle-aged man; and an anxious-looking man with a pretty young wife, who, in spite of the warm day, was swathed in a long cloak, which she refused to remove, saying she was susceptible to draughts.

Bethany served them with tea and cake in the little parlour, hoping that this would help to calm frayed tempers, and then invited them to rest and refresh themselves in their rooms until dinner time. As usual when there were several guests, she gave up her own room, this time to the young couple, and after making it ready for them she went downstairs to help her mother prepare the vegetables for dinner.

'I suppose it's understandable that tempers are a little frayed,' she remarked as she entered the kitchen. 'It's unseasonably warm today.'

'Yes. It can't have been very pleasant being cooped up in a stuffy old coach for most of the day,' Emily agreed.

'Not so much of the 'old coach',' Percy Jenkins, the coachman, said good-humouredly. He was sitting in the corner of the kitchen drinking a pint of beer as part of his payment for the custom he brought to the inn. 'I'll have you know my coach is as good as any you'll travel in today.'

'And that's not saying much, on these roads,' Emily replied with a smile.

Bethany didn't join in this exchange. She was frowning as she began to peel carrots. 'I do hope Mrs Peterson, I think that's her name, isn't ill. She refused to take off her cloak, even indoors. She said she feels the cold, but it isn't cold today.'

Emily brushed her hair back with her forearm. 'Far from it,' she said, opening the oven door to check the mutton pies. 'It's more like a summer day.' She nodded towards the open window, through which Sarah and Reuben could be seen sitting on the bench outside the woodshed, drinking the beer that Zack had taken down to them. 'Aunt Sarah and Reuben are making the most of the sunshine, too.'

'I don't blame them.' Bethany put the carrots in the pot and set them on the stove, her mind still on the young wife. 'I think there must be something wrong with her. I must say she looked rather pale.'

'Who? Aunt Sarah?' Emily looked up in surprise. 'She's as fit as a flea.'

'No, not Aunt Sarah, Mrs Peterson.'

'Oh, she's probably tired after a long journey, that's all. It's understandable on a day like this. Did they say where they'd come from?' Emily was expertly fluting the edge of a pie crust as she spoke.

'Somewhere the other side of Chelmsford, I believe.'

'I suppose they're making for the continent. Well, if the weather stays like this they should have a smooth crossing.'

Percy Jenkins went to help Zack see to the horses and Bethany and Emily worked in companionable silence. After a while they were joined by Sarah, who had come in to lend another pair of hands and relate the odd bits of gossip Reuben had passed on to her. Bethany had laid the table in the little parlour and the meal was almost ready to be served when there was a knock at the door from the passage and Mr Peterson came in to ask diffidently if a tray might be sent up for himself and his wife as Mrs Peterson was not feeling well enough to come downstairs for the meal.

'I'm willing to pay extra for any inconvenience, of course,' he added hurriedly.

'Oh, it's no trouble,' Bethany said with a smile. 'I'll bring a tray in about ten minutes.'

'But if Mrs Peterson is indisposed perhaps we should send for a doctor,' Emily said anxiously.

She couldn't bear the thought of illness, in the house or anywhere else, for that matter.

'No. No, I'm sure that won't be necessary, thank you all the same. I'm sure my wife will be fully recovered when she's had a night's rest,' he assured her.

'He does look a bit worried,' Sarah remarked when he had gone back upstairs. She was standing at the stove stirring custard.

'Yes. I do hope she hasn't got anything catching,' Emily said with a frown, emptying potatoes into a warm vegetable dish.

'No doubt I'll find out when I take up the tray,' Bethany said.

Emily's head shot up and she nearly missed the vegetable dish. 'Well, don't go inside the room. Just in case. We don't want plague . . . '

'Oh, Mama. Plague died out years ago.'

'You still get the odd case, even now,' Sarah said sagely, although she didn't appear worried. 'It wouldn't be good for business, if it's plague. It wouldn't be good at all. And just as we've got back on our feet, too.' She nodded towards the dining room. 'Better not say anything to the others. Don't want to frighten them.'

'Frighten them!' Emily was already twitchy. 'What about us?'

'Oh, it's probably nothing. I expect she's caught a chill,' Sarah said dismissively.

The words were hardly out of her mouth when the door opened and Mr Peterson burst in again.

'Please, can you help me? I don't know what to do,' he was almost beside himself with a mixture of terror and anxiety, 'I believe my wife is . . . ' he dragged at his collar, 'That is to say, she's with child and I'm afraid she is about to be delivered . . . Oh, dear God, I don't know what to do.' He slumped down on a chair and put his head in his hands. 'She complained of back ache earlier but we thought it was the jolting of the coach and that she simply needed to rest.' He looked up and gulped. 'We had thought there was another month to go before . . . You see, we were on our way to Amsterdam, where Ellen's mother lives.' He got to his feet again. 'Oh, dear, I shouldn't leave her. She is in great distress. But I'm a man and I don't know what I should do for her. What shall I do? What shall I do?' He looked helplessly at the three women.

Emily stared at him like a frightened rabbit. 'She can't be confined here, we have dinner to serve,' she said quickly. 'This is an inn. We've simply nowhere . . . '

Sarah had been standing by the stove taking it all in. Now she stepped forward and immediately took charge. Giving Emily's arm a shake, she said, 'Oh, for goodness sake, pull yourself together, woman and set a large pan of water on the stove. Bethany, you go and find Zack. I think he's in the bar tapping the new barrel. Tell him to go and find Matthew, wherever he is, and ask him to come. Tell him he's needed to deliver a child. Meantime, I'll go upstairs and see what I can do.' She eyed Emily, who was looking white and shaken. 'Oh, don't worry, Emily. I can see it's no use asking you to come and help me,' she said with a hint of impatience. 'But you'll have to serve dinner on your own. I reckon you can manage that, can't you?'

Emily nodded. She would have agreed to do anything rather than be forced to accompany Sarah.

'I'll come with you, Aunt Sarah,' Bethany volunteered, coming back into the room.

'Good girl. I thought you would. It'll be better if there's two of us.' In truth, Sarah, childless herself, was no expert in midwifery but she had helped to deliver calves and foals at the farm over the years and she judged that the process couldn't be that different.

'Oh, I don't think she should come, Aunt Sarah,' Emily protested. 'It's hardly the place for a young girl . . . '

'Rubbish. She's got to learn sometime.' Sarah turned to Bethany, fastening a clean white pinafore over her dress. 'Has Zack gone for Matthew?'

'Yes. He's taken Peggy because he'll go quicker on horseback and there's no telling where Matthew might be if he's not back at his house.'

'Good. Now, take this poor man into the bar before he collapses at our feet. Reuben's in there, isn't he?' A nod from Bethany and she continued. 'Ask him to pour Mr Peterson a stiff brandy. On the house. And when he's drunk it, he's to give him another and to look after him until . . . well, until we come down. Then put on a clean pinafore and come upstairs.'

Bethany did as Sarah asked and then, with some apprehension made her way up to the bedroom. She had no idea what to expect because her only knowledge of babies' beginnings had been gleaned from Iris Bellingham, a rather flighty girl she had met at the art classes they had both attended in London. Iris always stayed behind to help Monsieur Artur to tidy the studio after everyone else had gone home. But the graphic details that she provided of what went on then seemed to include very little in the way of tidying and caused Bethany's eyes to widen in astonishment. The other girls, drinking in the details as eagerly as Bethany but most of them slightly more worldy, had warned her that what she described so explicitly could lead to 'trouble' but Iris had said airily that Artur was very careful — whatever that meant. However, it transpired that Artur had not been careful enough because Iris suddenly stopped coming to art class, but not before a tell-tale thickening at the waist had begun to appear to the discerning eye. Bethany never saw Iris again but in a way she was grateful to her for dispelling the myths of gooseberry bushes and doctors' bags.

Although Iris had been quite explicit as to how babies were made she had never been able to explain exactly how they came to be born and now that she was about to find out Bethany was not quite sure whether her heart was thumping from fear or excitement.

She pushed open the door and immediately the reason for the enormous cloak was apparent. Even under the bedclothes the huge bulge of Mrs Peterson's stomach could be seen as she writhed in pain. Aunt Sarah was beside her, wiping her face with a cool cloth as she tossed her head from side to side, moaning.

'Ah, good, Bethany. You can come and do this for Ellen,' Sarah said, looking up. She smiled encouragingly down at the girl. 'We can't keep calling you Mrs Peterson, now, can we.'

For hours, it seemed, Bethany bathed Ellen's face, smoothed her tangled hair and when the pains got really bad let her hang on to her hands and arms whilst Aunt Sarah was busy at the other end of the bed. It seemed to go on for such a long time that her arms felt as if they were being pulled out of the sockets and her back ached with the effort of supporting the girl on the bed. She had never in her wildest imaginings realised what physically hard work a birth could be; no wonder it was called labour. And every birth was the same. It was hardly surprising so many women died enduring this. She found herself offering up a quick prayer, 'Please, God, don't let Ellen die.'

Suddenly, the girl let out a scream.

'That's it, my girl. Give a good push,' Aunt Sarah was saying, although Bethany couldn't really see what was happening, except that there was a lot of blood on the sheets. 'Now, another. That's right. You're doing well. One more . . . '

There was a thin wail and Aunt Sarah caught the tiny, slimy creature as it emerged. 'A little boy,' she announced, busily doing things that Bethany couldn't see with scissors and cord. Then she wrapped the baby in a blanket and put him beside his mother. Tired and exhausted, Ellen kissed her son and smiled weakly.

Bethany looked at the tiny, red-faced miracle

178

in the crook of his mother's arm and then slumped down on a chair and pushed her hair out of her eyes. She realised that at some point over the last hours the lamps had been lit but she didn't remember it happening. She felt as if she had worked almost as hard as Ellen to bring this tiny child into the world. Now, all she wanted to do was go to sleep.

'Don't go to sleep, Bethany. I want you to go downstairs and fetch another kettle of water,' Sarah commanded.

Bethany dragged herself to her feet and Sarah, looking as exhausted as Bethany felt, went to the door with her. 'There's something not quite right,' she whispered. 'There's too much blood for my liking. And she still seems to be in considerable pain. I don't understand it.' Her brow furrowed. 'I do wish Matthew would come.'

'Shall I tell Mr Peterson he's got a son?'

Sarah hesitated. 'Yes, you can tell him that. But tell him he can't see his wife yet.'

Sarah went back into the room and Bethany went into the bar and gave Joe Peterson the news that he had a son. Then, leaving him to celebrate in ignorance of the drama upstairs, she fetched a kettle of water from the kitchen and went back to watch helplessly with Sarah as Ellen, still in pain, lay moaning on the bed.

'I do wish Matthew would come,' Sarah said under her breath as she made the baby comfortable in a drawer as a makeshift cradle. 'He would know what to do. I wish to God I did.'

As if on cue they heard a heavy tread on the stair and a few seconds later Matthew came into the room, his coat discarded and his sleeves rolled up, just in time to catch a second baby as it emerged, screaming lustily, from its exhausted mother.

'Twins!' Sarah and Bethany said together, looking at each other incredulously.

Sarah sank into the chair by the fire, tears streaming down her cheeks. 'So that's what it was,' she whispered. 'Thank God. I thought I'd done something wrong and she was dying.'

Matthew had wrapped the second baby up and laid her beside her mother. 'You've done well, Mrs Peterson,' he said softly. 'A boy and a girl.' He watched for a moment, then took the baby from her. 'Now, we must take your lovely daughter and put her with her brother because you must rest.'

Ellen looked drowsily up at him. 'Twins. I had no idea there were twins. Are they . . . ?'

'They look fine. Small, but perfect.'

'Oh, thank God for that. Can I see my husband?'

'Only for a few minutes,' Matthew said.

Sarah and Bethany went downstairs and Bethany went to give the news to Joe while Matthew made Ellen comfortable. Emily, tired out from cooking and serving the meal for the visitors and then single-handedly clearing up afterwards, had been waiting impatiently for news in the kitchen. Now, she made a welcome cup of tea, which Sarah could hardly drink because her hands were shaking so.

'I didn't know what to do. I thought there was something I ought to have done that I hadn't,' she said, reaction setting in after the night's trauma. 'I thought she was going to die. And it would all have been my fault.'

'But you hadn't done anything wrong, Aunt Sarah. You couldn't have known she was having twins,' Emily reassured her. 'Just think. Your first confinement and you delivered twins!'

'I hope to God it will be my last, too.' Sarah's words were heartfelt. 'I never want to go through that again.'

But Emily was more worried about her daughter. 'It was hardly the place for Bethany. I'm surprised you allowed her to stay, Aunt. There must have been things a young girl of her age should never have seen,' she said primly.

'I couldn't have managed without her,' Sarah said wearily, putting her head on her hands.

'All the same . . . '

Before they could argue further Matthew came into the kitchen, saying he must make arrangements for a live-in nurse from the village to come and look after Ellen and the twins.

'You see, she'll need constant care for a few days,' he said, drinking the tea Emily had poured for him. 'She's very weak and the babies are small. But Mrs Wright will be the best person to call. She'll know exactly what to do. She lives alone in a cottage at the end of Maltings Yard.'

'Shall I get someone to go for her now?' Sarah said. 'Or is it too late, tonight?'

'No. No. It's not too late. She'll need to come right away. Say I've sent for her. She's quite used

181

to being called out of bed in the middle of the night.' He looked at his pocket watch. 'Oh, it's not too much past ten o'clock. That's not bad at all.'

Sarah went off to the bar and Matthew followed her to take another look at Ellen, rolling down his sleeves as he went. He met Bethany at the foot of the stairs.

'You did very well, Bethany,' he said, smiling at her. 'Your first birth?'

She nodded, biting her lip. 'It was a miracle. And then, when Joe went in and I saw them all together . . . they looked so happy . . . a perfect little family . . . Oh, Matthew . . . ' suddenly, she burst into tears and began to sob as if her heart would break, all the time saying she was sorry, because it was all so beautiful and how stupid it was to cry.

He gathered her into his arms and began to stroke her hair. 'Hey, hey, now. It's all right. It's all right to cry. It's all right,' he crooned. 'You're very tired and you've had a very emotional experience tonight. You've seen not one baby born, but two. It's enough to make even the most hardened midwife shed a tear.'

He held her close until her sobs subsided, then he bent his head and allowed his lips to brush the top of her head, so lightly that she would never know. But he knew and he would value the knowledge to the end of his days.

'Better now?' he asked gently, as he released her.

'Yes, I'm better now,' she hiccupped, giving him a watery smile. 'I'm sorry. I don't know what came over me.' She brushed away her tears with the heel of her hands. 'Whatever must you think of me, being so stupid.'

He took her hands briefly in his. 'I don't think you're stupid at all, Bethany. I think you . . . ' he broke off. 'It can happen to the best of us at times.' He finished rolling down his sleeves. 'Now, I'll just go up and make sure Ellen is comfortable and then, as soon as Mrs Wright gets here I'll be off,' he said, in his best professional manner. 'But I shall drop by every day to see how things are going.'

'Why don't you wait for her in the little parlour,' she said. 'I'll bring you a drink. What would you like? A cup of tea?'

'I've already had a cup of tea. A whisky would be what I'd like more than anything,' he said, smiling down at her.

'I'll get that for you.'

They both turned at the sound of Zack's voice. Neither of them had noticed him standing watching them in the half darkness and Bethany wondered uncomfortably how long he had been there.

15

The following month was the busiest Travellers' Inn had ever known. Apart from the general day-to-day running of the inn there were the two small babies and their mother, who was understandably still very weak, to be considered, plus the not inconsiderable demands of Mrs Wright in the execution of her duties towards them. Bethany soon began to appreciate how smoothly things ran in the normal course of events. It didn't help that Mrs Wright, who cared for Ellen and the twins with no-nonsense efficiency, irritated Sarah.

'She's only been here five minutes yet she's ordering everyone about as if she owns the place,' Sarah complained at the end of the first week.

'I know, but you mustn't get cross with her, Sarah,' Matthew said, when he paid his daily visit. 'She used be matron in the IFW so . . . '

'What's the IFW?' Emily interrupted.

He looked uncomfortable. 'The Infirmary for Fallen Women,' he said, quickly adding, 'so she's used to things being done the way she wants them. I must say she's looking after her patients extremely well, too. The babies are thriving, even though they were so small and in about another week Mrs Peterson will be out of bed for a few hours.'

'Oh, dear. Not for another week! However much longer are they likely to stay?' Sarah's face was a picture of dismay.

'I don't mind the extra work. I like having them here,' Bethany said happily. 'Ellen is so grateful for everything and the babies are such dear little scraps. You can see them changing day by day.'

'Victoria and Albert, that's what they're to be called, after the Queen and Prince Albert,' Emily said, anxious to impart her news. 'Isn't that nice?'

'Hmph,' was Sarah's only reply. She had had her fill of these babies and their trappings after the trauma of their birth and couldn't wait to be rid of them.

Joe Peterson stayed for ten days and then, with some reluctance, left his wife and children in Mrs Wright's capable hands and went back to his work in Chelmsford. But not before he had written to Ellen's mother, who was married to a Dutch diamond merchant in Amsterdam, to tell her the news. A letter came back by return to say she would be arriving as soon as she could book passage, and would be bringing a nursemaid for the babies.

'Hm. Bringing a nursemaid, is she! The sparks will fly when Mrs Wright hears that,' Sarah remarked when she heard the news.

In the event, there was hardly time for the sparks to ignite, let alone fly.

Mrs Van der Hogh, a large, autocratic woman, her hands and neck an ample showcase for the commodities her husband dealt in, arrived complete with nursemaid and private convey-ance. She stayed two nights and then whisked her daughter and grandchildren off to Holland.

'I warned her that Mrs Peterson is really not yet strong enough for a long journey,' Matthew said, shaking his head.

'And the twins are still very tiny,' Mrs Wright added, between pursed lips that signified her disapproval far more eloquently than words.

'What will Mr Peterson think of his wife and children being taken away like that?' Bethany asked nobody in particular.

'Oh, he's agreed to it,' Emily said, full of importance. 'Mrs Van der Hogh told me all about it when I admired her jewellery. She told me that Mr Peterson is to join them in Amsterdam as soon as he's worked out his notice at his present firm. Apparently, he's to work in Mr Van der Hogh's business, where, of course, he will receive a much higher salary.'

'Something of a *fait accompli*, by the sound of it,' Sarah remarked. 'I wonder if he had much of a say in the arrangement.'

'Ellen told me he was quite excited at the prospect,' Emily said, adding wistfully, 'and at least there'll be no shortage of money.' She sighed. 'Oh, I did like Mrs Van der Hogh's rings. She showed them all to me. And her necklaces. Real diamonds.'

'I thought they looked vulgar,' Sarah said, her expression sour. She felt patronised because Mrs Van der Hogh had presented her with a more than generous cheque to cover the incovenience that Ellen's untimely confinement had caused to the running of the inn. Yet it had been an inconvenience, there was no doubt about that;

the whole place had revolved round Ellen and her babies for nearly a month. So it was not unreasonable that the inconvenience should be paid for. Which Mrs Van der Hogh had done. Generously. But Sarah still felt patronised; as if she had been patted on the head like a good dog.

Life at the inn reverted to its usual rhythm. No longer did the laundry woman have to come in every day and they were able to dispense with the extra help with cleaning and cooking that Sarah had been forced to employ. Bethany found that once again she even had time to herself in the afternoon.

'You haven't been along here for a week or two,' Zack said, catching up with her one hot, sultry day as she walked along by the hedgerow to reach the river. 'In fact, I've hardly seen you at all.'

'Well, I've been busy. You know that. In fact, we all have.'

'It gave Dr Matthew an excuse to call every day, I noticed.'

'Of course. He came to see Mrs Peterson and the babies.'

'I thought that woman in the starched apron was supposed to be looking after them.' He shuddered. 'God, she was fearsome. I kept out of her way.'

'Matthew still needed to keep an eye on them.'

'Yeh. I know. Kept an eye on you, too, I reckon.' He kicked a stone into the field, where green corn shoots were just beginning to appear.

'I don't know what you're talking about.' But she did. She suspected he had seen her weeping on Matthew's shoulder on the night of the twins' birth and was jealous. He had no need to be, of course, but she wouldn't tell him that.

They reached the river bank. 'It's a pity the tide's out,' she said, surveying the expanse of black mud with barely more than a trickle of water running through it. 'There are no boats to watch.'

'Well, it's spring tides so it's about as low as it ever gets,' he said, picking up a stone and throwing it as far as he could across the mud. It landed with a dull plop. 'At springs it goes out further and comes up higher. When it's neeps there's not so much tidal difference. It doesn't come up so high and doesn't go out so far. It's all to do with the moon.'

She turned to look at him. 'Where did you learn all that?'

'I lived at Harwich for a good part of my life. You don't live at a port and not learn about these things.'

'No, I suppose not.'

He threw another stone into the mud, then sat down and patted the bank beside him. 'Have you ever been mudlarking?' he asked.

She sat down. 'No. What's that?'

'Larking about in the mud. Me and my mates used to do it a lot when we were boys. It's a bit dangerous, though, if you don't know the river.'

'Why?'

'Because you could sink in, that's why. In places where the mud's very soft it can act like quicksand. You have to sort of skate over it so you don't put too much weight down.'

'Show me.'

'Not likely. I'd get filthy. My mudlarking days are over, thank you very much.'

They sat together, gazing out at the wide expanse of mud, so black that it had an almost blue sheen, watching the seagulls padding about, patterning the mud with their footprints as they searched for worms and squabbled over their finds. After a bit, Bethany got to her feet and brushed her dress.

'It's very nice sitting here, but I think I should get back and help Mama prepare the vegetables for tonight's dinner,' she said with some reluctance.

He looked up at her. 'The bluebells are out now in Farthing Wood,' he said carelessly. 'We could go and pick some tomorrow, if you like.'

She looked away, hoping he hadn't noticed the flush that she knew had spread across her face at the mention of Farthing Wood. He had probably forgotten what had happened there, but she hadn't.

'I don't know if I can manage tomorrow,' she said, not wanting him to think she was too enthusiastic.

'Suit yourself.' He got lazily to his feet. 'But they'll be over before many more days so if we don't go soon you'll be too late.'

'Well, all right, then. We'd better go tomorrow.'

Bethany's prayers were answered and the day dawned clear and bright. She hurried through her chores and even did a bit of extra polishing so that nobody could accuse her of neglecting her work. Then, after a lunch of bread and cheese and pickles, which Sarah always thoroughly enjoyed but was rather too rustic for Emily's taste, she left her mother and aunt to rest for an hour and went upstairs to put on her blue muslin, which was her favourite dress. Then she combed her unruly copper mane and secured it with a blue ribbon before perching her best straw hat on her curls and tilting it forward over one eye.

As she went through the kitchen she saw the little cakes that her mother had baked that morning on the cooling tray. On impulse she took two and popped them into her reticule. Then she went outside.

Zack was waiting for her. 'Very nice,' he said admiringly.

She dipped a mock curtsey. 'Thank you, kind sir.' She noticed that he had smartened himself up, too. His hair was still wet from being dowsed under the pump.

They walked across the road and over fields peppered with buttercups to the wood. They reached the stream and she was half-relieved, half-disappointed to see that it was reduced to a trickle because it was some time since there had been any rain.

'Pity. I don't need to carry you across today,' he said, as they both stepped over it in little more than a stride. The way he smiled at her she knew he was thinking of the last time, too.

The wood was fragrant with the scent of the bluebells, which spread a mist of blue between the trees in all directions.

'Oh, it's just beautiful,' Bethany breathed. 'I've

never seen anything like it. It seems a shame to pick them.'

He laughed. 'Oh, I guess the few you'll pick won't be missed.'

They walked on through the wood, following a barely discernable path through the bluebells. He had taken her hand to steady her as they crossed the stream and apparently forgotten to release it.

After walking for some time they reached a clearing.

'Oh, this is where we came before. This is where I picked primroses,' she said delightedly. 'On the bank there, near the stream. And look, this stream hasn't dried up.'

He released her hand and flung himself down on the grass, patting a spot beside him invitingly. 'That's because it's fed from a spring. I told you that, last time.'

'So you did.' She sat down beside him and took the two small cakes out of her reticule and handed him one.

He grinned at her. 'Not exactly what you might call a picnic but near enough,' he said, taking a bite. 'Mm. Tasty. Did you make them?'

'No, Mama has taken over the baking and she doesn't like anyone else to interfere. Not that I mind,' she said with a laugh.

'They're very good. Did you bring any more?'

'No. Greedy. Be satisfied with one.'

'Oh, I'm never satisfied, you ought to know that,' he said softly. He leaned towards her and suddenly she felt a charge of something between them — she had no name for it but she knew it was there and sensed that he did, too. 'You've got a crumb on your chin.' The words were mundane enough, as gently he put out his hand and brushed her chin with his thumb. 'There, that's better.' He looked into her eyes. 'Remember the last time we were here, Beth?' he whispered.

'Yes. I remember.' She could hardly speak; his face was very close, close enough to kiss. She knew that if she turned away the spell would be broken; she also knew that if she didn't break the spell now, this minute, it would be too late.

She put up her hand and drew him to her.

He was very gentle. He kissed her, loosening her hair from its pins and spreading it over her bare shoulders as he unfastened her dress and caressed her. There was no turning back. They both knew that this was why they had come to the wood; the knowledge of it had hung between them since they left the house and she was as eager as he was, helping him when he fumbled with her buttons, undoing his shirt and the buckle on his belt. And it didn't hurt much; the pleasure by far outweighed the pain.

When it was over they lay side by side, looking up through the trees at the blue sky.

'Do you still want to pick bluebells, Beth?' he asked lazily.

'Some other day, perhaps,' she answered, leaning up on one elbow and tracing his profile with her finger. 'Tomorrow, perhaps?' She knew she was being wanton and she didn't care. It was a wonderful feeling.

He caught her hand and kissed her palm.

'Can't come here every time, sweetheart. Mrs P will get suspicious,' he said thoughtfully.

'Where, then?'

'You can always come to my room. You can make an excuse to fetch something from the tack room; my room's above so you'll only have to slip up the stairs.' He began to stroke her shoulder. 'And you can slip across the yard after everyone is in bed. That way we'll have all the time in the world . . . ' He pulled her down to him again.

When she got home she was surprised neither her mother nor Aunt Sarah noticed anything different about her; she felt as if the glow inside her must show on the outside. But all Aunt Sarah said was, 'Been for your walk? It does you good to get out into the fresh air.' And all her mother said was, 'I think I'll bake potatoes in the oven tonight so you won't need to peel any.'

It was quite amazing.

As Zack had predicted it was easy enough to go to his room after everyone else was in bed and every night after she had gone to her room she would wait impatiently for the sounds that told her it would soon be safe to leave; the closing of her mother's bedroom door, the creak of springs as Aunt Sarah got into bed.

Zack was always waiting for her and he would lift the covers so that she could slip into the narrow bed with him. She never stayed too long, always fearful that she would fall asleep and not wake till morning, but it was long enough to learn all he could teach her of the delights of love-making and to teach him some that she invented herself.

When she didn't visit his room for several nights he sought her out as she scattered corn to the chickens scratching about in the yard.

'What's the matter? Tired of me?' he demanded, a scowl on his face.

'No, of course I'm not tired of you, Zack,' she said, trying to laugh.

'Then why didn't you come? I stayed awake all night, waiting.' He followed her into the barn and pinned her against the wall.

'Zack! Somebody will see us,' she whispered fiercely, trying to twist away.

'Well, if you don't come to me tonight, I shall come to you,' he said, refusing to release her.

'No, you mustn't do that. What if somebody saw you?' She was horrified.

'Heard us, more like,' he said with a grin. 'You don't make love quietly, my girl.'

She flushed. 'Well, I can't come tonight.'

'Why not?'

She turned her head away. 'Don't you understand. It's . . . I can't do it when I'm . . . unwell.'

'Oh, I see.' His face cleared. 'Why didn't you say so, then?' He bent his head and kissed her, his hand cupping her breast. 'Well, it'll be all the better next time because I'm getting hungry.' He bit her lip gently.

He released her quickly at the sound of Reuben hawking as he came across the yard. 'Tuesday?' he whispered.

She nodded, gathering up kindling wood in

her apron. 'Tuesday.'

'Hev you got enough kindlin' there? I've jest come up to chop a bit more,' Reuben said, peering as his eyes became accustomed to the gloom.

'Yes, thanks, Reuben. I've got enough here to lay the fire in the parlour.'

'Yew don't need no fire this time o' year,' he said with a chuckle.

'No, but I like to have it ready to put a match to in case the evenings get cold,' she replied, making her escape without a backward glance because she knew Zack was still standing there, grinning, in the shadows.

She crossed the yard, her heart singing. She had always wondered what it must be like to be in love. Now she knew.

16

That summer was the happiest Bethany had ever spent. Basking in Zack's love, with the added frisson of excitement gained from stealing over to his room practically every night and the stolen kisses whenever there was the slightest opportunity, she sang about her work and had a ready smile for everyone.

She gave no thought to the future. The possibility that he might leave the inn and move on was a prospect she couldn't bear to consider. The fact that he might tire of her never crossed her mind. She was amazed that neither her mother nor her aunt detected the change in her, although she was always very careful not to betray her feelings for him when anyone else was around. The secrecy was part of the excitement.

Sometimes, when Matthew called, she found his eyes resting on her in a way she found slightly disconcerting. He was a doctor. Had he detected a change in her? But she dismissed her fears. Even if he had he could hardly know the reason for it.

At harvest time the whole village turned out to help, as they always did. Zack trundled barrels of beer down to the field to slake the thirst of parched workers and then stayed to help with the reaping, while Bethany and Sarah joined the women in binding and stacking the stooks. Working in the fields was not at all to Emily's taste, she insisted that too much sun would spoil her complexion. She preferred to stay in the kitchen baking mutton pies and apple tarts and receiving the compliments Isaac Walford passed on to her when he came to the kitchen to fetch more. She was flattered that the farmer himself came for replenishments, and even more that he was happy to stay for a chat and a cup of tea before going back to the field.

The Harvest Home followed the same pattern Bethany remembered from the previous year, only this year Emily joined in as happily as everyone else, sitting at the long table with Bethany and Sarah to eat roast beef followed by treacle pudding, all made by Mrs Kraft, the farmer's housekeeper.

'This treacle pudding is very nice but I would rather have had apple pie,' Bethany announced, nevertheless holding out her plate for a second helping.

'I just love apples.'

'So I've noticed,' Sarah remarked. 'Every time I've looked at you lately you've been munching an apple.'

Bethany shrugged. 'Well, I like them. They taste so much better when you can pick them straight off the tree.' Even the thought of them, hanging rosy and shining on the trees in the little orchard at the bottom of Sarah's garden made her mouth water.

Billy Shovel picked up his fiddle and the dancing began. Bethany joined in with a will. She was no longer a stranger in the village, all the men who came to drink at the inn knew her and wanted to dance with her. Zack only managed to claim her twice.

'You're not trying to avoid me, are you, Beth?' he said with a grin.

She laughed up at him. 'As if I would! But it wouldn't do for us to dance together too often.'

'No, you're quite right. In any case, I've got my eye on Harry Day's daughter.' He winked at her. 'She's a pretty little thing.'

'Where is she?' Bethany felt a sudden stab of jealousy although she was sure he was only teasing.

'She's over there, dancing with Doctor Matthew.' He steered her so she could get a good view of the willowy blonde being partnered by Matthew.

She tried to stifle the almost overwhelming feeling of sick jealousy that swept over her. 'Well, make sure you don't dance with her too many times or she might think you're setting your cap at her.' She managed to smile as she said the words.

'Well, if I can't dance with you . . . ' He left the words hanging in the air.

She didn't enjoy the rest of the evening, she felt sick and dizzy, but whether it was caused by too much energetic dancing or naked jealousy as she watched Zack twirling Elsie Day round she couldn't tell.

It was as she was dancing with Matthew that it happened.

They were in the middle of a rather unruly and ragged version of Sir Roger de Coverley — the dancing always degenerated towards the end of the evening in direct proportion to the amount of beer consumed — and Matthew had been remarking, when he could make himself heard above the noise, that the country air clearly suited her.

'I must say you're looking very well these days, Bethany,' he said, looking down at his feet as he concentrated on the steps. 'And I do believe you've even put on a little weight.'

'Yes, I know. It's all my mother's fault,' she said lightly. 'She's become a very good cook since we came here to live and I can't resist her cakes and pastries.'

'Then she's to be congratulated. It suits you. I've never seen you look so . . . '

The rest of his words were lost as he spun her round and went to hand her on to the next man. But even as she twirled she felt the barn spinning as well. Then there was a drumming in her ears and everything went black. The next thing she knew she was lying on a sack of straw in the open air, looking up at the harvest moon. Matthew, her mother and Aunt Sarah were all bending over her anxiously. She struggled to sit up, her first thought to try and see through the open barn door whether Zack was still dancing with Elsie Day. She saw that he was and with it came the realisation that she was about to be sick.

Emily and Sarah took her home, walking one each side of her and taking it in turns to scold her for drinking too much.

'It's what's expected of the farm labourers, and even their wives, at the Harvest Home,'

Sarah said, 'but I would have thought you had more sense.'

'It was hardly the behaviour of a lady,' Emily added primly. 'You made me feel really ashamed of you, Bethany.'

Bethany felt too ill to protest that she had, in fact, had very little to drink because for some reason even the smell of beer turned her stomach. Sarah and Emily continued chastising her, but she let the words wash over her head, wanting only to go to bed and forget the sight of Zack dancing with Elsie Day. She could hardly admit to them that it was pure jealousy that had made her sick.

'Matthew said he would come along in the morning to see how you are,' Sarah said.

'Oh, I'm sure there won't be any need. I shall have recovered by then,' Bethany said weakly.

She did feel slightly better by the morning although she still felt sick when she thought of Zack dancing with Elsie Day, and even worse at the thought that he might have walked her home. Emily, with motherly concern, had insisted she remain in bed until Matthew had seen her, although she did it more as a punishment for drinking too much and showing herself up in public than because she thought it necessary.

By the time he arrived it was almost midday and she was sitting up in bed munching an apple, impatient to be allowed to get up.

'Oh, thank goodness you've arrived,' she greeted him. She looked over his shoulder at Emily, who had accompanied him into the room.

'Now, Mama, perhaps you'll let me get out of bed.'

'You're feeling better, then?' he asked, giving her a searching look.

'Yes. I'm perfectly all right. Can I get up now?'

'I'll just examine you, now I'm here.'

'Oh, Matthew. Is it really necessary? Mama, tell him I'm perfectly all right.'

'I think you should let Matthew examine you. After all, you were rather violently sick.'

'Had you been drinking too much?' he asked, with a smile.

'Mama and Aunt Sarah said I had but it wasn't true. I only had one glass of beer and I didn't finish that. I don't much like it, to tell you the truth, although I wouldn't like Aunt Sarah to hear me say it.'

'Are you feeling better this morning?'

'Oh, yes.'

'Not still feeling sick?'

'No. Well, not very.'

All the time he was speaking he was examining her, looking in her eyes, at her throat, then pulling down the covers and pressing her abdomen. 'Your monthly courses. Are they regular?' he murmured without looking up, his tone completely professional.

She flushed to the roots of her hair at such a personal question and Emily cleared her throat in embarrassment, although there was no need because Matthew was completely at ease.

'Oh, yes, quite regular,' she muttered.

'And when was the last one?' He still didn't look up.

'Oh . . . ' Suddenly she realised that it was at least two months since her 'flowers' as she called them. She hadn't thought anything of it, simply glad that it hadn't come and hampered her nights with Zack. 'June? July? I can't really remember.'

He straightened up then, a strange, closed expression on his face. 'I think you know exactly what's wrong with you, Bethany, don't you?' he asked, his tone clipped.

She shrugged. 'Eating too many apples?'

'Don't play games with me, Bethany,' he said harshly. He turned to Emily. 'I can only assume Bethany hasn't seen fit to confide in you that she is pregnant. Some three months pregnant as far as I can ascertain.'

'Pregnant!' Emily and Bethany both said the word together and it was difficult to know which of them was most surprised.

He shot round. 'But you must have known, Bethany. You must have . . . ' Now, in spite of his profession he was lost for suitable words.

Bethany looked stricken, her gaze passing from Emily to Matthew and back again. 'I didn't know . . . I thought he . . . I thought he was being careful . . . I didn't think . . . '

'Just *who* did you think was being *careful*, Bethany?' Emily asked icily, her face white with a mixture of shock and anger.

The girl lifted her head defiantly. 'Why, Zack, of course. Who else? We're in love.' Zack had never actually said in so many words that he loved her but from the way he behaved Bethany was in no doubt that he did.

202

Neither she nor Emily noticed the expression of pain that crossed Matthew's face at her words. He left soon after, saying briefly that Bethany only had to call him if she needed anything. At Emily's request he sought out Sarah as he left and asked her to go to Bethany's room. She was, as usual, in the garden, and he offered no explanation when she raised questioning eyebrows.

'You'll see,' was all he would say as he swung up into the saddle and trotted off.

Puzzled, Sarah removed her boots, unhitched her skirt and washed her hands at the pump. Then she went upstairs.

Bethany was sitting up in bed looking nearly as white as the pillow behind her. Emily was sitting on a chair by the window, wringing her hands and looking twenty years older than she had at breakfast time.

Sarah frowned in alarm as she looked from one to the other. 'What's the matter? What's wrong with Bethany? We can afford the best doctors in the county if necessary.' She strode over and laid her hand on Bethany's forehead. 'What is it, my girl?'

'She's pregnant,' Emily said flatly. 'That's what's wrong with her. The stupid little slut,' she added vehemently.

Sarah sat down on the bed with a bump. 'Is this true, Bethany?' she asked incredulously.

'It's not something I'm likely to lie about, is it?' Emily almost shouted at her. She pulled herself together with an effort and put her fingers to her temples. 'We shall have to arrange for her to be married with all possible speed . . . '

'Married? Who's she going to marry?'

'The father, of course. Zack,' Emily spat.

Sarah turned, almost in slow motion, to Bethany. 'Is Zachary the father of this . . . this child?'

Bethany nodded.

'Does he know?'

'Of course he doesn't know. We've only just found out ourselves,' Emily said impatiently.

Sarah took no notice of her outburst. 'Well?' she said to Bethany.

Bethany shook her head. She licked her lips. 'I didn't think it would happen. I thought he knew what to do. I thought men could take care of . . . ' Her voice trailed off. Once again she remembered Iris Bellingham, who thought her Art master had taken care . . .

'Did he say so?' Sarah snapped, interrupting her thoughts.

'No, but I thought . . . '

'Tch.' Sarah made an expression of disgust. 'You thought! Have you no sense, girl? Do you think the poor people in the village would be overrun with children if they *knew what to do*, as you put it? If you do the thing that makes children, then children will come, as sure as night follows day.' A brief note of sadness crept into her voice. 'Unless, of course, you're barren, like me.' She shook her head. 'I'm surprised at you, Bethany. I'm surprised, disgusted and disappointed.' She paused, then pulled back her shoulders. 'Now, having said all that, we must think what is to be done.'

'We know what is to be done. She must be married. With all possible speed. Zack must marry her,' Emily said firmly.

'Be quiet, Emily. Let me think,' Sarah waved her hand in Emily's direction.

'Well, there's no alternative.' Emily refused to be quietened. 'We can't have the child born out of wedlock.'

Sarah lifted her head. 'I don't see why not,' she said thoughtfully. 'It'll be a disgrace; a nine-day's wonder in the village, of course, but no doubt we shall survive the gossip. And there will be three of us to bring up the child, so it will want for nothing.'

'Except a father,' Bethany said, her voice bitter to think her future was being decided for her.

Sarah nodded. 'Yes. Except a father. Because Zack will have to go. And the sooner the better.'

'You don't like Zack, do you, Aunt Sarah,' Bethany accused. 'You never have.'

'With good reason, it seems,' Sarah said, nodding towards Bethany's stomach.

'It's no use, Aunt Sarah, I simply couldn't face the shame of Bethany having a child out of wedlock,' Emily interrupted, tears beginning to stream down her cheeks. 'I think Zack will have to marry Bethany. I like him, even though he's behaved so badly, taking advantage of poor Bethany the way he has.'

'It wasn't like that . . . ' Bethany began but her aunt silenced her.

'Be quiet. What's done is done and can't be undone. The question is what's to be done about it.'

205

'As I was saying, Zack is a great asset to us,' Emily continued. 'He does all the heavy work and he's always helpful and cheerful. I really don't know what we would do without him. Just think about last winter when it snowed and Reuben was so ill. I don't know how we should have managed without him.' She lifted her chin. 'I think he should stay and they should be married.'

'Hmph,' Sarah said. 'That may be what you'd like but I guess when the word marriage is mentioned he'll be off and that'll be the last we'll see of him. I've seen men like him before.' She stood up, her back straight. 'We shall manage, the three of us. And as long as we hold our heads high we shall get over the shame of it all.' She nodded towards Bethany and said more gently. 'You needn't worry, my girl. There's no question of us turning you out, although there's a good many that would. No, we shall stand by you and your child and see that it's brought up decently. There's no need for you to think you've got to marry the man.'

Bethany took a deep breath, trying to keep her temper in the face of her mother and aunt deciding her future without even consulting her. 'But I *want* to marry Zack, Aunt Sarah. I love him and he loves me. I've no doubt, in time, he would have asked me to marry him, anyway.'

'Well, it's a pity he couldn't wait to sample the goods until he'd bought them, that's all I can say,' Aunt Sarah said crudely. She jerked her head towards the door. 'You'd better get yourself out of that bed and go and tell him the news. But if I don't miss my mark he'll solve the argument for us because when he hears what you've got to tell him you won't see his heels for dust.'

Bethany got dressed and went to find Zack. After seeing him with Elsie Day last night she wasn't quite as confident as she had made out to her mother and aunt that he loved her and would want to marry her. Perhaps he was tiring of her, although he had never showed any sign of it when she went to his room at night. Perhaps he had found a new love last night. In Elsie Day.

Tormenting herself with these thoughts she made her way down to the orchard, where she could see him picking apples.

★   ★   ★

About half a mile from Travellers' Inn Matthew dismounted from his horse and stood leaning on a five-barred gate overlooking the recently harvested field and the river beyond. Was it only yesterday that the field had been full of harvesters, men with red neckerchiefs and battered straw hats, women in faded bonnets calling happily to each other and laughing as they worked, without a care in the world? He stared over the field of golden stubble to the river beyond, where the water glinted in the sun and a red-sailed barge moved majestically up towards the quay at Mistley, but he saw none of it. His thoughts were turned inward to the girl he had just left and the blackguard that had played fast and loose with her in her innocence. He clenched his fists. He was normally a mild man but he had murder in his heart at what that scoundrel had done to Bethany.

And she thought he loved her. He made a sound of disgust. He had seen men like Zachary Brown before, taking what they wanted and then leaving the girl ruined, with a child to care for and no man, for not many would be willing to take on another man's leavings.

But he would. If Bethany would have him he would marry her. The thought struck him like a thunderbolt because he had thought he would never, ever think to marry again. Not after Celia, the love of his life, had died giving birth to his child. He had vowed never to marry again and subject another woman to that risk by his lust. But Bethany was different. She was what, nineteen? And he was twenty-six. Seven years older. Old enough to love and protect her as a father might. He closed his eyes. Who was he deluding? The feeling he had for Bethany was not at all fatherly; he wanted her for his wife. He wanted her so much that he was prepared to take her with another man's child in her womb, God help him.

17

As Bethany reached Zack, who was up a tree in the orchard picking apples, he threw one down to her.

'Here, catch! Right off the top of the tree, a nice juicy one. I know how much you like 'em.'

She caught it and because she couldn't resist it, bit into it greedily, the juice running down her chin. Impatiently, she wiped it away with the heel of her hand.

'Will you come down, Zack. Please. I've got something important to tell you,' she called urgently, taking another bite.

'Hang on a minute. I'll just finish filling this basket.' He began to whistle as he worked.

'No, Zack. You must come down right away. I need to talk to you. It's important, I tell you.' She almost stamped her foot in her agitation.

'All right, don't get your dander up,' he said mildly, beginning to climb down the ladder. When he reached the ground he leaned over and kissed the tip of her nose. 'Well, what is it that's so important it can't wait two minutes?' He grinned. 'Do you want to come to my room? Right now? In broad daylight?' He wiped his hands down his trousers. 'I'm ready if you are, but I don't know how we'll explain to Mrs P, 'cause I'll bet her beady eyes'll be on us, watching where we go.'

Bethany shook her head. 'It's too late, Zack.

We don't need to explain anything to Aunt Sarah, she already knows,' she said miserably.

He gave a low whistle. 'How did she find out? I thought you said you never came across to me till they were all asleep. Has she been following you?'

'No. Nothing like that.'

'What then?'

She couldn't look at him, fearful of what she might see in his face. She began to cry. 'I'm sorry, Zack. I didn't think it could happen. I thought you would know how to stop it. I didn't understand. And now it has and I'm afraid you'll go away . . . '

He took her by the shoulders and gave her a little shake. 'What in the world are you talking about, woman?'

She stole a glance at him. 'I'm pregnant, Zack. I'm having a baby,' she whispered.

'Ah, so that's it.' He shrugged. 'Well, we've really been going at it, so it's hardly surprising, under the circumstances.' He leaned against the trunk of the tree and took the apple out of her hand and took a large bite. After several minutes he said carefully, 'So, you're in pod and they've found us out. What now? Am I to be turned out for leading you astray?' He grinned at her. 'Not that you needed a lot of leading, I must say.'

'Not unless you choose to go,' she answered, equally carefully, ignoring his last words. 'Although that's what Aunt Sarah expects you to do. 'We shan't see his heels for dust when he finds out,' were her words.'

'Well, I suppose if I went of my own accord it

would save her the trouble of sacking me,' he said with another shrug. 'She's never had a very high opinion of me, I know that.'

'She's always very appreciative of the work you do.' Almost against her will she rushed to her aunt's defence, adding quickly, 'Mama doesn't agree with her. She thinks you should stay and we should be married.' She spoke quickly, trying to stifle the feeling of sick despair that had welled up in her at his words.

He bent and picked a blade of grass and began to chew it. 'And what do you think, Beth?'

'I thought . . . well, until last night I thought . . . ' she broke off, unable to voice her fears.

He looked up, frowning. 'Last night? What about last night?'

'Elsie Day.' She wouldn't look at him. 'You seemed to be having such a good time with Elsie Day at the Harvest Home that I thought you were tired of me. She's very pretty . . . '

He caught her by the shoulders and gave her a little shake. 'You were jealous!' He burst out laughing. 'Well, that made two of us, because I only danced with her so many times because you seemed to be having such a good time in Doctor Matthew's company.'

'In Matthew's company?' she looked up at him, puzzled. 'But he's only . . . well, he's just a friend of the family, that's all.'

'I'm glad to hear it.' He thought it wiser not to mention that he had seen the way Matthew had been looking at her, and that it was not at all in the manner of a friend of the family.

The worried look returned to her face. 'So what am I going to do, Zack?' she asked anxiously.

'About what?' He seemed genuinely puzzled.

She put her splayed hand on her stomach. 'About this?'

He looked down at her hand. 'How far gone are you?'

'Matthew reckons about three months.' She pressed her lips together but it was no use, her face crumpled into tears. 'Oh, Zack, you should have seen his face! He thought I already knew, but I didn't! I had no idea. Oh, Zack, what am I going to do?'

He stepped forward and put his finger gently under her chin. 'I think you should do what every good girl does,' he said, smiling at her. 'You should do as your mother tells you. You should marry me.'

He caught her just in time and held her to him as her legs began to buckle under her with relief.

'Do you mean that, Zack? Do you really love me? Do you really want to marry me?' She looked up from the circle of his arms, smiling through her tears.

'Of course I want to marry you, you silly little goose,' he said, kissing her soundly. 'I've wanted to marry you ever since I came here.'

* * *

Bethany and Zack were married at Mistley church one morning very early without any fuss. Only her mother, Aunt Sarah and Matthew were there to witness the event. Afterwards, Matthew shook Zack's hand and said he was a lucky man, kissed Bethany on the cheek and went on his rounds with a heavy heart. He hoped Bethany would be happy with her new husband, he told himself firmly; he really did. But there was an uncomfortable feeling lurking at the back of his mind which wouldn't go away and which he couldn't put a name to. He didn't think it was entirely caused by jealousy.

Bethany, ecstatic on her new husband's arm, went back to the inn with her mother, who was equally delighted, and Sarah, who was less so although she did her best to hide it, to begin the day's work. The only sign of celebration was that Emily cooked Zack's favourite steak and kidney pudding and Bethany's favourite apple pie, of which Bethany had three helpings and then felt sick. Reuben joined them for the meal and ate noisily and heartily and drank too much beer. He liked Zack. More than that, he had been secretly glad to hand over all the heavy work to him without actually having to admit that it was becoming too much for him to cope with. He was relieved that there was now no danger of Zack leaving Travellers' Inn and he raised his tankard to toast Zack and Bethany so many times that they became 'the Gride and Broom' and 'Back and Zephany'. Finally, Sarah, herself more than slightly mellowed by her best brew, refused to fill it up any more.

After that, life went on much as usual. Coaches came and went, some stayed overnight, some didn't. Sarah was both surprised and gratified to find that Zack didn't abuse his new position as 'man of the house' and continued to work as hard as he had ever done and to defer to her as and when he thought necessary or expedient. The only subtle difference, which Sarah didn't see because she rarely visited it, was in the bar, where his attitude gradually became slightly more proprietorial and autocratic. However, this was not a problem because it was no more than the customers expected.

The biggest change, of course, and one which was at first a cause of some embarrassment to all three women, was the fact that he now shared Bethany's bedroom instead of going back to his own room across the yard. Zack didn't share their embarrassment. He took it as a matter of course, glad of the comfort of a feather bed and an eagerly compliant wife. As far as he was concerned life couldn't be better.

All too soon autumn slipped into winter. Sarah had harvested her vegetables and stored them and had helped Emily preserve the apples and plums. Now that it was too cold to sit with Reuben on the bench outside the woodshed in the sunshine they sometimes sat inside for an hour or so, looking out at the garden where the seeds she had planted in October slept, snug in the warm earth, waiting for spring. But when the winter cold really bit Reuben often stayed by his own fireside, nursing his rheumaticky limbs and coaxed out only by the thought of Emily's mutton pies or Zack's beer.

As Bethany's pregnancy progressed and the baby grew heavy inside her, she was glad of

Sarah's help with some of the household duties, especially when there were guests. Bethany was never sure of Sarah's motives. She suspected it was more that her aunt was anxious to keep her swelling figure away from the eyes of guests — especially the men — than that she had any desire to wait on tables or empty slops. But whichever it was, Bethany was glad of it, particularly when her ankles began to swell and she became increasingly lethargic. She was more than happy just to sit by the fire and sew clothes for the coming baby, or gently doze the day away.

Neither Emily nor Sarah saw anything wrong in this.

Quite early on, Matthew had suggested, his voice kind but at the same time impersonal and businesslike, that when the time came for Bethany's confinement they should call on Mrs Wright as the best person to attend her. Although naturally, he had added, if anything gave them cause for concern they should call him immediately. Emily had been ready to protest, surprised that he should even consider not being present at such a time, but Sarah understood; she had seen the way Matthew looked at Bethany when he thought he was unobserved. So she had laid a hand on Emily's arm, silencing her before she could speak. When Sarah told her what Matthew had said Bethany was glad. Remembering the indignities Ellen Peterson had suffered during the birth of the twins she had no wish that Matthew should witness her in the same plight.

Nevertheless, when his duties permitted, Matthew visited Travellers' Inn for a quiet drink. After questioning Zack carefully about Bethany's health he would spend the evening in the snug with Isaac Walford, often discussing the progress of the railways and how much difference it would make to the district if, or more accurately when it reached their corner of Essex. They speculated as to the route it would take to Harwich and laid mild bets as to whether the line would come from Ipswich or Colchester. They both agreed it was only a matter of time before the navvies would appear to begin carving up the country-side.

'Then you'll be a rich man, Isaac,' Matthew said with a smile as he picked up his hat ready to leave. 'If they want the lines to run over your land they'll pay a good price for it.'

'Ah, but I might not want to sell it,' Isaac said getting to his feet. 'Then they'll have to pay even more.'

'Or go the other side of the river,' Matthew replied. 'Then you'll get nothing at all.'

'Well, we shall see. They've only just reached Colchester so it'll be a few years before they reach us. From what I've heard they've got to find more money before they can proceed any further.'

They walked out through the bar and Isaac left.

Matthew waited behind. He leaned over to Zack. 'Is Bethany well?' he asked quietly.

Zack nodded. 'Well enough. She's getting near her time now.' He nodded towards the kitchen.

'Go and see her. She'll be in the back there with the others.' He glanced up at the clock on the wall. 'Ah, no, she'll be in bed by now. She doesn't stay up late, these days. But Em and Mrs P are there. They were saying only yesterday that they don't see much of you, these days.'

'No, well, it's winter. I'm always more busy when it's cold.' It wasn't strictly true but it served as an excuse. He knew he was being cowardly and he promised himself that he would visit again when Bethany had been safely delivered of her child.

Early in the morning of the last day of March Zack, who for the past month had been banished to sleep on the bed in the kitchen, was woken by Sarah and told to go with all haste for Mrs Wright. He struggled, bleary-eyed, into his trousers but the cold blast of night air soon brought him to his senses and he ran the whole two miles, arriving too breathless to speak.

'Haven't you brought the dog cart?' she demanded, knowing what he had come for without being told.

He shook his head. 'No time,' he managed to say.

'Of course there's time.' She waved him away. 'Well, you'd better go back and fetch it. I'm not walking all that way at this time of night carrying my bag. It's heavy.'

'I'll carry it.' He grabbed it from her. 'Mrs P said I was to hurry.'

Mrs Wright wrapped herself in a voluminous cloak. 'Oh, very well,' she said with a sigh. 'But we'd have got there quicker if you'd stayed to harness up the dog cart. I can't walk very fast.'

'Well, I'll go on ahead and tell them you're coming,' he offered.

'You will not. If I've got to walk then you'll walk with me. It's the first, isn't it?'

He nodded, willing her to walk faster.

'Then there's no hurry. The first one always takes its time.'

Zack didn't believe her. He expected to hear the lusty cry of his child as soon as he opened the door, but all was silent. He looked at her in alarm.

She patted his arm. 'You go back to bed, boy. You've done your bit. I told you, these things take their time.' She lumbered off up the stairs.

Twenty-four hours later she sent Zack to fetch Matthew.

'She's exhausted,' Mrs Wright told him as soon as he arrived. 'She hasn't got the strength left to push the baby out.'

He went over and quickly summed up the situation. 'Please God, not again,' he prayed fervently as he put his hand on Bethany's brow. She opened her eyes. 'I'm so tired, Matthew,' she whispered.

'I know, my dear. But you've got a bit more work to do.' He laid a hand on her belly and felt the muscles contracting. He nodded to Mrs Wright who was already there, knowing exactly what to do. 'Now, when I tell you. Hold on to Mrs Wright and push as hard as you can. I'll help you. Now!'

She clutched at Agnes Wright, looking up into his face. 'And again!'

218

'I . . . can't . . . '

'Yes, you can.' He willed her to do as he commanded and she complied, too exhausted to do anything else.

Then, suddenly, after a timeless, pain-filled age, she felt a slithering between her legs and the pain left her.

He picked up the baby. 'You've got a daughter, Bethany. A beautiful daughter.' As if to echo his words the baby began to cry.

That was the last thing Bethany heard for three days.

Later, they told her how ill she had been, but she had no recollection of how the fever had raged and they had all thought she would die. She only knew she woke with a raging thirst and a feeling of surprise that her enormous stomach was now nearly flat. She frowned as Mrs Wright lifted her head to give her a drink of pure water from the well. 'The baby?' she whispered, trying to look about her.

'She's here.' Mrs Wright picked the child out of the cradle and put her in Bethany's arms.

Bethany gazed down at her. 'She's beautiful,' she breathed. The baby yawned and opened one eye. 'And she has lovely dark eyes, just like her papa. Has he seen her?'

'Oh, yes, he's seen her. But only for a minute, because you've been so ill we wouldn't let him stay long. I'll call him now.'

Zack came in. He looked pale and haggard, but whether it was through worrying about Bethany or from the hangover he suffered after too many men in the bar bought him drinks to 'wet the baby's head' was difficult to tell.

'Oh, Beth,' he said, kissing her. 'You had me scared. Are you all right now?'

'Yes, I'm all right now,' she said, smiling up at him. 'And look at our beautiful little daughter.'

'She's just like you, Beth,' he said, kissing her again.

'But she's got your lovely dark eyes, Zack.' She put up her hand and touched his face.

And that was how Matthew found them when he came to pay his daily visit.

'Matthew,' she said delightedly when she saw him. 'Have you see her? Isn't she beautiful? Did you know she was born?'

Matthew gave a quirky smile. 'Yes, Bethany, I knew she was born,' he said. He didn't add, 'Oh, yes, I knew. I was here. I practically pulled her out of you and afterwards, when you were on the point of giving up I willed you to live and wouldn't let you die. I never left your side for two days and two nights in case you slipped away when I wasn't there to call you back.' Nor did he tell her that when he was certain she would live he went home and got drunk.

But Mrs Wright wasn't so reticent. 'If it hadn't been for Dr Oakley I doubt if you'd be here now,' she said, after unceremoniously bundling the proud father out of the room.

'Oh, were you here, Matthew?' Bethany looked up at him in surprise. 'I don't remember anything. Except the pain, the terrible, unbearable pain.' She frowned. 'And the hand. There was a hand and I knew I mustn't let go of it because if I did I should be lost.' She gave a little smile. 'The funny thing was, when I felt I couldn't hold on to it any longer, instead of feeling it slip from my grasp it seemed to grip mine more tightly. Strange, wasn't it.'

'Yes, very strange,' Matthew agreed. He turned to Mrs Wright, his voice businesslike. 'Has the wet nurse been?'

'Oh, yes, Doctor. She lives in one of the farm cottages so she doesn't have far to come to suckle the child. Mrs Brown's mother and aunt wouldn't hear of her taking the baby away and it suits Mrs Partridge, too, because she's got quite a brood of her own, without taking this one. If she gets restless in between feeds I give her sugar water.'

'That's good.' He turned away and in a low voice asked Mrs Wright several other searching questions, which she apparently answered to his satisfaction because he said again, 'Good. I'm glad you've got everything under control.'

'You will come and see us again, Matthew, won't you?' Bethany asked anxiously.

'Oh, yes, I shall come and see you again, Bethany,' he said with a smile.

'That's good.' She closed her eyes and fell asleep.

18

Bethany's recovery took several weeks and a number of bottles of medicine which Matthew brought to her and which he called enigmatically 'tonic'. But whatever the bottles contained they — together with hours spent sitting in the sunshine sewing, or simply watching the baby at her side gurgling in her crib — eventually brought the colour back into Bethany's cheeks and started her energy flowing again. Matthew visited every week, sometimes twice, and on the rare occasions when he had half an hour to spare, allowed himself the luxury of sitting with her in the garden. Bethany enjoyed this, too, for she was very fond of Matthew; she had never forgotten how kind he had been to her and her mother on that fateful journey from London to Travellers' Inn and she had always regarded him as the first real friend they had found in their new life.

But Zack was her love. And there could be no doubt that he loved her, too. Even Sarah could see that. Whether he was working in the garden, rolling barrels into the house or yoked to the buckets of water he was carrying up from the well for the new brew he would always find time to give her a cheery smile or a wave, or he would drop a kiss on the top of her head as he passed, asking, 'Are you all right, Beth? Anything you want?' And she would reach up and squeeze his hand. 'I'm fine, love, thank you.'

But he had little interest in Tilly, short for Matilda, and most of the time he ignored her. Fortunately, she was a contented child and seldom cried, but when she did, especially if it was in the middle of the night, he would become annoyed and tell Bethany to give her a good smack or put her in another room where he couldn't hear her cries. This upset Bethany and she would comfort the child, saddened that he should show so little regard for his daughter.

She spoke of Zack's attitude to Tilly to her mother, adding, 'You must have noticed, Mama.'

'You can't expect men to be interested in babies,' Emily said philosophically, nursing her granddaughter in a way that more than made up for her father's lack of interest. 'Especially girl babies. It'll be different when she starts chattering and running about. And different again when he has a son. Men always want sons. You'll see.'

'I just hope you're right, Mama,' Bethany replied.

But if Zack didn't show any interest in his daughter, everyone else made up for it. Tilly soon stole the hearts of the whole household with her ready chuckle and sunny nature. Even Reuben looked for her whenever he came to the house, calling her 'the little maid'.

'Where's the little maid?' he would ask and if she was lying in her crib in a shady corner of the garden he would go and talk to her, telling her about the rabbit he had seen in the field or the blackbird's nest he had found. And as soon as she was old enough to hold them in her hand he fashioned little wooden peg dolls for her, which Sarah dressed from scraps in the patchwork bag and Emily trimmed with bits of lace or embroidery.

Sarah, equally doting, called him a 'silly old fool' but she was always eager to lead him to the crib and the two of them would sit watching and bickering over her just as they bickered over everything else.

'Put that dirty old pipe away, Reuben Scales. Don't you dare bring it near Tilly, she's all freshly bathed and clean.'

'You're a good one to talk, Sary Pilgrim. Look at your filthy owd sack apron. You're never gonna pick that little maid up with that dirty owd pinna on, are ye?'

'I never said I was.' Annoyed that she had forgotten she was still wearing it, Sarah whipped the sacking apron off and picked Tilly up. 'There, my little pretty one, what can you see? Can you see that old reprobate? Go on, pull his whiskers. That'll make him shout.'

Tilly, as if she knew exactly what was being said, stretched out her hand and took a handful of whiskers and gave them a tug, chuckling all the time. Reuben gently took her tiny hand in his gnarled and calloused one and marvelled at the perfection of it.

As soon as she was able Bethany resumed her former duties, because it was a busy summer for Travellers' Inn. Coaches carrying passengers taking advantage of the fine weather for a trip to the continent on the packet boat made it a regular stopping place because they knew they could rely on a good meal and clean, comfortable beds.

Mostly, these visits were uneventful. There was an established routine: Zack looked after the horses and saw that the coachman had all he needed; Sarah provided and prepared all the fruit and vegetables for Emily to cook; Bethany kept the rooms clean and waited on the tables in the little parlour. Fortunately, Tilly was a happy child as long as she was kept out of her father's way, and as she got older, was allowed to 'help', it all worked very well.

There was the odd hiccup, of course, such as when an irate father banged on the door at nearly midnight to reclaim his daughter, who had eloped with an army officer. He was too late; by the time he arrived the marriage had taken place and been thoroughly consummated, as the young lady informed him in a voice that left the whole household in no doubt and her new husband slightly embarrassed. Faced with this *fait accompli* the father was given a stiff whisky and a bed for the night, and family harmony was eventually restored the next morning over a hearty breakfast.

It became a bar legend that over the years lost nothing in the telling.

But such excitement was rare. Mostly, people came and went, some staying frequently so that they became almost like old friends, others on fleeting visits, like the proverbial ships that pass in the night. But all received the same caring attention, good food and clean, comfortable beds.

'You treat them too well, that's your trouble,' Zack complained one day as he followed Bethany, who was carrying a bundle of bed linen, down the stairs. 'Those people who've just gone only stayed one night so the sheets can't be that dirty. Why don't you leave them and let them do another night. It'd save you a bit of work.'

Bethany knew what he was getting at. She had been too tired to respond when he reached for her the previous night and that had made him irritable. 'We pride ourselves on clean beds, Zack,' she said over her shoulder. 'And Mrs Bridges does the laundry so it doesn't really make any extra work for me.'

'Well, I think it does. And it's all extra expense, too. If you didn't change the sheets so often you could wash them yourself.' He prodded her roughly in the back as he spoke, pushing her off-balance so that she fell the last three stairs and caught her head on the newel post.

He was beside her immediately, cradling her in his arms. 'Oh, Beth, I'm sorry. Was it my fault? I didn't mean . . . '

She rubbed her head, where a lump was already beginning to form. 'No, it wasn't your fault, Zack. I think I must have caught my foot or something,' she said, unwilling to admit he was to blame. She leaned against him and closed her eyes, glad of a few moments respite.

Tilly came trotting along the passage sucking a

stick of candy that Reuben had brought for her. Seeing her mother sitting on the floor she hitched herself on to her lap.

'Oh, leave your mother alone,' Zack said, giving her a push.

'No, Zack, she's all right.' Bethany put her arms round the little girl and held her.

'She never gives you five minutes peace,' he said. 'She's always trailing about behind you.'

'That's because you like to help Mama, don't you, sweetheart,' Bethany gave her a kiss.

Tilly nodded. 'Yes. Me help.' She looked up at her mother. 'Can we go to the river today, Mama?'

'Yes, we'll go this afternoon.' She bent and whispered something in Tilly's ear.

Tilly looked at her uncertainly, then turned to Zack. 'You come, too, Papa?' she asked, clearly at her mother's instigation.

'No, I've got too much to do,' he replied briefly.

'Come a nuvver day,' She slid off Bethany's lap so that Bethany could get to her feet.

'Maybe.' He rubbed the bump on Bethany's head. 'Are you all right now, Beth?'

She smiled at him. 'Yes, I'm fine. A walk in the sunshine will do me good.'

After dinner was cleared and Tilly had reluctantly had her afternoon rest they set off for Tilly's favourite walk, down to the river. She skipped along ahead of her mother, a flowered sunbonnet tied over the copper-coloured curls she had inherited from Bethany. As she skipped she pointed out the cows in the field on the other side of the hedge, wanting to know why some were brown and white and some were black and white; she picked a handful of little white flowers and a few taller pink ones and wanted to know what they were called, chanting 'shirt buttons, ragged robin' to herself as she skipped along after Bethany had named them. Then she nearly fell over her feet as she tried to see where the birdsong in the tree was coming from. Everything was interesting, every question needed an answer. Bethany smiled at the sight of her little daughter, bobbing along in front of her; and thought what a blessing she was.

They reached the river. The tide was full and there were several boats in full sail, making their way majestically up-river.

'Where are they going, Mama?'

'They're probably taking their cargoes to the quay at Mistley. Or perhaps some of them are on their way to Sudbury.'

'Where's Sudbury?'

'Further upriver.'

Satisfied, Tilly went to play at the water's edge, her shoes and stockings removed and her dress hitched up and secured with the ribbon Bethany had brought for the purpose. It was a spring tide so the water was high enough to encroach several feet on to the salt marsh, making little warm pools and runnels among the sea lavender, thrift, and marsh samphire where Tilly could paddle and splash to her heart's content.

Bethany unpacked the picnic they had brought with them. It was a beaker of milk and one of Emily's special cakes for Tilly and a drink of cool well water for herself. It was not much of a feast but it satisfied Tilly's idea of what a picnic should be.

'Don't go too near the edge of the marsh or you'll fall in the mud,' Bethany called, one eye on Tilly and the other on spreading the picnic cloth, without which the picnic wouldn't be complete. She was not in any real danger because the tide was barely covering the vegetation so the edge of the marsh was still clearly visible.

But Tilly wasn't listening. She had found a piece of stick and was busily stirring bits of grass and sea lavender into a pool of greenish grey soup. Then she jumped in it, splashing herself right up as far as her bonnet.

'Look at me, Mama,' she called, jumping and splashing even harder. Then she took a running jump to make the splashes even higher, screaming with glee.

'Be careful, Tilly, you'll fall in. You're much too near the edge.' Even as she shouted Bethany was scrambling to her feet and she reached the child just as she slid into the water.

It was not deep, less than twelve inches, but there was a layer of thick, black mud at the bottom, which Tilly, screaming and flailing her arms and legs, stirred up into a stinking black soup as her mother dragged her out on to the bank.

'I fell in,' she sobbed, lying filthy and woebegone. She held up her hands. 'Now, I all dirty.'

'I should think you are! And not just your

hands!' Bethany smiled. She was too relieved to be cross with her. 'Just look at you! Even your bonnet strings are covered in mud!'

Tilly sat up and wiped her muddy hands down her once-white pinafore, which was now dripping wet and streaked with mud. Then she examined them. 'That's better,' she remarked, holding them out and smiling at her mother through her tears.

Bethany looked at them. 'Yes, a bit better, but not much.' She got to her feet and held out her hand for Tilly to take. 'I think we'd better pack up our things and take you home and put you in the tub. You're soaking wet and covered in mud. It smells terrible.'

'But we haven't had our picnic,' Tilly wailed. 'I want our picnic.'

'Not today.' Bethany was packing the picnic basket as she spoke. 'We're going home.' She wiped the mud off Tilly's feet and legs as best she could with the towel she had had the foresight to include in the picnic basket. Then, with much protesting on Tilly's part, she managed to put her shoes and stockings on.

'Can't put clean stockings on dirty feet, Mama,' she said, pulling her feet away.

'Well, it's either that or you must walk back with no shoes and stockings on at all,' Bethany said, beginning to lose patience.

'No, the stones will hurt Tilly's feet.'

'Then let me put your stockings on.'

She watched as Bethany buttoned her shoes. 'I'm cold,' she said, shivering.

'Yes, I daresay you are. You're wet through.'

Bethany got to her feet. 'Here, put the towel round your shoulders, then we'll hurry home. That will help to warm you.'

They hurried back up the field and through the garden, singing nursery rhymes as they went to keep Tilly's spirits up.

When they reached the yard Zack was just coming out of the brew house. His jaw dropped when he saw the bedraggled-looking pair, because Bethany was nearly as muddy as Tilly; their skirts were both liberally caked in the stuff and Tilly's face was streaked with a mixture of mud and tears. Her bonnet had fallen back and there were even traces of it in her hair.

'What in the name of thunder have you been doing?' he asked. 'I thought you were going for a picnic.'

'I fell in the river an' I got all muddy, Papa,' Tilly said proudly, her good spirits restored. 'Mama fished me out.'

He rounded on Bethany. 'What in the world were you doing to allow her near the water?' he shouted. 'She might have drowned!'

Bethany stared at him, surprised at the vehemence in his tone. She had never known him show any interest, let alone anxiety over his daughter before. 'There's no cause for concern, Zack. It was a very high tide and she simply slipped off the marsh into the water,' she said calmly. 'I pulled her out very quickly. No harm was done.'

'We didn't have our picnic,' Tilly said, pouting.

Zack looked from Tilly to Bethany and back again. The little girl was hopping from one foot to the other, playing a kind of hop-scotch on the cobbles, obviously none the worse for her escapade.

'Never mind, poppet. Papa will take you for a picnic another day,' he said, ruffling her curls where her bonnet had fallen back.

She immediately stopped hopping. 'Ooh, yes, I would like to go to the woods. Can we go tomorrow, Papa?' she asked, determined to make capital out of her father's unaccustomed attention.

'We'll see. But you'd better go with Mama now and get yourself cleaned up.' He held his nose in an exaggerated gesture, grinning at her. 'That old mud you're wearing stinks, even when it's dried on.'

She went off with Bethany and he went back to the brew house and sat down on a rack. The surge of feeling that had swept over him at the sight of his bedraggled little daughter when he realised that she could so easily have drowned had shaken him. He had never paid much attention to her, never cared much for her, always considered her as something of a nuisance, someone claiming Beth's attention, coming between him and Beth. And he had thought Mrs P and Em were fools, the way they made such a fuss of her. And Reuben . . . well, sometimes he'd thought the old man must be soft in the head, the way he made all those little wooden toys for her and called her 'the little maid'. But suddenly, as she had stood there, filthy and wet, her face streaked with black mud, delightedly telling him of her mishap, her only complaint being that she had missed her picnic, he had seen her as a little girl, a personality in her own right, not just a crying bundle of baby clothes. He had seen something else, too, that he had never noticed before because in all her three years he had never bothered to look at her properly. She was a very pretty little girl with her mother's glorious hair and a sunny, outgoing nature. There was nothing prissy about her, either; she was full of fun and didn't care that her clothes were all filthy with mud. He smiled to himself at the memory of her hopping about on the cobbles. True, she wasn't the son he had hoped for but that was hardly her fault. He reckoned she was the next best thing. Moreover, at the very moment he could so easily have lost her he was proud of her and he knew that he could easily love her. The realisation shook him to the core.

19

It didn't take Bethany long to notice the difference in Zack's attitude towards Tilly. Instead of rebuffing her when she tried to talk to him he would get down on his haunches to be nearer her level and listen to what she had to say. And he allowed her to 'help' him, something he had always been too impatient to encourage before. He made sure she had her own little fork and rake so that she could help him in the garden and he even went so far as to ask Reuben to make her a little yoke from which he hung tiny buckets so that she could carry water up from the well, 'just like Papa'. Sometimes, and Tilly liked this best of all, he would let her watch as he fed and groomed the coach horses when they were stabled overnight, but he always warned her never to come too close to them because their behaviour was uncertain and there was always a danger that they might shy or kick out. Not like Peggy, who never minded if Tilly sat on her back and held on to her mane and would eat carrots, which the little pony loved, out of her hand, nuzzling after more, which tickled and made Tilly giggle.

'I saw Tilly following you up from the well with the water for the brew house today,' Bethany said, lying in bed in the circle of Zack's arm. 'It's nice seeing the two of you together, because I know she loves being with you, Zack.'

'Yes, well, she's old enough to talk to, now. I can tell her things and she'll listen. And she's forever asking questions. She's a bright little thing, you know. Must take after her mother.' He leaned over and gave her a peck on the cheek. 'I reckon it's high time she had a brother.'

'I know.' She sensed a rebuke in his tone. 'But it doesn't seem to happen. I'm sorry, Zack.'

He pulled her to him. 'We'll just have to try a bit harder, sweetheart, won't we,' he murmured, pulling her nightgown aside.

She stared up into the darkness as he took his pleasure. It wasn't like it used to be before they were married, when they couldn't get enough of exploring each other's bodies; now, he rarely even kissed her, but simply took what he wanted, then rolled over and went to sleep, not even bothering to consider what her feelings might be. Perhaps that was why there was no sign of the son he was so anxious for. She thought it might very well be so, but it was not something she felt she could speak to him about.

Trade was good at the inn during the hot summer. Every night the men from the farms came in to slake their thirst and play shove ha'penny or skittles, to relay the latest gossip and to discuss the railways that, according to unreliable rumour, were already covering most of the country with their gleaming metal lines.

This was something of an exaggeration, although since most of them had never seen a railway track, let alone the trains that ran along it, it didn't make much difference whether or not it was true.

235

'My sister's brother-in-law saw a train come into Colchester all the way from Lunnon town,' Fred Bowler said, swelling with importance. 'He said that made a powerful noise, a-snortin' an' grindin' an' makin' the ground all of a shake.'

'Ah, that don't sound safe to me,' an elderly prophet of doom said from the corner. 'You mark my words, nuthin' good'll come of it.'

'Nah. You wouldn't git me on a trine, nor was it ever so,' Reuben agreed, licking the froth off his moustache.

'Oh, I dunno.' Zack said, thoughtfully wiping down the bar. 'I reckon it'd be a bit of all right to go on a train. I hear they can go at over thirty miles an hour.'

'Git away with yer! Thass rubbish! Nothin' could travel that fast!' There was a chorus of derision.

'I don't hold with the railways,' Peter Goodwin, a fat, self-opinionated man, remarked pompously. 'They ain't natural. If the Good Lord had meant us to travel as fast as that He'd have given us wheels instead o' feet.'

There were murmurs of agreement.

'Anyways, that won't happen in my lifetime so I ain't goin' to worry about it,' Reuben said, slamming his mug down on the counter.

'I wouldn't be too sure about that, Reuben,' Zack replied. 'I've heard the navvies are already starting to dig out the track between Colchester and Ipswich and I've heard it'll pass through Manningtree.'

'Bah! I'll believe that when I see it,' Reuben said, putting an end to the conversation. 'Draw us another pint, Zack an' let's talk about somethin' sensible.'

While this conversation was taking place in the bar, a place that was strictly out of bounds to Tilly, she was trying to go to sleep in her little room just above. But it was difficult. Not because of the noise of men's voices coming from below, she was used to that, but because she was excited. She was excited because Mama had told her that the pedlar was on his way — he had already been seen around Mistley — and would very likely arrive tomorrow. And what made it even more exciting was that Tilly had a farthing to spend. She had already made up her mind what she wanted, she was going to buy a little doll that could be made to dance on the end of a stick. She had seen the pedlar do it the last time he visited; he held the doll up by its strings and stood it on the stick. Then he made it jiggle up and down and dance by banging the other end of the stick. Tilly thought it was very clever and she couldn't wait to try it for herself.

The next morning she was up early and after breakfast she went out to watch for him, scanning the empty road for what seemed ages before she saw him coming. There was no mistaking who he was, a tall, lanky man, with a battered stovepipe hat, stripey trousers and a green velvet coat that had seen better days.

She ran back into the yard. 'He's coming! He's coming! Quickly, Mama, come and see!'

By this time he had arrived, wreathed in smiles and bidding everyone a cheerful good morning as they gathered round him. He was carrying a large tray, supported by a thick strap that went round the back of his neck, and this he opened out to reveal all manner of wonderful and colourful things; buttons, ribbons, needles and pins, pegs, elastic, braid, hair slides; more things than Tilly could count. And hanging from the tray were the wonderful dolls: boy dolls, girl dolls, dolls dressed like Columbine and Harlequin, dolls dressed as milk maids and shepherd boys and dolls dressed in scraps of material that represented nothing in particular. Tilly didn't know which one to choose. In fact, by the time she made her choice, Grandmama had already bought one of the saucepans that were hanging from a string tied round the pedlar's waist, and Mama had purchased quite a long piece of pretty material and several reels of cotton. Aunt Sarah didn't buy anything; she said at her age she'd got everything she wanted, which Tilly thought was very strange. She couldn't imagine a time when there would never be anything she would want. But she was quite content for now and spent the rest of the day trying to make her dolly — the only one with a black painted face — dance, which was quite difficult until Papa showed her how it should be done, then it was easy.

For most people, especially those living in outlying districts, the coming of the pedlar meant more than the wares he had to offer because he was also their source of news and gossip. He brought news of babies born — both in and out of wedlock — of village scandals and of those who had died.

'Well, I can't say he told us much we didn't

already know,' Emily remarked, disappointed, standing in the yard and watching as the pedlar went on his way, pots and pans jingling from his waist, a mutton pie and a pint of best brew in his belly.

'What do you expect? Of course we know it already. The bar here is the fount of all gossip,' Sarah said with a laugh. 'In fact, news travels so fast in this place that I sometimes think we hear about things before they've even happened.'

'Did you hear him say that there was a lot of sickness about in Colchester?' Bethany asked anxiously. Her voice dropped. 'They think it might be cholera.'

'There's always going to be a certain amount of illness in a place that big,' Sarah replied, waving her hand disparagingly. 'And somebody's only got to eat a few green apples and get belly ache and everybody starts talking about cholera. In any case, Colchester's twelve miles away. It's not going to affect us, out here in the country, is it?'

'We get coaches coming in from Colchester,' Bethany said, not convinced.

'We get coaches coming in from Harwich and heaven knows what diseases there are on the other side of the sea, but we don't get them here, do we. In any case, everyone knows that it's bad smells that cause cholera. And we make sure we don't have bad smells at Travellers' Inn.' That clinched the argument as far as Sarah was concerned. She pulled on her boots. 'Now the pedlar's gone perhaps I can get on with picking the beans for dinner.' She stomped off down the garden.

Emily sniffed the air. 'Aunt Sarah's right, you know. All I can smell is wood shavings from the barn and malt from the brew house. Good, clean, healthy smells. I'm sure there's no need for us to worry, Bethany. And you know what the pedlar is like. If he hasn't much news to tell he's not above a bit of embroidery to make things sound worse than they are.' She turned to go inside, then turned back. 'Has Zack heard anything in the bar?'

Bethany shook her head. 'Not that he's told me.'

'Well, then, there's nothing to worry about.'

Bethany smiled at her mother. 'That's very true.' But she still couldn't help the nagging feeling of unease that had taken root at the back of her mind.

The gossip Zack related three nights later did nothing to allay her unease.

'Peter Goodwin was in the bar tonight,' he said as he pulled his nightshirt over his head. 'I can't say I like the man, he's too full of his own importance, but he was in a rare state about what happened to his granddaughter. Couldn't stop talking about it. I felt right sorry for him.'

'Why? What's happened to her?' Bethany yawned as she sank gratefully back into her pillows. She was tired. It had been a long day.

He blew out the candle and climbed in beside her. 'Well, it seems the girl, Nellie, I think he called her, was in service at a big house in Colchester.'

'How old is she?' She tried to show a bit of interest although all she wanted to do was go to sleep.

'Fourteen, I believe he said. Well, anyway, she got belly ache and had to keep running to the privy — been eating too many plums, Peter reckons; he knows how she loves plums and this is the right time of year. But the lady of the house had got wind of this cholera scare and as soon as she heard Nellie wasn't well she sent her packing.'

Bethany sat up, wide awake at the mention of cholera. 'Oh, that was unkind. But I suppose you couldn't blame her. How did the girl get home?'

'She walked part of the way. Then she got a lift with the carrier. But by all accounts she had to keep asking him to stop so she could nip over the hedge. By the time the poor mite got home she was in a poor way and all her clothes were messy where she hadn't been able to . . . well, you know.'

'Oh, dear. How is she now? Is she any better?'

'Yes, Peter said he thought she was a little better when he saw her today. But she's very weak and she can't eat anything.'

'Do you think I should take her something? An egg custard perhaps?'

'Haven't you got enough to do here, without running round the village playing Lady Bountiful?' He sounded totally unsympathetic.

'I only thought . . . '

'You think too much.' He climbed into bed and turned his back on her, wriggling himself over so that she was forced to the edge of the

241

bed. 'Well, goodnight, Beth.'

'Goodnight, Zack.' She closed her eyes, grateful that he wasn't in the mood to make love. Love. She smiled grimly into the darkness. There wasn't much love attached to what he did to her these days.

★　★　★

Matthew came to the inn a few days later. At Zack's request, he didn't go straight to the snug with his drink as he usually did but went through to the kitchen, where the three women were sitting round the table, Sarah and Bethany with their mending, Emily with her embroidery. It was a warm evening and the back door was open, letting in the last of the day's sunlight.

A visit to the kitchen was a luxury Matthew rarely allowed himself, partly because the cosy, cluttered kitchen and the warm, welcoming atmosphere at Travellers' Inn was in such stark contrast to his own cheerless hearth. But it was not only that. Of course, he still missed Celia, his dead wife; she would always hold a special place in his heart. But each time he saw Bethany he realised that he was falling ever more deeply in love with her; he loved her unruly copper-coloured hair, which she didn't seem to be able to tame but she always brushed until it shone; he loved the tilt of her head, the look in her clear grey eyes and her mouth — oh, how he longed to kiss that mouth. But she was another man's wife and he had no right even to think of her in that way. Consequently, he considered that it was better that he stayed away from her lest he should give himself away by a look or a gesture.

He ducked his head as he went through the door from the passage. 'Good evening, ladies,' he said with a smile. 'Zack said you wanted a word with me.' He looked at each in turn, his eyebrows raised questioningly.

'It's good to see you, Matthew,' Emily said warmly. 'Do come and sit down.' She patted the chair between herself and Bethany.

'Thank you.' He put his whisky down on the table and sat down. 'Well?' he asked quizzically, 'and what can I do for you?'

'Oh, you can't do anything for me, I'm past all help,' Sarah said, although her cheeky smile belied this. 'It's Bethany. She's the one who needs help.'

He swivelled round to look at her and saw her flush with embarrassment.

'It's probably nothing, Matthew,' she said uncomfortably. 'But we heard about this cholera scare in Colchester and then Peter Goodwin's granddaughter got sent home from the house where she was in service because of . . . ' she didn't know how to finish delicately so she bent her head over her mending.

'Nellie Goodwin. Yes. I've been to see her.' He took a sip of his whisky. 'She's still quite poorly. And unfortunately she seems to have passed it on to her little brother.'

'But it's not the cholera, is it.' It was more a statement than a question from Sarah.

'I don't think so. But it's really too early to tell,' he replied honestly.

'What causes it?' Emily asked.

'The general opinion is that it breeds in bad smells,' he said thoughtfully.

'There! I told you so, didn't I!' Sarah said triumphantly.

Emily laid her hand over her heart. 'Thank goodness. It means we're all right here.'

He nodded. 'Oh, yes, I should think so. It's usually worst in towns and places where there is a lot of poverty and overcrowding.'

'See? I told you so. Now you can stop fretting, Bethany.' Sarah got up and went over to the stove, putting an end to the conversation. 'Is there more of your nice stew left, Emily? I'm sure Matthew could manage a little, couldn't you, Matthew?'

'Well . . . '

Bethany smiled at him. 'Of course you can, Matthew. You know how much you like Mama's stews.'

He smiled back at her in a rare moment of intimacy. 'Well, if you put it like that . . . '

After she got to bed that night and Zack lay snoring beside her, Bethany remembered Matthew's smile and was shocked to find herself wondering how it might be if it was Matthew and not Zack lying in bed with her. She was even more shocked to realise that she wished it could have been. Feeling guilty at such a wicked thought, she laid her hand on Zack's shoulder. He immediately woke and rolled on to her.

'Ah, like that, is it?' he murmured, as he thrust himself into her.

She closed her eyes. No, it wasn't 'like that' at

all, she thought miserably. All she could think of was that his breath smelled of beer and pickled onions.

* * *

Every week Zack took the dog cart and went to buy malt and flour. Recently, he had begun to take Tilly with him, and she loved nothing better than to sit up beside him on the driving seat with her little hand on a loop of Peggy's reins.

Bethany went out to the stables where he was harnessing up the little pony.

'I don't think you should take Tilly with you today, Zack,' she said, putting her hand on Peggy's flank.

He looked up from tightening the girth. 'And why not? She likes to come and I like to take her.'

'Well, with all this illness about . . . And they think it might be cholera . . . '

His face darkened. 'Don't be ridiculous, woman. Of course it isn't cholera. It happens every year. The poor gorge themselves on blackberries from the hedgerows and scrump apples from the farms and then they wonder why they get the gripes.'

'All the same, I wish you wouldn't take her today, Zack.'

He straightened up. 'And I wish you wouldn't keep trying to tell me what I can and can't do.'

'I'm only asking . . . '

'Well, don't ask. I'm taking her with me and there's an end of it.' As he spoke he caught her a stinging blow to the side of her face.

She stared at him without moving, her hand up to her face where he had hit her. He stared back at her, aghast at what he had done.

Suddenly, he stepped forward. 'Oh, Beth, I'm sorry.' He gathered her into his arms, full of remorse. 'I didn't mean to do that. I don't know what came over me, really I don't. Please forgive me.' He was kissing her hair, the red mark on her cheek, her lips, all the time murmuring how sorry he was and that if she didn't want him to take Tilly then he wouldn't and would she please, please say she had forgiven him and promising that he would never, ever do such a thing again.

Bethany laid her head on his shoulder, savouring the touch of his lips and the gentleness of his touch. This was just how things used to be and the old feeling of love for him welled up inside her.

'I'm all ready.' Tilly came dancing into the stable. 'Oh, are you coming too, Mama?'

'No, I'm not coming. But you go with Papa, darling.' She lifted her up on to the driver's seat.

Zack dropped a kiss on Bethany's forehead and then climbed up beside Tilly. 'Thanks, sweetheart,' he said. 'I'll look after her.'

'Yes, I know you will.' She waved as they went off and then turned and went back into the house, ashamed of her own unreasonable behaviour.

20

Tilly returned from her visit to the village with her father full of excitement and enthusiasm. Sitting at the meal table that evening Bethany watched her little daughter's face, alight with happiness as she recounted everything that had happened during the afternoon, from the blue tit swinging upside down on a bramble to get at a succulent blackberry to the man at the maltings who spoke with such a loud voice that she had to put her hands over her ears.

'And then Papa bought me a lollipop,' she finished, looking round for approval.

'I'm glad you had such a lovely time, darling,' Bethany said, smiling at her.

'She wouldn't have done if you'd had your way,' Zack reminded her, helping himself to another slice of ham. 'I hope you won't try to stop me taking her again. After all, you know I'd never let her come to any harm.'

'No, of course you wouldn't. I know that, Zack,' Bethany replied, carefully keeping her voice neutral.

Emily, busily getting a large apple pie out of the oven, didn't notice this exchange, but although she said nothing, it was not lost on Sarah, sitting opposite Bethany.

'I don't know what's come over young Zack,' she confided to Reuben the next day as they sat together on the bench outside the potting shed

247

stringing beans. Or rather, Sarah was stringing beans while Reuben watched, smoking his pipe. 'He seems to be getting rather belligerent these days, especially with Bethany.'

'Well, she's his wife. If she don't toe the line he's bound to git stroppy with 'er.' He shrugged complacently.

'Hmph.' Sarah didn't agree with his line of thinking but she wisely didn't say so.

'Nah. You don't need to worry about Zack, he's all right, Sary Pilgrim,' he went on, spitting copiously and accurately into the bushes. 'He's a good bloke.' He jabbed the stem of his pipe in her direction. 'An' I'll tell ye this much. He won't hev no nonsense in the bar. No puttin' drinks on the slate. Pay on the nail or there's no beer. An' he's got a way with them as has had a drop too much to drink. They're outside the door afore they know what's gooin' on.' He drew on his pipe. ''Cept for his mates, o' course. He ain't quite so strict with them.' He patted her knee, at which she immediately slapped his hand away. 'I reckon Zack's on'y trouble is he works too hard.'

She sighed. 'You're probably right.' There was no denying that Zack worked hard. He was up with the lark and rarely in bed before eleven o'clock at night. Travellers' Inn was doing better than it had ever done; coaches stopped there regularly, knowing there would be a good meal and a clean bed as well as good stabling and Zack's beer was becoming quite famous in the district. 'I reckon you're right; I worry too much.'

'I reckon you do.'

But a few days later there was cause for worry, although it had nothing to do with Zack.

It was late one afternoon. Emily was resting on her bed before preparing the evening meal and Sarah had taken Tilly to pick blackberries. Zack had gone to fetch new barrels from the cooper and Bethany was savouring a few quiet moments, sitting by the back door in the sunshine as she stitched the hem of a new dress for Tilly, when Matthew arrived. Without being asked, which was unusual, he went in and slumped down on a chair by the table and put his head in his hands.

Bethany put down her sewing and followed him in. 'Matthew? What's wrong? Are you ill?' she asked anxiously.

He looked up, shaking his head. His face was grey with tiredness. 'No, I'm not ill,' he said wearily.

'Then what is it?' But before he could answer she asked sharply, 'When did you last eat?'

He frowned and waved his hand vaguely. 'I don't remember. Yesterday, I think. But that's not what I came for. I came to tell you . . . '

She went over to the stove and ladled broth into a bowl. 'Eat this. Then you can tell me,' she ordered, placing it on the table in front of him.

He gave her a fleeting smile. 'You spoil me.'

'Oh, Matthew, it's a good thing somebody does,' she replied sadly. 'I just wish . . . ' Her voice tailed off. She couldn't say what was on her mind.

But he guessed. 'So do I, Bethany,' he said

quietly, looking up at her with a wealth of love in his eyes. 'So do I.'

They said nothing more but the unspoken words hung between them until he broke the spell. 'That was good,' he said, smiling at her as he finished the broth. 'I hadn't realised how hungry I was.'

She smiled back at him and picked up her sewing again. 'Good. Now, what was it you wanted to tell me?'

Immediately, the smile left his face to be replaced by a look of defeat. 'I thought you should know. It's cholera,' he said wearily. 'I was hoping it was nothing more than the usual diarrhoea that happens all the time, but it isn't. It's much worse. People are dying. It's mostly in those crowded yards down by the walls, but I'm afraid it's spreading. There have been twenty cases already.' He put his head in his hands. 'And, God help me, I don't know what to do about it because I don't know what's causing it.'

'I thought you told me once that the medical men thought it was caused by — what did you call it? 'Miasma in the atmosphere', whatever that is,' she said, puzzled.

'Bad smells, in common language. And it's true, that's what the general medical opinion is.' He shook his head. 'But those yards are all down by the river. Surely, even though the cottages are old and squashed together the air should be pure enough there.'

'I don't know about that,' she said grimly. 'Sometimes the river smells pretty foul and you can't wonder at it, the amount of rubbish that gets thrown into it as well as all the filth that drains into it, especially when the tide's going out and the sun's on the mud. I've stopped taking Tilly down to the river when the tide is on the ebb because of the dreadful smell.'

He nodded thoughtfully. 'Then perhaps that's what it is. Perhaps it is bad smells that cause these epidemics. But the smells are always there, yet outbreaks of cholera are fairly rare, thank God.' He sighed and shook his head. 'I don't know. I really don't know what to think.'

She took his empty bowl. 'I'll pour you some more broth. You look as if you could do with a good meal but I'm afraid it's not ready yet and I guess you won't want to wait.'

He shook his head again. 'No, I've several more calls to make yet.'

'Then come back when you've finished your rounds. I'll keep something hot for you.' She held her breath, waiting for his answer.

He looked up at her and smiled. 'Thank you, Bethany. I should like that,' he said, and she realised with a jolt just how badly she wanted to see him again.

It was quite late when he returned. Zack was still in the bar, Emily had gone to bed and Sarah was dozing by the fire, muttering from time to time that she ought to go to bed but making no effort to do so. She woke with a start when Matthew arrived.

'You're very late, my boy,' she said, surprised.

'I know. I nearly didn't come back, but I thought it would be rude if I didn't,' he said, 'since Bethany had promised to keep a meal for

251

me.' He smiled at Bethany as he spoke.

Sarah got to her feet and peered at the plate that was keeping hot over a saucepan of water. 'I don't think it's quite dried up,' she said with a yawn. 'But now I'm on my feet I'm off to my bed, if you don't mind.' She looked him up and down. 'You look as if you could do with your bed too, Matthew.'

'He can go as soon as he's eaten,' Bethany said, laying a place for him at the table.

'Aye, he'll sleep better with a full belly,' Sarah agreed. 'Well, goodnight to you both.'

After she had gone Bethany sat down opposite Matthew as he ate the mutton pie and gravy she had saved for him. Now and again there was the sound of raucous laughter coming from the bar.

'It sounds as if Zack's got some of his friends in tonight,' she said, jerking her head towards the direction the sound was coming from.

'Will it wake Tilly?' he asked, looking up.

'No, she's getting used to it.'

'Why? Does it happen often?'

'Often enough.' She got up and poured him a mug of beer and then sat down again, leaning towards him, her elbows on the table.

He took a long draught, then put the mug down carefully. 'I've been thinking,' he said, speaking slowly. 'I'm wondering if this outbreak could have anything to do with the water.'

'What? The river?'

'No, the drinking water.'

'But don't they get it from the pump?'

He nodded, his mouth full of pie.

'Then I don't see how . . . '

He looked up and grinned. 'No, neither do I. It's just that people who live at the other end of the village and use the other pump haven't been affected.'

'Yet.'

'That's true. I just hope to God it doesn't spread that far.'

He finished his meal and drained his mug and got to his feet. The sounds from the bar had quietened as the customers left.

Bethany glanced at the door to the passage. 'Yes, you'd better go. Zack will be through in a minute.' She looked up at him and flushed at the implication of her words. 'Not that he would think . . . ' she stopped, confused.

'No, of course not.' He smiled at her. 'All the same, better not risk upsetting him. Thank you for the meal, Bethany. And for your company,' he added softly.

A few minutes later Zack came through to the kitchen. He was only a little the worse for drink.

'Why aren't you in bed?' he asked, surprised.

'I had things to do. And I kept a meal hot for Matthew. He's very busy at the moment. There's cholera in the village.'

'Yes, so they were saying in the bar.' He looked round. 'Where's Mrs P? Gone to bed?'

'Yes. She went up a few minutes ago.' It was only a small lie.

'Well, come on, let's do the same.' He caught hold of her roughly. 'It's time you tried a bit harder to give me a son, my girl. It seems to me you're too busy all the time trying to do things for the travellers who come here so you don't bother to consider my wants.' He bent her back over the table and began to fumble with her skirt.

She tried to push him away. 'No, Zack. Not here. Someone might come in.'

'What if they do? You're my wife, aren't you?' His eyes were alight with lust at the thought of taking her on the kitchen table and she had no defence against him. She closed her eyes and waited for it to be over. Then she got to her feet and pulled down her skirt.

'Don't you ever treat me like that again, Zachary Brown,' she said through gritted teeth.

He caught her arm. 'You're my wife, so I shall treat you any way I like, my girl,' he said, pushing his face close to hers so that she could smell the beer on his breath. He gave her a shove. 'Now, get up to bed. I haven't finished with you, yet.'

No, she thought wearily as she climbed the stairs, but I'm beginning to think I've finished with you, Zachary Brown. Only there was no escape.

The following day Zack announced that he was going to the farm because he was low on straw for stabling.

'Then will you take Farmer Walford this apple pie, Zack?' Emily asked, a faint blush spreading over her cheeks. 'I made it yesterday thinking it might be needed for those people who stayed last night, but they didn't want it and Isaac . . . Farmer Walford is particularly fond of my apple pies so he might as well have it.'

'I suppose we could eat it ourselves,' Sarah said, winking at Bethany.

'No, we don't need it because I'm going to make a pie with the blackberries you picked yesterday with Tilly,' Emily said quickly. 'Do you want to help me, Tilly?'

Tilly put her head on one side. 'I'd quite like to help you, Grandmama, but I think I'd rather go with Papa because then I can see the little piglets at the farm.' She turned to Zack. 'Can I come with you, Papa?'

A look of alarm crossed Bethany's face. 'You're not going to the village, are you, Zack.' It was a statement rather than a question.

'Might be. Might not,' he replied, deliberately aggravating her. He ruffled Tilly's curls. ' 'Course you can come with me, sweetheart. You like a ride in the trap with you old pa, don't you.'

Bethany bit her lip, knowing it was useless to say more.

But she was anxious all the time they were gone because knowing Zack as she did she wouldn't put it past him to take Tilly into the village simply to spite her. Yet on the other hand, she couldn't believe he would deliberately put his daughter's health at risk. In any case, he was unlikely to take her anywhere near the walls and that was where Matthew had said the outbreak was situated. Nevertheless, she still worried and was relieved when they arrived back, Tilly wreathed in smiles and full of chatter about the fourteen piglets Farmer Walford had shown her.

'And his dog Bess has had five puppies, Mama, what do you think of that!' she announced, her eyes shining. 'Papa says when they're big enough I can have one. Can I have one, Mama?'

'Of course you can, darling, if Farmer Walford can spare one.'

Tilly nodded, her copper-coloured curls bouncing up and down in her excitement. 'He says he can. He says I can choose which one I would like and I've already chosen. He's light brown and Farmer Walford says I should call him Sandy because he's the colour of sand.' She put her head on one side. 'I don't think I've ever seen sand so I don't know what colour it is,' she said thoughtfully.

'I'll take you to the seaside one of these days,' Zack said, grinning at her. 'You'll see plenty of sand there.'

'But now, finish your tea and then it's time for bed,' Bethany said, her eyes warm with love for her little daughter.

Tilly pushed her plate away. 'I don't want any more,' she said. 'I'm not hungry tonight.'

'But it's honey from Aunt Sarah's bees,' Emily said in surprise.

'I suppose she's not hungry because I bought her a toffee apple at Mrs Green's,' Zack said.

Bethany's head shot up. Mrs Green's sweet shop was in the heart of the village. 'I thought you weren't going into the village,' she said sharply.

'I never said I wasn't,' he replied. 'I said I might not. Well, I remembered I needed some more malt, so I had to go and get it. We weren't there long. Don't make such a fuss.' He pushed his chair back and leaned across the table, pointing a finger at her. 'I don't have to answer to you for every move I make, woman. I go where I like and I do what I like. And if I like to take my daughter with me then neither you nor anybody else is going to stop me.' He straightened up. 'Time I went and opened the bar,' he said and went off, before she could open her mouth to speak again.

Sarah pursed her lips. 'That young man's getting above himself if you ask me,' she remarked.

'Oh, I expect he's tired. He does work very hard,' Emily said, defending him.

Bethany said nothing. She knew it was nothing to do with tiredness. Zack was disappointed — furious might not be too strong a word — because she hadn't given him the son he craved and he used every opportunity to vent his frustration on her. That his frustration had, on occasion, ended in violence was not something she could ever speak about, particularly to her mother and aunt.

Later in the evening, when Zack was busy in the bar and the three women were sitting round the kitchen table, Sarah and Bethany with their mending, Emily with her embroidery, Matthew arrived. It was becoming something of a habit for him to drop in after he had finished his rounds and as far as Bethany was concerned this was the best part of her day. She always made sure there was a meal waiting for him — just in case.

'How nice. You've come early tonight,' Emily greeted him with a smile. 'It's usually so late before you get here that I've gone to bed.' She moved up to make room for him beside her. 'I don't keep late hours, you know.'

'I could wish I didn't have to,' he replied ruefully, sitting down to the plate of stew and dumplings Bethany placed before him. 'Ah, this looks good.'

'You look as if you need it, too,' Sarah remarked. 'Look at you. You're as thin as a rake.'

'It's because you're so worried about this cholera epidemic, isn't it, Matthew,' Bethany said. 'Is there no sign of it ending?'

'No, not really, but I ... Oh, wait till I've finished this delicious meal and then I'll tell you. It'll be good to talk over with you all what I believe I may have discovered. If you don't mind, that is?' He looked round at them all, his eyebrows raised. 'After all, I realise it isn't a very pleasant subject.'

Emily got to her feet with a shudder and swept up her embroidery. 'I think I'll go to bed,' she said. 'I don't think I wish to hear about unpleasant medical matters, if you don't mind.'

Matthew got to his feet, immediately contrite. 'Oh, I do beg your pardon, Emily. I didn't think ... I'm so used to these things. But if it offends you I promise I won't speak about it. I realise it's hardly the subject for polite conversation.'

'Oh, let her go,' Sarah said, waving Emily away. 'She's always been squeamish. Bethany and I are all agog to hear what you've got to say. Now — ' as the door closed behind Emily ' — Tell us. What have you discovered?'

21

Matthew looked from Bethany to Sarah and back again. He could see they were really interested in what he had to tell them and he knew they would listen without the hostility he had encountered earlier among the councillors. For his own part, he would be grateful to talk his ideas through once again; he felt sure he was right, but there was always the possibility that he could be mistaken.

'Come on, then, tell us,' Sarah said, a trifle impatiently. 'It's getting past my bedtime.'

'Very well, if you're sure you want to hear?'

They both nodded.

'All right. Well, I've been reading an article by a man named Dr John Snow.' He spread his hands. 'I've been reading articles by a lot of people but this one really struck home to me because like me, he has an idea that these cholera outbreaks have a lot to do with the water supply.'

'Water supply? Not bad smells?' Bethany asked, surprised.

'He seems quite convinced it's something in the water supply, although I can't believe bad smells don't have some part to play in it.'

'Go on,' Sarah encouraged.

'After I'd read his article I began to look at where the people in the village live who are most affected by the epidemic.' He began to draw lines on the table with his finger. 'Look, as you can see, most of the worst cases have been down by the walls. One or two at the other end of the village and a few at the top of the hill.'

'Isn't that where Peter Goodwin's grand-daughter lives, at the top of the hill?' Bethany asked.

'That's right. Luckily, she survived, but sadly her little brother didn't. But they were fairly isolated cases. As I say, most of the worst cases have been down by the walls.' He looked up. 'And almost without exception they draw their water from the old pump at the cross roads.'

'And you reckon the pump is the cause of the trouble?' Sarah asked, leaning back in her chair. 'No, I think that's a bit far-fetched, myself. I don't see how the pump could carry the disease.'

'It could if the well that the pump draws its water from had been contaminated by sewage — especially cholera-infected sewage.' Matthew's eyes were bright with enthusiasm.

'But how could that happen?' Bethany asked with a frown. 'It's not as if it was an open well where people could tip their rubbish.'

'No, but what about the stream? People use that stream for all sorts of things: to wash their clothes, to tip all manner of rubbish, not to mention emptying . . . well, I needn't go into that, but you know what I mean.'

Bethany frowned. 'Yes, but I still don't see . . . '

'If that same stream should leak into the well that supplies the pump — and it could, because it runs quite near it before it discharges into the river — it could easily contaminate the water people are drinking and cause disease.'

'I can see what you're saying, but I still think it's a bit far-fetched,' Sarah said, shaking her head.

Matthew sighed. 'Yes, so did the councillors I spoke to tonight.'

'So you're not really any further forward,' Bethany said sadly.

He grinned. 'Well, actually, yes, I am. I persuaded them to allow me to remove the pump handle, just as an experiment. If it hasn't made any difference in a week then I'll put it back and admit I was wrong. But if there are significantly fewer cases — ' he spread his hands, ' — I shall have proved my point.'

'I suspect the people living down by the walls won't be too happy fetching their water from the other end of the village,' Sarah said. 'It's quite a trek to the other pump.'

'If I tell them it will prevent them getting ill I'm sure they'll accept it,' he said. 'In the meantime I've taken a sample of the water from the pump. I'll put it under the microscope in my laboratory at home, although I don't know whether it will tell me anything.' He looked up, his eyes alight with enthusiasm. 'But I'll tell you something else I've noticed. Very few of the men who live down by the walls have gone down with the disease. Why do you think that is?'

The two women looked blank. Then Bethany said with a laugh, 'Not many men drink water, they all drink beer.'

He slapped his knee. 'Exactly! And that's

another reason why I'm convinced it has something to do with the water supply.'

'Oh, I do hope you're right, Matthew,' Bethany said with a sigh.

'Well, I've only got a week to prove I am,' he replied as he got up to leave, 'so wish me luck.'

'It's not luck you need, my boy, it's cast-iron evidence,' Sarah said. She gave a yawn. 'Well, if you'll excuse me, I'm ready for my bed. My old bones don't like late hours, these days.'

After she had gone, Bethany said thoughtfully, 'At least we should be safe enough, if you're right about the disease coming from the water in the village pump, Matthew, because we draw our water from our own well.'

'And you make your beer from your own well water, too' he said, 'so if my theory is right you've no need at all to worry.'

He got up to leave and still thinking over what he had been saying, Bethany went over and took his hat from the hook by the door where he had hung it when he came in. As she reached up, her sleeve fell back, revealing angry black and purple bruises along the length of her arm. Quickly, before he should see, she pulled down her sleeve and turned to hand him his hat.

But she was too late.

'Did he do that to you, Bethany?' he asked quietly, taking her hand and pushing up her sleeve again.

'No, I . . . ' she began.

He gave the hand he was holding a little shake. 'Don't lie to me, Bethany,' he said savagely. 'I've seen this sort of thing too often to be fooled.' His expression softened. 'Oh, my dar . . . ' He broke off and his voice became more businesslike. 'Does he often strike you, Bethany?'

She looked away, biting her lip. 'He can be — violent, at times,' she admitted. 'He's got a temper and when things don't go his way he takes it out on me. And he's desperate for a son. He blames me because . . . ' She couldn't go on. Guilty at revealing her awful secret, yet at the same time relieved to be sharing it, her eyes filled with tears. 'He's not always unkind,' she finished in a whisper. 'He can be very loving.'

'Loving? Dear God, if he treats you like that the man's a monster! What's he thinking of? Why doesn't he cherish you? Why doesn't he appreciate what a brave and wonderful wife he's got?' Then, because he couldn't help himself he gathered her into his arms. 'Oh, Bethany, I can't bear to think of you being treated like this. I just wish I could protect you, take you away, love and cherish you as you deserve . . . ' He broke off and released her, suddenly embarrassed. 'I'm sorry. I shouldn't have said that. Please forgive me. I don't know what came over me.'

She took a step back. 'That's all right, Matthew. I realise you didn't mean it,' she said trying to smile. 'We all say things we don't mean in the heat of the moment.'

He shook his head. 'No, you don't understand. That's the problem, Bethany. I did mean it. I meant every word,' he said, his voice quiet. 'But you're another man's wife. I've no right to tell you how much I love you.'

'And I've no right to tell you that I love you,' she said, looking up at him, her eyes shining. 'But God help me, I do, Matthew. And I can't tell you what a comfort it is to know that you care for me, too. But what can we do?'

He kissed the tips of her fingers and then laid them on her lips. 'We can't do anything, my darling. We must continue to act as if we are nothing more than good friends.'

'But how can we do that when we know how we feel?' she cried desperately.

He gave a wry smile. 'It's possible. Remember, I've been doing it for some time, my love. But I'll admit it's not easy.' He leaned his forehead against hers briefly. 'But we must, otherwise I shall have to stay away from Travellers' Inn altogether.'

'I don't think I could bear that,' she said quietly.

'I couldn't, either. But if Zack were to suspect . . . '

She shuddered. 'Oh, don't. I think he'd kill you. Or me. He's a jealous man.'

'Then we have no alternative, sweetheart.'

'It's not enough.'

'It has to be.' He put his arms round her and held her close for a long moment, then he bent his head and kissed her, a lingering kiss that held the knowledge that this was all they had, all they would ever have. Then, suddenly, he broke away and was gone, leaving her alone, her face wet with tears. She went up to bed, her mood swinging between euphoria because Matthew loved her and despair because they could do nothing about it. This, she realised, was how it would always be.

* * *

But two nights later, all her own feelings were swept to one side and Matthew's hopes were dashed as the dreadful and irrefutable proof came that he had been mistaken in his theory about the cause of the cholera outbreak.

Tilly had been off-colour all the previous day and had eaten practically nothing. In the middle of the night Bethany heard her crying and in spite of Zack's insistence that she made too much fuss of the child she went in to her and found her doubled up with griping pains in her stomach. Tilly spent the rest of the night on the chamber pot while Bethany propped her up and sponged her face and hands, comforting her as best she could.

In the morning she was vomiting too and Bethany hardly dared to give her even the sips of water that she craved in case it made her worse.

When Zack came into the bedroom, cheerfully telling her she must have been eating too many green apples, he took one look at her and the smile left his face.

'I reckon I'd best fetch Matthew,' he said grimly.

'Yes, Zack, I think you had,' she said as she changed Tilly's nightgown yet again.

By the time Matthew arrived the little girl was lying in Bethany's arms in an exhausted sleep.

It didn't take him long to diagnose the dreaded cholera.

'Oh, dear God.' At his words Bethany felt as if an icy hand had clutched her heart.

Matthew laid a hand on her arm. 'She's got a good chance,' he said quietly. 'She's healthy and well fed, not like some of the poor mites down by the walls. Keep her warm and give her little sips of water. I know it's no use suggesting you should let anyone else look after her so hang a sheet soaked in vinegar at the door and keep everybody else out. There's no point in exposing the rest of the family to risk.' He smiled gently at her.

'Of course not.'

'And make sure you wash your hands very carefully if you leave the sick room and particularly before you touch any food.'

'I'm not likely to touch any food. I'm so worried about Tilly that I can't even bear the thought of it,' she said with a shudder.

'You must keep your strength up, Bethany,' he said urgently. 'I couldn't bear it if you . . . ' he broke off and looked away. Then he said in a more normal voice, 'It'll be best if you don't let any coaches put up here until she's better.'

'There's no danger of that once they know there's cholera in the house.'

He left then, thoroughly depressed and disappointed. He was anxious about Tilly and worried sick about Bethany, but what depressed him more than anything was the fact that Tilly contracting the disease had made a nonsense of his theory that it was the pump at the crossroads that was to blame for the outbreak. Yet he had been so sure that he was on the right track. Late last night when he had examined the sample of pump water under the microscope it had shown up the curious white particles so indicative of cholera diarrhoea, convincing him that the effluent from the stream was somehow leaking into the well and contaminating the water. And he was pretty sure that Peter Goodwin's daughter, who lived at the top of the hill, would have rinsed the soiled clothes from her sick children's beds in the stream. It was what the women did; it saved them having to carry extra water to their houses. It all added up.

Except Tilly didn't drink water from the pump at the crossroads. She always drank the pure, clear water from the well at Travellers' Inn.

For the next two days Travellers' Inn was quiet. Too quiet. It was as if the heart had gone out of the place. Sarah and Emily crept about, banned from the sickroom yet desperate to know how things were on the other side of the vinegar-impregnated sheet. But all they could do was to leave tasty dishes outside for Bethany to eat or to tempt Tilly with. Mostly, they were left where they had been placed.

Reuben came every day to ask after his 'little maid'; Sarah was surprised and touched at the depths of the old man's affection for the little girl. Sometimes as they sat quietly in the kitchen talking about her and the funny little things she said and did Reuben would surreptitiously wipe away a tear when he thought Sarah wasn't looking and Sarah would blow her nose and complain that this was a bad time to catch a cold.

To keep herself busy, Emily cooked mountains of cakes and pastries, which would probably never be eaten.

At night, a few of the regular customers still came into the bar but they drank quietly and then went home. One or two of them had already experienced a death in the family from the dreaded disease so they could offer little comfort. Zack was pale and hollow eyed, full of remorse that he had left it so long before he had begun to appreciate his delightful little daughter.

After visiting Tilly late one evening and finding no improvement Matthew went into the bar for a stiff whisky. All the men had gone home and Zack was there alone, tidying up. He poured himself a whisky and came and sat with Matthew.

'Is she any better?' he asked anxiously.

Matthew shook his head. 'No, there's no sign of any improvement.' He couldn't tell Zack, any more than he could admit it to Bethany, but there were clear signs that Tilly wouldn't last the night. He drained his glass and held it out for another.

'I was so sure I'd found the cause of this outbreak,' he said, putting his head in his hands. 'It all made sense. Pretty well all the people affected used the pump at the crossroads; as far as I could see it had to be the water from that well that was causing it.' He looked up. 'The men who drink here haven't caught it. The people who use the pump at the other end of the village haven't caught it. It all seemed to add up. But now Tilly's gone down with it so it can't be water that causes it after all because the water in your well is the purest for miles.' He shook his head. 'I don't know what to think, Zack.' He drained his second glass. 'The only consolation is that there haven't been any new cases in the last few days, in fact, not since I got the handle taken off the pump.' He gave a weary shrug. 'So maybe it has got something to do with it, or maybe the disease has just played itself out. I'm damned if I know.'

Zack refilled Matthew's glass and his own. He sat for a long time, staring down into the amber liquid, then he looked up. 'If I tell you something will you swear never to tell Beth or the other two?' He jerked his head towards the kitchen.

Matthew frowned. 'I don't usually betray confidences,' he said stiffly. He didn't want to hear. He was tired and worried and had too much on his mind to bear the added burden of playing Father Confessor to Zack. But it seemed he had no choice.

Zack took a deep breath. 'Well, I'll have to trust you because I must tell somebody.' He shrugged and gave an uncomfortable laugh. 'It's probably got nothing to do with it so when Tilly's better we'll be able to forget all about it.'

'Forget about what?' Matthew asked suspiciously.

'Well, I took her with me the other day when I went to the farm for fresh straw. Then I remembered I was low on malt so we went to the village. Beth had said Tilly wasn't to go there but I didn't see any harm in it, after all, she was only sitting up beside me in the trap. Well, she'd been a good girl and sat quietly while I was getting the malt so I bought her a toffee apple at Mrs Green's sweet shop.' He shook his head, a half smile on his face. 'My word, you never saw such a mess as she made with that blamed toffee apple, she was sticky all over her hands and face. I said to her we'd have to clean her up before her mother saw her or we'd get a right rollicking. So I stopped off at the pump . . . '

'The pump at the crossroads,' Matthew said, cold fear clutching his heart.

He nodded. 'When I'd dipped a bit of rag in the water and cleaned her up she said she was thirsty so I let her have a drink . . . ' He looked up. 'I swear I never let her use the iron cup chained there, I made her cup her hands and hold them under the pump. There couldn't be any harm in that, Matt, could there? That couldn't have made her ill? I was careful not to let her use the cup left there for all and sundry.'

Matthew hesitated. 'I can't prove any-thing . . . '

'But I never let her use that cup,' Zack insisted. He peered into Matthew's face and saw no comfort.

'As I say, I can't prove anything. All I can say is that there have been no new cases since I had the handle removed from the pump.'

Zack put his head in his hands. 'Oh, Christ. What have I done!'

'You couldn't have known there was any risk,' Matthew said quietly. Heaven knew, he didn't like the man but just at that moment he felt nothing but pity for him.

Zack looked up. 'Promise me you'll never breathe a word of this to Beth or the other two,'

Matthew shook his head. 'Not if you don't choose to tell them yourself.'

Zack was quiet for a long time. Then he looked up. 'Of course, Tilly being ill might not have anything to do with that pump. You don't know for sure, do you? You said yourself you can't prove the water from the pump caused the outbreak. It might not have had anything to do with it.' He leaned back in his chair, his conviction growing. 'Nah, I don't reckon it was the pump water made her ill. Could've been something she picked up in the garden, or down by the river. Yes, that's it, she picked it up down by the river.' Now he was busily salving his conscience. 'I've told Beth time and time again not to take her down there near that stinking mud, there's no telling what filth she might pick up, never mind falling in it.' He warmed to his theme. 'I shall tell her . . . '

Matthew got up, scraping his chair back on the sawdust. His pity for the man was rapidly turning to disgust. 'I'm tired. I must go home. I'll call again in the morning,' he said briefly. 'Unless I'm needed before.'

Zack waved him away, his good humour restored. 'No, you go home and get a good night's rest. She'll be fine,' he said cheerfully.

But Tilly wasn't fine. At three o'clock in the morning Zack heard Bethany calling for him to fetch Matthew.

'Is she worse?' he called anxiously from

271

outside her door, all the while hopping from one foot to the other in his haste to get his trousers on.

'Yes, go quickly. And tell Matthew to hurry.' He could hear the sob in Bethany's voice.

Less than twenty minutes later Matthew slipped behind the vinegar-soaked sheet and into the sick room. He left Zack pacing up and down outside, too worried to go far away but too frightened of the illness to actually enter the room.

Matthew took the limp little body from Bethany's arms and laid her gently on the bed and closed her eyes.

'You were too late,' Bethany said dully. 'She died five minutes ago.'

'I'm so sorry, Bethany. I came as quickly as I could.'

'You couldn't have done anything, I know that.' She turned grief-filled eyes up to him. 'I just wanted you here, Matthew,' she whispered.

He sat down beside her and took her in his arms. 'I'm here now, my darling,' he whispered, stroking her hair as the tears began to flow.

He let her cry, holding her close as she clung to him, whispering words of love because he couldn't help himself and because he knew her grief was too deep for words of comfort.

After a while he put her gently from him. 'We should tell Zack,' he murmured.

She looked at the little figure lying on the bed. 'I can't bear this, Matthew,' she sobbed, clinging to him again. 'Tell me it isn't true.'

'Oh, my dear love, I wish I could,' he said. He

kissed her briefly on her forehead. 'I'll fetch your husband,' he said, bringing them both back to reality.

'I don't want you to leave me.'

'I know. But you know I must, Bethany. I must go and tell Zack.'

'You'll come back?'

'Of course.'

He left and she sank down beside the bed, holding Tilly's little hand and kissing it over and over. 'My little girl,' she whispered. 'Why did it have to be you? Why wasn't it me?'

Zack came in and his grief was terrible to see. He threw himself down beside Bethany and buried his head on her shoulder, harsh, dry sobs shaking his body. Consumed by her own anguish Bethany had no energy left to prop him up in his grief and all she could do was to pat his shoulder and stare over his head at a future that was empty and hopeless because Tilly would have no part in it.

'I'm sorry, Beth,' he said, over and over again. 'I'm so, so sorry.'

'Yes, so am I,' she answered woodenly, 'but it won't bring her back, will it.'

He tried to take her in his arms so that they could weep together but she pushed him away. She didn't want him near her. He was Tilly's father and he had every right to be there, every right to weep, but until recently he had never taken any interest in Tilly so Bethany couldn't understand why he should be so grief-stricken. She just wished he would go away and leave her alone with her little girl. More than that, she

273

wished Matthew would come back. It was Matthew she wanted by her side, Matthew who could comfort her, not Zack. The realisation burned through her grief and she had neither the strength nor the will to deny it.

22

The next few days were the worst Bethany had ever known. She couldn't eat, she couldn't sleep. Everywhere she looked she saw Tilly. Everything she did was automatic because all she could think about was Tilly. Only Tilly wasn't there any more because Tilly was dead. Her pretty, vivacious, loving little daughter was dead.

She was beyond comfort. She shut herself in Tilly's room and scrubbed every inch of every surface with the disinfectant that Matthew gave her, washed the walls and curtains and boiled the bed linen. What couldn't be washed or scrubbed she burned on a bonfire at the bottom of the garden.

'She'll work 'erself to death if she carry on like this,' Reuben said, sitting in the shed with Sarah and watching as Bethany fed the fire with the feather bed from Tilly's room. 'P'raps we oughta go an' give 'er a hand.'

'No, she has to do it all herself. It's the only way she can cope,' Sarah said, shaking her head. 'Grief takes us all in different ways. Look at Emily. She does nothing but cook. She cooks meals that nobody has the appetite to eat and she's made that many apple pies we shall never eat half of them. And we can't give them away because people are still afraid they'll catch . . .' her voice trailed off and she shut her eyes tightly against the tears that were never far from the surface.

'Ah, thass a bad job an' no mistake,' Reuben said, unashamedly wiping his rheumy eyes with a large, once-white handkerchief. 'I can't believe we shall never see the little maid skippin' down the path again. That don't seem right that she should've been took when you an' me old codgers are still here.'

'If I was a religious woman I'd say it was the will of God and get some comfort from thinking it,' Sarah said. 'But I can't believe that a God who could create all the beautiful things there are in the world would be cruel enough to stand by and let little mites like Tilly suffer as she did if He could do anything about it.' She looked up towards the sky. 'No, I reckon, if there's a God up there He suffers as much as we do because of what we've done with His creation.'

Reuben knocked his pipe out on the leg of the stool he was sitting on. 'Well, I ain't never heard you talk like that afore, Sary Pilgrim,' he said. 'Meself, I jest git on with me life as best I can an' hope when I meet my Maker at the Pearly Gates, He'll say 'Well, I dunno as you've done much good in the world, Reuben Scales, but you ain't never done nobody any harm so I reckon you can come in'.' He sniffed. 'Yes, thass about all I ask. 'Cept, I hope He's lookin' after little Tilly.'

'I reckon He is. Jesus said, 'Suffer the little children to come unto me.' He'll look after her.'

Reuben wiped his nose on the back of his hand. 'I just wish He hadn't chosen our little maid to suffer like she did.'

'That's not what was meant by suffer,' Sarah said impatiently. 'He meant *Let* the little children come . . . '

'Well, I reckon it comes to the same thing in the end,' he answered, turning bleak eyes on her.

Zack arranged Tilly's funeral; purple-plumed black horses pulled the purple-draped carriage containing the tiny white coffin. The undertaker's mute leading the cortege looked hardly older than the child on the hearse. It didn't help that it rained.

Not that Bethany noticed. She went through the funeral in the same dazed manner she had spent the previous days, tightly buttoned up inside herself, allowing nobody near enough to comfort her because the one person she wanted had no choice but to keep his distance. As the coffin was lowered into the ground she stepped forward and dropped a single white rose into the grave. Then she fell to the ground in a dead faint.

When she came to she found she was lying in bed. She lifted up her arm and saw that she was wearing her nightgown and her hair was lying in a thick plait over her shoulder. Her new black mourning dress was draped over a chair by the window.

'Oh, Bethany, thank God. We thought we'd lost you, too.' It was her mother's voice. Bethany turned and saw that she was sitting by the bed.

She frowned. 'I think I must have fainted,' she said, her eyes filling with tears. 'I only remember . . . '

'Shh. That was two days ago,' Emily said,

laying a hand on her arm. 'You had to be carried home, then Matthew gave you something to help you to sleep. He said you'd worn yourself out. You were completely exhausted.'

'I thought I could stifle the pain with hard work,' she whispered, the tears still flowing. 'But it didn't work. It's still there.' She turned her face into the pillow. 'I can't bear it, Mama.'

'I know, my dear. I know how hard it is for you,' Emily said softly. 'But we've all tried to cope with it in our different ways. Zack has hardly spoken to anybody, he's spent his time repainting the bar, although it didn't really need it. But it meant he could shut himself away and not talk to anybody, because of course the bar hasn't been opened.' She paused and stared out of the window, biting her lip to prevent the tears, wanting to be strong for Bethany. After a few minutes she went on, 'Aunt Sarah clings to Reuben. They spend all day just sitting in the garden shed, talking. All of a sudden, I realise that Aunt Sarah begins to look old. I suppose, come to think of it, she is quite old. It's funny, I've never thought of her that way, but I suppose she must be nearly seventy.'

'I'm sure it's hit them hard because they both loved Tilly,' Bethany said. It was the first time she had said her daughter's name.

'Yes, I know they talk about her all the time.' Emily squeezed Bethany's hand. 'That's how they'll keep her alive in their hearts. We should do the same, Bethany. While we talk about her and remember her she'll always be with us.'

Bethany nodded. 'She'll always be in my heart.

And even though she's gone now, I shall always be grateful that I had her to love, even though it was for such a short time.'

There was a heavy tread on the stair and a knock on the door and Matthew came into the room.

'Look, she's awake, at last,' Emily said. She turned to Bethany. 'He's been in every day, you know, sometimes twice a day.'

'Just checking on you, Bethany,' he said with a smile. He came over and picked up her hand, checking her pulse with his watch. 'Now she's woken up I daresay she's ready for a cup of tea,' he said over his shoulder to Emily.

When Emily had left the room he dropped the pretence of taking her pulse and turned her hand over and pressed a kiss into the palm. Then he closed her fingers over it. 'You have to be strong, Bethany,' he said gently. 'I promise you, although the pain of your loss doesn't get any less you will get used to it; it will become a part of you, a burden you carry alongside all the other things life throws at you. Believe me, I speak from experience. I know what it's like. There is a corner of my heart that will always belong to Celia.' He put his hand over her fist, still closed on the kiss he had planted there. 'But since I met you I've realised that it doesn't mean I can never love again, although I never thought I would.'

'I love you, too, Matthew,' she said, tears filling her eyes. 'But what can we do?'

'We can't do anything, my darling. Like I told you the other day, we must continue to act as if we are nothing more than good friends.'

'It's not enough.'

'It has to be. Apart from anything else I can't risk getting myself struck off the medical list for improper conduct with a patient.' He grinned. 'Much as I would enjoy the improper conduct.' His smile faded and he gripped her hand. 'Be strong, my love. What we have is better than nothing.'

There was the sound of Emily coming up the stairs and he dropped a kiss on Bethany's forehead before he went to open the door.

'Ah, tea. Just what the doctor ordered,' he said in his best professional voice. 'And you've brought a cup for me as well as yourself, Emily. How thoughtful.' He handed a cup to Bethany. 'One sugar, or two, Bethany? I can never remember.'

'I don't take sugar at all, Matthew,' she reminded him, catching his mood. 'I would have thought you'd have known that by now.'

He gave an elaborate sigh. 'I take tea with so many of my patients. Some have sugar, some have milk, some have sugar and no milk, some have milk and no sugar, some have lemon. Can you wonder I can't keep up with it all?'

'Well, I take two sugars, Matthew,' Emily said as she reached for the sugar tongs. 'But I wouldn't expect you to remember that, either.'

They talked trivialities while they drank their tea, then Matthew said, 'I have to go to London next week, to a meeting, but I'll call and see you before I go.'

'What's the meeting about?' Bethany asked,

immediately interested.

He hesitated, realising his mistake, then said briefly, 'To report my findings on the cholera epidemic.'

'Is it quite over?' she asked quietly.

'Yes. It's over.'

'Is that all you're going to say about it?'

'What more is there to say except thank God it's over?' he said, getting up from his seat.

'Aren't you going to tell us your findings?' she persisted.

'It was as I had suspected. It came from the water supply at the pump. There was a leakage from the stream into the well and that was the cause of it.' He hadn't expected Bethany to question him and he realised he was on dangerous ground. 'Well, mostly that was the cause of it,' he added quickly. 'There were, of course, a few isolated cases that were not related.'

'Like Tilly,' she said quietly.

'And one or two others.' He picked up his hat. 'I'll call and see you all when I get back,' he promised. 'In the meantime, Bethany, you need plenty of rest. At the same time, you need a bit of company, so it won't hurt if the coaches are encouraged to stop here again. I'm sure there's no longer any risk of infection.'

'That will be nice,' Emily said thoughtfully after he had gone. 'I've missed having people to stay.'

'You've changed, Mama,' Bethany said, smiling at her. 'Don't you remember, when we first arrived here, how you were afraid we'd all be murdered in our beds if strangers stayed overnight?'

'Yes, well, I suppose I've got used to it.' Emily shrugged, then added a trifle sheepishly, 'but I always sleep with a poker under the bed, just in case.' She stared out of the window for several minutes. 'Such a lot has happened since we came to Travellers' Inn, I can hardly remember what it was like to live in London.' She looked down at her hands, no longer white and carefully manicured. 'And I don't know what my Seymour would say if he could see me now.'

'Do you still miss him, Mama?'

'I don't think he would have fitted in very well with our lives here in the country,' she said ambiguously. 'He was very much a town man.'

'But you like it, here in the country?'

'Oh, yes, I'm very happy here.' She got up and went over to the window and looked out. Then she waved and a blush spread across her face.

'Farmer Isaac is just coming down the road with a big bunch of chrysanthemums. I expect they're for you, dear. I'll go and let him in.'

'The flowers may be for me but I expect he's come to see you, Mama,' Bethany said half under her breath. But Emily was already on her way downstairs and wouldn't have heard.

Over the following weeks Bethany wept many tears for her little daughter, but gradually she became able to speak of her and to keep her memory alive by talking about the things she had said and done. Zack too had taken Tilly's death hard and although they were both able to speak to Sarah and Emily about her they found it difficult to talk to each other.

Until one night, as she blew out the candle, Bethany said, 'I could never understand how Tilly caught that dreadful illness, Zack. Matthew said it came from the pump at the crossroads. Are you sure you didn't take her there?'

'No, why should I?' he said irritably.

'It just seemed strange that she caught it after you had taken her to the village,' she said thoughtfully. 'I'd asked you not to take her there.'

'Oh, don't start that again. I only bought her a toffee apple, for God's sake.'

'Maybe there was something in the toffee. Maybe Mrs Green used water from the pump to make it . . . '

Suddenly, he reared up beside her and delivered a stinging blow across her cheek. 'Will you stop accusing me! What about the times you took her down to the river? What about the times she played in that stinking mud? How do you know she didn't catch it there?'

'But it couldn't have been that. I hadn't taken her there for a long time,' she protested, holding her cheek.

'That's what you tell me. But if you had I wouldn't expect you to admit it.' He turned his back on her. 'Oh, shut up about it, can't you. I need to get some sleep.'

Bethany lay staring up into the darkness. It was no use speculating as to how Tilly had contracted the illness. They should be comforting, not blaming each other for her death. She fingered her cheek, still stinging from the blow he had dealt her. Instead of drawing them closer together, she thought sadly, their grief seemed to be driving them further apart.

Business at the inn gradually began to pick up. As the winter progressed coaches once again began to stop for a few hours respite from the weather and the bad roads. Some used it to recover from an unpleasant sea crossing, grateful for a good meal and a comfortable bed now that they were back on dry land, some seeing it as a last chance for the same before embarking on their journey cross the sea.

Emily was kept busy doing what she enjoyed most, which was cooking for appreciative customers. She basked in their praise and concocted ever-more complicated and delicious meals to tempt jaded appetites. As the weather grew colder and it became too cold for Sarah and Reuben to sit on the bench outside the shed, or even inside it, the two of them would spend hours sitting like sentinels, one each side of the kitchen stove, Sarah preparing vegetables, Reuben smoking his pipe. Emily found this mildly irritating because she had come to regard the kitchen as her private domain, but she was wise enough not to say so, except when Sarah surreptitiously helped herself and Reuben to one of the scones she had just taken out of the oven.

'Well, you can spare us one,' Sarah said innocently. 'After all, we're only testing them to see if they've got enough fruit in them.'

'I know they've got enough fruit in them,' Emily exploded. 'I weighed it out, like I always do.'

'They ain't bad,' Reuben mumbled through crumbs. 'But I could judge better if I had another one.'

'You're not having any more,' Emily said, her face red from bending over the oven.

'Shut the door, boy, there's a terrible draught,' Sarah called, putting a stop to the argument, as Zack wheeled a new barrel of beer in.

'Hold on. You might let me get through it before you start shouting for me to close it, Mrs P.' he said cheerfully. 'You're getting soft in your old age, sitting by the fire all day.' He went whistling through to the bar.

'Not so much of your sauce, Zachary Brown,' she called after him, enjoying the banter. 'Old age, indeed!' She leaned forward to warm her hands at the fire.

'You shouldn't be hard on 'im, 'e's a good man,' Reuben remarked, chewing his whiskers.

She sat back in her chair. 'Yes, he is. I confess I wasn't too happy when Bethany married him but I can't deny he's proved a real asset to the place.' She sighed. 'Truth to tell, I don't know what we'd do without him now. And he's always cheerful.' For her part she was becoming more and more contented to simply sit by the fire when the weather was cold. It had been a gradual process but over the winter she had tended her garden less and less, leaving Zack to do what had to be done and as spring approached it was Zack who did the planting when he had dug the ground, although he always deferred to Sarah as to what she wanted planting and when. He said he found working out in the

285

open air a pleasant change from all his indoor tasks and was more than willing to add it to his daily workload. Occasionally, she would don her old brown coat and battered old hat and boots and trudge down the garden path between the vegetable beds and pull up a few weeds, but she found this aggravated her already painful arthritis so she didn't do it very often.

But Zack was indefatigable, up early every morning to wash beer mugs, clean tables, empty spittoons and put down fresh sawdust in the bar. That was always the first job of his day. After that he attended to the brew house and stables and was always ready with fresh horses for coaches in a hurry or to stable those who were putting up for the night.

Bethany, too, was always busy. She made sure that the guest bedrooms were kept ready for visitors, with clean bed linen and towels and well-polished furniture, and the dining room, as the little parlour was now re-named, set with spotless table linen and polished silver.

She couldn't bear to be idle because only hard work helped her to bear the pain of losing Tilly. And Matthew. Sometimes she was not quite sure which hurt most, the fact that she would never see her little daughter again, or that on the rare occasions when she saw Matthew she knew she must keep him at a distance.

23

Life at the inn gradually resumed its old pattern. Several of the men who came for a drink and a game of dominoes had lost at least one member of their family to the dreaded cholera so there was no lack of sympathy for Zack. Most evenings someone would raise a glass and toast 'absent friends' and a brief silence would descend as they remembered their loved ones. It had been a difficult time and one that would not easily be forgotten by any of them.

But gradually the conversation began to be dominated by speculation over the coming railway. Navvies were already at work extending the line from Colchester to Ipswich and it was rumoured there was going to be a station at Manningtree. This was received with a mixture of excitement and trepidation because tales were rife of the wild behaviour of the navvies, many of them Irish and far from home, who were anxious to convert their hard-earned wages into drunken oblivion at the local pubs.

But this was of little concern to Zack. Travellers' Inn was situated well out of the village and nowhere near the proposed railway line. His main concern and the speculation that dominated talk in the bar centred more on how long it would be before a branch line was extended to Harwich, because railway travel, so much faster, would surely put an end to the coaching trade.

Each day, over breakfast, he recounted what he had heard in the bar the night before.

'Well, if the railway extends as far as Harwich it'll surely put an end to us as a coaching inn,' Sarah said sadly. 'Just as we're picking up nicely and getting back on our feet again.'

'I don't see why it should,' Emily countered. 'Who, in their right mind, would want to travel on a dirty, noisy, smelly, uncomfortable, not to mention dangerous railway train when they could travel in the comparative comfort and safety of a coach?'

'A good many people,' Zack answered, draining his cup and pushing it over to Bethany for a refill. 'The main thing is, it's so much quicker. And now they've covered in the carriages and padded the seats it's more comfortable, too, by all accounts. Oh, there's no doubt the railways are the thing of the future.'

'And coaching inns will be a thing of the past,' Sarah said, shaking her head.

'Yes, but don't you worry about Travellers' Inn, Mrs P. Matthew says it'll be some time before the line's extended to Harwich, so we'll have coaches stopping here for a good many years yet,' Zack assured her.

'Oh, has Matthew been in?' Bethany said, carefully keeping her voice casual as she slid another egg on to Zack's plate.

'Yes, he was in the snug last night.' It must have been her imagination that detected a note of something like triumph in his voice. 'He'd been to see the Squire and Squire told him that the line won't be built yet because nobody will put up the money.'

'I believe Isaac . . . Farmer Walford has been approached to sell some of his land, but he refused because they weren't offering a very good price for it,' Emily said, turning pink.

'How do you know that?' Sarah asked, frowning at her.

'I saw him yesterday. He brought me some cooking apples and asked if I would make an apple pie for his housekeeper, Mrs Kraft. She's hurt her foot so she's had to stay at home.' She flushed again. 'I made two, one for him. If Mrs Kraft can't cook for herself she can't cook for him, either.'

'Funny you should say that,' Zack said, rubbing his stubbly chin. 'Farmer Walford asked me only last night if we did mutton pies. We could do that, couldn't we? Mutton pies and mash in the snug. It might be popular, especially with the likes of Farmer Walford and the doctor. The two of them often sit in the snug together putting the world to rights.'

'Why don't they sit in the bar?' Emily asked innocently.

'Because the locals wouldn't feel comfortable drinking with them, Mama,' Bethany said with a trace of impatience.

Emily nodded. 'Ah, no, I suppose not.' She took a bite of toast and marmalade. 'I think it's a good idea of yours to serve pie and mash in the snug, Zack. Just to a few of our favoured customers, not to any old Tom, Dick or Harry, of course.'

'You mean just to Farmer Walford and the doctor, Em,' Zack said, grinning at her.

'Well, no, not exactly,' she said, although that was precisely what had been in her mind because she liked the idea of Isaac enjoying her mutton pies.

'I'll tell them,' Zack said, pushing back his chair and getting to his feet. 'Well, I can't sit here gossiping all day. I've got work to do. Have you noticed the carrots are coming through, Mrs P?'

'No, I'll go and take a look later on. I'll thin them out when they're big enough. I can do it now the weather is getting warmer.'

'Don't you worry yourself about that, Mrs P. I'll do it when the time comes. We don't want you hurting your back, now, do we.' He went off, whistling.

'He's a good man,' Sarah said, for the umpteenth time. 'I don't know what we'd do without him. I never thought I'd say it, but I'm becoming very fond of Zack.'

'So am I. And he's thoughtful, too,' Emily agreed. 'Always makes sure there's plenty of fuel at hand for the stove without me ever having to ask him.'

'We couldn't run the place without him, that's for sure.'

Bethany began to clear the table, saying nothing. She saw a different side of Zack; a side that was carefully hidden from other people because he always made sure that he hit her where the bruises wouldn't show.

It had been worse since Tilly died.

Although he had grown to love her he had always been disappointed that Tilly hadn't been the son he craved. He had blamed Bethany for this and for the fact that she seemed unable to conceive again. Bethany was equally disappointed. She longed for another baby to love, not to replace her beloved Tilly but to fill a little of the yawning gap she had left in all their lives. But her disappointment was nothing to Zack's fury as each month went by with no sign of the child they both so desperately wanted.

'Bitch!' he would say, knocking her to the ground in the privacy of their bedroom. 'Barren bitch! What's the matter with you!' And he would kick her again as she struggled to her feet, each kick accompanied by an oath. By the time he had finished with her she was like a limp rag, with no energy or strength left to oppose him. But nobody knew about this because he was always careful never to bruise her where it might show. And she was too ashamed of her failure to conceive, too ashamed of the way he treated her to let anybody know what she suffered.

In any case, Zack was doing nothing wrong in the eyes of the law. A man was entitled to beat his wife as long as the stick he used was no thicker than his thumb and Zack never used a stick. His fists and his boots were sufficient.

The strange thing was that he was always filled with remorse after he had beaten her and he would cradle her in his arms, telling her over and over again how sorry he was, that he didn't know what had come over him and that he would never, ever do such a thing again. He would bathe her bruises and put soothing ointment on them, kissing her and telling her how much he loved her, his cheeks wet with remorseful tears.

Although she loathed him and hated herself for submitting to his tender ministrations, she was too shocked and battered to resist them; yet such were his powers of persuasion that by the time he lifted her up and laid her carefully into the soft comfort of her bed she was almost ready to believe him when he promised it would never, ever happen again.

But of course it did. Time and time again. And Sarah and Emily never suspected a thing.

Pie and mash in the snug became a twice-weekly occurrence for Matthew and Isaac. It suited them both very well, even after Isaac's housekeeper, Mrs Kraft recovered. Matthew in particular was glad of a meal that hadn't been kept hot for several hours over a saucepan that had long since boiled dry. He missed the meals Bethany used to save for him, meals that he could eat with her sitting opposite to him in the intimate confines of the kitchen at Travellers' Inn. But those days were gone; she was another man's wife and it was better that he should stay away. He knew he had been wrong to declare himself; it had been a moment of unforgivable weakness in what he knew was a hopeless situation. Yet he couldn't bring himself to regret it because now he had the comfort of knowing that Bethany shared his feelings. But the situation was still hopeless and it wasn't helped by the fact that he found Zack was growing increasingly arrogant and self-opinionated.

He carried his beer into the snug on a Tuesday evening in April. Isaac was already there with his tankard in front of him. They both looked forward to these evenings, when they could enjoy a quiet chat over a good meal, because over the years they had become good friends.

As soon as Matthew entered the room Isaac got up and went over to the bell pull to ring for their supper. A few minutes later Emily came in with a tray holding two plates of steaming roast beef and yorkshire pudding. It was nearly always Emily who brought their meal although she never waited on the tables in the dining room, as the little parlour had now become known. Matthew had noticed this; he had also noticed the admiring way Isaac often looked at her and the way she flushed when he spoke to her. He wondered, in fact he rather hoped, that there might be a romance gently blooming between them, although he knew that Isaac was a very shy man with ladies and also quite set in his ways. Wisely, he kept his thoughts to himself.

'We've got travellers in tonight and I was cooking a roast so I thought you might like a change from pie and mash,' she said with a smile as she put it in front of them.

'I must say it looks very good, Mrs Emily,' Isaac said warmly, smiling back at her. 'But your meals are always very good. I look forward to them.'

'Thank you.' Usually, she hurried back to the kitchen after she had served them, but tonight she lingered by the door. 'Matthew, do you remember the night there were twins born here at Travellers' Inn?' she asked.

Matthew laid down his knife and fork. 'Oh, I do indeed. What a night that was! And what a surprise, not least to their parents! A boy and a girl. They called them Victoria and Albert, as I remember. Isn't that so?'

'Yes, that's right.' She nodded.

'They must be, what? Three or four years old now, I should think.' He turned to Isaac. 'The young man and his wife were on their way to Holland for the young lady's confinement — not a wise thing to do under the circumstances, as it proved because the twins came rather sooner than they anticipated. However, thanks to Mrs Pilgrim and Bethany everything went well, although, as you can imagine, it was something of a shock for all concerned.'

'It was, indeed.' Emily gave a little laugh and shook her head. 'But those twins are not three or four, Matthew. They are now six years old. They've come off the boat from Holland with their parents and are at this moment sitting in the dining room with their parents, tucking into roast beef.' Her eyes shone with pleasure as she imparted the news.

'Six years old? Well I never! How time flies. And how long are you expecting them to stay this time?' Matthew asked.

'Oh, they'll be leaving in the morning.'

Matthew grinned. 'That was the intention the last time they stayed.'

'Yes, but they really will be leaving this time.'

'Then I must pay them a visit tonight, for I

can't let them go without seeing them. Are they all well?'

'Yes, very well. I'll ask Bethany to tell them you're here and that you'll be in to see them shortly, shall I?'

'Yes, please do.' He began to tuck into his meal, still shaking his head to think that it was a full six years since the night the twins were born.

Emily went to the door, then hesitated. 'I've made a treacle tart for pudding in the dining room but there's plenty,' she said, speaking now to Isaac. 'Would you like me to bring you some?'

'I would, indeed, Mrs Emily,' Isaac said. 'What about you, Matthew?'

'Oh, yes, please. It's one of my favourites,' Matthew said with a grin. 'Goodness me, six years,' he said again after she had gone. 'How time does fly.'

'How often we say time flies, when it is we that are passing away,' Isaac mused. 'I don't know who said it but it's true.'

'It's also quite depressing.' Matthew finished his meal and got up from the table. He slapped his friend on the back as he passed him. 'I'll go and see these twins and bring you another beer on the way back. That'll lift your spirits.'

He slipped off to the dining room and introduced himself to the twins, a pair of serious-looking children who were not a bit alike: Victoria was the bigger of the two and very like her father, Albert was smaller and favoured his mother. Both were pleasant and well mannered and Albert had a mischievous twinkle in his eye that Matthew was pleased to observe.

It never ceased to amaze him that children born of the same parents should show such different characteristics and appearance. Both parents looked happy and prosperous; the move to Holland had clearly been successful. He stayed talking for a few minutes then excused himself and left them to finish their meal.

Just outside the door to the dining room he met Bethany, on her way to clear their table.

'Oh, I see you've been to visit the twins,' she greeted him, talking rather quickly and carefully not meeting his eyes. 'I could hardly believe they are six years old. How those years seem to have flown . . .'

'How are you, Bethany?' he asked quietly, cutting across her words, trying to see her face in the dim light of the passage.

'I'm very well, thank you. At least . . .'

'I understand.' He linked his fingers with hers. 'Do you remember the night they were born, Bethany? How you cried on my shoulder?'

She nodded, still not looking at him. 'Oh, yes, I remember. You were such a comfort.'

'I wish I could always comfort you, Bethany,' he whispered.

'Oh, Matthew, if only . . .' She raised her eyes to him and he saw tears glistening there.

'Bethany, are you in any trouble,' he asked, immediately alarmed.

She shook her head quickly. 'No, no. Of course not.' She released her fingers from his. 'I must go. It's time to serve the coffee.' She hurried off before he could speak again.

He watched her go. Something was troubling

her, he was sure of it.

The next morning the yard was full of the hustle and bustle that always accompanied a coach leaving. There were the horses to harness and the bags and cases to load while the guests were at breakfast. Then there was the last-minute panic over things that might have been left behind before the coachman climbed up to his perch and with a crack of his whip in the air the wheels rumbled and the coach turned out into the road and was off at a cracking speed.

It had always been the custom for them all to assemble in the yard to wave off coaches as they left and today was no different. When it had disappeared in a cloud of dust Sarah and Emily hurried indoors.

'He was a nice little lad, that Albert,' Zack remarked to Bethany as she made to follow them.

'They were both nice children,' Bethany replied. 'I thought Victoria was quite a pretty child.'

'Yes, and if you hadn't been careless and let my little Tilly go down to the river we might still have had a pretty little daughter,' Zack said almost carelessly.

Bethany stopped short. 'How dare you blame me for Tilly's death! We hadn't been near the river for weeks,' she said, stung into retaliation. 'No, if anyone is to blame it's you, Zack. It's far more likely that she picked up the disease when you took her to the village. I'd asked you not to take her there but you took no notice. You even bought her a toffee apple and goodness knows what that might have had in it.' She made to stalk off but he caught her arm in a vice-like grip and swung her round.

'So now it's my fault, is it? You'll be blaming me next because you're barren.' He bent his head towards her. 'I should have had a son like the young lad that's just left,' he hissed in her ear. 'It's what every man wants, a son to follow him. What kind of a wife are you that you can't give me one? My God, the women down by the walls breed like rabbits but I can't even get a son on you, although heaven knows it's not for want of trying.' He let her go with a push that nearly knocked her off her feet. 'Oh, get out of my sight. You're neither use nor ornament.'

She straightened her cap and brushed down her skirt, then, with her head held high she went back into the house to continue the day's work. Sometimes she could hardly believe that the man she was married to was the same one she had been so besotted with when she was eighteen. She sighed as she went upstairs to strip beds and clean bedrooms. She had learned a lot in the past six years.

24

April gave way to May. The apple blossom smothered the trees in a pale pink froth and cushions of primroses and polyanthus bordered the garden path. Now that the winter had gone and the days were becoming warmer Sarah had regained her lost energy and she happily thinned out the carrots, and planted peas and beans in the ground Zack had dug for her. When he was not sitting in the sun watching Sarah at work Reuben chopped sticks from the logs Zack had sawn.

'You're a lazy old devil, Reuben Scales,' Sarah said to him one day as he sat on the bench outside the shed watching her hoeing between the carrots. 'All you do is sit in the sun all day smoking that filthy old pipe.'

'You need somebody to keep a eye on you, Sary Pilgrim,' he replied unrepentantly through a haze of smoke. 'Make sure you don't work too hard. But I shall go an' chop a few sticks in a minit or two. Then, if I'm lucky, Bethany'll come out an' say, 'thass a dry owd job you're doin', Reuben. I better pull you a mug o' beer.' An' I'll say, 'I don't like to drink on me own so you better pull one for Sary as well.' That way we'll both git a drink.' He got to his feet. 'Come to think of it I am a bit dry. I'll go an' do it now.'

Sarah continued hoeing and before long he

came back down the path with a mug of frothing beer in each hand.

'There y'are. What did I say?' he said, plonking himself back on the bench. 'You'd better come an' drink yours afore the froth's gone, Sary.'

'You weren't gone long enough to chop many sticks,' she remarked as she came and sat beside him. She took her mug from him. 'You're a crafty old devil as well as a lazy one,' she said with a sniff. She took a draught of beer. 'Ah, that's a good brew. I must say young Zack knows how to brew a good beer.'

'Well, he had a good teacher,' Reuben said, wiping the froth off his whiskers. 'You an' your John made the best beer in the district an' you've taught Zack to do the same.'

'Yes, he's turned out to be a good man,' Sarah said. 'I didn't want Bethany to marry him because I though he'd taken advantage of her, but I've had cause to be glad she did.'

'Ain't like you to admit you was in the wrong, Sarah Pilgrim,' he said with a grin. He wetted his finger and made a mark on the shed. 'I'll chalk that one up.'

'Cheeky beggar.' She gave him a playful nudge.

'Don't do that, you'll spill my beer.' He took a long draught then wiped his mouth with the back of his hand. 'I thought Bethany was lookin' a bit peaky when she poured the beer,' he said sadly. 'I dessay she's still grievin' over the little maid even though it must be nigh on a year since she was took. Ah, that was a bad business an' no mistake.'

'Aye, you're right, it was.' Sarah took a drink of her own beer. 'But I've got an idea there might be something coming along that'll help to take her mind off her loss,' she said enigmatically without looking at him.

'What d'you mean?' He frowned at her, then, seeing her expression, his face cleared. 'You mean there might be another little 'un?' He beamed. 'Now, that *would* be a treat, wouldn't it.'

'I'm saying nothing. And you're not to, either, Reuben Scales. But all the signs are there. She's finicky over her food and several times I've seen her rush to the privy.' She shrugged. 'But I could be mistaken. Time will tell.'

Sarah was not mistaken.

Bethany was overjoyed when she realised she was pregnant again and Zack's delight knew no bounds. He insisted on bringing her breakfast in bed, which she felt too nauseous to eat and of course the beatings ceased. He had never been more solicitous and caring towards her, in fact, he was more like the old Zack she had fallen in love with nearly seven years ago. She tried very hard to revive that feeling, but the very fact that she had to try so hard meant that the spark had gone, killed by the way he had treated her. But he was still her husband; it was her duty to love and care for him and so she did her best, hiding her true feelings deep within her.

Ever since Tilly's death, Bethany visited the graveyard every week, whatever the weather, and put flowers on her tiny grave. In winter, when there were no flowers to be had, she arranged

301

evergreens and berries to brighten up the corner of the churchyard where, sheltered by enormous yew trees, Tilly was laid to rest. And each week she would talk to her, telling her of the things that had happened at Travellers' Inn and often confiding her innermost thoughts as she arranged the flowers and tidied the grave.

'I've got some wonderful news for you today, Tilly,' she whispered as she made a posy of the very last of the primroses that she had found on the bank down by the river. 'You're going to have a little brother. Or sister. I really don't mind which, although your papa is desperate for a son. Come to think of it, perhaps a son would be better because no daughter could ever take your place, my darling.' She finished arranging the flowers, shedding a few tears as she always did and wiping them away with a handkerchief edged with black lace. Then, reluctantly, she got up off her knees to leave. But as she got to her feet the whole churchyard seemed to spin crazily and she staggered and sank to the ground again, one hand to her head, the other fishing ineffectually in her reticule for her smelling bottle. She couldn't find it and felt too ill to search further, so she closed her eyes and rested her head against the cool marble feet of the angel on Tilly's headstone and waited for the world to right itself and her strength to come back.

She didn't know how long she had been there, half lying, half sitting, when she caught the sharp ammonia smell as her smelling bottle was held

302

under her nose. This immediately revived her and she gave her head a little shake and opened her eyes.

'Matthew!' she said, surprised to see him crouching beside her. She smiled at him weakly. 'What on earth are you doing here?'

'It was a lucky chance,' he said, automatically feeling for her pulse and laying his hand on her clammy forehead as he spoke. 'I'd been to visit the vicar and I was coming back through the churchyard when I saw someone lying huddled next to Tilly's grave. I knew it must be you. Goodness knows how long you've been here. I was with the vicar nearly an hour.'

She sat up and looked at the watch pinned to her black mourning dress. 'Not long, I think. I must have fainted when I got up off my knees.' She smiled. 'It's nothing, Matthew. It's happened before. Several times, lately.'

His eyes searched her face, noting the pallor and the circles under her eyes. His professional gaze then rested briefly on her breasts, full and rounded and he knew.

'I'm very glad for you, Bethany,' he said quietly, although it cost him a great deal to say the words. 'A baby is exactly what you need.' He bowed his head and turned away. 'God help me, I wish it could have been mine,' he whispered.

She heard him. 'I wish that, too, Matthew, with all my heart,' she said quietly. She put out her hand to him. 'But it can never be. We both know that. Zack is my husband and he loves me. I know he loves me,' she added rather too firmly.

She went on, 'You should find yourself a wife, Matthew.'

'Oh, yes? And where do you suggest I should start looking?' he asked with a bitter twist to his mouth. 'Since the wife I loved is dead and the only other woman I could ever love is married to somebody else?'

'Oh, don't be like that, Matthew,' she pleaded. 'You know as well as I do there can never be any future for us together. There's no point in wasting your life waiting, hoping for something that we both know can never be.'

He got to his feet and helped her up. 'I'm not wasting my life, Bethany. I have a very fulfilling career, which I'm pleased to say takes up a great deal of my time. I could never take a wife simply for the comfort of a warm bed at night and at the moment I can see no other reason to want one.' He took her hands in his. 'You told me that Zack loves you but you didn't say that you love him, Bethany. Tell me, do you love him?'

She shook her head. 'Not any more. But he's my husband, I have a duty to remain faithful to him.' She looked up at him and there were tears in her eyes. 'But you are my very, very good friend, Matthew. And I hope you always will be.'

'I'll settle for that, Bethany,' he said quietly.

Bethany's pregnancy didn't go well. She felt continually ill and her back ached. But she carried on with her work without complaint, doing her part to keep up the tradition of Travellers' Inn as a place where good food and good clean beds were always to be found. And when she was tempted to feel a little sorry for

304

herself she thought of the women she had seen working in the fields, picking up stones or potatoes, helping with the harvest almost till the day they gave birth, or the tales she had heard — she could hardly believe they were true — of pregnant women working down coal mines and even giving birth down there in the dark, and she gave thanks for her life of comparative ease and comfort.

Zack was full of concern for her. She could hardly believe this was the man who had punched and kicked her so often in the past but she was thankful for the change in him and she looked forward to the baby that would be born in the winter, hoping that it would help her to be contented with her lot. She prayed for a boy because this was what Zack wanted so badly and she feared more beatings if she let him down by producing another girl. Another girl. But no girl could ever replace Tilly.

Soon it was strawberry time and Sarah's carefully tended strawberry beds yielded a better crop than anyone could ever remember. They all ate their fill and Bethany was reminded of how, last year, Tilly had helped herself to strawberries and then, with juice all round her mouth, innocently wondered how Bethany knew what she had been doing. It was just another precious memory to be preserved.

Meantime, Emily served up strawberries and cream night after night in the dining room, and Sarah and Bethany made jam although the smell of the hot jam made Bethany feel sick and Sarah didn't look well, either.

'I reckon I've eaten too many, they've given me pains,' Sarah said, rubbing her stomach.

'Yes, I'm almost thankful this is the last of them,' Bethany agreed as she tied down the last few pots of jam. 'But it will be gooseberries next, I suppose.'

'There aren't so many of them,' Sarah said, 'Thank goodness.' She sat down on a chair by the table and got up again immediately. 'Oh, dear, I must run,' she said and dashed out of the door down to the privy. When she came back she looked grey and pinched. 'I think I'll go and lie down on my bed for an hour or so. Perhaps it'll help me feel better,' she said, hugging herself and shivering.

'Wait a minute. I'll get you a hot water bottle,' Emily said, already at the stove filling the stone bottle with water from the kettle. Then she put it in its red flannel cover and handed it to her.

'Oh, thank you. That's lovely. Even though the sun is shining I can't seem to get warm.' She took it gratefully and wrapped her arms round it.

'It's not like Aunt Sarah to go to bed in the middle of the day,' Bethany said anxiously after she'd gone up. 'I hope she'll be better tomorrow.'

'I expect she will,' Emily said. 'We've all eaten rather a lot of strawberries this year and they can upset some people.'

At first Zack laughed at Sarah's indisposition; he had eaten more strawberries than anyone, with no ill effects. But when she was not much better the next day he insisted on fetching Matthew, who came and examined her, diagnosed dyspepsia and left her medicine that she flatly refused to take.

'You won't get better if you don't take it, Auntie,' Emily said, holding out the glass.

Sarah sniffed it. 'I'm not taking it. I don't know what's in it,' she said stubbornly.

'It's indigestion mixture. Matthew told me that's what wrong with you, indigestion.' Bethany said.

'He didn't call it that. I heard what he said, it was disappearance or some such word.'

'It was dyspepsia. It's another name for indigestion.' Bethany said patiently.

'Well, if that's what it's for I don't need to take it. I haven't got indigestion.'

Emily raised her eyes to the ceiling. 'I thought you'd got pains in your stomach.'

'I did have. They're better now. I've starved them out. I think I shall get up.' Sarah was obviously feeling better and getting back to her old cantankerous ways. She waved them away. 'Go on, off you go. I don't want you watching me and counting how many petticoats I put on.'

Reluctantly, Emily and Bethany left her to dress herself and went downstairs with the medicine bottle. Zack was in the kitchen, stacking logs by the stove. He looked up when they entered.

'How is she?' he asked, full of concern.

'She says she feels better. She's getting up,' Bethany said, rubbing her aching back. 'There's no arguing with her. She's as stubborn as a mule.'

'Well, it's a nice day, so I reckon it won't hurt her to sit in the garden in the sunshine,' Zack said straightening up. 'In fact, it'll do her good. I'll fetch a comfortable chair out for her. Poor old Reuben is sitting on the bench down by the shed looking as if he's lost a guinea and found a farthing. He's like a lost soul when he hasn't got his mate to argue with so it'll cheer him up, too.'

A few minutes later Sarah appeared, looking white and holding on to things as she walked.

'Zack's putting a chair in the garden for you, Auntie,' Bethany said. 'It'll be more comfortable than that wooden bench.'

He came in as she spoke. 'Hullo, Mrs P. I must say you're still looking a bit peaky. Come on, I'll take you out into the sunshine, it'll do you good.' He offered her his arm. 'You can lean on me, I'm as good as a stick,' he said with a grin. 'I've put you a chair near your old friend. He's lost without you.' He whispered something in her ear as they went out of the door and she turned to smile at him.

'Do you know, I think I might just fancy that,' she said, nodding.

He looked back and winked at Bethany. 'She fancies a glass of beer.'

'Well, don't give her too much and make her tiddly. Remember she hasn't had anything to eat,' Emily warned.

'A little won't hurt her, Mama. It's nourishing,' Bethany said, glad that Sarah was on the mend.

Emily put her head on one side and studied her daughter. 'Then perhaps you should have some, too. You don't eat enough to keep a sparrow alive.'

'Ugh! I can't even bear the smell of it these days,' she said, shuddering.

Sarah stayed in the garden with Reuben till the sun went down, then Zack helped her indoors and she went back to bed. The next day she didn't get up at all but the following day she felt stronger again. And so it went on; some days she was well enough to sit in the garden, some days she kept to her bed, but it was evident to them all that she was becoming weaker.

Zack was tireless in helping to look after her, taking her the drinks and tasty snacks that Emily prepared because he was anxious that Bethany shouldn't tire herself by continually going up and down stairs to the sick room.

Matthew visited as often as he could, worried that she seemed to be getting no better, but he said there was little he could do if Sarah refused to take the medicine he prescribed for her.

'I'll try and get her to take it,' Zack said. He was as worried as Emily and Bethany. 'I manage to get her to eat a little sometimes so perhaps I can get her to take her medicine.'

'Yes, you seem to be able to twist her round your little finger,' Emily said with a smile. 'She'll do things for you that she won't do for us.'

He grinned. 'That's because I'm a man and I make a fuss of her,' he said with a wink.

'Are you saying we don't?' Emily said, bridling.

'No, I'm saying I'm a man,' He went off up the stairs with the bottle and glass. When he came down he was smiling. 'I managed to persuade her to take it,' he said triumphantly, putting the bottle down on the table. 'You see? All you have to do is leave it to Zack.' He went back outside, whistling, obviously pleased with himself.

But although Zack persuaded Sarah to take her medicine it was to no avail. She got steadily worse until all she could take were a few sips of water.

'I don't understand it,' Matthew said when he came to see her. 'The medicine should have helped. I've examined her and I can find no sign of any growth that might cause the pains and sickness yet she seems to be getting steadily weaker.'

'I suppose that's because she's eating practically nothing,' Bethany said. 'Even Zack can't get her to take more than a drop of water.'

He rubbed his chin. 'I really don't know what else to do for her,' he said. 'So I think perhaps the time has come to call in a specialist from Colchester, if you are willing.' He looked a little uncomfortable. 'Of course, there will be a fee.'

Emily waved her hand dismissively. 'We'll pay whatever he asks if he can make her better,' she said.

But the specialist was never needed because the following day Sarah's heart gave out and she died.

25

Emily and Bethany were both distraught at Sarah's death. To their knowledge she had never suffered a day's illness in her life and that she should sicken and die within a matter of weeks shocked them to the core. They simply couldn't believe that they would never again see the tall figure in her old brown coat and floppy hat striding up the garden path, nor be given the benefit of her somewhat cantankerous wisdom and blunt opinions.

'I simply can't believe it's true. I can't believe she's gone,' Emily said when all her tears were spent. 'It just doesn't seem right that she's not here any more. The place just isn't the same.'

'I think Tilly's death must have affected her even more than we realised,' Bethany said sadly. 'Heaven knows, we all grieved — we still grieve, there isn't a day that passes . . . ' She pulled herself together and went on, 'But maybe we didn't realise . . . After all, Aunt Sarah was quite old . . . '

Emily nodded. 'Yes, sometimes these things take a long time to surface. And it's barely a year . . . '

They sat in silence for some time, each busy with her own thoughts. Then suddenly, a ghost of a smile crossed Bethany's face.

'Do you remember what it was like when we first came here, Mama? No sheets on the bed, no

311

blankets, everywhere covered in dust and cobwebs . . . '

Emily shuddered. 'As if I could ever forget! And Aunt Sarah wasn't exactly welcoming, was she?'

'No, we only persuaded her to let us stay because I pretended to faint.' Bethany's smile deepened. 'But it worked out well and I know she became as fond of us as we were of her.'

'Yes, and although she didn't want to admit it I believe she was glad we wanted to open up the inn again . . . '

'Of course it helped when we found she had money in the bank.'

Emily shook her head in bewilderment. 'Fancy her not knowing about that, Bethany.'

'Well, with Uncle John dying so suddenly, and her not being able to read or write, how could she know?'

'And to think I used to visit her and Uncle John when I was a child and I never knew that,' Emily said, shaking her head.

'Well, I don't suppose she was exactly proud of the fact.' Bethany poured yet another cup of tea for them both. 'I wonder if she knew how much we loved her,' she mused. 'She was not a woman to encourage open affection.'

'Only with Zack. He could twist her round his little finger in the end.'

'Yes, I think she became very fond of Zack.'

'Somebody mention my name?' Zack, wearing his best suit came into the kitchen.

'We were just saying Aunt Sarah became very fond of you,' Bethany repeated.

'Yes, well, she was a good old thing, we got on well together. I shall miss her.' He sat down and took the cup of tea Bethany gave him. 'I've been to see the undertaker and the funeral's all arranged. I think I've thought of everything.'

'Thank you, Zack,' Emily said. 'And did you go and see Reuben?'

'Yes, the poor old chap's very cut up. I never understood why those two never got wed. They were like an old married couple, the way they bickered and argued.'

'Yes, they were funny.' Emily wiped away a tear. 'That's another thing. I can't believe we shall never see them sitting together outside the shed in the garden again.'

'She was a good age,' Zack said. 'I guess she'd had well over her three score years and ten.'

'I don't care. She was still too young to die,' Bethany said. 'And she'd never had a day's illness in her life.'

'Till now,' Emily said quietly.

'Yes, till now.'

Sarah's funeral was meant to be a quiet, family affair, but practically the whole village turned out and the church was full, echoing with Sarah's favourite hymns, which they only knew because they'd sometimes heard her humming 'All things bright and beautiful' or 'Rock of Ages' as she went about her work.

After the funeral there was free beer and fruit cake in the bar, which Zack dispensed. Everyone it seemed had a memory of Sarah, a funny thing she had said or done, or some kindness she had shown. These anecdotes brought her back to life

313

as nothing else could have done and the gentle laughter was a fitting tribute to her.

Reuben, in the dusty, moth-eaten black suit he had bought for his mother's funeral fifty years earlier, sat in his corner of the bar chewing his whiskers and drinking steadily, saying little. He had seemed to grow smaller in the days since his old friend's death and Bethany resolved that he would have to be watched carefully lest he pined for her. It was late before the last mourners left, a few of them none too steady on their feet.

In bed that night, Bethany was really too tired to listen as Zack outlined some of the improvements he would like to make to Travellers' Inn.

'Isn't it a bit soon, Zack?' she said with a yawn. Worn out from the emotional strain of the day and still feeling ill from her pregnancy, she wasn't as enthusiastic as he was. 'Aunt Sarah is hardly cold in her grave and you're already talking about making changes to the place.'

'Well, I've been thinking about it for a long time.'

He was quiet for some time and Bethany was just dropping off to sleep when he started off again.

'We'll sell the dog cart and buy something bigger, say a wagonette, so we can fetch people from the new station at Manningtree, and put them up for the night before they go on to Harwich by coach. And we can build . . . '

'You seem to have got it all cut and dried, Zack,' she said a little sharply.

'Well, I can see where improvements can be

made. I used to talk about it a bit to Mrs P but she was never very keen. She reckoned things were all right as they were. But you and me, Beth, we're modern, go-ahead people. We need to keep up-to-date with things. I'm wondering if we might have this new gas laid on . . .'

'That would cost quite a lot of money, wouldn't it?'

'Well, I reckon Mrs P has made quite a little packet out of the place these past few years, hasn't she? After all, she hasn't spent a lot. The whole place could do with a coat of paint.'

'I don't know how much money she made, Zack. I've never asked.'

'You should have. It's always good to know how things stand.'

'I've never thought it was any of my business. You've been paid a decent wage and we've always had everything we've needed. I know Matthew sometimes took money to the bank for her when he went into Colchester and now and again she asked me to write a cheque for her — not often, because she didn't understand how cheques worked so she didn't trust them — but I don't know any more than that.'

'Well, we shall have to make it our business to find out.' He put his arm round her and started playing with a strand of hair. 'I've got plans for Travellers' Inn and I shall need somebody to keep proper accounts. And that somebody will be you, Beth.'

'But I shall have a baby to look after. Have you forgotten that?'

'No, of course I haven't.' His hand slid down

to her stomach, only just beginning to bulge a little. 'It's our son's future I'm thinking of, sweetheart.' He was quiet for several minutes, then he said, 'Perhaps we can go to the bank tomorrow. No sense in wasting time.'

But by the time Zack had cleaned up the bar from the previous night, done several other necessary jobs and was ready to harness up Peggy, a rather smart gig, drawn by a chestnut mare, pulled into Travellers' Inn. A portly man dressed in a black frock coat and a black top hat, the neatness of his dress rather spoiled by untidy grey whiskers, got stiffly down from it.

'I'm Abraham Thickbroom, Mrs Pilgrim's solicitor,' he introduced himself a trifle breathlessly as Zack came forward, more than a little annoyed at being held up further. 'Is Dr Oakley here? I arranged for him to be here when I arrived. Eleven o'clock was the time we agreed.'

'Solicitor? I didn't know she had a solicitor,' Zack said a trifle grumpily, ushering him into the house and introducing him to Emily. 'Do you know what this is all about?' he asked her accusingly.

'No, Zack, I don't,' Emily said. She looked anxiously at Abraham Thickbroom. 'Is something wrong?'

'No, indeed, nothing at all,' Mr Thickbroom said, pulling at his whiskers. 'Quite the contrary, in fact. I've come with Mrs Pilgrim's will. And I arranged with Dr Oakley that he should be here when it was read, since he was principal witness.'

'I've never heard anything about a will, have you, Em?' Zack asked, puzzled.

Emily shook her head. 'No, Aunt Sarah never said anything to me. Perhaps Bethany knows about it.'

'Well, here's Matthew, smack on time,' Zack said, looking out of the window as Matthew rode into the yard. 'So we'll soon find out.'

'Perhaps you'd like to take some refreshment,' Emily said, not quite sure how to proceed. 'And I'll call my daughter since I presume this is a matter that concerns the whole family.' She hesitated. It didn't seem quite the right thing for such an important thing as the reading of the will to take place in the kitchen so she led the way to the dining room, which had been cleared of breakfast and not yet laid up for dinner.

A little later, with coffee and Emily's best home-made biscuits in front of them, they waited expectantly, all eyes on Mr Thickbroom at the head of the table, with Matthew and Emily on his right and Bethany and Zack opposite to them on his left.

The solicitor shuffled his papers importantly, cleared his throat and began, 'The will is quite straightforward. Mrs Pilgrim left the sum of fifty pounds to her lifelong friend Mr Reuben Scales, one hundred pounds to her great niece, Bethany Stanford and the residue of her estate, which comprises the inn known as Travellers' Inn and any money left after the bequests to her niece, Mrs Emily Stanford.'

Zack's face darkened dangerously. 'What about me? Don't I get a mention after the way I've slaved my insides out over this place?' he shouted. 'Why did she cut me out?'

Mr Thickbroom looked up at him over the gold rim of his spectacles. 'I can only tell you what is written in the will, Sir,' he said mildly, 'And your name is not mentioned anywhere.'

'When is the will dated, Mr Thickbroom?' Bethany asked anxiously, seeing Zack's temper rising.

'The thirtieth of June, Eighteen-Forty.'

'I took her to see Mr Thickbroom the same day that I took her into Colchester to see her bank manager,' Matthew explained. 'It seemed sensible to get everything done at the same time. Did she never mention this, Emily? Bethany?'

They both shook their heads. 'No. Never.'

He turned to Zack. 'It wasn't a case of cutting you out, Zack. I don't believe Mrs Pilgrim even knew you at that time.'

'No, you didn't come to work here until after harvest, that year,' Emily said.

'And we certainly weren't married, Zack,' Bethany added. 'Look, the hundred pounds is left to me in my maiden name. Does that make any difference, Mr Thickbroom?'

'None at all, provided I can see proof of your marriage.'

'Didn't she ever make a new will?' Zack persisted.

'Not to my knowledge,' Mr Thickbroom said.

'I certainly never witnessed another one,' Matthew said.

'Have you looked?' Zack turned accusingly to Emily.

'Of course I haven't looked, Zack. Why would I, since I didn't know she'd made a will in the

318

first place,' Emily said sharply.

'What about you, Beth?'

Bethany shook her head wearily. 'In any case, does it matter, Zack? Nothing's going to change, is it, Mama?'

'No, of course not,' Emily said. 'Why should it?'

Zack got up and pushed his chair back angrily. 'No, that's the trouble with this place,' he muttered as he left the room. 'Nothing's ever going to bloody well change.'

After he had gone Matthew said, 'I'm sure if Sarah had made another will I would have known.'

Bethany shook her head. 'I don't suppose she ever gave it a thought. Once you'd sorted out her finances for her, Matthew, she was content to let things be. I know you used to go to the bank for her sometimes and I wrote the odd cheque for her but I don't suppose she had any idea what she was worth.'

'Which is quite a substantial amount,' Mr Thickbroom said. 'Several thousand pounds, in fact.' He smiled at Emily. 'You're quite a rich woman now, Mrs Stanford.'

Emily looked down at her hands, not quite as white and soft as they had once been. 'I think I shall buy myself a diamond ring. I've always wanted a diamond ring,' she said complacently.

Fortunately, Zack didn't hear that remark. He was busy furiously going through the desk in the snug looking for secret compartments that might have held a later will, but although he found two secret drawers they were empty except for the skeleton of a mouse. It was obvious there was no other will.

That night Zack drowned his disappointment in drink.

He stumbled up the stairs at half past midnight and fell into the bedroom, waking Bethany from a deep sleep.

She got up and tried to help him into bed while he cursed and swore.

'Why didn't that old bitch leave the place to you, then I could have done what I wanted with it,' he shouted. 'I'd got plans. Big plans.'

'Oh, do be quiet, you'll wake Mama,' she said, trying to half push, half lift him into bed.

'Bugger Mama,' he swore. 'She'll hang on to every last penny, mingy old cow. That's the trouble with you women, afraid to take risks. Expand, that's what we should do. Expand.' He flung his arms wide, catching her on the side of the face.

'You can't say that, Zack. I'm sure Mama will be generous. When you tell her what you want to do I'm sure she'll be happy to pay for it.'

'Why should I have to ask her for every penny I want? A man shouldn't have to ask for every penny he spends . . . ' he was off again, ranting and waving his arms and kicking out at her as she tried to get him on to the bed. 'Aaaah, get off me,' he shouted, catching her with a vicious kick in the stomach as she tried to catch his foot to unlace his boots, sending her sprawling to the other side of the room. She lay there, doubled up with pain, her arms protectively round her stomach.

'The baby,' she moaned. 'My baby.'

But Zack didn't hear. He was snoring in a drunken stupor.

Bethany didn't know how long she remained on the floor, holding her stomach against the pain of his kick. It felt like hours. But at last she managed to pull herself up and crawl over to the bed and climb in beside him. There she turned her back on him and lay on her side with her knees up, praying that no harm had come to the child she was carrying.

She didn't sleep and the pain didn't lessen.

At six o'clock she began to feel a warm trickling between her legs. She got out of bed and folded up a towel to lie on, then shook Zack, trying to wake him.

'Wassamatter,' he muttered, turning over and going back to sleep.

'Zack. You must wake up. You must go and fetch Mrs Wright.' She shook him again, urgently. 'It's the baby. She'll know what to do.' She shook him again. 'Zack! Wake up! I think the baby's coming!'

He sat up in bed and shook his head. 'God, my head feels like a ton of bricks,' he moaned. 'And why am I still wearing my boots?'

'Because you were drunk and I couldn't get them off you. Zack, will you please hurry. Fetch Mrs Wright. She'll know what to do to save the baby.'

'Save it?' He swung round and blinked owlishly at her. 'What are you talking about? It's not due for months yet.'

'I know. That's why you have to go and fetch

Mrs Wright. Quickly. Oh, please, Zack. Hurry.'

He blundered out of bed. It was fortunate he was still wearing his boots and trousers because he had enough trouble finding his shirt and buttoning it. Then he clattered off down the stairs, still cursing and moaning about his head.

Bethany lay quite still, praying that this precious baby hadn't been harmed. Her stomach was still very sore and the pain seemed to be getting worse. She wished Zack would hurry.

It was a full half hour before she heard steps on the stairs and Mrs Wright came into the room. She pulled back the covers and lifted Bethany's nightgown. The tell-tale blood stains and the huge bruise forming on her abdomen, together with Zack's constant complaining about his head on the way, told their own story.

'How far gone are you?' she asked.

'A little over three months, I think.' Bethany looked up at her, fear in her eyes. 'Will it be all right?'

Mrs Wright laid a hand on her stomach. 'I can't say, at this stage. Are you in much pain?'

'A bit. But it might be from . . . where I fell and hit myself.' Bethany knew Mrs Wright was not taken in by the lie but it was the best she could think up.

Ethel Wright nodded. She'd seen it all before and it hadn't taken much to put two and two together. Zack, obviously hungover, complaining about his sore head and the boot-shaped bruise on Bethany's stomach told their own tale, a tale Bethany was anxious to keep to herself. She pulled the covers up over her gently. 'Well, there's nothing to be done but wait and see. Stay in bed with your feet higher than your head, that's the best thing, and wait and see what happens.'

'Can't you give me anything?' Bethany asked desperately.

'No, I'm sorry, love.' She shook her head and a faint smile played about her lips. 'It's something I'm not often asked for, to tell you the truth. More often, the women are desperate for something to get rid of it.' She laid a hand on Bethany's arm. 'The only thing you can do is rest and let nature take its course.'

She left then, promising to come back if she was needed. But she knew, and by that time so did Bethany, that there was nothing to be done.

26

'I can't understand it. Why wasn't she more careful? What did she fall over, for God's sake?' Zack thumped his fist on the table with every question.

Emily looked at him from the other side of the table, an enigmatic expression on her face. 'Is that what she told you? That she fell over?' she asked quietly.

He frowned. 'Oh, I dunno. I can't remember exactly. She said she fell over, or bumped into something.' He thumped the table again. 'But whatever it was she's lost me my son, stupid, careless bitch.' He stared at Emily. 'What are you looking at me like that for?'

'Because I'm going to tell you exactly what did happen, Zack. And you're not going to like it.'

'What do you mean? She's already told me what happened.'

Emily shook her head. 'No, she hasn't. She obviously wanted to spare your feelings. But I'm going to tell you because I won't have you blaming Bethany for something that was your fault.'

'How could it have been my fault?'

'Because you kicked her in the stomach. And that's what caused her to lose the baby.'

His jaw dropped. 'Don't talk such rubbish. I'd never do such a thing!' He leaned over the table and jabbed a finger at her. 'I wanted her to have this child. Do you hear me? I want a son!'

'That's as maybe. And I agree you wouldn't do a thing like that when you were sober. But you were so furious that Aunt Sarah left the inn to me — no, don't shake your head and try to deny it because you know it's true — that you got yourself blind drunk. Bethany was trying to get your boots off and get you to bed and you lashed out at her with your foot ... ' Emily spread her hands.

He slumped in his chair and put his head in his hands, thinking about what she had said. After a long time he sat up straight and said belligerently, 'Well, then, it was her own fault. She knows what I'm like when I'm drunk. I don't know what I'm doing. I'm not responsible for my actions. If she'd had any sense she'd have left me alone and let me be. So she's only got herself to blame.'

'I can't believe you said that, Zack,' Emily said incredulously. 'I can't believe you're going to blame Bethany for what you did. Heaven knows, she's upset enough as it is, without that.'

He shook his head. 'No, I shan't say anything about it to her. She's proved she's not barren so it's not the end of the world,' he said magnanimously. 'But perhaps it'll teach her to be more careful next time.' He got up from the table. 'I've got to get on. This business has put me all behind with my work. I've got to draw water from the well for the brew house.' He paused. 'Now you've got all this money you might consider having the water piped up to the house instead of me having to cart it all up by the bucketful.'

'I'll think about it. But I've got other things I want to do first.'

'Like what?'

'That's my business.'

He went out and slammed the door.

Emily sat for a long time after he had gone out. She had always liked Zack; she still did, but she was learning that he never accepted the blame for anything. If anything went wrong he would always find a way to lay the fault at somebody else's door. She shook her head. As if Bethany hadn't enough to bear without being blamed for this. She hoped he would keep his word and never repeat to her what he had just said.

Bethany was in bed for a week. During that time Zack was loving and concerned for her. He brought her meals to her, saying it would save Emily's little legs, and there was always a posy of flowers on the tray that he had picked for her. Together they cried over the lost child and together they resolved that soon there would be another. He was just as he had been when they were first in love, caring and considerate. Bethany allowed herself to enjoy his attention, pushing to the back of her mind the suspicion that this was his way of showing remorse for what he had done.

Emily waited until Bethany had been back on her feet for several days before she announced, 'I've an appointment with the bank manager in Colchester on Thursday and you're coming with me. It's Mrs Barton's scrubbing day so she'll be here to look after things if meals are needed. I've told her where everything is and what to do so I'm sure she'll manage.'

'Colchester? Who's going to take us? Zack?' Bethany asked in surprise.

'No. Not Zack. He can't be spared. We need to leave somebody in charge. We shall go by ourselves. I've hired a gig and a driver and it'll be here at ten o'clock sharp.' She hunched her shoulders conspiratorially and grinned at Bethany. 'It will be quite an adventure for the two of us and it will do you the world of good to get away from the place for a few hours; perhaps it'll put some roses back in your cheeks.'

'What does Zack say about it?' Bethany asked anxiously.

'He isn't very pleased but there's not much he can do about it because he knows the three of us can't be away at the same time.'

'I expect he thinks I shouldn't go,' Bethany said, looking worried. 'I wouldn't want him to feel left out, Mama, it was bad enough that he wasn't mentioned in Aunt Sarah's will.' She wasn't sure whether she was more concerned over Zack's feelings or his temper, which was likely to be taken out on her.

'Oh, don't worry, I'll make it right with him. He wants me to have water piped up to the house from the well.'

'And . . . ?'

'I've told him I'll think about it.'

★　★　★

In spite of her misgivings over Zack, Bethany found herself really looking forward to her trip to Colchester and she was quite excited when the day arrived.

The gig was there in good time and she managed to ignore the thunderous look on Zack's face as she kissed him goodbye. It helped that the day was warm and sunny and as they bowled along the hedgerows the blackberries were just beginning to turn from red to black and the dog roses were bright with scarlet hips. In the fields the corn was tall and golden, reminding them that soon it would be time for harvest. Although they were both saddened by the thought that Sarah wouldn't be there to join in the festivities this year, neither of them mentioned it.

Emily's business at the bank didn't take long, although she was somewhat annoyed by the bank manager's attitude. He seemed to think she was incapable of managing her own affairs and when she pointed out that she had her daughter to help her, he made a disparaging remark to the effect that it was not the same as having a man to look after things.

'I thought that was your job, Mr Threadgold,' she said with some asperity.

'Only if I see you getting into difficulties,' he replied smoothly.

'Then I don't anticipate we shall trouble you overmuch, since I don't intend to get into difficulties,' she said with a lift of her chin. 'I am not an imbecile, Mr Threadgold.'

'Indeed, no, madam, I would never think that,'

he replied, holding open the door for them to leave.

'Odious man,' Emily said when he was barely out of earshot. 'Well, that's got that out of the way. Now, we'll go to The George and have some lunch and then we'll buy a few things. We can do that now we've got a little money of our own.'

'Do you think we should, Mama?' Bethany said anxiously. 'Zack wants to make some improvements, you know.'

'I know. But I think we should treat ourselves a little first, dear. We need new dresses.'

'But we're in mourning, Mama.'

'I know, but you know how Aunt Sarah hated black. She never wore it herself and she hated to see us in it.'

'That's true,' Bethany admitted.

'Therefore we'll have new dresses made, not in bright colours, that wouldn't be at all suitable, but in dove grey, lilac, pale mauve, those sort of colours. Yes?'

Bethany couldn't resist the idea.

'But first we must go to the jewellers. We had to sell nearly all my jewellery when we came to Essex so I think it's time I replaced some of it.'

'Oh, wouldn't that be a bit extravagant, Mama?' Bethany said, horrified.

Emily stopped in the middle of the pavement and put her hands on her plump little hips. 'I've been to the bank. I know how much money I've got and I've decided that I can spend a certain amount on what might be deemed extravagances. When that money is gone we'll go back to the frugal ways of Aunt Sarah's time — well, not quite so frugal as she was, perhaps, but well within our means. Have I made myself clear?'

'Abundantly so, Mama,' Bethany said, looking nervously at the passers-by who were obviously enjoying the scene.

Emily was not extravagant — she only bought herself one ring to replace several that had had to be sold when they left London — but she bought Bethany a double string of pearls and earrings to match. Then they went to The George and in a private room enjoyed a very good meal while they examined their purchases in great detail, Bethany admiring Emily's emerald ring — diamonds had proved a little too extravagant — and Emily helping Bethany to fasten the clasp of her pearls. After they had eaten they went to the dressmakers and ordered dresses, then on to buy shoes and hats. Emily also bought a hat for Zack from the men's department, which Bethany was sure he would never wear since he preferred a cap.

Then, in spite of Bethany's protests, Emily ordered new curtains and carpet for the dining room.

'Are you sure these are necessary, Mama?' Bethany whispered as Emily tried to choose between velvet and brocade for the curtains.

'Yes. It's time we brightened the place up a bit. Nothing has been replaced since long enough before we came to the inn and we've been here six years or more.' She looked up at the waiting assistant. 'Yes, I think the brocade, thank you.' She rummaged in the voluminous bag she had brought with her. 'These are the measurements of the windows and we shall need a matching pelmet.'

'And would Modom like us to come and hang the curtains when they are made?' the shop-walker intervened obsequiously.

Emily hesitated. 'Yes, I think that might be a very good idea.' She smiled at him in her old patronising way as he escorted them to the door of the recently opened department store when all the purchases were made.

'Well, I think that's enough for one day,' she said happily as they waited for the gig which had been ordered for four o'clock. 'All we have to do now is to wait for the carrier. The curtains and carpet should be delivered within a week and the dresses a week after.'

They piled their other purchases into the gig and set off for home.

'Have you enjoyed the day?' Emily asked.

'Oh, yes, Mama, indeed I have,' Bethany said with a contented sigh, 'It's such a long time since we haven't had to turn every penny over twice before we spend it.'

'Well, times are different now,' Emily said happily. 'Because I have the purse strings.'

It was probably a mistake to show off their purchases to Zack, but since he helped them down from the gig and carried the parcels in there was really no choice.

'I don't see what you wanted to waste money on two pairs of shoes each, since you hardly ever leave the premises,' he pointed out, his face black with anger. 'And six hats! What do you want six hats for?'

'Three each, to match the three dresses we've ordered,' Emily said excitedly, ignoring his black looks. 'But we haven't left you out, Zack. Look, we've bought you a hat, too.'

He looked with disgust at the black top hat she was holding. 'What do I want that for? I always wear a cap,' he snapped. 'It's a waste of money, I tell you. I'd rather have the water piped up from the well.'

'All in good time, my boy,' Emily said. She was obviously delighted with herself. 'First things first. And giving Bethany a treat and a day out after . . . ' she hesitated, ' . . . what happened to her, seemed the right thing to do.' She looked at Bethany's flushed cheeks and sparkling eyes. 'Yes, it was definitely the right thing.'

'That's only your opinion. I reckon the money could have been better spent on some of the things I've got planned, instead of that rubbish,' Zack said, still furious. 'You get a bit of money left to you and all you can think about is getting rid of it as fast as you can on a lot of folde-rols you'll never wear, instead of letting me handle it.'

'And why should I do that?' Emily asked, her eyes glittering dangerously.

'Because I'm a man and men know how to handle money better than women.' He gave another scathing look at the purchases laid out on the table. 'I'd never have spent money on such fripperies. I've got more sense.'

Emily drew herself up to her full height, which was almost to Zack's shoulder. 'I know exactly what I'm doing, Zachary,' she said and the use of his full name should have warned him that he was treading on dangerous ground. 'I allowed a specific sum to spend on Bethany and myself. Before we came here we were used to a life of comparative luxury and I for one have missed it. We've both worked hard over these past years so I decided we could both do with a little pampering. So that's what I've done and I don't regret it.' She gave him a look as scathing as the one he had given their purchases. 'You needn't worry, Zack, there will be money for some of the things you want to do. But it will be in my time, as and when I think fit. Travellers' Inn belongs to me now and what I say goes. You're not dealing with Aunt Sarah now.'

Bethany had never heard her mother use such an aggressive tone before; clearly she was still smarting from the bank manager's patronising manner.

Zack glared at her and opened his mouth to speak, then changed his mind and turned to go. 'Oh, by the way, Beth, Matthew called,' he said over his shoulder, as he reached the door. 'He'd heard you were under the weather and he called to see if you were better. I said you gone gallivanting off to Colchester with your mother so he knew there couldn't have been a lot wrong with you.' He slammed the door as he went out.

After he had gone Bethany kissed her mother and thanked her for her generosity, then took her purchases upstairs to her room. Zack's reaction had put a real damper on the day. She had known he wouldn't be pleased but she hadn't expected him to be quite so vehement in his displeasure. She took off her pearls and laid them carefully in their velvet box. It was fortunate he hadn't noticed them, she thought as she unclipped the earrings, or he might have dragged them off her neck and broken them in his temper. She wouldn't have put it past him.

Yet, in a way she didn't blame him. He worked hard and there were a good many things that could be done to make his life easier. And her mother had told him they would be done, later. All he had to do was to exercise a little patience. But Bethany knew Zack wasn't good at being patient. She frequently had bruises to remind her.

She sat down on the bed. Her stomach ached a little because she had been on her feet all day and she curled her arms protectively round it. Only there was nothing there to protect now, she reflected sadly. She wished she had been at home when Matthew called. It had been a legitimate call, on medical grounds, so there would have been nothing for Zack to object to and it would have been an opportunity to see and talk to him, an opportunity that came so rarely these days. She closed her eyes. Oh, how she missed him, her very, very good friend. All the pretty clothes and all the pearls in the world couldn't make up for the gap in her life that only he could fill.

That night, in bed, after she had submitted to Zack's demands, feigning an enthusiasm she was far from feeling, she thought it was safe to speak about her day out with her mother.

'I'm sure it will be all right, Zack,' she said, rubbing his shoulder the way she knew he liked. 'Mama had a long talk with the bank manager and I'm sure there will be plenty of money to do what you want here. You shouldn't begrudge her spending a little on luxuries. You simply can't imagine the life we led in London, Zack, and although she doesn't say much I know she misses it.'

'What she doesn't realise is that if she was to give me a free hand she could have a life like that again,' he said, his voice surly.

'Oh, I don't think so, Zack,' she said, a smile in her voice. 'We had a large house, with big rooms and high ceilings, beautiful furniture and servants to look after us . . . '

He leaned up on one elbow. 'Are you suggesting I couldn't get that for you again?' he said roughly.

'Well, I don't see how. I don't think there's *that* much money, Zack.'

He flung himself back on the pillow. 'I had plans,' he said, speaking as much to himself as to her. 'I thought when the old girl died she would leave it all to you. After all, it was you who brought the place back to life again.'

'But Mama was her niece. I was only her great niece. Of course it went to Mama. It was only right that it should. Anyway, what difference does it make?'

'It makes a world of difference. If it had all come to you there would have been nothing to stop me making all the alterations and improvements I wanted and then we could have sold it at a handsome profit.'

'That's ridiculous. Why on earth would you have wanted to sell the place?'

He stretched his arms luxuriously above his head in the darkness. 'Because, my sweet wife, then we could have emigrated to America.'

'America! But I wouldn't want to go to America, Zack,' she said, alarmed at the thought. 'And neither would Mama.'

'Oh, we wouldn't be taking the old girl. Just you and me.' He turned to face her. 'There are rich pickings to be had over there, Beth. Mountains made of gold, there for the taking. And with the sort of money we'd have in our pockets . . .'

'Oh, Zack, don't talk such nonsense. Anyway, even if it was mine, which it isn't, I wouldn't want to sell Travellers' Inn.'

'If it was yours you wouldn't have any choice, my love. Not if I wanted to sell it,' he said softly. 'Because you're my wife and by law, what's yours automatically becomes mine.'

She didn't answer. He was right, of course.

But Travellers' Inn had been left to Emily, not to her, so it was in safe hands, because Emily would never agree to sell it.

27

Bethany had guessed there would be trouble when the carrier's cart arrived with all Emily's purchases from Colchester, and she was right. Zack refused to help the carrier to unload and so it was left to Bethany to help. The boxes that contained the new dresses weren't heavy but it was a struggle to get the new carpet indoors and she knew it would be left to her and Emily to move furniture and lay the large turkey square, for Zack was still smarting and would have nothing to do with it.

It was even worse when two smartly dressed and well-manicured men arrived to hang curtains. Zack went about muttering about men who could only do women's work and didn't know what a real day's work was, but he had to eat his words when he saw them roll up their sleeves to shift all the furniture and lay the carpet as well.

He had the grace to offer them a mug of beer when they had finished, which they each drank at a single draught and held out their tankards for more, complimenting him on his excellent brew. In spite of himself, Zack was both flattered and impressed; he had obviously misjudged them and as the man of the house he magnanimously gave them sixpence each as they left.

'The new carpet certainly gives the place a

touch of class,' Emily said, as she and Bethany stood at the door of the dining room admiring it. 'I think perhaps we should turn our attention to the bedrooms next. They could all do with smartening up.'

'You promised Zack you would have the water piped up from the well, Mama,' Bethany reminded her. She was still sore from a punch in the ribs he had given her the previous night.

'And there'll be worse if you don't persuade the old girl to get a move on. I'm fed up with carrying water up in a bucket,' he'd said.

'You only carry the water for the brew house,' she'd retorted. 'I fetch the water for the house, myself.' She had begun to do that when he started to agitate for a tap in the yard because she knew that the more he agitated the longer Emily would make him wait. It was a cat-and-mouse game between them and Bethany sometimes felt like a piece of cheese in the middle.

Emily pinched her lip. 'I'll think about it after harvest,' she said. 'Farmer Isaac has asked me if I'll make all the apple pies again this year.' She leaned towards Bethany. 'He says my pastry is so much nicer than his housekeeper's. He's bringing me the apples when he comes to the snug tomorrow evening.'

Bethany smiled at her. 'I think he's a little sweet on you, Mama,' she said.

'Oh, go on.' Emily blushed and gave her a little push. 'What nonsense. A woman of my age! What must you be thinking!'

'I'm thinking he probably only needs a little encouragement.'

'Well, he's not going to get it from me!' Emily bridled. 'The very idea. It's not the done thing at all for the woman to make the running.'

'It is if she likes him and the man is very shy,' Bethany said, teasing her. 'And you do like him, don't you, Mama?'

'Yes, I think he's a very nice man,' Emily said primly. 'And now it's time to stop talking nonsense and do some work. I can smell my cakes are ready to come out of the oven.' She went out into the passage and paused, rubbing her hand over her chin thoughtfully. 'We could really do with a new runner for this passage and a new stair carpet. But the walls would need to be redecorated beforehand, wouldn't they.' She sighed. 'Everywhere needs money spending on it because it's looking rather shabby. In fact, it's difficult to know where to start first.'

Bethany closed her eyes and prayed that it would be the piped water. Yet she knew Zack well enough to realise that once he had piped water he would begin to agitate for something else. Gradually he would get his own way and make all the improvements he had in mind, but then what? Would he manage to persuade Emily to sell Travellers' Inn? And even worse than that, how far would he go in forcing her, Bethany, to support him against Emily in his madcap scheme to emigrate to America?

★ ★ ★

339

The good weather held until the harvest was in and the Harvest Home went with a swing, due in a large part to the particularly potent beer Zack had brewed for the occasion.

Emily decided to wear her new dove-grey silk and insisted that Bethany wore the pale-green checked taffeta, bought at the same time.

'After all,' she remarked. 'Where else do we go these days to dress up? It's not like it was when we were in London. We were always calling on people, going to theatres and dinner parties.' She gave a deep sigh. 'Here, we're always at work.'

'Do you miss London very much, Mama?' Bethany asked gently.

Emily thought for several minutes, then she said, her face breaking into a smile, 'Do you know, I don't believe I do, Bethany. I suppose it's because I rarely have time to think about it, I'm always so busy these days.' She laughed. 'I used to think I was busy when we lived in London, but I can see now that what I was really doing was finding things to do to fill up my time. Here, I feel that what I do really matters. I feel useful. It's a good feeling.'

Bethany nodded. What her mother said was true. There was a great sense of satisfaction in knowing that when visitors left Travellers' Inn she and her mother had ensured that they had been well fed and were refreshed after a good night's sleep. And it was always gratifying when visitors returned again and again. Like Emily, Bethany realised that she wouldn't want to go back to her old life.

'Well, go on,' Emily said, breaking into her

thoughts. 'Go and do as I say, put on the green taffeta or we'll never be ready in time.'

Bethany smiled to herself as she dressed. Since there was no-one to help with buttons and hooks these days Emily had sensibly insisted that they bought dresses fastened at the front and they had both adopted hair styles that were easily managed. As Bethany did up the little buttons down the front of her bodice she reflected that it really did feel good to be wearing a dress that rustled as she moved, making her feel almost attractive. In that she did herself an injustice. The pale-green taffeta suited her coppery curls and her clear, creamy skin. Although she would never be beautiful, with her regular features and wide, smiling mouth she was nevertheless strikingly attractive. It was only in her grey eyes, which had once held a mischievous twinkle, that there was an air of sadness; these days her laughter rarely reached her eyes. But only those who were close to her, those who really cared for her, saw this.

It didn't escape Matthew's notice.

'You must have one dance with me, Bethany,' he said, leading her on to the floor, already crowded with dancers in various stages of inebriation.

She smiled at him. 'Of course, Matthew. It might look a little odd if I didn't dance at least once with my very good doctor friend.'

'Indeed, it might.' He looked down into her eyes. 'And it would be even more odd if I missed the chance to hold you in my arms,' he whispered.

They said nothing more, savouring the opportunity to touch, to hold, although Bethany frequently cast a glance over to the corner where Zack was embroiled in a good-humoured argument with several other, equally tipsy cronies. Soon, she feared, the argument would turn nasty and into a brawl. It happened time after time late at night in the bar at Travellers' Inn, disturbing both her and Emily as they tried to sleep upstairs.

But for now she gave herself up to feeling Matthew's arm round her and his hand in hers, to feel the way their steps matched and their bodies swayed together — but not too closely — to catch the distinctive smell of the special soap he always used for his hands because he had the idea that disease could be carried on hands that were not clean. She felt his hand tighten on hers and returned the pressure gently. She knew as well as he did that their love could never find fulfilment but it was so hard to regard him as nothing more than a friend and although she had once urged him to re-marry, what she dreaded more than anything was that one day he would come to tell her he had found himself a wife.

They were in the shadows as the music ended and for one brief second he held her very close and dropped a kiss, as swift and as light as a butterfly's wing, on her hair. Then he released her and took her back to her seat beside Emily, who was sitting with Reuben. Bethany had noticed before how he seemed to have shrunk since the death of his old friend; his smock hung so loosely on his shoulders that he had to roll the sleeves back and it reached almost to his ankles, making it look as if it was several sizes too big.

Matthew fetched mugs of beer for them all and sat down with them.

'And how are you, Reuben?' he asked, placing his beer in front of him.

'Fair t' middlin',' Reuben replied, taking a long draught and then wiping his mouth with the back of his hand. 'Mustn't grumble.'

'We don't see you as much nowadays, Reuben,' Emily said.

'No, well, t'ain't the same up there now that owd besom's gone,' he said, his tone truculent to hide the hurt. 'I ain't got nobody t'argify with.'

'You could come and argue with me,' Emily said with a smile.

He looked her up and down. 'I couldn't argify with the likes o' you, not like I used to argify with *her*. Her an' me near as don't matter grew up together.'

'I can't see what difference that makes,' Bethany said.

He stared at her. 'No. Well, you wouldn't,' he said enigmatically.

'What's that supposed to mean?' she asked, raising her eyebrows.

'Nothin'.' He sniffed and took another draught of his beer.

Emily took several sips of her beer, then said, 'Well, my pile of kindling wood is getting well down so I'd be glad if you could come and chop some more for me.'

'Zack can do that,' he said stubbornly.

'Zack's busy,' Bethany said.

'So'm I.'

'No, you're not,' Emily said, rounding on him. 'I'll wager you spend all your time sitting in the chair in your cottage feeling sorry for yourself.'

'No, I don't.'

'Yes, you do. Look at you. You don't even feed yourself properly.'

'I don't git hungry.'

'Well, you must eat.'

'Don't hev to. Not if I don't want to.'

'Yes, you do.'

'No, I don't.'

'You're getting as thin as a rake, you silly old fool. Why don't you come up and have your dinner with us like you used to?'

' 'Cause t'aint' the same.'

'It's not the same for us, either, remember,' Emily chided him. 'But we're missing two, since you don't come now.'

'I'll think about it.' He dragged out his old pipe and began tamping it down.

'And don't say you haven't got anybody to argue with,' Bethany said, looking at Matthew. They both broke into laughter.

'No, indeed,' Matthew said. 'It was just like old times to hear the way you and Emily have been going at each other.'

Reuben shrugged uncomfortably. 'Well, I ain't gonna be told what to do.'

'Of course not, Reuben,' Matthew said, agreeing with him. 'But I suggest a compromise. You help Emily out by chopping some sticks for her and then perhaps she'll give you a spot of dinner. How does that sound?'

'I'll see.' The old man refused to be drawn further. In any case, speech was becoming difficult because of the noise coming from the corner where Zack and his cronies were playing an increasingly aggressive game of dominoes.

Suddenly, the table was upended and all the dominoes cascaded on to the floor as somebody, it was impossible to see who, struck the first blow. After that it was a free-for-all. Women screamed, grabbed their children and ran outside as benches were hurled and bales of straw thrown. The beer barrel was upended and the last dregs dribbled out over the floor, crockery was smashed and what little food was left was trampled underfoot.

Farmer Isaac jumped up on to a table and called for calm. In return, a stool was hurled that missed him and knocked down one of the oil lamps fixed round the walls. There was a gasp and everyone backed away as a tongue of flaming oil shot across the sawdust-strewn floor and caught the nearest hay bale. Several men rushed forward and tried to trample the flames with their heavy boots but this made the sparks fly in all directions and as fast as they put them out in one place they had spread to another. It was all happening with frightening speed, often fanned rather than extinguished by befuddled men, who tried ineffectually to beat the fire out with whatever came to hand, which was mostly their own coats and hats.

The women clutched their children to them

and ran outside, where they watched, mesmerised, as the flames and sparks rose higher and higher in the moonlight. Luckily, someone had the presence of mind to call for help to get the horses out of the stables and lead them to safety in case the fire spread. Then a woman's voice was heard.

'The tide's full in. Git buckets, everybody. Let's make a chain.'

In a matter of moments, buckets had appeared as if from nowhere and a chain of men, women and the older children were passing buckets full of water up from the river for the men to douse the fire with, whilst Granny Simmons took the little ones up to the farmhouse for bread and milk.

Bethany and Emily joined the chain with the rest. Emily found herself halfway down the field with her foot in a cow pat, whilst Bethany's dress was torn to ribbons by brambles because she was standing in a gap in the hedge.

'Dunno if we're doin' much good,' the woman next to Bethany said breathlessly as she handed on yet another bucket. 'Thass loike tryin' t'empty a well with a teaspoon.'

'I think they must be concentrating on damping down everything nearby,' Bethany said, equally breathlessly. 'I don't think there's much chance of saving the barn itself.'

'As long as the fire don't git to the house,' the woman panted. 'That belonged to Farmer Isaac's great-grandfather an' 'e set great store by lookin' after 'is great-granddad's property.'

'Oh, I'm sure there's no danger of that,'

Bethany said. 'It's a good distance away from the barn.'

'What a way to end the Harvest Home,' the woman on the other side of Bethany remarked. 'Two minutes more and I'd have missed all this. I was just goin' to take my little 'uns home to bed. Thass well past their bedtime.'

The chain went on, seemingly for hours; full buckets passed up from the river, empty buckets passed down to it. Bethany felt as if her arms were being torn from their sockets and she gave a fleeting thought to her mother, further down the line, who had never so much as carried a cup of water up from the well before this.

At last, word came from the top of the chain to stop.

'We can't do any more,' Farmer Isaac's voice was heard to say. 'The barn's wrecked but we'll leave a couple of men here to keep watch in case it flares up again; everybody else is welcome to come to the farmhouse for bread and cheese and pickles.'

It was a sorry crowd that straggled into the kitchen at Marsh Farm. Everyone was exhausted; men with scorched and fire-blackened faces and clothes, women with their best dresses soaked in river water and bespattered with filthy mud. The two men at the river end of the chain were caked in mud up to their knees.

'Good thing Farmer called a halt when 'e did,' one of them said. 'That woulda bin too dangerous for us to carry on much longer takin' water from the river. The tide's well on the ebb now so that mud's gettin' treacherous.'

Isaac rapped the table with a wooden spoon. His face was black and his beard and hair were badly singed. 'I want to thank you all for what you've done tonight,' he said, with a break in his voice. 'I've lost my barn, which is bad enough, I know, but we've managed to save all the other buildings and the stacks, so it could have been worse. And thank God no lives were lost. Granny Simmons looked after the little ones and as far as I know nobody's missing.'

'Where's owd Reuben?' somebody called.

''E's all right. Ted Child's took 'im 'ome when he went to fetch more buckets,' someone else shouted.

'Ah, thass all right, then.'

'Now,' Isaac said, 'As I told you, I can offer you bread and cheese and pickles, but not a lot else. I fear it may be a bit like sharing the loaves and fishes at the feeding of the five thousand, but you're more than welcome to what there is.'

Several people murmured that they had eaten so much at the Harvest Home that they couldn't touch a morsel; others said the shock of the fire had taken away any appetite they might have had, but there were others who made no such excuses and soon there weren't even enough crumbs left to tempt a mouse from a hole in the skirting boards.

Then, in weary and dejected twos and threes they left, the holiday spirit of the Harvest Home killed by the fire that had ended it. Soon only Bethany and Emily were left with Isaac and a little later Matthew appeared. He had spent most of his time in the dairy attending to burns and other minor injuries.

He looked at the three tired faces at the table. 'Where's Zack?' he asked.

They looked at him and then at each other. 'I don't know. Hasn't he been with you?' Bethany said. 'I assumed that's where he was.'

'No.' Matthew shook his head. 'I haven't seen him since the fire started.'

'No, I can't say I have, either,' Isaac said, frowning. 'Although, come to think of it, I don't know if it was him I saw just before the roof collapsed . . . '

Emily put her hand to her mouth and glanced at Bethany, who had gone pale but said nothing.

'Come on, Matt. I'll get a lantern.' Isaac got to his feet, shedding his weariness. 'We'd better go and take a look.'

After they had gone Emily and Bethany sat either side of the table without speaking. They both knew that, depending on what Isaac and Matthew found in the yard, from now on their lives could be very different.

28

Bethany sat opposite her mother, waiting, hardly daring to allow the thoughts that kept trying to push their way into her mind to surface. She twisted the heavy gold wedding ring round and round on her finger. Zack was her husband; she should be praying for his safety. But she couldn't. All she could think was that there would be no more talk of making improvements to Travellers' Inn so that it could be sold, no more talk of gold digging in America; no obstacle to marrying Matthew if Zack were to be . . . She shook her head, determinedly pushing such disloyal thoughts away. Of course she wanted Zack to be safe. What would she and her mother do if he wasn't there? He was the prop and mainstay of Travellers' Inn. How could they possibly manage without him, two women on their own? And she was still fond of him in spite of the way he treated her when he was drunk. He didn't beat her when he was sober, at least, not often and he could be very kind and loving. They had a good life together, in spite of everything. They did; they really did.

Muddled and confused after the evening's events, she put her head in her hands and wept.

Emily sat watching her daughter. She knew how Bethany felt about Matthew; she knew, too, that Zack was sometimes cruel to her. But that was commonplace. Husbands did beat their wives. Seymour had beaten her on occasion and it had been almost worth it for his abject tenderness later. It was how she had extracted her most expensive jewellery out of him. And Zack had his good points.

In fact, Emily was very fond of Zack. She liked the way he flirted with her, knowing just how far to go without giving offence. He was hard-working, too, and could turn his hand to almost anything, although he was becoming a little tiresome over the business of improvements to the inn. Emily liked Travellers' Inn as it was; she saw no need for all these new-fangled ideas. And as for having the new gas laid on ... There was no question of that! It wasn't safe. They'd all be poisoned by the noxious fumes. Or burnt in their beds. She shuddered. The events tonight had convinced her even further of the horrors of fire.

She leaned over and put her hand on Bethany's arm. 'Shall we have a cup of tea while we wait, dear?'

Bethany lifted a tear-stained face and nodded. She pulled out her handkerchief and blew her nose. 'Yes, that would be nice, Mama.' She looked up at the grandfather clock, ticking in the corner. 'How long have they been gone?'

'Twenty minutes or so, I think. I didn't really look at the clock before they went.'

'Surely they should have found him by now, Mama.'

'These things take time.' Emily tried to sound

matter-of-fact. 'Ah, it sounds as if they're coming now.'

They both held their breath and turned towards the door.

★ ★ ★

Whilst the two women waited, Isaac and Matthew went to look for Zack. As they stepped out into the yard, the air was still filled with the acrid smell of burning and the pall of smoke that hung over everything obscured the light of the full, harvest moon.

They went over to the barn. Blackened beams stood drunkenly propped against each other, outlining the skeleton of the barn and inside the smouldering remains a few embers were still glowing red.

Matthew heard an involuntary gulp, almost a sob, from Isaac at the sight and he laid a sympathetic hand briefly on his friend's shoulder.

'A bad business, this, Mr Isaac,' said one of the two men who had been left to rake over the embers to prevent the fire flaring up again, shaking his head sadly.

'Aye, that it is, Sir,' the other agreed.

'Yes, it's a sad night's work,' Isaac said. 'I never thought to see my great-grandfather's old barn reduced to this.' He pulled himself together with an effort. 'But have either of you seen anything of Zack? He hasn't been into the house and we don't know where he is.'

'No, Sir, ain't seen nothin' of 'im,' one said.

'No, we aint seen nothin' of 'im since . . . well, I dunno . . . ' the other said, shaking his head.

'Well, keep an eye open as you rake over the . . . ' he stopped, realising the dreadful implications of what he was about to say. 'Just keep an eye open,' he muttered. 'Matt and I'll go and have a look round.'

'Yes,' Matthew said. 'It's quite possible he could be lying hurt somewhere near.'

Isaac led the way, holding the lantern high and Matthew followed. They searched all round by the stacks and the pig pens, which were mercifully far enough away to remain untouched by the fire, then they went to the stables, empty now that the horses had been moved to safety. It was as they were leaving, the stalls still smelling strongly of horse but eerily quiet and ghostly in the lamplight, that Matthew caught Isaac's arm.

'Listen. Can you hear anything?'

Isaac stood still. An owl hooted and there was the rustle of rats in the straw but other than that all was silent. Then, from the tack room beyond, came the unmistakable sound of snoring.

The two men exchanged glances and went to the door at the end of the stables. Isaac held the lantern high and saw Zack, spread-eagled among years of accumulated rubbish, an empty tankard still clasped in his hand. His snores reverberated round the room, so loud that they jangled the bells of an old harness hung from the ceiling above him.

They went over to him and taking an arm each

dragged him to his feet.

'Well, at least we haven't had to dig him out from under the cinders,' Isaac said with black humour. He looked at Matthew and they both began to laugh uncontrollably, the tensions of the night finally released.

Zack looked owlishly from one to the other. 'Wassamatter? Wassofunny? What you doin' here? Where am I?'

'You're in the tack room.' Isaac told him.

He rolled his head from side to side. 'Well, I dunno how I got here. I only came outside for a leak, then I seem to remember I couldn't find the door to get back in. Don't remember anything else. Must've fallen asleep.' His head lolled forward again.

'Oh, come on, Isaac. Let's dunk him in the water butt, that'll sober him up,' Matthew said impatiently as they dragged him outside.

'No water in it. It was emptied to put out the fire,' Isaac reminded him. 'And so was the cattle trough and the pig trough.'

Zack's head rolled up. 'Fire? What fire?' He stared as they reached the yard. 'Where's the barn? What's happened to the barn?'

'That's where the fire was,' Isaac told him. 'We've spent half the night putting it out.'

'Well, I'm buggered,' Zack stared at the heap of smouldering ashes where the barn once stood, the sight sobering him up more quickly than anything else could have done. 'And to think I never knew a thing about it.'

★ ★ ★

It was a long time before Zack lived down the night of the fire.

'Can anybody smell burnin'?' became a common phrase in the bar, accompanied by loud sniffs.

'Ask Zack. If 'e ain't asleep,' was inevitably the answer.

As for Bethany her relief at seeing Zack safe and sound was tempered by the guilty knowledge that for a split second, when he appeared in the doorway propped between Matthew and Isaac, her reaction had been one of dismay and disappointment. But this was a secret she kept locked in her heart and admitted to nobody.

One good thing that came out of it all as far as Zack was concerned was that soon after the fire Emily arranged for the water to be piped up from the well at Travellers' Inn to a pump in the yard, although she was forever complaining about how much it had cost. But even she had to admit that it made things much easier all round, since water for the brew house and the stables only had to be carried a matter of yards and it was handy for the house as well.

'I don't know why we didn't do it years ago,' she remarked, although in fact it made little difference to her since, apart from the night of the fire, she had never handled a bucket of water in her life.

'I did keep asking,' Zack reminded her. He knew that his disappearance on the night of the fire had frightened both women, making them realise just how much they depended on him.

355

This was evident in Bethany's extra loving behaviour in bed and the fact that Emily cooked his favourite meals. But cooking his favourite meals was not enough; there were more things he wanted to do to the inn before he could begin to persuade Emily to sell up. He was determined to make capital out of the situation.

'There's the business of having gas laid on,' he said. 'I've seen how you strain your eyes with your embroidery, Em. Look at you, needing spectacles when you sew. It doesn't do you any good, you know, sitting at the table to get the best light from the oil lamp. With the new gas you probably wouldn't need to wear those spectacles and you could sit anywhere in the room — in a comfortable armchair, even.'

'I don't want to sit in a comfortable armchair to do my sewing, Zack,' Emily said, looking at him over the gold-rimmed spectacles in question. 'I need to sit at the table. And I don't trust this new gas. I don't think it's safe. I'm told it's poisonous, anyway.'

'Only when it leaks,' Bethany said. 'It's not poisonous when it's lit.' She spent her time desperately trying to balance keeping Zack happy with not allowing too many of his schemes to come to fruition.

'Well, I'm not paying for it and that's that,' Emily said firmly.

'Then perhaps you'll pay for a new roof for the stables and the brew house,' he said. 'That won't cost you as much.'

Emily cut off a length of thread and rethreaded her needle. 'You're quite determined to part me from my money, aren't you, Zack?' she said with a smile.

He grinned back at her. 'Whatever makes you think that, Em!'

'Oh, just the odd word you throw in here and there. But let me tell you this, it's my money and I'll spend it how I choose and not how you tell me I should, Zachary Brown.' She was still smiling at him but there was a warning behind her words.

Bethany said nothing. She wondered what her mother would say if she had any idea of Zack's plans for the future.

$$\star \quad \star \quad \star$$

Throughout the winter Isaac and Matthew took supper together in the snug at least once a week and sometimes twice.

'Are you thinking of rebuilding the barn?' Matthew asked as they sat enjoying Emily's delicious steak and kidney pudding one evening. He thought enough time had elapsed for Isaac to have made his mind up what he would do.

'I should like to,' Isaac replied, chasing a piece of kidney round his plate with his fork. 'But I really don't know if it's worth it. Times are not easy in farming, there's not the money in it there used to be and I've still got the small barn near the house, so I'm still undecided as to what to do, to tell you the truth.'

'Pity. It was a lovely old barn.'

'Yes, as you know, my great-grandfather had it built.'

'Well, then . . . '

Isaac smiled. 'If I had it rebuilt it wouldn't be the same, would it? It wouldn't be the barn my great-grandfather built.'

'No, I suppose not.'

They fell silent as Emily came in to take away their plates and replace them with dishes of steaming lemon pudding.

'My, that looks delicious, Mrs Emily,' Isaac said admiringly.

She smiled, obviously pleased. 'It's a new recipe. It seem's to have turned out rather well.'

'The proof of the pudding . . . ' Matthew said, digging his spoon in. 'Yes, quite delicious.'

When Emily had left the room Matthew said with a wink, 'She'd make somebody a splendid wife, Isaac.'

Isaac nodded soberly. 'You're right, Matthew, but I'm afraid, in spite of all your hints and innuendos, that it won't be me.'

'Why not, my friend?' Matthew asked in surprise. 'You two are ideally suited.'

'I would have thought it obvious, Matt,' he said, looking down at his plate. 'I've got an ailing farm and she's inherited a thriving inn.' He looked up at Matthew. 'Under those circumstances, how could I propose marriage? Whatever my feelings it would look as if I was only after her money.'

Matthew nodded. 'I see your dilemma.'

Isaac gave a crooked smile. 'I guess we're both in the same boat to a certain extent, Matt.'

'What do you mean?'

'Oh, come on, my friend. I can see as far

through a brick wall as most people. You and Bethany . . . '

Matthew closed his eyes briefly. 'Oh, God, is it that obvious?'

'Only to those who know you well. And I count myself privileged to be one of that number because I know how few there are.' He smiled. 'Your secret is safe with me, Matt, as I know mine is with you.' He gathered up his mug and Matthew's. 'I think all these unaccustomed confidences call for more beer. I'll go to the bar and fetch it.'

While he was gone Matthew mulled over his words. It was true what Isaac had said, he had very few real friends, which was why he had always valued his friendship with the women at Travellers' Inn so highly. The fact that this had ripened into love for Bethany was, he supposed, as inevitable as it was doomed to remain unfulfilled. But at least he had once known the joys of married life, which was something his shy bachelor friend had never experienced.

★ ★ ★

The inn was not very busy over the winter. People didn't travel by coach on roads that were muddy and rutted or slippery with ice unless they were forced to. And now that the new railway track was open many preferred to take their lives in their hands and travel by train between Colchester and Ipswich, although the breakneck speeds, the noise and the filthy smoke from the engines still daunted all but the intrepid.

However, since the railway didn't yet reach Harwich, although there was little doubt that it eventually would, Zack began to agitate for Emily to buy a smart gig.

'Oh, Zack, whatever next!' she said with a laugh when he spoke of it over their midday snack. 'What do we need a gig for?' She put a basket of freshly made rolls on the table, together with cheese and pickles.

He helped himself to a generous helping of everything. 'Hasn't Beth told you my idea?' he cocked a questioning eye at Bethany.

Bethany shook her head. 'I didn't think you were serious,' she said with a shrug, which was not quite true.

'Of course I'm serious,' he said angrily. 'I want to turn this place into a thriving concern, so that when we sell it . . . '

'Sell it? I'm never going to sell Travellers' Inn!' Emily said furiously. 'And I can't think what's ever given you the idea that I might.'

He held up his hand. 'No, of course not, Em. I didn't mean *when*, I meant *if* for any reason we had to sell it we could do so as a profitable venture.'

She shook her head. 'I can't think of any reason why I should want to sell my home, Zack. I love it here and so does Bethany, don't you, dear?'

'Yes, I do. I should hate to move from here,' Bethany said.

Zack took a deep breath, keeping his temper

with difficulty. 'Well, yes, so should I,' he said. 'That goes without saying. But we could make things better for ourselves, couldn't we.' He leaned forward. 'If we had a smart gig, we could run it between here and Manningtree station, fetch the passengers on their way to Harwich, feed them and give them a bed for the night ready to pick up the Harwich coach in the morning. And in reverse, we could take passengers from Harwich, who had stayed the night, to catch their train in the morning.' He leaned back. 'But we'd need better transport than we've got at the moment, you must agree. Smart folks from Colchester and London would look down their noses if I rolled up with old Peggy and the dog cart, wouldn't they.'

Emily pinched her lip and nodded. 'Yes, I guess you're right.' She nodded again. 'I must say it seems like a good idea, on the face of it. But of course, they'll extend the railway to Harwich eventually, then what you're suggesting won't be needed.'

He waved his arm deprecatingly. 'Oh, that won't be for a year or two. They haven't decided exactly where the line will go yet and anyway they haven't got the money. We could make ourselves a tidy little packet, Em, but we need to get in first, before Mistley Thorne and the other places get the idea.'

'What do you think, Bethany?' Emily asked, still undecided. 'Do you think it's a good idea?'

'Yes, but we should have to employ extra help for Zack. He couldn't do everything himself,' Bethany said. 'And we could do with extra help in the house, too. I've been thinking that for some time.'

'Employ too many people and you'll eat up all the profits,' Zack warned tetchily, glaring at her.

Bethany said nothing. She had been careful not to disagree with Zack, but she knew that his long-term plan to persuade kind-hearted Emily to sell up would be thwarted if there were employees to consider.

29

As spring came and once again people began to travel both Emily and Bethany had to admit that Zack had been right. Knowing that they would be met at the railway station in the new gig, emblazoned with the name 'Travellers' Inn' in gold lettering and drawn by a friendly mare with the unlikely name of Clara, passengers from London or Ipswich and bound for Harwich were only too happy to take the train as far as Manningtree and then be whisked off to spend the night in the comfort of Travellers' Inn before finishing the journey by coach.

But, as Bethany had predicted, although the inn prospered with the increased trade, it inevitably made a great deal more work for them all. With some reluctance, Zack allowed Emily to employ a man from the village to do the rough outside work and to look after the vegetable garden, although Reuben was still always happy to chop sticks and do some of the lighter jobs. But Zack refused to relinquish working in the bar, saying he enjoyed the company of other men in the evenings, since he lived in a house of women. Bethany and her mother could hardly argue with that.

Zack also refused to let anyone else meet the train. It appealed to his not inconsiderable vanity to roll up at the station in the brightly painted gig wearing his Sunday suit, the well-groomed and well-behaved mare waiting patiently as he stowed the luggage and handed up the passengers, palming the tips into his pocket with just the right amount of deference. This money was kept in a tin in the brew house, where nobody knew about it so no questions were asked. It wasn't that he thought he would need it, not once he had managed to persuade Emily to sell the inn, but his early life had taught him that it was always as well to have a little strictly personal money to fall back on in case of need and it was a habit he found hard to break.

As well as the scrubbing and laundry women who always came twice a week, Emily employed a willing young girl to help in the house wherever she was needed. The eldest of a large family, Tansy was grateful to escape the drudgery of looking after eight younger brothers and sisters. It made no difference to her whether she was emptying slops, helping Bethany to keep the guest rooms clean, polishing silver, washing dishes or preparing vegetables for Emily, she was happy and she sang as she worked. And she idolised Zack, who teased her and called her a baggage.

One sunny afternoon in late June, Bethany sat on the bench outside the shed shelling peas, remembering that this was just what Aunt Sarah used to do. It was a fairly mindless task and she was grateful for a few minutes of peace and quiet as she worked, savouring the sunshine and watching the butterflies flitting among the flowers in Aunt Sarah's border. The last of the polyanthus and primroses were fading now and the lacy lady's needlework would soon take their place with pink and white phlox standing sentinel behind them. While her flower border flourished there would always be a reminder of Aunt Sarah, Bethany mused. It hardly seemed possible that she had been dead almost a year — she often felt so close that Bethany fancied she could almost talk to her.

She let her hands rest in her lap for a moment. It was soon after Aunt Sarah died that she lost the baby, too. Tears filled her eyes and she dashed them away, wondering if the kick Zack had given her that night had done more damage than she realised, because she had not yet conceived again. Maybe Zack wondered this, too, because he had stopped accusing her of failing to give him a son.

A little smile played round her mouth. In spite of all that had happened she and Zack were not unhappy together now. The ache for Matthew would always be with her, she accepted that. By mutual consent they didn't often meet, although she knew he came to the snug for a meal at least once every week and she took comfort in the knowledge that he was never far away. Zack had never said anything more about emigrating to America, for which she was profoundly thankful. He was working hard to make the inn successful, with ambitious — sometimes harebrained — schemes for its improvement and often accused Emily — sometimes to her face — of being tight-fisted when she wouldn't give him the money to have them carried out.

'It's simply not necessary to have the whole of

the yard roofed in,' she said when he put forward this latest idea.

'But it would mean that passengers would always alight under cover,' he argued. 'They wouldn't get wet when it rained.'

'They don't get wet now. It's only a step into the house and we have umbrellas,' she said. 'And it doesn't rain all the time. No, Zack. I will not countenance spending the enormous amount of money it would cost for something I don't consider necessary.'

'Well, what about extending the dining room? It's a bit small for the number of guests we have now.'

She turned the corners of her mouth down thoughtfully. 'Mm,' she said, nodding. 'That might not be such a bad idea. We used to call it the little parlour and it's true it's a bit cramped when we have several visitors.'

He rubbed his hands together. 'I'll go and see the builder tomorrow.'

'Not so fast, Zack,' she said, holding up her hand. 'We need to give it a bit more thought before we commit ourselves.'

'And we all know what that means,' he said with a sigh, raising his eyes to the ceiling.

'Oh, Zack, don't be so impatient,' Bethany said mildly, smiling at him.

'*Impatient!* I don't know how you can say that, Bethany. Every time I suggest something should be done your mother says, 'We'll have to give it a bit more thought. We'll have to think about it.' And that's all she ever does — think about it.' His face darkened. 'But, trust you to side with your mother instead of your husband.'

'That's not fair, Zack. I don't always side with Mama. I was very anxious to get the water piped . . . '

'That was ages ago,' he interrupted. 'And what have we done since to improve the place? Bugger all.'

'Please mind your language, Zack,' Emily said tartly. 'And you're being quite unreasonable in saying I've done nothing to improve the place. I've had the guest rooms redecorated. I've bought new curtains and carpets.'

'That was all to smarten up inside the house,' he argued. 'What about making my life easier?'

'It's important the place doesn't look shabby. Anyway, you've got the new gig you wanted so much.'

'Which was a very good idea indeed, wasn't it, Mama.' Bethany put in eagerly, trying to redress the balance of loyalties.

'Yes, I agree. It was,' Emily said. 'But I don't see you've got cause to complain, Zack. Money doesn't grow on trees, remember. And Aunt Sarah's money won't last for ever if we start throwing it around on unnecessary things.'

Suddenly, he smiled at her disarmingly. 'No, you're quite right, Em. I'm sorry. I agree, I do let my ambitions run away with me sometimes. It's just that I can see what could be done to make the place so much better and I can't wait to see it happen.'

'We can make it better without changing the atmosphere of the place. We don't want to get *too* commercial,' Emily reminded him gently, glad he was coming round to her point of view. 'And we don't want to be in too much of a hurry, either.'

He looked at the new pocket watch she had bought him and got up from the table. 'I must go and meet the three-thirty train,' he said. As he passed Emily he dropped a kiss on the top of her head. 'Wise woman. As always,' he said, winking at Bethany.

After he had gone Emily set Tansy to prepare vegetables whilst she made pastry and Bethany went to lay up tables in the dining room.

It was true, Bethany mused as she edged her way between the two long tables, the dining room was getting too small for the number of guests. She pushed a table nearer to the wall to make a little extra space and spread the starched damask tablecloths before laying out glasses and silver. As she worked she thought about the conversation that had just taken place. Zack and Emily often had these arguments and it was sometimes difficult to keep the peace between them. She knew that it was never a good idea to side with Emily, even if she agreed with her, but at times she felt she had to speak her mind, even though she knew she would suffer for it later. There was also the uncertainty of Zack's motives. There had been no mention recently of gold-digging in America, but she knew Zack well enough to realise that this didn't mean he had given up the idea. Sometimes, she felt she was living on the edge of a volcano, never knowing whether it was sleeping or about to erupt.

She heard the noise of the gig returning and

looked out of the window to see six young men spilling out of it into the yard. Her heart sank. It had happened before, several times; a group of rich young men from London with nothing better to do would decide to go across to the continent for a few days and a good time; a good time which often started at Travellers' Inn with drinking and roistering well into the small hours. Zack welcomed them, said it was good for trade, but both Bethany and Emily hated the noise, the drunken behaviour and the mess that had to be cleaned up after they left. It was not at all unusual for food to be flung across the dining room or trodden into the carpet and wine flowed freely, almost as much of it on to the floor as down throats. Added to that there were always breakages — glasses, plates, chairs and benches — not to mention the disruption to any other guests that might be staying. Fortunately, there were no other guests today.

Bethany glued a smile on to her face and went to greet them and show them to their rooms, three to a room to conserve more money for drinking. Not that they would spend much time in bed; they would be drinking well into the night and then they would have to be up at dawn in order to reach Harwich in time to catch the packet.

She was relieved to find her misgivings unfounded. They appeared to be a relatively well-behaved group. Nobody tried to pinch her bottom when she served the meal in the dining room and several of them sent compliments to the cook on her delicious roast beef and succulent plum pie. They also waited until she was out of the room before telling bawdy stories and risqué jokes, which wasn't always the case. When this happened she feigned not to understand — sometimes she didn't even have to pretend.

'They seem to be a very well-mannered group, tonight,' she said as she took a stack of empty plates back to the kitchen, where Tansy was already busy washing up.

'Oh, thank heaven for that,' Emily said. 'I'm so tired. I can do with a good night's sleep. Cooking for these parties wearies me far more than it ever used to.'

Bethany glanced at her mother. Emily was rather flushed and her hair was sticking out untidily from under her cap.

'Why don't you go to bed, Mama? Tansy and I can manage here. We've only got to clear up once the men have gone to bed.'

'Or to the bar, more likely,' Emily said sagely. 'But I would be glad to go up, if you don't mind, dear.'

It was not like Emily to go to bed before everything was done and the breakfast table laid for the morning, but cooking for six hungry young men was hard work and Bethany noticed that she did indeed look very tired.

After the men had done as Emily had predicted and gone into the bar, Bethany cleared the dining table and put the wine-spattered tablecloths and napkins out for the laundry woman. Then she cleaned up the room, which didn't take long because there was relatively little mess and went back to help Tansy with the last of the dishes before they both went up to bed.

'Thank goodness it looks like being a quiet night,' she said as she followed the girl up the stairs. 'They're a very well-behaved group. I don't think we shall have any trouble with them.'

'I never hear anything anyway, Mrs Beth,' Tansy said, starting to climb the narrow attic stairs. 'Not from up here.'

'That's good, because you have to be up early in the morning. Goodnight, Tansy.'

Tansy yawned. 'Goodnight, Mrs Beth.'

But Bethany had been over-optimistic. The noise started almost before she had climbed into bed. First it was one or two singing bawdy songs, then others, including the regular drinkers, joined in and those that couldn't sing kept time by stamping their feet and banging their tankards on the table. This went on for over half an hour, interspersed with raucous laughter, then argumentative voices began to rise above the noise of the singing and finally the singing stopped. Beth lay staring up into the darkness — with the racket going on downstairs there was no prospect of sleep — waiting for the inevitable crash that would signal that a fight had begun. It wasn't long in coming. She could hear the shouts and scuffles, the splintering furniture and above it all, Zack's voice shouting,

'Gentlemen! Gentlemen! Can we have a little order here, please!' which was totally ignored.

Then she heard the sound of breaking glass and let out a sigh of irritation. It was less than a month since, against her better judgement,

Emily had paid quite a lot of money for a long mirror to be put up at the back of the bar. Zack had persuaded her that it was the modern thing to do, saying it would make the bar look bigger and the whole place lighter. Now, it sounded as if someone had thrown a chair at it and smashed both the mirror and the glasses that stood in front of it. Well, she knew her mother well enough to predict that she wouldn't pay for a replacement, however much Zack might try to cajole her. She turned over and pulled the covers up over her head to shut out some of the noise from downstairs and tried to sleep.

Miraculously, she was just dropping off when Zack burst into the room.

'Quick! You'd better get up. Beth,' he said, shaking her. 'There's been an accident. A couple of the chaps downstairs were fighting and they fell through the window.'

'Are they badly hurt?' Beth was scrambling out of bed and into her clothes as she spoke.

'One of them has cut his head and the other one's gashed his hand quite badly. We need something to stem the blood till Matt gets here. Someone's gone for him.'

'I've got some old sheets I can tear up.' She began rummaging in a drawer. 'I'm not surprised there's been an accident. There's been enough noise down there to wake the dead.' She pulled out a sheet and some old towels. 'Where are they? Still in the bar?'

'Yes. We thought it best not to move them. There's a lot of blood . . . '

She followed him downstairs to the bar. A

quick glance round showed absolute chaos, chairs and tables overturned, beer spilled on the floor, overflowing spittoons and overall the stench of stale beer and stinking bodies. The waft of fresh night air that was coming through the broken window was the only thing that stopped her from gagging.

On the floor by the window a young man she had seen earlier was lying in a pool of blood. He was unconscious, bleeding from a gash in his temple. The other one was sitting propped on a chair, half-fainting, supporting one hand with the other, both hands covered in so much blood that it was impossible to see where the wound was or even which hand was damaged. She took in the scene at a glance and quickly made a towel into a pad and told a rather green-looking man standing nearby to hold it to the man's head while she attended to the other man. She was trying to bathe both hands to see where the damage was when Matthew hurried in.

'This chap's going to need a couple of stitches in his head,' he said, examining the man on the floor, at which the green-looking man fell down in a dead faint. 'Oh, get him out of here and give him a drink of water,' he said impatiently, giving him no more than a cursory glance. He looked up towards Bethany. 'Can you help?' he asked. 'I need to do it before he comes round.'

She nodded. 'Yes. But I think there are bits of glass in this man's hand,' she said.

'They'll keep till I've stitched his head.'

It was amazing how quickly the bar emptied at Matthew's words. Even Zack kept his distance as

Bethany helped, holding the man's head steady as Matthew worked. When he had finished and bandaged him up two of his friends, who had been waiting outside, carried him up to bed. Then he attended to the other man, with Bethany supporting him and helping wherever she could.

'The amount of blood always looks alarming,' he said as he worked, 'but most of these cuts and lacerations are not deep. However, he won't be able to shake a dice with these hands for a week or two, so that should save him a few pounds.' He looked up into the man's decidedly pale face, his eyes screwed up in pain. 'Are you a betting man?'

'What? Oh, I have the odd flutter. Ouch! Have you nearly done?' He looked down at what Matthew was doing and then away again quickly.

'Won't be long now.' Deftly, Matthew finished what he was doing and bandaged the injured hand and then got to his feet.

'There. You'll do. But perhaps it will teach you not to get involved in drunken brawls.'

'That's the beggar of it. I wasn't the one who was drunk,' the man said gloomily. 'It was the other bloke. And now there's no point in carrying on.' He held up his hands, swathed in bandages. 'What can I do with these? I can't even hold a knife and fork, let alone a hand of cards.'

'Your friends will put you to bed tonight, then you'll just have to stay here and wait till they get back from Holland,' Matthew said cheerfully. 'I'm sure you'll be well looked after. Mrs

Bethany is very capable. In fact, seeing how she's coped here tonight I'm convinced she would have made an excellent doctor's wife.'

He picked up his bag and went to the door, issuing instructions to Bethany on the care of the two injured men as he went.

'I hope I'll remember all you've told me,' she said with a frown.

'Remember the last bit, about making a good doctor's wife, that's the important thing,' he whispered close to her ear. Then his voice rose. 'Don't worry, I'll look in again tomorrow.' He looked at the clock on the wall, 'Or, I should say, later on today.' He smiled at her. 'Not that either of them would take any harm for a day or two,' he added quietly. 'But it gives me a legitimate excuse to see you, Bethany. I miss you.'

'I miss you too, Matthew. But . . . '

'I know.' His voice dropped again. 'I know there's no future for us, Bethany, but that doesn't stop me from holding you in my heart.'

She closed the door behind him and stood with her back to it, her eyes closed, savouring his words.

'Come on, then. Aren't you coming to bed?' Zack's voice broke into her thoughts.

'Yes. Yes. I'm coming.' She followed her husband up the stairs.

30

As Matthew had promised, he called in every day to see his patients and Bethany helped him where she could. Sometimes she wondered if she was more of a hindrance than help but there was always some small thing that he called on her to do. From the way he smiled at her she knew it was her presence rather than her assistance that he wanted and this gave her a warm feeling inside. For her part she never tired of watching his long fingers at work, so deft and at the same time so gentle, nor of seeing the way his hair curled into the nape of his neck, refusing to lie flat, as he bent over the wounded hand or examined the gashed head.

'I don't see why he needs to come in every day,' Zack remarked as Bethany returned to the kitchen after seeing Matthew out. 'Both men seem to be making a good recovery. I can tell that by the amount they drink every night in the bar.' He glared at her. 'And why do you always have to be there? Can't he manage on his own?'

'He probably could, but he's glad of a little help.' Bethany raised her eyebrows. 'But would you like to be there instead of me, Zack? Would you like to unwrap bloody bandages and check to see if the stitches are healing? I'll tell Matthew . . . '

'No, there's no need.' Zack gulped, as she knew he would because in spite of his pride in his masculinity he couldn't bear the sight of blood. 'The others will be back in a couple of days. I take it the two invalids will be fit to travel back with them?'

'Yes, Algy can manage a knife and fork now . . . '

'Oh, Algy, is it?' Zack sneered.

'Oh, don't be silly. I can't keep calling them 'Sir' all the time and Mr Blackwood and Mr Arbuthnot sounds dreadfully formal. Anyway, as I was saying, Algy can manage a knife and fork now and Theo's head is healing up nicely.' She turned to Emily, who was putting the finishing touches to a rabbit stew. 'Do you know, Mama, he had a four-inch gash over his eye? It was a very deep cut, too. Right through to the bone. Matthew reckons he'll always have a scar there.'

Zack gulped again and pushed back his chair noisily. 'I must be off. I want to check the new brew,' he said, snatching up his cap and hurrying out of the door.

The two women exchanged glances and burst out laughing.

'I'll make a cup of tea,' Bethany said, pulling the kettle forward.

Emily settled herself in the chair by the fire. 'Yes, I could do with a cup. I seem to get very tired, these days. I don't know why I should. After all, I used to be able to spend all day baking and not feel tired, but I can't now.'

'Well, Mama, you're getting older, you know.'

Emily waved her hand dismissively. 'Oh, I know that. But I still don't think I should be feeling as weary and listless as I do. And I get rather a lot of indigestion, too.'

'I'll speak to Matthew,' Bethany said, pouring out the tea and giving a cup to her mother.

'No. No. Don't do that. He'll think I'm making a fuss,' Emily said, a note of alarm in her voice.

'Oh, don't be silly, Mama. Of course he won't,' Bethany said impatiently. 'He knows you're not like that.'

'All the same, I forbid you to speak to him about me. I'm perfectly all right. A little tired, that's all. It's probably because we're getting more visitors now that the weather has improved.'

'Yes, I expect you're right.' Bethany sipped her tea and gazed out of the window. Aunt Sarah's garden was a riot of colour and beyond it the blossom had gone from the trees in the orchard, leaving the fresh green leaves to protect the tiny budding fruit. Reuben was sitting on the bench outside the garden shed, a lonely figure with a mug of beer at his side. Zack would have taken that to him; he looked after Reuben and when he could spare the time he would sit with him for a few minutes, listening to him reminisce about the days when Sarah was alive. Zack was very good with old people, Bethany mused, remembering how he had cared for Aunt Sarah during her illness.

She turned her attention back into the room, waiting for her eyes to adjust to the dim light. 'You haven't drunk your tea, Mama.' She nodded towards the full cup still standing on the table.

Emily shook her head. 'No, I didn't fancy it, after all. It tasted funny. All my food seems to taste funny these days, I don't know why.'

Bethany frowned. 'You're really not at all well, are you, Mama?'

Emily shrugged. 'A little tired, that's all.' She got to her feet. 'I must get on. I promised Algy and Theo dumplings with their rabbit stew tonight.'

That night Bethany forced herself to stay awake until Zack came up so that she could speak to him about Emily.

'Have you noticed she doesn't seem quite herself, Zack?' she asked anxiously.

'She still seems a bit tired, I must say. I thought she was working too hard; that's why I suggested employing Tansy,' he said.

It had been Emily who had suggested employing help, not Zack, as Bethany recalled. Not that it mattered.

'Perhaps she just needs a tonic,' he went on. 'I could get her some of that stuff that the chemist makes up for her. She always swears by that.'

'Yes, perhaps that's what she needs,' Bethany agreed.

'I'll get some for her next time I'm in the village. Can't have Em crocking up, can we.'

'No. Goodness knows how we'd manage if she was ill.'

He gave her a squeeze. 'Don't worry, Beth. We'll soon have her better. Now, seeing as you're awake . . . '

The following day the four young men returned from their trip to the continent full of tales of their adventures, most of which, Bethany suspected as she served their meal in the dining room, were exaggerated for the benefit of the two who had been left behind.

'Ah, but we've had the exclusive ministrations of Mrs Beth and enjoyed the delicious cooking of Mrs Emily,' Theo replied, determined not to be outdone.

'Not to mention the expert treatment from Dr Oakley,' Algy added. 'Look, my hand is practically healed. I have no trouble wielding a knife and fork and I can even do up my own buttons. And now his bandages are off Theo is sporting nothing more than a very rakish scar over his eye.'

'Yes, I'll tell the ladies it was a duelling injury,' Theo said, casually. 'That should get their sympathy.'

'They certainly won't sympathise if you admit you got it being thrown through a window in a drunken brawl,' his friends said, laughing. 'Don't admit that or we'll all get a bad name.'

Bethany was relieved that in spite of their high spirits the six friends spent the evening relatively quietly in the bar. Nevertheless, she was not sorry to see them pile into the gig with their luggage the following day and she waved them goodbye without regret as Zack drove them off to the railway station.

'I hope Zack will remember to call at the chemist to get that tonic for you,' Bethany said as she and her mother went back into the house.

'I don't really think that's necessary, dear. I'm just a little under the weather, that's all,' Emily said. 'Ah, look Tansy's made us a cup of tea. That's thoughtful of you, dear. It's just what I fancy.'

Bethany regarded her mother thoughtfully as she sipped her own tea. Only the other day Emily was saying that she didn't like tea any more. Now here she was, drinking it with obvious enjoyment. And she was looking better, she even had a little colour in her cheeks. Perhaps she had been worrying about her unnecessarily. Nevertheless, she decided to have a word with Matthew as soon as she got an opportunity.

Almost as if in answer to her thoughts there was a tap at the door and Matthew walked in.

'You're too late to see the invalids,' Emily greeted him with a smile. 'Zack's taken them to catch the train back to London.'

'Oh, I didn't realise they were going to leave quite so soon, although they're both pretty well on the mend now. However, it looks as if I'm not too late for a cup of tea,' he said, rubbing his hands together and sitting down at the table with them.

Tansy bustled about pouring tea, then escaped to tidy bedrooms. She was clearly overawed by the fact that Dr Oakley was actually sitting at the kitchen table, the very table that she scrubbed every day. And drinking tea as if he was entirely at home, too. It quite put out her idea of the proper order of things.

Zack came back before Matthew had finished drinking his tea.

'Oh, you're here,' he said rather rudely. 'Well,

you're too late. They've gone.' He was disgruntled at the meagre tip he had received after he had taken the trouble to load their bags right on to the train.

'So I understand. I hope they left a forwarding address,' Matthew replied, his mouth twisting into a rueful smile. 'Because they left without paying my bill.'

'Oh, dear. That's awful. And after all you did for them, too, Matthew,' Bethany said, horrified. She turned to her mother. 'Did they leave an address when they settled up with us, Mama?'

'They didn't settle with me. I thought they'd settled with you . . . '

'No, they told me . . . ' Beth's voice trailed off.

'Oh, my goodness, it looks as if we've been taken in all round, doesn't it.' Emily's shoulders sagged.

'Oh, what a thing to do! And after the way we looked after Algy and Theo all last week, too,' Bethany said crossly. 'And they seemed such nice young men, too, insisting we should call them by their Christian names. It just shows, you never can tell.'

'Well, there was nothing very Christian about the way they left, going off without paying their bills,' Emily said, furious at the way they had been taken in. 'I suppose what happened was the other four gambled all their money away over on the continent and expected Algy and Theo to pay for their lodging here.'

'Fat chance of that,' Zack said with a mirthless laugh. 'If you could have seen them in the bar every night, gambling on anything from dominoes — although Algy had a bit of trouble manipulating them — to who could down a pint of beer the fastest, you'd know those two hadn't a bean left between them, especially as they played with Billy French and you know what an old cheat he is. None of the locals will play with him.'

'Oh, Zack! You should have warned them,' Bethany said.

'Why should I? Most of the money Billy won he tipped down his neck at the bar so it came back to me in the end. The bar made a nice little profit, I can tell you.'

'Well, it's a good thing somebody did,' Matthew said ruefully.

'I think we should pay your bill, Matthew,' Bethany said.

'Indeed, yes,' Emily agreed. 'After all, the accident happened here.'

'You will do no such thing,' Matthew said, getting to his feet. 'I won't hear of it.' He picked up his hat and prepared to leave. 'It's not the money that concerns me, it's the fact that those young men were so irresponsible. They disrupted the bar . . . ' he turned to Zack. 'Did they pay for the damage they caused?'

'Did they hell! No, of course they didn't,' Zack said savagely.

'No, I thought not. And the two injured ones took advantage of your hospitality and my services for a whole week and probably had no intention of paying for a thing. It makes my blood boil. And there's not a thing we can do about it because we've no way of tracing them. In truth, I'd be surprised if they gave you their real names.'

'You could be right. Algernon Blackwood and Theodore Arbuthnot,' Bethany said slowly. 'Fairly unusual, to say the least.'

'But very aristocratic. A nice touch. And the others?'

Bethany shrugged. 'I don't think I ever knew. Dick? Fred? Sid? Quite ordinary names like that were what I believe they called each other, but I'm not sure.'

'I wonder if they spend their time going round the country tricking people like that.' Matthew said. He went to the door. 'I'll report this to the constable but I doubt he'll be able to do much because I guess they won't stay in London. They'll be on their way to Birmingham or Bristol, or even to Manchester, before he can get word to the right places.'

'I suppose we should count ourselves lucky,' Bethany said thoughtfully. 'This sort of thing has never happened before. People have always paid their bills before they left and have often been very complimentary to us. Travellers' Inn has a good name in the area. I suppose we shall just have to put it down to experience and watch it doesn't happen again.'

'Put it down to experience! Watch it doesn't happen again!' Zack got to his feet, his face red with fury. 'Is that all you can say? We've been tricked, woman, we've had those ba . . . those men sponging on us for all that time and you're prepared to shrug it off. Well, I'm not. We've been tricked and I don't like being tricked.'

'So what are you going to do, Zack?' Bethany asked quietly. 'You heard what Matthew said, they'll be well away by now. There's no chance of catching them. So what *can* we do?'

He sat down and said reluctantly, 'No, I suppose you're right, Beth. All right, we'll put it down to experience.' He thumped his fist on the table. 'But I shall make bloody sure it doesn't happen again. It's cost us a fortune, keeping those b . . . '

'Don't exaggerate, Zack,' Emily said wearily. 'You said yourself the bar made a good profit out of them, even if it was in a roundabout way, so you've no cause to complain. And all the fruit and vegetables they ate had been grown in the garden . . . '

'Oh, very well.' Knowing he had lost the argument Zack got up again and went to the door. 'I can't sit here arguing all day, I've got things to do,' he said. He turned back into the room. 'And I expect you have, too, Matt,' he said pointedly.

'Yes, you're right. I must be on my rounds.' Matthew went out with him.

It was only after he had gone that Bethany remembered that she'd had no chance to speak to him about her mother.

In the event there was no need. The tonic Zack had purchased for her at the chemists did the trick and she was soon her old self again, working as hard as ever and keeping an ever-tightening rein on the purse strings.

This irked Zack, who still cherished dreams of

expanding the place and then selling it.

'We shall never sell the place the way it is at the minute,' he complained to Bethany when they were in bed, the only place where they could talk privately.

'Mama has no plans to sell, she likes it the way it is,' Bethany replied. 'You know that.'

'I'll change her mind when the time comes. You'll see, Beth. I can twist her round my little finger, you know that.'

'You haven't managed to twist her far enough to pay for the roof over the yard,' she reminded him.

'I know. She's a bit stubborn over that. But now she's feeling better I daresay I shall be able to get round her. Especially when I tell her my plans for America. I reckon she'll like the thought of going there to live.'

So now he was intending that Emily should go with them on his wild-cat adventure. She made a face up into the darkness at the thought of her mother being asked to face the deprivations of travelling by wagon train across America, whether or not there was unlimited gold at the end of the journey.

'I wouldn't bank on it.' she said dryly.

The summer was hot and dry and the harvest was good, the work in the fields washed down by copious amounts of Zack's beer.

Emily made pasties and her own special harvest cakes and took them down to the field where Bethany was working with the other women.

After distributing them around she sat down

under a shady tree with Bethany.

'I really don't know which is the hottest, working out here in the fields with the sun beating down or working in the kitchen over a hot stove,' she said, fanning herself with a large hat as she ate her pasty.

Bethany took off her bonnet and shook out her mane of hair.

'Cooking isn't quite so hard on the back,' she said, flexing her shoulders. 'But it's more sociable here because you learn all the gossip. I've heard quite a lot since I've been helping, I can tell you. I know who's having a baby and who will have to get wed in a hurry. I know who will have the empty cottage now that Granny Styles has died and I know who is jealous because they wanted it.' She laughed and tossed her head. 'Oh, I've heard it all these last few days' She finished her pasty and stretched out on the grass.

Then, suddenly, she sat up again. 'There's something else I've heard this morning, too.'

'Oh, yes?' Emily was repacking the basket.

Bethany leaned forward. 'I don't think it's common knowledge yet but I heard a whisper that Farmer Isaac has been made another, better offer for some of his land.'

Emily looked up, frowning. 'By whom?'

'Oh, Mama! By the railway company, of course. If he agrees to sell it will mean the railway will run through his land and extend as far as Harwich.'

'Then I hope he won't sell. We don't want noisy, smelly railway trains running past the bottom of our garden.' She leaned forward. 'You must realise, Bethany, that it wouldn't do our business any good at all if the railway was extended, because we should lose all the coaching trade. I shall speak to Farmer Isaac. I'm sure he'll listen to me.'

'Oh, Mama, I don't think you should do that. It's really none of our business,' Bethany said, alarmed.

'Anything that affects Travellers' Inn is my business,' Emily said, with uncharacteristic sharpness.

Bethany said no more but if this was Emily's reaction to the coming of the railways she could well imagine what her mother would say when she discovered Zack's ambitious schemes to sell the inn and go to America.

31

Bethany said nothing to Zack concerning what she had heard about Farmer Isaac and the coming of the railway. He didn't mention it, either, which she found strange, because she couldn't believe it hadn't been talked about in the bar. Even the closest secrets somehow found their way there, usually mysteriously gleaned from a mythical figure known as 'Miles's Boy' and repeated with much tapping of the side of the nose and warnings to let the news go no further. There was no quicker way to spread a rumour round the village.

The Harvest Home took its usual form, with plenty to eat and drink followed by dancing to Billy Shovel's fiddle. The only difference was that this year, since the barn hadn't yet been rebuilt, it was held in the yard, with long trestle tables shored up at the corners to keep them level and planks supported by bricks or lumps of wood for seating. Fortunately the weather had held and it was a warm autumn evening with a huge harvest moon shedding benevolent light on the proceedings as darkness fell. But even while the beer flowed freely the party was a little subdued because the huge space where the barn had once stood was a constant reminder of last year's fire, making everybody extra careful with lanterns and candles in hollowed-out turnips.

'I'm afraid my housekeeper's cooking is not

quite up to your standard, Mrs Emily,' Farmer Isaac said as he led her to a quiet corner after a rather boisterous dance. 'But I felt you had quite enough to do at the inn without taking on cooking for an extra thirty people.' He looked at her, his face concerned. 'Especially since I've heard you've not been very well.'

'Oh, it was nothing. I got a little overtired, that's all. I'm quite better now.' She smiled at him.

'You're certainly looking very well, if I may say so,' he said gallantly.

'Thank you.' She paused, then said hesitantly, 'Farmer Isaac, there's something I want to ask you, if you wouldn't mind.' She gave him a half smile and then looked away.

'You can ask me anything you like. But please drop the 'Farmer'. Isaac will do nicely.'

'Very well, Isaac.' She paused again, then said in a rush. 'It's about the railway. I've heard you are going to sell some land to the railway company so that the line to Harwich can be put in. Do you think this is a good idea . . . Isaac?' She pulled her shawl round her a little more closely. It was a nervous gesture, not because she was cold but he saw it and said quickly, 'You're chilled. Would you like to come into the kitchen where it's warmer and we can talk more easily. Billy Shovel is tireless on his old fiddle but what with that and the stamping of feet it does make serious conversation difficult.' He stood up and led the way into the brightly lit farmhouse kitchen, a large, stone-flagged room with a long, scrubbed table in the middle. This was piled with pots and pans from the feast that had been washed up by willing hands and were waiting to be put back in their proper places. He ignored these and led the way to the two high-backed chairs set either side of the fire. Emily noticed that apart from the things heaped on the table the room was fairly bare. A dresser with what remained of a dinner service displayed on its shelves, together with heaps of papers was at the end of the room, and a long oak settle that in her opinion would have improved with a few brightly coloured cushions stood on the wall opposite the fireplace. Several pairs of boots were ranged just inside the door. It was a far cry from the cosy clutter of the kitchen at Travellers' Inn.

'Now,' he said when he saw she was comfortably settled, 'What were we discussing? Ah, yes. The railway.' He smiled ruefully. 'News does travel fast round the village, doesn't it.'

'Yes. I'm afraid secrets are not secrets for long,' Emily agreed.

'Well, it's not exactly a secret that the railway company has approached me with a view to purchasing some of my land,' he said, rubbing his beard. 'Up until now I've resisted, but if the price was right . . . ' he shrugged. 'Who knows?'

Emily frowned. 'Would you really sell to the railway company, Isaac? Would you really be happy to have those great railway trains rattling across your land, belching thick black smoke?'

'It wouldn't affect me too much, here in the farmhouse,' he said slowly. 'The fold in the land would protect me from the worst of the smoke and noise. But I realise that Travellers' Inn wouldn't be quite so well placed; so I wouldn't dream of making any final decision without consulting you,' his voice dropped, 'Emily.'

Glancing at him she saw that he was looking slightly uncomfortable. And well he might, she thought sharply; that railway line would affect me in more ways than the smoke and the noise.

'You do realise that my business depends to a large extent on the coaching trade, which of course the railway would kill,' she said bluntly.

He nodded. 'Yes, I know that. But I also know that Zack does very well with the bar. His beer is the best in the district.'

'It wouldn't be enough to support us all,' she said.

He leaned forward. 'But would it be enough to support Zack and Bethany if — well, if you . . . um . . . made other arrangements?' He leaned forward and poked the fire to cover the fact that a dull flush had spread across his face.

'I'm not sure about that. But as I'm not likely to make any other arrangements the question doesn't arise, does it.' She held out her hands to the warmth.

'It all depends.' He leaned back in his chair. 'You see, it's like this, Emily. Contrary to what a lot of people think, I'm not a rich man. What with a run of bad harvests and prices dropping due to cheap imports now the Corn Laws have gone, I haven't even seen my way clear to rebuild the big barn yet. But if I was to sell part of my land for a good price, and I should stick out for that, because they're more anxious to buy than I am to sell, then I should be in a much better position. You see, I have my pride and if I was to ask a lady to be my wife I should want my financial situation to be at least comparable to hers, if not better. At the moment this isn't the case, but a nice fat cheque from the railway company would set me up quite nicely and enable me to . . . ' He hesitated, then said in a rush, 'Emily, my dear, if I was in such a position would you consider doing me the honour of becoming my wife?'

Emily looked up, startled. She wasn't absolutely sure she had heard right.

'Isaac . . . '

He held up his hand. 'You don't have to answer me now, Emily. You need time to think about it, I realise that. But you must know the high regard I have for you. No, more than that, you must know how I've grown to love you in a way I have never thought to love anyone. To have you always sitting opposite to me, at my own hearth, just as you are doing now, my dear, would give me more joy than I have ever experienced in my whole life. Of that I am quite sure.' He stroked his beard nervously several times. 'Please forgive me,' he said, 'I've never made quite such a long speech before.' Then he added quickly. 'But don't misunderstand me, I meant every word.'

'Thank you, Isaac. I'm very honoured by what you've said,' she said gently.

'And you'll think about it?' he asked eagerly.

'Oh, I will, indeed.' She paused. 'To be truthful, if I only had myself to consider I shouldn't need to stop and think . . . but there's

Bethany. And Zack. My life is so bound up with them and Travellers' Inn that I can't make decisions without . . . ' She put her fingers to her temples. 'Oh, dear, I don't know what to do. If I say yes you'll sell your land and the railway will ruin trade at the inn but if I say no . . . ' She looked up at him. 'Oh, Isaac, how can I say no when I want so much to say yes?'

He came over and knelt beside her and took both her hands in his. 'I'm sorry, my love. I've put you in a dreadful situation. But I can't marry you and expect you to live in the frugal way I have become used to, not when it's in my power to give you so much more.' He kissed her hands, one after the other. 'We'll say no more about it now, my dear. Talk it over with Bethany.' He smiled up at her. 'I'm confident she won't stand in your way.'

She smiled back at him. 'You're probably right, Isaac, but I'm not so sure about Zack.'

Isaac was right. Bethany was overjoyed to think that the gentlemanly farmer had proposed to her mother and to Emily's surprise Zack was equally happy about it.

'But you do realise that Isaac intends to sell land to the railway company, which will affect trade at Travellers' Inn, don't you,' Emily said, anxious that they should fully understand the situation.

'You don't need to worry your pretty little head over Travellers' Inn, Em,' Zack said expansively. 'Just make it over to Beth and you can forget all about it.'

Emily sat bolt upright in her chair. 'Indeed, I

shall do nothing of the sort,' she said firmly. 'It's mine. Aunt Sarah left it to me and I don't intend to part with it.' She shook her head. 'It would be a violation of her trust.' She smiled at them both. 'But having said that, this is still your home. I realise its days as a coaching inn might be numbered, but Zack makes the best beer in the district and I've no doubt you can build on other things — '

'Like what?' Zack said, his voice suddenly cold.

Emily shrugged. 'I don't know. Meals?' She sighed. 'Of course, all this is idle speculation. It may all come to nothing between Isaac and me. Especially if you aren't both happy about it . . .'

'No, you go ahead. Don't worry about us. We'll scratch a living somehow.' Zack got up from the table, knocking the chair over as he did so and flung himself out of the door.

'Oh, dear,' Emily said sadly. 'I think I must tell Isaac I won't marry him after all.'

Bethany got up and dropped a kiss on her mother's head. 'You'll do nothing of the kind, Mama. I think it's the best news I've heard for a long time. Zack will soon come round. You'll see.'

But Zack continued to be morose and short-tempered, both with Emily and with Bethany, although he was never violent with Emily. Before long, the tension in the house began to tell on Emily and she became tired and listless, and her indigestion returned so that she ate hardly anything.

Bethany went out to the brew house one day to talk to Zack.

'If you were to be a little less bad-tempered I might be able to persuade Mama to make the inn over to me,' she said desperately. 'Then you could do what you've always wanted to do, sell it and go gold-digging in America.'

He turned and looked at her, an excited gleam in his eye. 'Do you really think she would?' he asked eagerly.

'I can but try,' she said. 'But she won't do anything if you continue to be so horrible to everybody.' She paused. 'She might put the date of her wedding forward, though. Then, of course, legally, Isaac will have control of everything. Not that he would exercise it, of course, he's far too nice a man,' she added, with a sly dig at him.

'By God, yes. I hadn't thought of that,' Zack said, either unaware of or ignoring her barb. 'Poor old Em. I've given her a hard time these past few weeks.'

'And not only Mama,' Bethany said, rubbing her bruised ribs.

He put his arms round her. 'I'm sorry, Beth. But I get so frustrated when I see what could be done . . . '

She turned her face up for his kiss. 'Well, before long you may get your own way.'

He grinned. 'And then . . . America, here we come!'

She didn't join in his enthusiasm. Now was not the time to tell him she had no intention of accompanying him halfway across the world — to search for something that might not even exist — even though she had no idea what she would do instead.

The tension in the house eased a little but in spite of the tonic that Emily always swore by her condition didn't improve. In fact, if anything it worsened, with diarrhoea and vomiting that sometimes kept her in bed for days at a time.

Bethany wanted to call Matthew but she flatly refused, always saying it was something she had eaten. She wouldn't even let her tell Isaac when she was ill and Bethany suspected that she was afraid he wouldn't want to be saddled with an ailing wife. She was at her wit's end to know what to do, so one afternoon, when Zack was harnessing up the gig to meet the train, she said,

'How many people are you meeting today? Will there be room for me in the gig? I want to do a bit of shopping in Manningtree.'

'I'm sure there'll be room and if not you can always ride up on the box with me,' he said. 'What are you going to buy? Can't I get it for you?'

'Mainly some embroidery silks for Mama.'

'Oh, you'd better come, then. I don't know anything about that sort of thing.'

She didn't tell him that she wanted to have a word with the chemist about her mother, since Emily refused to let her even speak to Matthew about her condition.

She had to admit that Zack looked very smart in the suit he always wore to meet the train. It would be a pity when there was no longer any need for Travellers' Inn to provide this service; Zack had built up quite a good business and most nights there were visitors wanting a meal and a bed for the night. She couldn't quite see how they were going to compensate for the money lost, but wisely she didn't voice these fears to her husband.

He put her down in the high street and she went to buy embroidery silks that her mother didn't need before going to the chemists.

Here, she discussed Emily's problems and purchased yet another kind of medicine that the chemist said should bring her some relief.

'Although I really think, from what you've described, your mother should see a doctor,' he said, shaking his head. 'She sounds quite poorly to me.' He held up the bottle. 'I've found this to be very good but if it doesn't help, you must persuade her to seek further advice.'

'Thank you.' She smiled ruefully. 'But you've no idea how stubborn my mother can be.'

She left the shop and a few minutes later Zack came bowling along with three people in the gig. She climbed up beside him on the box, pulling her shawl more closely round her because although it was a cold day it gave her an opportunity to talk to him without interruption.

'I've been to the chemists for medicine for Mama,' she said. 'He's given me something that should help her. It was a bit expensive.'

'Never mind the expense as long as it does her some good. I don't like to see Em so poorly,' he said, his voice full of concern.

'No. Neither do I. I just wish she would let Matthew see her.'

'I'll have a word with her. She'll listen to me.'

Bethany smiled. 'Yes. You could always twist her round your little finger, couldn't you.'

'Not always,' he replied seriously.

'Well, nearly always.'

They reached home and there was the usual flurry of settling the visitors in and making them a meal. Zack carried the bags upstairs, then put the gig away and attended to the horse.

'How is Em?' he asked, when he came in a little later.

'I think she's a tiny bit better. She fancies a little bread and milk,' Bethany said.

'I'll take it to her when it's ready, if you like,' he said. 'I can see you're busy.'

'No, it's all right. I'm sure you've got other things to do.'

'Maybe I have, but I can always spare a few minutes for Em. I like to try and cheer her up a bit.'

Bethany had to admit that was true. Zack could make Emily laugh when nobody else could and he was always very solicitous when she was ill.

'I think she enjoyed it,' he said when he came downstairs again. 'She's gone to sleep now.'

'Did you give her some of that new medicine?'

'Yes.' He grinned. 'She said it tasted better than the last lot we got her.'

Bethany shook her head. 'It's silly. She really should see Matthew.'

'I'm not sure that he could do much more for her than we are. In any case, she says she's feeling better.'

The improvement continued for a few days

but then Emily was ill again. As Bethany went about her work a cold finger of fear clutched her heart as she reflected that Aunt Sarah's illness had been very similar to what her mother was suffering. But, with an effort she pulled herself together; it couldn't possibly be the same because Aunt Sarah had died. And anyway, Aunt Sarah was old.

But the idea persisted and Bethany tried to think what there could possibly be in the house that could have made Aunt Sarah ill and might equally be affecting her mother.

'I want the privy scrubbed out every day,' she announced at breakfast one morning.

Zack looked up from his plate of bacon and egg. 'I do it three times a week,' he protested. 'What more do you want?'

'I want it done every day,' she insisted. 'Especially while Mama is ill. And it could do with another coat of whitewash, too.'

'That was done a month ago,' he argued.

'Never mind. I think it should be done again. And Tansy, I want all the saucepans scoured.'

'But ma'am . . . '

'I know you did them yesterday but I want them done again today. And make sure all the vegetables are thoroughly washed before they're cooked.'

Zack frowned. 'What's got into you all of a sudden, Beth? To hear you talk anybody would think we live like pigs.'

She put her fingers to her temples. 'I'm sorry, Zack. But I think Mama might be suffering from the same illness that Aunt Sarah died from.'

'That's rubbish, Beth, and you know it. Aunt Sarah was an old lady and she ate too many strawberries. That's what killed her.' He shrugged. 'As for Em, well, I shouldn't be surprised if she's suffering from a bad conscience over the business of marrying Isaac and leaving us in the lurch.'

Her face cleared. 'Do you really think so, Zack?'

'Yes. I do.'

'All the same, I think you should scrub out the privy every day.'

He got up from his chair and dropped a kiss on the top of her head as he passed her. 'If it'll make you happy, then that's what I'll do, sweetheart,' he said. He reached the door and then turned back. 'I suppose you heard there was a bit of a rumpus in the bar last night,' he said. 'It wasn't anything much but one of the settles got a bit battered. Get Tansy to give it a polish, will you?'

She looked up and smiled at him. 'All right, dear. I know you like to keep the bar looking smart.'

'Well, it's important. Creates a good impression.' He went off, whistling.

Because she had set Tansy to scouring all the saucepans Bethany went to look at the settle in the bar. There was a deep gouge across the back which no amount of polishing would remove so she went to find Zack and ask him if he had some stain that would cover it. He was nowhere to be seen and Bethany guessed he was scrubbing out the privy so she went into the tack room, where she knew Zack kept paint and cleaning materials, to see if she could find anything suitable. Some of the shelves were so dusty it was obvious they hadn't been disturbed for years, others had rusty tins with labels so old that it wasn't possible to decipher what the contents had been. But eventually she was rewarded and found a tin of stain that would do what she wanted. She reached up to take it off the shelf but her sleeve caught a tin on the shelf below and knocked it off. Fortunately, the lid was rusted on so it didn't spill but as she went to put it back on the shelf she saw a tin half hidden behind it. The label on this tin was partly scratched off, but she could still make out the words Rat Poison in rather flowery gold lettering.

Her automatic reaction was to look round nervously and pick up her skirts and hurry outside, shuddering.

'Ugh. I didn't know we had rats.' She hurried across to Zack, who was just crossing the yard.

'Rats? What are you talking about? There aren't any rats.' He looked blank.

She frowned. 'Then what's that tin of rat poison doing in the tack room? I found it while I was looking for this.' She held up the tin of stain.

'Oh, yes, there is a tin of rat poison.' He hesitated, not meeting her eyes, then muttered with a shrug, 'I'd forgotten it was there. I bought it ages ago when I saw a rat in the brew house. I was going to get rid of it but I forgot.' His tone became belligerent. 'What did you want to go poking about in there for, anyway? You know I

402

don't like you meddling with my things. If you'd asked me I'd have got the stain for you. What did you want it for?'

'To cover up the scratches on the settle in the bar, of course, like you asked me.'

'Hmph.' Without another word he stalked off across the yard.

She carried on into the house, frowning. What on earth had got into him?

32

For a few days Emily seemed to take a turn for the better. She even managed to come downstairs and sit in the kitchen for an hour or two and when Isaac learned this he asked if he might visit her.

Emily was quite excited at the thought and insisted on wearing her best lavender silk and her pink paisley shawl when he came. Bethany noted with affection that her mother was almost pathetically pleased to see Isaac, who was full of concern as he sat down beside her and took her hand in his.

'I'm really feeling very much better, Isaac,' she replied with a smile when he asked after her health. 'Especially now you've come,' she added a little quietly and a little coyly.

He squeezed her hand. 'Well, as soon as you are well enough, my dear, I intend that we shall marry, then I can take you away for a nice long holiday. How would you like that?'

'Oh, I should really love that, Isaac,' she said, her face lighting up. Then she frowned. 'But wouldn't it be rather expensive?'

'Don't worry your head about that, my love.' He kissed the hand he held. 'Nothing is too expensive if it will help to make you well again, Emily.'

While Emily and Isaac talked Bethany was busy preparing the evening meal with Tansy's help. There would be two visitors in the dining room to cook for, plus Matthew and Isaac, because this was one of their evenings to eat in the snug.

Isaac watched as Bethany put a pan of potatoes on the stove to boil.

'If I might be so bold, Mrs Beth,' he said tentatively, 'wouldn't it make a little less work for you this evening if Matthew and I took our meal in the kitchen here? I'm sure Matt wouldn't mind and it would save you having to carry the plates through into the snug.' He gazed lovingly at Emily. 'And I should be able to spend a little more time here with Emily. Unless you're too tired, my love, and wish to retire early?'

'No. That would be lovely. I should enjoy it very much,' Emily smiled at him.

'And perhaps we might even persuade you to eat a morsel or two yourself, my dear?' he asked.

She nodded. 'I'll try, Isaac.'

Watching them, Bethany thought she had never seen her mother looking so happy, in spite of having been so ill; it was obvious that she and Isaac were very much in love.

It made Bethany equally happy to have Matthew there. It was a long time since he had eaten at the kitchen table and for some reason she felt a little shy as she served them with steak and kidney pie.

'I'm afraid it isn't quite as good as Mama makes,' she apologised.

'Maybe not, but it comes a very good second,' both Isaac and Matthew agreed with a laugh.

After the meal Matthew went and sat by

Emily's side and talked to her for a while, then he made his excuses and left.

Bethany accompanied him to the door.

He caught her hand. 'I'd like to stay longer with you, Bethany; I can't tell you what a pleasure it has been just to sit at your kitchen table with you again, my love,' he said quietly. 'It was just like the old days. But I think it diplomatic that I should go now. I wouldn't want Zack . . . '

'No, it's best that you go, Matthew, much as I would like you to stay,' she replied.

As he reached the door he stopped. 'I need to speak to you urgently about your mother, Bethany,' he whispered. 'Now is not the time, but can I come and see you tomorrow?'

She shook her head. 'No, don't come here,' she whispered back. 'Zack might be around and you know how awkward he can be.' She pinched her lip. 'I shall be going to tend Tilly's grave tomorrow afternoon. Could you meet me there? About three o'clock?'

'Excellent. I'll see you there.' He lifted the latch, then turned back. 'Bethany, do you always prepare your mother's food yourself?'

'Oh, yes. Not that she eats much,' she said with a smile.

'Good. Well, I'll see you tomorrow.'

Isaac left soon after Matthew and Bethany helped her mother up to bed and then took her a glass of hot milk and a small glass of the tonic the chemist had made up.

'I don't think I need that tonight, Bethany. I'm feeling so much better. I think I shall sleep very well without it,' Emily said, sighing happily. 'It was so nice to see Isaac. I was afraid he wouldn't want to marry me if I was ill but he still seems to care just as much.'

'I'm sure he does, Mama.' Bethany dropped a kiss on her mother's forehead and left her dreaming happily of a holiday in Italy with Isaac.

★ ★ ★

'I think that man's a snake in the grass,' Zack said when Bethany told him in bed that night how much Emily had enjoyed Isaac's visit. 'Can't you see, Beth? He only wants to marry Em so that he can get his hands on Travellers' Inn.'

'Oh, I'm sure you're wrong there, Zack,' Bethany protested. 'He's just as anxious as Mama that we should stay here and make a good living.'

'He's got a funny way of showing it, then, selling his land to the railway company. He must know it will ruin the coaching trade and when that goes the best part of our income will go with it. You know that, Beth, as well as I do.'

'Then what good would it do him if he did get his hands on Travellers' Inn, since you say there won't be a living to be made?' Bethany asked reasonably.

'No good at all. The best thing would be for Em to make the place over to you, Beth, then she can forget about it.'

'And she'll know Isaac isn't marrying her to get his hands on it,' Bethany said with more than a trace of sarcasm, which was lost on him.

'That's right. I think you should try to persuade her to do that, Beth.'

'What, so that you can sell it and go gold digging in America?'

'Of course. But you mustn't tell her that's what we plan to do or she'll never make it over to you.'

'You mean it's what *you'd* do. I don't want to go to America, Zack.'

'You'll do as I say, madam, make no mistake about that.' He turned on to his back and in a few minutes he was snoring.

But Bethany stared up into the darkness for a very long time. Zack was the one who was mistaken, she decided. And on three counts. Because she had no intention of doing as he said, no intention of going to America with him, and last and most definitely, no intention of suggesting to Emily that she should ever part with Travellers' Inn. She turned her back on him and eventually fell asleep.

The next afternoon was wet and windy but the weather never deterred Bethany, and most weeks she visited the tiny grave of her daughter, putting on fresh flowers or making sure the grass was neatly trimmed. While she worked she would tell Tilly what had been happening since her last visit; that way she could feel that her little girl was still a part of her, still not far away even though she couldn't see her. Today, since the last of the fresh flowers were finished, she had brought a small posy of white waxen flowers protected by a glass dome.

'I'll leave this here for the winter because all

the fresh flowers have finished now, dear,' she said. 'But don't worry. I shall keep the glass clean so that you can see the pretty white flowers.' As she put it carefully in place she murmured, 'Matthew will be coming soon. He wants to speak to me about something; I can't imagine what.' She got to her feet, still wondering what it could be that Matthew so urgently needed to discuss with her that was so secret that he couldn't have told her last night. After all, there had been plenty of opportunity, because Isaac and her mother had eyes for nobody but each other so they wouldn't have heard. She was pondering on this when Matthew arrived.

'I'm sorry to have dragged you out on such a dreadful day,' he said, as she turned and greeted him.

'Don't apologise, Matthew. I would have been here, anyway,' she said with a wry smile. 'I come to see Tilly nearly every week.'

'Still?' he asked, looking down at her.

She bit her lip. 'Oh, yes. I still come to see my little girl.'

A gust of wind nearly blew his umbrella inside out and when he had righted it he took her arm. 'Let's go and sit in the church porch,' he said. 'It will be a bit sheltered there.'

At least it was out of the wind and rain although the stone seats that lined the porch were cold. They sat down and he put his arm round her.

'It's all right. Only fools would be out in this weather,' he said, smiling at her look of alarm.

'And only stupid fools would be walking round the graveyard.'

'So what does that make you and me?' she asked, managing a little smile.

'Fugitives from the weather,' he said promptly.

'We could go inside the church,' she suggested.

He hesitated. 'I'd rather not, if you don't mind, Bethany. I'd rather say what I have to say here, outside.'

She twisted round to look at him, frowning. 'I don't understand.'

'It's about your mother, Bethany. While I was talking to her last night I noticed things that I wasn't happy about. She's been ill for some time, hasn't she?'

She nodded. 'Well, on and off. Sometimes she hasn't been so bad.'

'But gradually getting worse?'

She thought for a moment or two, then she nodded slowly. 'Overall, yes, I suppose she has. The attacks do seem to be getting worse and they do last longer.'

'Why didn't you call me in to examine her, Bethany?'

'I wanted to, but she said no and Zack said it was probably something she'd eaten. And then she would be better for a little while . . . ' Her voice trailed off, then she explained, 'We got her a tonic from the chemist. That did her good for a while, but then she was ill again so I went to see him again and got something different.'

'What was in this tonic?'

She shook her head. 'I don't really know. I

410

think he said something about quinine and iron.'

'That wouldn't do it,' he said, half to himself.

'Wouldn't do what?' she asked with a frown.

He turned to look at her. 'It wouldn't poison her.'

She gaped. 'Poison her? What are you talking about? Why should it poison her?'

He covered her hand with his. 'I'm sorry, Bethany, but I've every reason to believe that your mother has been taking arsenic in some form or other. I've done quite a lot of research into this and she has all the symptoms — her fingernails, the way her skin is flushed — have you noticed it flaking at all?'

She nodded. 'Yes. I put cream on it. But I didn't think . . . '

'And these vomiting attacks?'

'Again, we thought it was something she'd eaten; sometimes her stomach is rather delicate. She's rather anaemic, too.'

'I'm not surprised.' He nodded. 'I'm afraid it all adds up, Bethany. I'm quite sure somebody is trying to poison your mother.'

'Oh, Matthew, that's ridiculous. Who on earth would want to do that? And why? She's never done anybody any harm. In any case, how would they do it?'

'It would only need a little added to her food or drink over a period because it would have a cumulative effect. Or in that tonic. It's got quite a strong taste, hasn't it.'

'I don't know. I've never tried it. But surely the chemist . . . '

'Oh heavens, no. Mr Bradshaw would never,

ever do anything like that. I'd stake my life on it. In any case, why should he? He doesn't even know your mother, does he?'

'No. Not that I know of.'

'Well, then, it must be somebody in the family.'

'But there's only Zack and me. And Tansy, of course. And the women who come in to do the rough work.'

'Zack?' he asked quietly.

She laughed. 'Heavens, no. He thinks the world of Mama and he's always worried and concerned when she's ill. He takes her meals to her and looks after her, makes her drinks. He couldn't be more attentive if it was his own mother. In any case, where on earth would he get arsenic from, Matthew? The idea is quite ridiculous.'

'Is it, Bethany?' He was looking at her intently.

'Well, of course it is.' A note of uncertainty had begun to creep into her voice as she recalled the conversation last night in bed. 'Zack would never . . . In any case, where on earth would he get arsenic from?'

'Fly papers. Do you use fly papers, Bethany?'

She shook her head. 'No, I can't bear to see them covered in dead flies.'

'Rat poison? Are there rats about the place?'

She put her hand up to her mouth. 'I did find a tin of rat poison the other day,' she whispered. 'I thought Zack looked a bit strange when I asked him about it, but he told me he'd bought it when he saw a rat in the brew house. Not that he'd ever said anything about seeing rats . . . '

She shook her head and her voice became stronger. 'No, Matthew. It's nonsense. Zack would never do such a thing. Why should he, for goodness sake?'

'To get his hands on Travellers' Inn?' Matthew suggested quietly. 'I've often heard him talking in the bar about the things he'd like to do to it and the fact that your mother holds the purse strings and won't let him.'

She put her head in her hands. 'It's true. He wants me to persuade Mama to make the inn over to me so that he can sell it and use the money to go to America to dig for gold,' she said, her voice muffled.

'So there's his motive,' Matthew said flatly.

She looked up. 'No, I still can't believe . . . You're mistaken, Matthew. You must be.'

'I'm sorry, but I don't think I am, Bethany,' he said sadly. 'But clearly we need to prove it one way or the other. Look, I'll tell you what we'll do. I want you to get Zack to take your mother a drink. She likes milk?' Bethany nodded. 'Very well, a drink of warm milk. But make sure to warn your mother not on any account to drink it. Then you must somehow get it to me and I'll take it into my laboratory and analyse it.'

She shook her head. 'I don't think you'll find anything, Matthew.'

'Considering we're talking about a man who has beaten you till you were black and blue, I must say you're very trusting, my love,' he said, his mouth twisting bitterly.

She shrugged. 'I just can't imagine *anybody*

would do such a thing,' she said.

She made her way home, Matthew's words spinning round and round in her head until she thought she would go mad. It was not possible. She knew it was not possible because it would mean that Zack was cold-bloodedly poisoning her mother. The idea was quite ridiculous. Zack was very fond of Emily. Even if he was anxious to get his hands on Travellers' Inn he would never go to such lengths as to murder her.

Nevertheless, she found herself looking for Zack the minute she got home.

'Where's the master?' she asked Tansy, who was busy peeling vegetables for the evening meal.

'Upstairs with Mrs Emily. She went to lie down because she was tired and he's taken her a drink of warm milk to help her sleep. He said he'd take it to her as I was busy.' She smiled at Bethany as she spoke. 'He's very thoughtful, ain't he?'

'Indeed he is.' Bethany hurried up the stairs, shedding her shawl and hat as she went.

Zack was sitting on the side of the bed, trying to spoon milk from a mug into Emily.

'I really don't want it, Zack,' she was saying. 'I only came up for a rest, not for a sleep.'

'Well, now I've brought it you'd better drink it, you silly old . . . ' he turned as he heard Bethany enter. 'I'm trying to get Em to have a drink of milk. She hasn't had much else all day.' He turned back to Emily. 'You know, you'll need to keep your strength up if you're going swanning off to Italy, darlin'.'

414

She pushed it away. 'I'll drink it later,' she said.

Bethany went over to the bed. 'Perhaps she'll drink it for me, Zack.' She took the mug from him. 'I think there's somebody downstairs looking for you,' she lied. She turned to her mother and winked. 'You'll take a little for me, won't you, Mama?'

'I don't want it,' Emily said after he had gone. 'Anyway, it tastes funny. My food often tastes funny these days; I don't know whether it's my illness or what it is. What are you doing, Bethany?'

'I'm pouring the milk into this little bottle. Then I'm going to take it and the mug to Matthew. He thinks he knows what might be wrong with you, dear.'

'Oh, good. I suppose we should have consulted him before. What does he think it is?'

'I'm not sure.' She made a little parcel of the mug and bottle and went to the door. Then she came back and leaned over the bed. 'Listen to me, Mama. This may sound odd, but if Zack brings you anything to eat or drink, whatever you do don't touch it. The best thing will be to pretend to be asleep if he comes in. I shall be back in half an hour.'

Emily frowned. 'I don't know what you're talking about, Bethany.'

'It doesn't matter. Just do as I say, dear.'

Bethany put her wet shawl and hat back on and hurried out. Fortunately, Zack was nowhere to be seen as she crossed the yard and she walked as fast as she could the mile or so to the large house where Matthew lived alone. He answered the door himself when she rapped on the knocker.

'Oh, thank heavens you're here,' she said, thrusting the package into his hand. 'This is what you want. Zack was just trying to give it to Mama when I arrived home. She said it tasted funny.'

He glanced inside the bag. 'I must warn you that if this contains what I think it will I shall bring the constable with me when I come, Bethany,' he said quietly.

She nodded. 'I understand.'

She turned and hurried back along the road to the inn. It was still raining and the wind was howling in the trees as darkness closed in. She pulled her shawl more closely round her, holding her hat on with her other hand. She was beginning to wish she had brought a lantern with her but it had been barely dusk when she left so she hadn't given it a thought. Not that the darkness worried her. Aunt Sarah had always talked about friendly darkness and she had always tried to think about it this way. But with the noise of the wind howling and the rain beating down she had to admit it was distinctly unfriendly tonight.

Suddenly, without warning, she felt a heavy hand on her shoulder and she let out a scream.

'Don't be daft. It's me.' It was Zack's voice.

'Oh. My goodness, you startled me, pouncing on me in the dark like that.' She cried. 'What are you doing here?'

'Following you, my dear. I know exactly where you've been, so don't try to lie to me.' He gripped her arm. 'Why did you go there? And what was in that package you gave your fancy man?'

33

This was a nightmare. It couldn't be real. Alone on a lonely country road on a dark, wild night with a potential murderer. Bethany's mouth felt dry and she was shivering with fear as well as with cold.

'Well?' Zack shook her arm. 'What did you take your doctor friend?'

She thought fast. 'Oh, Zack, I know how squeamish you are. Do you really want to know? Matthew had asked for a sample of Mama's . . . '

'What? On a night like this? I don't believe you.'

'She took a turn for the worse,' she lied, thinking on her feet. 'But, why don't we wait until we get home, dear, then I'll tell you about it,' she said in her most wheedling tone. 'I'm soaking wet and very cold and you must be, too. Look, I believe I can see the lights from the inn in the distance. Let's hurry home and we can talk about it over a cup of tea.'

The inn still seemed an awful long way away but he was clearly mulling over what she had said as he walked along beside her, still clutching her arm. She managed to speed their steps so that it was not long before they reached home and it was with a sob of relief that she lifted the latch and stepped into the warm, familiar kitchen.

'I'll just go up and see how she is now,' she

said, taking off her wet shawl and hat for the second time that day and lighting a candle.

'I'll come with you,' he said, following her up the stairs.

Emily was sitting up in bed reading by the light of the oil lamp Tansy had lit. She smiled as Bethany entered the room. 'Hello, dear. He didn't come back . . . ' her voice trailed off as she saw Zack. 'Oh, hello, Zack. Have you been out in the rain, too?'

Although she had her back to him Bethany could see Zack's reflection in the mirror on her mother's dressing table as he came into the room. The expressions that flitted across his face when he saw Emily sitting up in bed looking bright and happy — shock and disbelief, followed by terror — told her all she needed to know.

He caught Bethany's arm and bundled her out of Emily's room.

'Be careful,' Bethany cried as he pushed her along the passage into their bedroom. 'Do you want me to drop this candle and set the house on fire?'

He took no notice. 'Do you realise what you've done?' he hissed. 'You've put a noose round my neck, you silly bitch. You took that milk to Matthew, didn't you? No, don't bother to deny it. I know you must have done because the old bitch is still breathing and there was enough rat poison in that glass to kill twenty people.'

'My God! You're a monster, Zack. How could you do such a thing?' She was horrified and had to put the candle down quickly because she was trembling with terror. 'Why do you want Mama dead? She's never done you any harm,' she asked, trying very hard to keep calm.

'You know very well why I want her dead, you stupid little cow.' He shook her arm. 'I want the money from this place and I'm tired of waiting for it. God knows, I've waited long enough. Years, I've waited. Ever since I first came to work on old Isaac's farm I liked the look of Travellers' Inn. I'd never had a place to call my own and I fancied owning it. I always get what I want in the end, even if it takes me years.' He began pacing up and down the room then stopped in front of her. 'But you've ruined everything, you stupid little fool. Now you've put your fancy man on my trail I can't stay here. After what I've done I'll end up at the end of a rope if I don't get away.' He slapped her face so hard that her head jerked back. 'But I need money. Go down to the bar and see what there is in the till. Get a move on now and don't try anything stupid because I shall be at the top of the stairs watching.' He prodded her in the back and began impatiently pacing up and down the room again.

When she came back with half the money that had been in the till he snatched it from her. 'Is that all there was?' He stuffed it in his pocket. 'I deserve this. I've worked bloody hard over the years. If it hadn't been for me the place wouldn't be as successful as it is today.'

'That's true,' she said, trying to keep her voice level and playing for time. 'But I thought you wanted to sell it and go to America?'

'Yes, my plans changed after I spoke to a chap

who stayed here one night. He told me about the gold in the Black Hills of the American West. He said it was there for the taking and hundreds of people were going after it. So I reckoned if I could get my hands on the inn and sell it I'd have plenty of money to travel there and set myself up as a gold miner and make a fortune. Then I'd never have to work again.'

'And where do I come in all this?' She was keeping him talking, stalling for time. Matthew seemed to be an awful long time coming with the constable.

'Oh, I've done with you. I only got you in the family way and married you to get my foot in the door,' he said carelessly, ignoring the stricken look that crossed her face. 'Then I put paid to the old girl because I thought she'd leave the place to you, but the old fool left it to her daughter instead.' He stopped his pacing and smirked a little. 'I was pretty clever over that. I only put a little of the stuff in her food at a time and gradually increased it. Everybody thought she'd eaten too many strawberries in the end. Well, she had, but there was a hefty dose of rat poison in the sugar she dipped them in and that finished her off.'

'You're mad!' Bethany breathed, horrified.

He caught her arm. 'Oh, no. I'm not mad, Bethany. I'm ambitious. And I'm determined not to let anything stand in my way,' he hissed in her ear. 'I'm going away now because I know what'll happen when your precious Matthew finds what's in that milk you took to him. But I shall be back, never fear, because I want the money

421

from this place and by hook or by crook I shall find a way to get it.'

'Where will you go?' she whispered.

'You don't imagine I'm going to tell you that, do you?' He glanced out of the window. 'Christ! I can see a lantern! I'll bet it's that bloody doctor and it looks like he's got the bloody constable with him. I'm off.' He flung himself down the stairs and out of the back door and was gone.

Bethany sat down on the bed, rocking back and forth and wringing her hands. She was shaking from head to foot, her teeth were chattering and tears were pouring unheeded down her face. She heard Matthew come into the house but when she tried to stand up her legs wouldn't support her and she hadn't even the strength to call out to him.

Moments later he came up the stairs and knocked on the door of her bedroom.

'He's gone,' she said dully without looking up. 'He saw you coming and ran.'

'Damnation. He must have escaped over the fields.' He shouted down to the constable who immediately gave chase. 'He can't have got far,' he said when he came back. 'The constable will catch him if anyone can.' He sat down beside her on the bed and took her hand in his. 'Has he been beating you, Bethany?' he asked quietly.

She shook her head. 'No. Well, yes, he hit me, but only once,' she corrected herself. She paused. 'It's worse than that. Did you know he'd killed Aunt Sarah, Matthew?'

He drew in a deep breath and blew it out. 'My God, is there no limit to what the man has done?

No. No, I didn't.' He was silent for several minutes, then he said, 'But now you tell me that I realise I should have seen there was something not quite right about her death. But she was an old lady . . . ' He shook his head. 'It doesn't excuse the fact that I missed the symptoms, of course.'

'You mustn't blame yourself, Matthew. You'd hardly have been looking for signs of poisoning, would you? And Zack was always so attentive, so kind to her, it was the last thing you would have expected.' She bit her lip. 'Then he told me he only seduced me and married me to get his hands on Traveller's Inn.' She turned and looked at him. 'That really hurt, Matthew, because I'd tried so hard to make our marriage work and I'd felt so guilty because I had stopped loving him.' She shook her head. 'And then to discover that he had never loved me at all and had only married me as a means to an end . . . '

He kissed her gently. 'My poor love. You've been through so much.' He put his arms round her and held her close. 'If only I could marry you and take you away from this place.'

She put her head on his shoulder. 'I wish you could, Matthew. I feel so safe with you. But while Zack is at large . . . and he says he'll be back . . . oh, what a mess everything is.'

'Don't worry, my love, I'm sure Charlie Blake will catch him and then he'll be brought to trial. He showed no mercy to your mother and aunt and there'll be none for him.'

She looked up at him. 'Zack isn't really a bad man, Matthew. He can be kind and gentle and

423

very thoughtful, you know. He's really very nice at heart. Or at least, I thought he was,' she added bleakly.

'Oh, he can be a charmer, all right,' he agreed. 'The fact is, we're none of us all bad, nor all good.' He paused. 'I think Zack's downfall was greed,' he said after a minute. 'He'd grown up with nothing and I guess until you experience what it's like to own nothing in the world you can't understand how great the craving for money and possessions is.' He cocked an ear. 'Ah, listen, I think that's Charlie back. We'd better go and help him with Zack.'

But Charlie was alone. 'Fred Cork helped me and we've combed the area as best we could but it's pitch black out there now so I doubt we'd see him if he was only ten yards away,' he said. 'There's no telling where he's gone to ground.'

'Did you search the stables and brew house?' Bethany asked.

'Yes. We've looked everywhere we can think of, Ma'am.'

Matthew pinched his lip. 'I don't think it would be a good idea for you and your mother to be here alone at night while he's at large, Bethany,' he said thoughtfully.

'We've got Tansy,' Bethany said, nodding towards the little servant girl, cowering in the corner, wide-eyed with fear.

Matthew cocked an eyebrow at her. 'I don't think Tansy would offer you much protection, my dear. I think you'd have to protect her.'

Suddenly, the door from the passage opened and Emily appeared, fully dressed although her hair was still in the plait she wore at night. 'What's happening? I couldn't stay in bed wondering what was going on so I got dressed.' She turned to Bethany and whispered behind her hand. 'I couldn't manage my stays. Does it notice?'

Bethany shook her head and suddenly dissolved into peals of hysterical laughter. 'Oh, I'm sorry,' she said, laughing and crying at the same time. 'But it's so funny. Zack's on the loose after murdering Aunt Sarah and trying to murder Mama and all Mama can think of is whether anyone will notice she hasn't managed to put her stays on.'

'Bethany!' Her mother said, shocked. 'Such talk! In front of gentlemen, too.'

'I can't help it, Mama. I just think it's so funny.' Bethany still couldn't stop laughing and tears were running down her cheeks.

Annoyed at being made fun of, Emily caught her daughter by the arms and gave her a good shake. 'Oh, for goodness sake! Behave yourself, Bethany!' she shouted.

Bethany stopped laughing, shocked at her mother's uncharacteristic behaviour.

'I'm sorry, Bethany, but you were behaving rather foolishly, weren't you,' Emily said, her voice still sharp. 'And what's all this talk about murder? Have you gone completely out of your senses, child?'

'No, Emily, I'm afraid she hasn't,' Matthew said quietly. 'It's quite true. Zack poisoned Aunt Sarah and he was trying to do the same to you.'

Emily's jaw dropped and she sat down with a

bump. 'Poisoned? Aunt Sarah? But I thought it was the strawberries . . . ' her eyes widened and she pointed to herself. '*Me*? He was trying to poison *me*?' She looked from Matthew to Bethany and back again.

Bethany nodded, still hiccupping, wiping her eyes with the heel of her hand. She was beyond speech so Matthew continued, speaking gently to Emily, 'That's why you've been feeling so poorly lately. Zack's been slowly poisoning you with rat poison. Fortunately we found out in time . . . '

Shakily, Emily put a hand to her throat. 'Is it . . . ? Will I . . . ?'

'You'll be fine, Emily. There's no need to worry. We discovered what he was trying to do before it could do any lasting harm.' He didn't add that he had found enough arsenic in the milk to kill a horse.

'Oh, thank God for that.' Emily put her head in her hands and began to weep.

Bethany came over and put her arms round her mother. 'I'm sorry, Mama. I didn't mean to embarrass you by laughing like that. It was just that . . . well, everything . . . Oh, I'm so glad you're going to be all right.' She buried her head in her mother's shoulder, unable to continue.

'I think a good strong cup of tea is what's needed. For everybody,' Matthew said firmly. He turned to Tansy, who was twisting her apron round in her hands, still unable to grasp exactly what was happening and smiled encouragingly. 'Pull the kettle forward, Tansy, and make tea for us all. Do you think you can manage that?' he asked gently.

She nodded and began scuttling around, warming the teapot and taking down cups and saucers, glad to do something familiar, the only sign that she was still terrified her shaking hand as she poured milk into the cups.

'Well, as I was saying earlier. I don't think you should be here alone while Zack's on the loose.' Matthew pulled out his pocket watch. 'I've one more call to make tonight, then I could come back and stay the night. I take it you've got a spare room?'

'Yes, we've nobody staying tonight,' Emily said. 'I think we'd like that, wouldn't we, Bethany?'

'Yes. It would be a great comfort. But we'll be all right till you come back,' Bethany said. 'The men will be coming in for their evening drink and game of dominoes soon. They'll protect us — if we need protecting, that is.'

'You'll be opening the bar, then, Missus?' Charlie Blake said in some surprise.

'Oh, yes. We'll keep opening as long as there's any beer to sell. Don't you agree, Mama?'

Emily looked uncertain. 'Who'll serve it?' she asked anxiously.

'Oh, I'm sure one of the regulars will act as barman,' Bethany said. 'And Reuben will keep an eye on things. He's always there and he'll tell us if anything isn't as it should be.' As far as she was concerned that was the least of their worries. 'We need to keep the bar open or we'll have no money, Mama,' she said gently. 'Because we're not likely to get very many people staying, unless we can get somebody to meet the train. And somebody to look after the horses . . . ' she put her fingers to her temples. 'Oh, dear, there's a lot to be thought about now Zack's not here.'

Emily looked up. 'We shall miss Zack, shan't we?'

'Oh, yes, but it'll be a good miss if he's bent on poisoning us all,' Bethany said firmly, pulling herself together. 'I'm sure we'll manage very well without him.'

'Well, I'm hiring a room for tonight. And a meal, if you can manage to prepare it,' Matthew said. 'And I've no doubt my good friend Isaac will join me when he finds out what's been going on.'

In that he was quite right. Charlie Blake called on his way home to inform Isaac what had been happening and it was not long before he arrived at Travellers' Inn. He was appalled to hear of Emily's narrow escape from death and could hardly be persuaded to leave her side even long enough to eat the meal Bethany and Tansy had prepared.

'What are you going to do, my love?' he asked. 'You can't stay here, can you?'

'For the present I think we must,' Bethany answered for her. 'In any case, where else would we go?'

'Emily can sell this place and you can both come and live with me,' Isaac said immediately. 'And Emily and I will be married as soon as possible.' He beamed at everybody. 'There. How's that for a solution?'

'It sounds very nice, Isaac,' Emily said, 'and I think it very likely that I shall sell Travellers' Inn, but that will take time.' She smiled at him. 'You mustn't rush me, dear.'

'But you and Bethany definitely can't stay here on your own, because you never know if Zack will turn up and murder you both in your beds.'

'Oh, I'm sure he wouldn't do that,' Bethany said quickly.

'Are you? I'm not. After all, he's already murdered once and tried to do it a second time. However many people he puts paid to now he can only hang once.' He turned to Matthew. 'It seems to me that the best thing would be for you and me to take it in turns to stay here every night, Matt. At least until things calm down a bit and that scoundrel is found and brought to justice.'

'We should certainly sleep more easily in our beds,' Emily said, relieved.

For the next three weeks it worked very well. The two men ate at the inn every night, then one or other of them stayed on until morning. In this time there was no sign of Zack although there were rumours that he had been seen as far afield as Colchester and Ipswich, and someone swore he had been seen in Harwich, boarding a boat for the continent.

Bethany didn't think that was likely. If he went anywhere it was likely to be to America and he hadn't got enough money for that.

Life at the inn went on. Not as smoothly as in Zack's time but nevertheless Bethany and Emily managed to keep things going well enough for Emily to put Travellers' Inn up for sale as a thriving business.

'What will you do when the inn is sold, Bethany?' Matthew asked her one evening when they were sitting alone in the dining room. It was his turn to stay the night and Emily had already gone to bed.

'I really don't know, Matthew,' she said. 'Isaac has offered me a home at the farm, but I don't think it would be a good idea for me to go there to live when he and Mama are married.'

'I've been thinking about it, my love. If I were to leave this place and set up my practice somewhere where neither of us are known I could take you there as my wife . . . ' He held up his hand. 'Oh, I know what you're going to say, my darling, and I know we can't be married while Zack is alive, but if you're prepared to take the risk, take my name and live 'in sin' — although anything less like sin I cannot imagine — with me, then I would be the happiest man on earth.'

'But if anybody found out, Matthew . . . ' she said uncertainly.

'I should be struck off the register, I know that. But if we went far enough away there wouldn't be much risk of that.' He took her hands in his. 'It's a risk I'm prepared to take, if you are.'

She shook her head. 'I couldn't jeopardise your career, Matthew. Your work is your life. If you had to give it up because of me I would never forgive myself and you would always blame me.'

'Never, my darling.'

But Bethany knew she was right and all the

time she felt she was tiptoeing about, metaphorically treading on eggshells, waiting for her husband to come back, half dreading, half hoping that he would so that he would be brought to justice and she could be rid of him once and for all.

And one cold, dark night he did.

34

There was a new moon the evening Bethany went out to the woodshed to fetch more logs for the fire. Beyond the shaft of light thrown by the windows of the house the darkness surrounded her like a cloak of black velvet, spangled with stars and the thin, white sliver of moon. She was a little annoyed that Tansy hadn't filled the log box while there was still daylight and she shivered and pulled her shawl more closely round her against the frosty night air. As her eyes became used to the dark she went unerringly to the log pile and filled her basket with enough logs to last the evening before making her way back to the house.

He came up so quietly that she didn't even know he was beside her until he took her arm and whispered in her ear,

'Don't scream or I'll kill you.'

She stopped, rooted to the spot, dropping the log basket so that the logs clattered out on to the frozen path.

'Stupid bitch.' His voice was raw with fear and impatience.

'What do you want?' she whispered.

'I want food. And money. And shelter. No,' he corrected himself. 'I want food and money. I've got shelter. I've been in my old room over the tack room for the past three days and I can stay there as long as I need to. But I'm hungry. And I could do with a blanket. It's cold up there of a night.'

'I don't know . . . '

He gripped her arm. 'Don't argue with me, just do as I say or I shall come and fetch it myself. And don't think I wouldn't. I've got a knife and I've already killed once, remember, so two or three more won't make much difference.'

'You're mad.' She was shivering with fear now.

'Then you'd better humour me, hadn't you. Don't forget. Food and a blanket. I shall be waiting. And don't you dare tell a soul I'm here or I'll cut your throat.'

He was gone as silently as he had come.

Bethany gathered up the logs as best she could and went back to the house. The kitchen was warm and cluttered and so wonderfully normal that for a moment she wondered if she had imagined the encounter with Zack.

'You've been gone a long time, dear.' Emily looked up from her sewing. 'And what's the matter? You're as white as a sheet. You look as if you've seen a ghost.'

Bethany put the log basket down and warmed her hands at the fire. 'It's very cold out there, Mama,' she said, surprised how steady her voice was. She gave a shiver and turned to Tansy. 'I'll make sure you don't forget to fill the basket another day, my girl, or you'll have to go and fill it yourself in the cold and dark.'

'I'm sorry, Mrs Beth. I won't forget again. I promise.'

Bethany threw a log on the fire, trying to calm her thumping heart, her mind racing as she tried to think of a way to get food and blankets to Zack. It wouldn't be easy. Isaac would be staying tonight; he was here already, looking after the bar. She smiled grimly to herself. Isaac and Matthew were taking it in turns to stay each night precisely in order to protect her and her mother against the very thing that had happened. And after what Zack had said she didn't dare to warn them.

She prowled about the kitchen, picking things up and putting them down again, unable to settle to anything.

'What *is* the matter with you, Bethany? You're like a cat on hot bricks,' Emily said, looking at her over the gold rim of her spectacles.

'I'm sorry, Mama.' She sat down at the table and began looking at a book, but after a minute she was up again, plumping up cushions, poking the fire, looking in cupboards.

Finally, when she could stand it no longer, she said, 'I think I'll go to bed. I'm cold and tired.'

'I should think that's a very good idea. You still look rather pale. I think you must be sickening for something,' Emily said. 'I'll wait until Isaac has finished in the bar, then I shall do the same.'

Bethany went up to her room and sat on the bed wringing her hands and dreaming up wild, impossible schemes to get rid of Zack. She didn't want to see him hang, although God knew, he had done her family enough harm to deserve it many times over; cold-bloodedly killing poor Aunt Sarah; killing darling little Tilly, albeit unwittingly; almost killing Emily . . . She hardened her heart when she recalled his part in

Tilly's death. In her mind he deserved to die for that alone.

At last, she heard Tansy go up to her attic; she heard the last of the men leave the bar and Isaac shoot the bolts; she heard Isaac go along to the kitchen and some time later she heard him and Emily come up the stairs and go to their separate rooms. Then she waited a bit longer before she crept down, a blanket under her arm, cut half a loaf of bread and a lump of cheese, drew a mug of ale and let herself silently out of the house and slipped across the yard.

As she went she recalled the number of times she had done this in the past; her eagerness to go to Zack, unable to get enough of his lovemaking. The knowledge that he had only been using her to get his hands on Travellers' Inn made her blush at her own naivety. But she had paid for it. Oh, how she had paid for it, in mental as well as physical cruelty.

She climbed the stairs to his hiding place. He had the stump of a candle, carefully shaded from the window and by its light she could see that his hair was straggly and matted and he had several days' growth of beard. His clothes were filthy and stinking and what she could see of his flesh was grimy. And this was a man who had always been fastidious in his appearance.

'Where have you been all this time?' she asked quietly as she watched him tear off lumps of bread and cheese and stuff them into his mouth. 'It's been nearly a month since you left.'

'Can't you see? I've been living rough.' He crammed more food into his mouth. 'I stayed a couple of nights with Reuben. He didn't want me there, I could see that, and anyway I thought they'd come and look for me there so I left.'

'He never said.'

'No, I warned him to keep his mouth shut.'

'I wonder it didn't kill him.'

'He's tough.'

She shook her head. 'You don't care, do you.'

'Only about number one.' He tapped his chest.

'So now what? You can't stay here, you know.' Even as she was speaking she had difficulty in keeping her teeth from chattering with fear and her mouth was dry.

He leaned forward. 'I've got a mate in Harwich. He's off to America. He said if I could get the money I could go with him. So that's what I've come for.'

'How much do you want?'

'A hundred pounds.'

'Don't be ridiculous. I haven't got anything like that.'

'Well, I've got a bit stashed away in the brew house.'

'How much?'

'Dunno. I haven't counted it lately.'

'Where did you get it?'

'Tips and that.' His voice roughened. 'Not that it's any of your concern. Have you got any more cheese?'

'No, I couldn't bring too much or it would be missed.'

'I'd like some stew. Some nice hot stew with dumplings.'

'Well, you'll have to settle for bread and cheese.'

'You can bring me some stew another night. With the money.'

'I told you, I haven't got that much money.' She was near to tears.

'Then you'll have to look after me here till you have. Or till my mate comes upriver with his boat to fetch me.' He stretched out on the truckle bed and covered himself with the blanket. Then he sat up again and reached under the straw mattress and brought out an evil-looking knife. 'I'll keep this handy. Might need it if you try to do something silly.'

Bethany crept back to the house and up to bed. She didn't know what to do. She didn't doubt that Zack would carry out his threat to kill her if she told anyone he had come back. She wracked her brain to think how she could get hold of enough money to be rid of him and hopefully never see him again, but it would take weeks of filching takings from the bar and payments from overnight guests — not that there were many of these now. And it would be noticed. And because there was nobody else to blame Tansy would be accused of stealing; poor innocent Tansy . . . She turned over and sobbed into her pillow. If only she could get hold of his knife she would kill the bastard herself for the anguish he was causing her.

During the next days she could neither eat nor sleep. She managed to slip over to his room with food and drink each night after everyone else was in bed and she gave him what little money of her own she had.

'We seem to be eating rather a lot of bread,' Emily said one morning as she began mixing up the dough for another batch. 'I don't usually make three batches in a week.' She glanced up at Bethany. 'And it's not you who's been eating it, you've not eaten enough to keep a sparrow alive and you're as jumpy as a cricket. I don't know what ails you, child.'

'I'm all right, Mama,' Bethany said, dragging herself together with an effort. 'I shall be better when the spring comes. This winter seems to be neverending.'

'I think you should speak to Matthew. Maybe he could give you something . . . '

'I don't *need* anything, Mama,' Bethany shouted, and slammed out of the room.

'Which just goes to prove that you do, my girl,' Emily said to herself, venting her feelings on kneading the dough. 'And I shall speak to Matthew.'

But there was no need. Matthew had loved Bethany for a long time now and he was sensitive to her every mood. He knew whether she was happy or sad, anxious or worried, without her ever having to utter a word. So he soon realised something was very wrong with her, however much she tried to deny it.

'Well, I'm a bit worried because I don't think we shall be able to continue here at Travellers' Inn for very much longer,' she prevaricated when he tried to discover what was troubling her. 'Especially now Isaac has agreed to sell some of his land to the railway company.'

They were sitting in the kitchen after everyone else had gone to bed. This was their special time, just as Emily and Isaac had a special time when it was Isaac's turn to stay.

He rubbed his chin. 'Emily will marry Isaac, of course,' he mused.

'Oh, yes. I'm very happy for them,' she said with a smile. 'They're so right for each other.' She sighed. 'They've asked me to go and live with them but I don't want to do that. I don't feel it would be right.'

'No, I agree with you.' He leaned forward and took her hands in his. 'Oh, Beth. If only you were free to marry me. I'd give the world . . . '

'Oh, so would I, Matthew,' she breathed. 'So would I.'

He stood up and pulled her to her feet, taking her in his arms. 'The offer is still there, my darling. I'll find a practice miles away — Scotland, Wales, anywhere where we wouldn't be known and we could live there as man and wife. Nobody would ever know.'

'You know that's not possible, Matthew,' she said, her voice muffled. 'It could ruin your career.' She looked up at him. 'Perhaps I could come and live at your house as your housekeeper?'

He looked down at her, then kissed her, long and hard. 'That would ruin your reputation as well as my career because I should never be able to keep my hands off you,' he said, holding her close. 'It's difficult enough when I'm staying here, knowing you're in the next room, but at

439

least there are other people in the house.'

'I wouldn't care, as long as I could be with you,' she said, clinging to him.

'And then when you become pregnant?'

'Oh, I don't think that's likely. After that miscarriage I seem to be barren.'

'We couldn't take the risk, my darling. Not that I wouldn't want children with you . . . '

She flung away from him. 'Oh, what's the use. He'll always blight my life, wherever he is. Even when he's in America . . . '

'How do you know he's going to America?' Matthew cut in quickly.

She sat down. 'I . . . I don't. Well, surely you must have known he'd been talking about going to America to dig for gold. That's why he wanted to get his hands on the inn, so that he could sell it and get the money to go.' She shrugged. 'I don't know, but I'm just supposing that's where he'll go now.' She pretended to yawn. It was very late. Zack would be getting impatient.

'Yes. Of course.' He pulled her to her feet and kissed her, more gently this time. 'I can see you're very tired. I think it's time for bed, my love, much though I hate to curtail these precious times together. But it is getting very late.'

They went to their separate rooms and Bethany waited impatiently till she heard him get into bed, then she waited again until everywhere was quiet before stealing out of her room and down the stairs.

She had hidden some ham and cold potatoes

earlier in the day and she took them across to Zack.

'Have you brought any money?' he asked, shovelling the food into his mouth. He had no need to light a candle because the moon was full, shedding a grey light over the filth in which he was living.

'Not tonight. I couldn't get any.'

'It doesn't matter. I've been down to the brew house and fetched my little store. There was more in it than I remembered.' He looked up at her and grinned. 'I'll be gone in a couple of days, Beth. Gone and out of your life so you can marry your doctor friend.' He speared another piece of potato with the end of his evil-looking knife and shoved it into his mouth. 'Except you can't, because you'll still be married to me, sweetheart.'

'There's always the chance that you'll die of yellow fever, or swamp fever, or be scalped by Red Indians,' she said, surprised at her own callousness.

'Trouble is, you'll never know,' he said. 'I'll be gone, but you'll never know whether I'm alive or dead. Not till I come back, rich as Croesus.'

'I could kill you,' she said quietly.

He held up his knife. 'Not as easily as I could kill you, my dear.'

She left him then, trying to contain her sobs of misery and frustration until she was out of earshot, and went back to the house, letting herself in as silently as she had left. She had nearly reached the door to the passage when she felt herself enveloped in strong arms and heard

Matthew say, 'It's all right, my darling, it's me. Now, are you going to tell me what all this prowling about in the dead of night is about? Or shall I tell you?' He stroked her hair. 'He's come back, hasn't he?'

She buried her face in the warmth of his shoulder, registering with some surprise that he was still fully clothed, and cried uncontrollably, trying to tell him at the same time how she had secretly been keeping Zack fed for the past three days and how he had threatened to kill her if she revealed his hiding place.

'He's got a knife, Matthew. A horrible-looking knife,' she finished, her tears and energy all spent.

He led her to a chair by the fire. 'Sit there while I warm you some milk and I'll give you something to make you sleep.'

'Shall I light the lamp?'

'No. Mustn't do that or Zack might see the light. Fortunately, the moon is bright enough for me to see what I'm doing, as long as I'm careful.' He put milk in a saucepan and set it on the still warm stove.

'What are we going to do, Matthew?' she asked in a small voice, curling her hands round the mug of milk when he gave it to her.

'We're going to bed — to our separate beds' he corrected himself with a rueful smile. 'And we're going to sleep. I've put something in your milk that should help. In the morning I'll have decided what's best to be done.' He dropped a kiss on the top of her head. 'You've done enough worrying about all this. Now you can leave it to me, sweetheart.'

'Don't forget he's got a knife,' she warned.

'I'm not likely to forget that, my love.'

'We mustn't tell the others. Zack would kill me if he thought I'd told you.' She was still wild-eyed with anxiety.

'We're not going to talk about it any more tonight. Finished your milk?' He took the mug from her. 'Then off to bed with you. I'll deal with Zack tomorrow.'

'But you don't know what he's like. He's already killed once, so he won't mind doing it again.'

He took her by the hand and led her up the stairs. At her door he kissed her. 'I'll see you in the morning. Sleep tight.'

She crawled into bed and closed her eyes, knowing there was little chance of that. When she opened them again, what seemed a few minutes later, daylight was streaming in through the window.

35

Matthew had left by the time Bethany got downstairs. Emily was at the stove, stirring a pan of porridge and Tansy was scuttling about doing her morning chores.

'You're very late this morning, dear,' Emily said anxiously. 'Are you not well?'

'Yes. I overslept, that's all.' Bethany sat down at the table and put her head on her hand. She felt strangely detached, almost light-headed. She supposed it was the effect of whatever Matthew had put in her milk last night. 'Did Matthew say anything before he left?'

'Only that he would be back tonight.' Emily frowned. 'But I think he must have made a mistake. I'm sure it's Isaac's turn to sleep here tonight.'

Bethany yawned. 'I expect they've worked it out between them. As long as one of them is here.' She wondered what Matthew was planning and what part she would have in it.

'Indeed.' Emily shuddered. 'Do you think Zack will come back, Bethany? He's been gone almost a month so it's not very likely, is it?'

Oh, how little you know, Mama, Bethany thought wryly. Aloud, she said, 'No, I don't think it's very likely. He's probably gone to America by now, to dig for gold.'

'And good riddance, too.' Emily showed her feelings by plonking a bowl of porridge in front of Bethany. 'Eat that. You'll feel better when you've got something inside you.'

'I don't feel ill.' But her mother was right. By the time she had eaten the porridge and drunk a cup of tea she felt more herself and she knew that the deep sleep had refreshed and strengthened her.

She tried to keep very busy during the day but Zack was always on her mind, like a dead weight she was forced to carry around with her. It had been like that for the past three days, ever since he came back. But now there was the added anxiety of Matthew. What did he intend to do? Had he made any plans? She hoped and prayed he wouldn't decide to go and confront Zack, or worse, come marching along with the constable, because she knew Zack was keeping a sharp eye on all the comings and goings.

Early in the afternoon she went up to her room to change from her plain 'morning' dress into one a little smarter. It was a habit left over from their life in London that both she and her mother had never relinquished. As she reached the top of the stairs she glanced out of the window as she often did, to look out at the river view. The tide was full and a frosty sun danced on the ripples in points of light. There was what to her inexperienced eye looked like a small fishing boat at anchor in the middle of the river. It hadn't been there yesterday, of that she was sure and her heart leapt. Perhaps this was Zack's friend, come to take him away. She hoped and prayed it might be so, although she knew he wouldn't feel it safe to leave his hiding place until after dark. She rested her aching head on the cool glass of the window; only a few more hours and he would be gone, thank God. What would happen to him after that she neither knew nor cared, she just wanted to be rid of him before he could do any further damage to her and her family. And that included Matthew, of course.

★ ★ ★

'Oh, I thought it was Isaac's turn to stay tonight,' Emily said when Matthew arrived that evening. She was obviously disappointed.

He took off his hat and the thick caped coat he wore on his rounds and hung them on the back of the door.

'I guess he's already here,' he said briefly. 'In the bar with the constable.'

'But . . . ' Bethany began, alarmed.

He held up his hand. 'It's all right, Bethany, don't get alarmed. Zack would need sharp eyes to have seen them arrive. We arranged last night that they should come on foot in amongst a few of the regulars.'

'So now what?' Bethany sat down at the table and began chewing her fingernails. It was a new habit, formed in the past few days.

'First, I'm going to put Emily and Tansy in the picture. It's only fair that they should know that Zack is back, hiding out over the tack room.'

Emily gasped and Tansy's eyes grew saucer-like as he told them what had been going on.

'No wonder you've been so jumpy these past

few days, Bethany,' Emily said. 'Why didn't you tell me?'

'I couldn't. I couldn't tell anybody. He said he'd kill me if I did.' she replied simply.

'But you told Matthew.'

'I didn't. He found out. There's a difference. Go on, Matthew.'

'Well, what I intend to do . . . '

'I don't think you need to do anything, as a matter of fact,' Bethany said thoughtfully. 'I've seen a fishing boat moored in the river opposite the end of the field and I'm pretty sure it belongs to Zack's friend. He said he was coming to fetch him. I reckon he'll be gone by morning and that'll be the last we shall see of him.'

'But where does that leave you, Bethany?' Matthew asked, spreading his hands. He answered his own question. 'Still married to a man who you'll never know is alive or dead. You'll never know where he is or whether you're a wife or widow. Is that what you want?'

She shook her head impatiently. 'No, of course it isn't. But more than anything I want him out of my life.'

'Well, if that boat you saw has come to fetch him we've still got just a few hours because they'll want to go downriver on a falling tide.' He took out his pocket watch. 'High tide is about two o'clock so my guess is it'll be soon after that. But Zack can't get out to the boat until there's enough water to row out to it, which won't be until midnight at the earliest.' He turned to Bethany. 'Has he got a pocket watch?'

She shook her head. 'I don't think so. In any

447

case, even if he had he wouldn't be able to see the time by it, he hasn't got enough light.'

'That's good. Now, Tansy, you stoke the fire up then go to bed like you always do.'

'I shall bolt me bedroom door when I go up,' Tansy said, shuddering.

'I don't blame you, child,' Emily said.

Matthew took out his own watch. 'It's a bit early but that's all to the good if he's watching the house. Now, don't forget to take your candle and let it shine out of the window. It'll make him think it's later than it really is.'

When she had gone, he drew his chair up to the table. 'Now, what Isaac and I propose is this, if Bethany agrees, of course.'

'Oh, I'll agree to anything if it gets rid of him,' Bethany said with feeling.

'You might not be too happy with this,' he warned. 'But we think it should work all right.'

Bethany nodded. 'Go on.'

'Well, what we propose is quite simple. I shall put on one of Bethany's dresses — you'll have to fetch down the biggest you've got, Bethany. I know it still won't be big enough but covered with a shawl and in the moonlight it'll serve the purpose. I'll take his food over, just like you do every night, Bethany, and because he won't be expecting it I should be able to overpower him and shout for the help that will be waiting below in the tack room.'

'Oh, I don't like this,' Emily said anxiously. 'I don't like it at all.' She turned to Isaac, who had just come in. 'Are you involved in this, Isaac?'

'Not directly,' he said, sitting down beside her.

'This was mostly Matt's idea.'

Matthew was becoming impatient. 'Well, what are you waiting for, Bethany? Go and fetch a dress for me while Emily gets some food ready for him.'

'No. I think it's a stupid idea and I'm having no part in it,' Bethany said flatly.

'Why?' Matthew and Isaac said together.

'Because you would have no chance of overpowering Zack, Matthew. He's a strong man, remember. He's used to humping heavy barrels and carrying heavy loads about, whereas you would be hampered wearing unfamiliar clothing that was far too tight and with skirts that would trip you up. And he's got that knife. I've seen it. It's an evil-looking thing.'

'Does he brandish it at you every time you go up there?'

'No. He keeps it under the mattress. But he could soon whip it out if he thought he might need it.'

Emily nodded. 'I agree with Bethany. It would never work.'

Matthew was obviously put out. 'Well, have you got a better idea?' he asked stiffly.

'Yes. I'll take him his meal like I've done each night. In fact, I could take him a bowl of stew,' Bethany said. 'It's what he's been asking for.'

'Then what? Are you going to overpower him?' Matthew's tone was bordering on sarcasm because like everybody else in the room he was on edge.

'No. But if I can keep him occupied for long

enough I'm hoping you'll do that,' Bethany said calmly.

'And how will you keep him occupied?' Emily asked anxiously.

Bethany turned to look at her. 'Mother, I'm his wife,' she said briefly.

Emily flushed to the roots of her hair. 'Ah, yes.'

'I don't like this,' Matthew said. 'It's too dangerous, Bethany. I can't let you . . . '

Isaac laid a hand on his arm. 'Bethany's right, Matt. It's the best way. You couldn't do it, I can see that now, not hampered up with skirts and such. And we'll be right there to see she doesn't come to any harm.'

Matthew nodded. 'All right. But I still don't like it.'

'Oh, stop arguing and let me go before I lose my nerve,' Bethany said impatiently. She went over to the stove and ladled some stew into a bowl while Isaac went and fetched a mug of beer, a signal to Charlie Blake that things were about to happen.

Bethany threw a shawl round her shoulders, put the things on a tray and taking a deep breath walked across the yard to the tack room and up the stairs, her heart thumping so hard she felt sure Zack would hear it.

'You took your time tonight,' he growled as her head appeared. 'I hope you've brought plenty because I'm hungry and I shall be off in a few hours.'

She forced herself to sit down beside him on the bed although the stink of his unwashed body made her feel sick. 'Look, I've brought you some stew. It's what you've been asking for, isn't it,' she said. She turned to him. 'It's good. It's lamb stew. Your favourite. See, I haven't forgotten what you like, Zack.' She spoke softly and moved nearer to him, rubbing her arm against him.

He began to shovel the stew into his mouth. 'Mm. Tasty,' he managed to say between mouthfuls.

She put up her hand and smoothed his matted hair, the thought crossing her mind that it could well be crawling. She tried not to shudder. 'You always took such a pride in your lovely hair, Zack. Now, look at it, all matted and filthy. Such a shame.'

'Yeh. Well, I shall be able to wash it when I'm on the boat.'

'Boat? What boat?' She feigned surprise.

He nodded briefly towards the window. 'See that boat down there in the moonlight? That's going to take me downriver to the ship in Harwich harbour that's bound for America.'

'Will you send for me when you're rich, Zack?' she asked seductively, leaning towards him and caressing the nape of his neck the way she knew he liked but with the other hand feeling under the mattress for the knife he kept hidden there.

'Maybe. I might.' He finished the stew and mopped up the last of the gravy with the bread she had brought. Then he took a long draught of beer and wiped his mouth on the back of his hand and put the tray away from him. He grinned at her in the gloom. 'Do you reckon you'll miss me, then?'

'I reckon I might, Zack,' she said softly, forcing herself to nibble his ear lobe. She didn't know how long she could keep this up. She'd had to give up trying to locate the knife; either it was pushed too far under the mattress or he had moved it, she had no way of knowing which. She couldn't understand why she hadn't been able to detect any sound from down below although her ears were straining to hear. She'd felt sure Matthew would have managed to send her some sign that he was there to back her up.

Suddenly, Zack pulled her towards him and began to kiss her, his slack mouth wet and stinking. He began to knead her breast 'Well, if you're going to miss me I'd better give you a little something to remember me by, hadn't I? You never know, after all this time it might even be a little Zack.'

In one movement he twisted her round on to the bed and pushed up her skirts.

It was all going too fast. There was still no sound from below. Where were they? Why weren't they coming to her rescue?

Kneeling over her he began to unbuckle his belt and she could see, silhouetted against the window the huge bulge in his trousers. She knew she was trapped and with his weight straddling her there was nothing she could do to help herself. She stifled a sob. She had been so sure she knew where the knife was hidden that was to have been her salvation.

In desperation, she screamed. 'I thought I felt a rat run over my feet.'

He put his hand over her mouth. 'Shut up, you

silly bitch.' He cocked an ear and froze as he heard a stair creak. 'Bitch! You set me up!'

In a flash he leapt off the bed, dragging her with him. Keeping one arm tightly round her he bent down and retrieved the knife from under the mattress and she realised it could only have been a hair's breadth away from her own fingers. Then he backed away from the stairs, still holding her with one hand, the knife in the other. As Matthew's head appeared she felt the cold blade at her throat.

'If you come any nearer I shall slit her throat,' Zack said, his voice frighteningly quiet and conversational. As he was speaking he was edging very slowly towards the window, dragging her with him.

Matthew took a step towards them and she could see Isaac and Charlie Blake behind him, their faces masks of horror. 'Let her go, Zack, for God's sake,' he said desperately.

'What? So you can have her? I'm telling you, if you don't keep back, by the time I've finished with her you won't want her, Matthew. And don't think I don't mean what I say.' Zack still spoke quietly, as if his words were no more than remarks about the weather, but she could feel his hand trembling as he pressed the knife blade flat against her throat.

'For goodness sake, do as he says, Matt,' she cried, her voice half strangled. 'Don't come near. He'll kill me.'

'I might kill you, anyway,' Zack said conversationally. 'I've never slit anybody's throat so it might be interesting. 'And I can only be

453

hung once so I've nothing to lose.'

'Christ, you're a monster!' Matthew cried and Bethany could see that it was only the fact that the other two men were holding on to his arms that was keeping him back.

Then suddenly, without warning, Zack slackened his grip and gave her a push that sent her flying across the room to land at Matthew's feet. Before anyone could move, he made a dive for the window and with a shattering of glass launched himself through it, landing on the muck heap from the stables that he himself had built in less troubled times. Then he was off, streaking down the garden and across the field towards the river, leaving a trail of blood behind him.

Isaac and Charlie dashed out of the stable and immediately gave chase, but Matthew was more concerned with Bethany. He picked her up and carried her down the stairs.

'I'm all right, Matthew, really I am,' she said when they reached the yard and he set her on her feet. 'Go with them They'll need you. He's still got the knife. Look, there he goes.'

Ahead, in the moonlight they could see Zack running like a hare over the field with Isaac and Charlie not very far behind him.

'Don't worry. He won't get far,' Matthew said grimly. 'They'll catch him when he gets to the river bank.'

'He's as strong as an ox so they'll still need you.' She gave him a push and watched as after a last look to make sure she wasn't hurt he turned and raced after the others. Then she staggered

454

indoors and immediately fell down in a dead faint.

But Matthew knew nothing of this as he tore down the field to assist Isaac and Charlie to overpower Zack at the river bank.

To their horror he didn't stop at the bank but ploughed straight on through the mud, desperate to get to the boat that was moored in the middle of the river. After the first few yards his pace began to slacken as the mud became wetter and more glutinous, and it took more and more effort, because as he dragged one foot out the other was sucked in deeper by the weight of his body. As they watched, his progress became slower and slower and they could do nothing but look on as he struggled, sinking deeper into the oozing mud with every step he tried to take.

They could see a man with a lantern on the moored boat and his voice came over the water, 'Goo back, ye silly bugger. Ye'll drown.'

But Zack took no notice and still struggled on trying to drag his foot out — his boots had been left yards behind — until he overbalanced and fell flat on his face. He was losing strength now and the more he struggled to keep his face out of the stinking, sucking, black mud the deeper he sank into it.

'For God's sake, help me!' They heard his desperate voice across the expanse of mud.

'We'll never get to him without a plank. It's too dangerous,' Charlie yelled.

'I'll fetch one. I think there's one in the stable.' Matthew raced back across the field and hurried back as quickly as he could, dragging a long plank and a coil of rope. The three of them manoeuvred the plank with some difficulty into place across the mud but although it almost reached him Zack was now too panic-stricken to even see it.

'I reckon I'm the lightest. I'd better go and fetch him,' Charlie volunteered, taking the rope. 'You two hold it steady.'

Lying on his stomach, Charlie inched his way carefully along the plank. In the moonlight they could see Zack, still flailing around, trying in vain to keep his head out of the mud and to find something firm to get hold of. But the more he struggled the deeper he was sinking and the deeper he sank the weaker his movements became. By the time Charlie reached him they had stopped altogether.

'I need help. I can't shift him on me own,' Charlie shouted. Then, after a minute, 'Jest a minute. P'raps if I can get the rope under his arms I can keep hold of him while you two drag the plank back in.' There was silence for several minutes. Then, 'I've got 'im. You can start pullin'. But for God's sake take it gentle-like or he'll hev me orf the plank and in the mud with him.'

Slowly, inch by inch, Isaac and Matthew eased the plank back across the mud while Charlie clung to Zack's inert body. The tide was rising now, which helped a bit but even so, Charlie was exhausted by the time he reached the bank.

'I wouldn't want to do that agin in a hurry,' he said, rolling off the plank and lying spreadeagled while Isaac and Matthew dragged Zack the last few yards. 'I thought every minute'd be me last. He was a dead weight. Nearly pulled me arms outa their sockets.' He lifted his head. 'Were we in time?'

Matthew, wiping the mud out of Zack's eyes and mouth, shook his head. 'No, I'm afraid not. He drowned in the mud.'

'God, what a horrible way to go,' Isaac said.

'Well there's nothing we can do except tie him on to the plank and carry him back to the yard,' Matthew said.

By this time several men from the bar had arrived so there were plenty of willing hands to carry Zack's mud-caked body back to the yard. Charlie, Isaac and Matthew followed wearily behind.

'We'd better put him in the tack room till he's been cleaned up,' Matthew suggested.

'There'll have to be an inquest, of course,' Charlie said, 'but there's no doubt the verdict will be accidental death.'

'Better than hanging, I suppose,' Isaac said grimly.

'Yes, I suppose so,' Matthew said.

The two men went into the house together to find the women they loved.

36

When Bethany stumbled into the house she knew nothing until the acrid smell of feathers being burnt under her nose brought her round. As the memory of her ordeal came back to her she put her hand to her throat where Zack had held the knife. To her surprise it came away spotted with blood.

'It's only a scratch,' Emily said, examining it. 'Thank God,' she added fervently.

They sat together, drinking tea liberally laced with whisky, listening for the men to come back with Zack.

'Do you know, I almost hope they won't catch him,' Emily said, shaking her head. 'I know he's done terrible things, but he could be such a *nice* man, couldn't he, and he worked very hard to make the inn a success. I suppose it was greed that made him like that. It's so sad.'

Bethany looked at her in surprise. 'How can you say that, Mama?' She shuddered. 'After all the dreadful things he's done and what happened to me tonight we could never again sleep easily if he was at large. He's totally ruthless, Mama.'

'Yes, I know.' Emily still sounded regretful.

'He tried to *kill* you, Mama. And he would have killed me, too. How can you feel sorry for him?'

'Yes, you're right,' Emily pulled herself

together. 'He deserves to hang.'

They sat in silence, each with her own thoughts, until they heard men's voices and a shuffling of feet. A minute later, Matthew and Isaac came in, both filthy with river mud.

'You caught him, then,' Emily said, her voice still tinged with sadness.

'No,' Matthew shook his head. 'We didn't catch him. He tried to get away and drowned in the mud.'

Both Emily and Bethany gave a gasp of horror.

'We've brought him back,' Isaac said. 'He's in the stables. A couple of the men have offered to stay there with him until they fetch his body in the morning.' He paused, then added, 'Not a nice way to die.' He turned to Matthew. 'I think we both need a stiff whisky, Matt. I've already told the men outside to go to the bar and get themselves a drink on the house. They deserve it, after what they've seen and done.'

Matthew went over to Bethany. 'Are you all right now, darling?'

'Yes, I'm all right now you're here, Matthew.' She took his hand. 'Stay with me, Matthew. Don't leave me. I don't want to be alone. Not while . . . ' she nodded in the direction of the stables.

'You've nothing to fear from Zack, Bethany.' He put his arm round her. 'He can never again cause you any harm. But I won't leave you, my love. If you want me to stay . . . '

She leaned her head against him. 'I do, Matthew. Oh, I do.'

★　★　★

Three months later, early in the morning, there was a double wedding at Mistley Church. It was a very quiet wedding, in view of the dreadful events of the recent past, but the two brides, mother and daughter, were radiantly happy as they came out into the sunlight on the arms of their respective bridegrooms. Bethany, the younger of the two, was looking particularly bonny. She had put on a little weight, especially round the waist, proving beyond all doubt that she was not, as she had once feared, barren.

After the wedding the four of them went back to Marsh Farm for a quiet celebration, after which Isaac Walford was taking Emily to the Italian Lakes for a month-long honeymoon. He was now a rich man, having finally given in and sold some of his land to the railway company. Navvies were already busy at work cutting the track for the trains that would soon put an end to the coaching business for ever. But Travellers' Inn was already up for sale and Emily had her new life to look forward to so this was no longer of much concern to her. She was looking forward to becoming a real farmer's wife, keeping chickens and helping her husband to make the annual Harvest Home into a truly memorable occasion.

Bethany was also looking forward to her new life as the local doctor's wife and making Beckford Lodge, the house where he had his surgery and laboratory into a real home, full of children's laughter. She made a promise to

Matthew that he would never again have to eat a meal kept hot over a saucepan of water and she kept her promise.

*   *   *

Travellers' Inn was never again occupied for any length of time and gradually the legend grew that it was haunted, some said by a man covered in mud and brandishing a knife. Bethany believed none of this. She was sure that if Travellers' Inn was haunted at all the ghost was a benign old woman in a brown skirt and a man's striped shirt striding up the garden path or sitting outside the garden shed drinking beer with a cantankerous old man wearing a smock and buskins and smoking a filthy old pipe.

We do hope that you have enjoyed reading this large print book.

Did you know that all of our titles are available for purchase?

We publish a wide range of high quality large print books including:
Romances, Mysteries, Classics
General Fiction
Non Fiction and Westerns

Special interest titles available in large print are:
The Little Oxford Dictionary
Music Book
Song Book
Hymn Book
Service Book

Also available from us courtesy of Oxford University Press:
Young Readers' Dictionary
(large print edition)
Young Readers' Thesaurus
(large print edition)

For further information or a free brochure, please contact us at:
Ulverscroft Large Print Books Ltd.,
The Green, Bradgate Road, Anstey,
Leicester, LE7 7FU, England.
Tel: (00 44) 0116 236 4325
Fax: (00 44) 0116 234 0205

Other titles published by
The House of Ulverscroft:

MOLLIE ON THE SHORE

Elizabeth Jeffrey

After the death of her mother, Mollie Barnes was taken in by her Aunt Rose and Uncle Sam. Rose, however, resents Mollie and makes her life a misery. Then Mollie inadvertently discovers the shocking truth about her parentage. James Grainger, the master of the big house on the cliff, is her real father . . . She vows that one day she will sit at his table. Mollie and Charlotte, the young Grainger girl, become friends and Mollie gains access to the house. But her plan goes awry when she becomes the unwilling object of James' son's affections. And then she realises she is falling for Mark Hamilton, a poor relation of the Graingers', whom Charlotte believes to be her own secret admirer . . .

THE WEAVER'S DAUGHTER

Elizabeth Jeffrey

When Anna discovers her father's plans to marry her off to an old widower, she flees from Holland with her sweetheart, Jan. They go to Colchester in England, the hub of the thriving cloth trade, where there is a substantial immigrant community. However, there is a great deal of animosity between the English and the Dutch, and riots often break out. On the advice of the local church minister, Jan takes up poorly paid work as a dyer, in very bad conditions. Anna is offered a place in the minister's house, looking after his pregnant wife. But she soon realises the true motive behind Minister Archer's generosity . . .

GINNY APPLEYARD

Elizabeth Jeffrey

When Ginny Appleyard's childhood sweet-heart returns after his racing season aboard the yacht *Aurora,* her hopes that he is bringing her an engagement ring are shattered, as Nathan disembarks with Isobel Armitage, the daughter of *Aurora'*s owner. Nathan tells Ginny that he is following Isobel to London to pursue his dreams of becoming an artist. Already distraught at the tragic death of her father, Ginny is further devastated to hear that Nathan and Isobel are to be married. More heartache is in store for Ginny when she realises that she is expecting Nathan's child . . .

TO BE A FINE LADY

Elizabeth Jeffrey

Found as a baby wrapped in a luxurious blue velvet cloak, Joanna was brought up by the cruel farmer who found her, and put to work on his land just as soon as she could walk. Despite such hardship, Jo dreams of a reunion with her true mother, convinced that she must be a fine lady. When local factory owner Abraham Silkin decides that she has the potential to make him a good wife, Jo believes her dreams are finally coming true, but she hasn't bargained on her forbidden attraction to Abraham's godson!

1	21	41	61	81	101
2	22	42	62	82	102
3	23	43	63	83	
4	24	44	64		
5	25	45	65		